DAVID ANNANDALE

RaveN
STONE

Crown Fire
copyright © David Annandale 2002

Published by Ravenstone
an imprint of Turnstone Press
607-100 Arthur Street
Artspace Building
Winnipeg, MB
R3B 1H3 Canada
www.TurnstonePress.com

Turnstone Press gratefully acknowledges the assistance of The Canada
Council for the Arts, the Manitoba Arts Council, the Government of
Canada through the Book Publishing Industry Development Program
and the Government of Manitoba through the Department of Culture,
Heritage and Tourism, Arts Branch for our publishing activities.

The Canada Council | Le Conseil des Arts
for the Arts | du Canada

Canadä

Cover design: Tétro Design
Design: Sharon Caseburg
Printed and bound in Canada
by Friesens for Turnstone Press.

National Library of Canada Cataloguing in Publication Data

Annandale, David 1967–
    Crown fire

    ISBN 0-88801-267-5
    I. Title
PS8551.N527C76 2002   C813'.6   C2002-910054-2
PR9199.4.A56C76 2002

CROWN FIRE

For Eric, Eleanor,
Michelle and Robert Annandale

ACKNOWLEDGMENTS

My thanks are too paltry, my debts too many. But here goes anyway.

Thank you to my family: Eric, Eleanor, Michelle and Robert Annandale. Their support and belief has been constant over the decades, and I dedicate this book to them.

Thank you to my editor, Wayne Tefs, who saved me from myself. To everyone at Turnstone, for taking a chance, and giving my dream flesh. To Beatrice Findlay, for providing me the keys to New York City, and to Mel Menscher, for showing me through the gates. To Stephen R. George, for support, feedback and advice beyond invaluable. To Bob Baxter, for the design of the lodge.

Thank you to Ann Howey, Shawn MacDonald and Max Verbrugge for matters military. To the gang at the Canadian Interagency Forest Fire Centre, for twelve years of information and support, and especially to Serge Poulin, who vetted the fire scenes. For support, comments and questions answered, thank you to Peter Armstrong, Doug Barbour, Scott Ellis, Sue Fisher, Hung Pin Kao, Tony and Melanie Hawkes Kavanaugh, Jane Magrath, Andrew O'Malley, Lesley Peterson, Paul Regehr, Dave and Jennifer Violago, Mary Beth Wolicky, Russ and Mary Wolicky, and Eric Wright. The accuracies are theirs, the cock-ups mine.

And finally, thank you to Leanne Groeneveld. I am indebted to her for far, far more than an author's photograph.

CROWN FIRE

PROLOGUE

DEAR GOD, THEY WERE RETREATING.

Stop it. Stop thinking about it. Get normal.

She opened her eyes. I'm here, not there. She was Corporal Jennifer Blaylock (Radio Operator, 1st Canadian Division HQ Signal Regiment), based in Kingston, but now on conquering hero's leave here in Winnipeg, on Harvard Avenue, in her parents' home, on the second floor, in her room, here, on her bed. Downstairs, she could hear the clink-clatter of the Victory Dinner being prepared. The television hummed with patriotic fervor. This, she thought, arms folded behind her head, is what it feels like to be flavor of the week.

It should have been fun. That was the point, wasn't it? She should be downstairs or out in the bars, getting in on the hearty party, the big blowout of 1991. Things were cool, after all. She and The Team had gone into Kuwait, helped

3

beat the bad guys, and all come back. Righteous. A Job Well Done. Okay, so it was mostly a question of helping out while the Big Uncle to the south did all the heavy lifting, but reflected glory was still glory, yes? So?

(They were retreat—) Stop it. Get normal. She stared at the walls, at the magazine-glossy reminders of her teengirl past. Her gaze slid over a Duran Duran centerfold from Tiger Beat. Simon LeBon was curling at the edges and turning an unhealthy yellow. Her lips twitched with contempt for the Jenny of ten years ago. But it was contempt leavened with a touch of affection. So Jenny hadn't had any taste. No harm done. She had learned. It was Jennifer, not Jenny, who had put up the Judas Priest posters a few years later.

She grinned. (Good. See? We're getting normal.) God forbid, of course, that her younger self should actually take down the old idols when the new ones went up. Not the Blaylock way, that. Accumulation, always accumulation. Never throw out the past. So Simon was bracketed on the left by the metal eagle off the album cover of *Screaming for Vengeance,* and on the right by the demon bull from *Defenders of the Faith.* Remember what they were called? Come on, she thought, name the monsters. The eagle was.... She struggled for it. The Hellion. Right. And the bull thing was the Metallion. Cool. Yes, she remembered them, the demon-gods of adolescent power fantasies. They'd set the tone for what had come later.

At eighteen, Jennifer had enlisted, barely taking the time to remove her high school graduation robe before marching hell-for-leather and take-on-the-world, Hellion and Metallion rolled into one, to the nearest recruitment office. Over the next six years, Jennifer had turned into Jen "Rammer" Blaylock. Well and good. And she'd found the time to take night courses in Human Geography and Political Science. Well and good too. The courses had opened the Rammer's eyes a bit wider than was entirely comfortable, but that was cool. It had been good for her. Nothing she couldn't handle.

Her memory slipped then, skipped to the thing that was harder to handle. The recent thing. On the last day of February, she'd found herself standing by the 6th Ring Road, the Jahrah Road, outside Kuwait City, looking at a huge convoy of blackened metal and flesh, gazing at the remains of over three thousand vehicles and tens of thousands of lives, staring at the charred results of a job well done, and had known that, in whatever small way, she had helped bring this about. The image of charcoal that had once been screaming flesh superimposed itself over the posters. She felt her stomach contract once more. They were retreating, she thought. It was a sentence that had become her mind's one-track chorus. They were retreating. They were retreating.

Stop it, stop it, that's *enough*. It was war. And in war, guess what: shit happens. SNAFU leads to FUBAR and that's the way of the world. Deal with it.

Footsteps coming up the stairs. Her door opened and Celia poked her head in. Little sister Celia: fourteen gangly years, a mouth full of orthodontic metal and eyes two Olympic torches of hero worship. Baby sister come to summon her down to dinner.

Dinner. The family and the groaning board: no warmer welcome possible for the returned conqueror. Jen took the scene in through her pores, absorbed the familiar and the oh-so-necessary. Home. Home. The Highway of Death fell back before the safety and comfort of the word. Home. Warmth coursed through Jen's veins. It was addictively good. Warmth for her stomach from dinner, warmth for her skin from the hearth, warmth for her ears from long-missed voices, warmth for her eyes from the faces and the architecture and the familiarity of home. The solidity of the dining room shoved the desert tents into another universe. Dark oak everywhere: hardwood floor, beams and paneling, matched by a heavy-as-stone table. The rest of the house followed suit: big, old and elegant, in one of the older, quieter neighborhoods of Winnipeg. River Heights: elm-shaded streets with names like Harvard, Yale, Oxford and Cambridge. Dignity. Outside, the calm was sealed by the weight of deep snow and the harsh snap-silence of a late Winnipeg March gone to cold again in the last roar of winter. Home.

There were no secrets in home, though. Jen's mother held off until dessert, then dug at Jen's secret. "There's something bothering you," Gail said.

"Well, you know: war, hell. The usual." She was not going to talk about the Highway with Celia sitting beside her.

"So you'll be leaving the service?"

Here we go, Jen thought. Mum seeing her fondest wish become possible. "No," she said.

"I see."

"It's what I do."

"You do other things well. You've almost finished your degree, for heaven's sake. There are all sorts of things that—"

Jen interrupted. "I said it wrong. The army isn't just what I do. It's what I am. The Poli-Sci is to make me a better soldier, that's all."

Jen's father said, "You prefer field work to the library."

She nodded. "No slight meant."

"None perceived." Howard taught political science at the University of Manitoba. Jen had taken his Corporations and the State evening course two years ago. It had kept her up nights, stewing. "But you know," Howard went on, "we do more than just sit and study."

"I know, Dad." Howard loved digging around hot-button topics. He loved telling people what he found. And the media loved to let him tell. "I just feel that I'm more effective out there."

"And were you?" Howard asked. "Was your war effective?"

Jen grimaced. "Thanks for putting it that way."

"Well, was it?"

Jen turned her coffee cup around in her hands. "We shouldn't have stopped." The Highway flashed through her mind as she spoke, but she believed what she said.

"Why not?"

She thought for a moment. "The war wasn't complete."

Howard smiled. "That sounds like an esthetic argument."

"Could be."

Celia broke in. "It was all about oil, anyway."

Jen turned her head to look at her sister. "That right? So much for hero worship, I guess."

"You're cool. But it was still about oil."

"Indoctrination, Dad?" Jen asked. She kept her eyes on Celia.

"Critical thinking," he answered.

"Going to be a radical?" Jen asked Celia. "Going to be out there in the streets?"

"Don't tease." Celia got up from the table.

"I'm not. You go for it, Cee. Do it." Jen glanced at her mother. Gail was looking at her hands.

No secrets in home. They were doing the dishes when Jen got at her mother's. The phone rang. Howard passed the dishrag to Jen and went to answer. "What is it, Mum?" Jen asked as soon as Howard was out of the kitchen.

"Why are you a soldier?"

This again? And yet there was a quality to Gail's voice, a deep-soul quaver, that Jen hadn't heard before. "Because I am. And because somebody has to be."

"And was this war necessary?"

Jen didn't answer. In the corridor, she heard Howard say, "No." Then again: "No, I won't."

Gail leaned her hands against the counter. "You see, I'm not sure what upsets me more: that you feel some people need killing, or that you believe you're one of those chosen to do the killing."

"God, I don't think of it like that. And I wasn't anywhere near actual combat."

"What about next time?"

"Mum." She took her mother into her arms, her mother who, needing comfort, suddenly seemed so small.

Howard appeared at the kitchen doorway. He hovered there, looking like he wanted to talk. Jen mouthed "wait" to him, and he disappeared off to the living room. After a minute, Gail sighed and pulled away. "I'm sorry," she said, and sniffed.

"You shouldn't be," Jen said. She gave her mother's arm a squeeze. "I'll be right back."

Howard was sitting beside the fire. In the light of the low flames, his face had a gray sheen. Jen asked, "Something up?"

"I wanted to ask your advice."

"That's a reversal."

His smile was wan. He looked cold, frail, even more shrunken than Gail had seemed.

"You're freezing," Jen said. "Let me get some firewood, then I'll be wise."

Outside, she kicked through the snow, deep-breathing the frost. There was a woodshed at the bottom of the yard. She stepped in and loaded up with logs. She felt a queasy thrum in her chest. She didn't like seeing her parents vulnerable, especially not both at once. Her father had seemed fine until a couple of minutes ago, but not now. Now he was definitely not fine. Jen was okay handling Celia's adolescent traumas. Jen could remember how those worked. Helping Mum and Dad, though, that was going to take some care. Arms full, she stepped out of the shed.

Even over short distances, the difference in speed between sound and light is detectable. She saw the house explode a fraction before she felt it. A billow of light shot up from the basement, Hell breaking through. The light became a scream of fire that took out every window in the house. Then the shock wave hit her. She flew backwards, her cry swallowed by the roar and blaze of home flashburning into a pyre.

1

Flanagan never saw it coming.

Arthur Pembroke asked, "Who have you got for me?"

Karl Noonan slid the file across Pembroke's desk. "Mike Flanagan. In Shipping."

Pembroke placed a finger on the file's cover. "Tell me why you picked him."

"He's hungry, but he's a team player. He's been here two years, with top-notch work straight down the line. He's beginning to move up, gettin' his first taste of the honey. He's pumpin' up the efforts, so he wants more. But he never, ever rocks the boat. Doesn't play politics except when he's being peacemaker, gets along with everybody, wants everybody to like him."

"Puppy dog," Pembroke sniffed.

Noonan shrugged. "But a smart one. I made sure he got tossed a couple of curveballs recently, and he hammered them. He just does the job. And doesn't ask questions."

"Sounds too good to be true."

"Checkitout: it's all in the file. Mr. Friendly all through university. Does student politics, but only as secretary, treasurer, social convener, that kind of thing."

"Visible but non-controversial."

"You got it. Sat on a couple of committees that did squat, but were good for the resumé."

Pembroke smelled promise. He opened the file now. The first thing he saw was Flanagan's picture. Generic New England handsome. Early thirties. Mid-length hair with just that touch of wave. Clean-shaven. Eyes women probably thought of as soulful, but that Pembroke now read as desperate to please and not be hurt. "Okay, what about politics?"

"Republican Lite. Middle of the road. Up with money, but doesn't yell about it. Bit of the guilt thing. Radicals scare him. Get in his face and he backs down."

Pembroke leaned back in his chair. "We still need the safety factor. What have you got for leverage? Any wife, kids, parents?"

Noonan shook his head. "Never married. Had a couple of girlfriends, but nothing serious for the last year. The parents are dead. Heavy smokers. Kicked off pretty close together three years ago. But there is a sister."

"Something in your tone tells me she's a winner."

"Oh yeah." Noonan grinned, showing fangs. "Holly Flanagan. Ten years older. Divorced, one kid, aged eight. Student counsellor. Ready for the kicker? Some kid pulled a gun on her four years ago. Bullet damaged the spine. She's paralyzed from the waist down. Wheelchair city."

"And they're close?" Pembroke asked.

"He visits her every week. Helps out with medical expenses."

Pembroke spun around in his chair. He looked out the curving windows of his office at the stone spires of New York City's hunting grounds, thinking. Flanagan sounded perfect. But. "Are there any other possibilities?" he asked without turning around.

"A couple. None as good. Either the leverage isn't as strong, or they're shit-disturbers. Always something. I say we go with Flanagan and get this show rolling."

Pembroke let himself imagine the big picture for a moment, and saw a giant machine, every cog meshing smoothly. Time to let it go to work. "Do it."

A Friday morning of early April and life was fine. Flanagan looked up at the Integrated Security building as he approached, and gave it a smile. The building was a sixty-storey cylindrical column of black glass and steel. Needle thin, it shot up from the block-end formed where Greenwich and Trinity converged at Edgar. In Midtown its attitude would have been swallowed effortlessly by the classical-to-postmodern mix of skyscrapers, but here it was aggressively out of synch with the white stone of the surrounding buildings. It made the World Financial Center look like the dowager guardian of tradition. It was an architectural middle-finger salute to the Financial District. When Flanagan smiled at it, the building didn't smile back, but he still sensed that it was glad to see him. InSec had always treated him well, and lately had been treating him better. But the rest of the world had smartened up lately as well. The weather had cleared, the rains making way for the kind of New York spring day the tourist board sacrificed goats for. And he'd managed to go a full week now without stepping into any conversational minefields. The last month had been weird that way. He couldn't talk to anyone without accidentally hitting some hot button of theirs. He wasn't sure what curse had blighted his usually smooth social sailing, but it seemed to have lifted now, and he'd had seven consecutive nights of going to bed without the nagging chest-pinch memory of having given offense. He was cruising again, rock and roll. "Looking sharp," he told the building, and stepped through the revolving door.

Sleek and airy, the lobby was dominated by a fountain that shot a narrow jet of water three storeys high. Boutiques lined the perimeter of the lobby, exercises in quiet taste that attracted only the most select public. Nearer the elevators were a newsstand and sandwich counter, as neat and attractive as the jewelry snob-shop. Nothing but the best at InSec.

A security turnstile blocked the way to the elevator bank.

"Morning, Derek," Flanagan said to Derek Hirsch, who was guarding the drawbridge.

"Good morning, Mr. Flanagan." Formal and correct as ever, not a hint of familiarity after two years, but what the hell, that was Hirsch. Flanagan swiped his pass through the sensor and passed through the turnstile. He joined the crowd waiting for the elevators, then rode forty floors to the Shipping department and cubicle-land. Spacious cubicles, granted, and ones where there was minimal shuffling, so you could make yours as close to a home environment as you could manage, but cubicles nonetheless. Not for Flanagan, though, not for the last six months. He wove his way through the rat maze, smiling and launching good-mornings for all he was worth, doing his damnedest to carry the rest of the department along in the wake of his mood, and got to his office. It wasn't a window office, but still, it was an honest-to-God office, and just outside was his honest-to-God secretary, proof positive that, if he hadn't arrived just yet, his plane was at least on final approach.

"Morning, Mon—" Flanagan covered his stumble with a cough. "Mary. Lovely day outside." He'd almost called her "Moneypenny." Bottomore looked a lot like a latter-day Lois Maxwell, and Flanagan was getting a little too comfortable thinking of her that way. He wasn't sure she'd appreciate the joke. He picked up his messages and hurried into his office before his face, eternal stoolie, gave him away with a flustered blush. Still, no harm done, still sailing smooth. He settled down and flicked on his computer. Main order of business was finishing the report on the new InSec fleet. There was a proposal on the boards to purchase eight new superfreighters. The decision to buy was not Flanagan's (God forbid), but a report on feasibility and costs was expected from him. Input without responsibility. He rather liked that. As far as he was concerned, the fleet was a stellar idea. InSec's shipping was on a steady rise, and he'd seen projections that called for some colossal tonnage transfers in the near future. He marshaled his arguments and got to work.

Noon had just rolled around when there was a knock on his door. Rebecca Harland, from Foreign Accounts, poked her head in. "Hey hey," she said.

"Hey yourself."

"Lunch?"

"Two shakes. Let me put some last touches here. Have a seat."

Harland parked herself down to wait. Flanagan's fingers danced over the keyboard as he came up to the big finish. His conclusions were solid, his numbers were impeccable, and his prose shone. He had the tingle he got when he was on a winning track, when he *knew*, goddamn *knew*, that he was producing excellence. He was more than earning his keep, and he loved it. When he got to the last sentence, his momentum almost kept him going. He leaned back, clicked on SAVE, and grinned.

Harland said, "Enough with the swallowed canary act. Let's go eat."

Flanagan stood up. "In the sun?"

"Yeah. Shame to waste it."

Forty floors back down and out into a day that had

bloomed the promise of the morning. Flanagan squinted against the light as he and Harland walked the block up to Trinity Church. They angled right on Rector, found a vendor on Broadway, grabbed some bagels, and entered the churchyard. There was a dozen or so other office workers taking lunch in the grounds. There was no reason why the mere fact of stepping through a low wrought-iron gate should make the sounds of the city drop away, but it did. Flanagan could hear birds. The force of Wall Street receded, respectful. They sat down on the steps of the central monument.

"All right," Flanagan said after swallowing his first mouthful of bagel. "I can tell you have news. Let's have it."

"Well, it's like this. You know Terry Chatman?"

"Know *of* him." Flanagan wasn't sure exactly what Chatman's official position in the company was, but he had a habit of turning up in pictures with upper stratosphere politicians. Heavyweight. "Haven't been up to his pad lately, though," he quipped.

"Ho ho," Harland's response was mechanical. Cue for Flanagan to start taking this seriously. "The MAI talks are starting up all over again in Paris at the beginning of May."

Flanagan whistled. That was big news. Negotiations for the Multilateral Agreement on Investment by the twenty-nine wealthy nations of the Organization for Economic Cooperation and Development (OECD) had been an on-again off-again deal since the '90s. The last collapse in 1998 had put paid to the idea, or so it had seemed. Ostensibly the accord laid down standardized rules for global business investment, for the purpose of saner, smoother trade. In practice it had the potential for opening up all sorts of areas the transnationals had previously been denied access to. Flanagan had heard some Wall Street sharks refer to it as Master And Invade. All he knew was that every time there were rumors of the OECD having another kick at the can, his stock options went up. "For real?" he asked. "For real and for true?"

"Call your broker. So anyway, Terry is flying over to be InSec's rep at the talks."

"And. . . ." Flanagan prompted. He noticed Harland's use of the first name. She moved in higher circles than he had suspected.

"And he wants me in Paris as his aide."

Flanagan ate his bagel in silence for a moment as he absorbed this. "Wow," he finally said. "For how long?"

"For the duration."

Flanagan looked at Harland. Her face was both excited and uncertain. "Well. Congratulations, yes?"

Harland shrugged. "Thanks, yes, I guess. I mean, it is an unbelievable step up."

"But. . . ."

"Christ, Mike, why is InSec so keen on the MAI? Think about it."

Flanagan didn't want to. Smooth sailing often required an absence of thought. "That's not your problem."

"Isn't it?"

"No. No broken laws, no problem."

"But the consequences—"

"—are for the people who are in charge of those things to work out. Worry about your own consequences. Imagine what would happen if you said no." Silence. Harland kept her eyes on the cobblestones. "You hear it, I know you do," Flanagan said. "That hard *clunk* sound. That, my dear, is the sound of the glass ceiling falling into place. You say no to Chatman tomorrow, and you can say hello to the first day of the rest of your life."

Harland didn't say anything for a couple of minutes. Then: "You really are a cold fish son of a bitch."

Flanagan felt something open a deep lesion. He tried to ignore it. "No. I'm just realistic." He looked Harland in the eyes. "You ace this thing, and you're gold, and not just with InSec." He paused for a moment. "Then you can get out," he said quietly.

Harland wiped her hands with her napkin. They were already clean. "What about you?" she asked. "You the team player forever?"

"Until the big score," Flanagan said. "Give me my big score and I'll bear the children of the first headhunter who comes calling."

Harland leaned back, lifting her face to the sun. "And when we're gone, someone else will step in and do exactly the same thing." Her eyes were closed.

"Which is why we don't worry about things now, and we'll worry about them even less when we're gone." He stood, lunch done, wanting to banish the shadow of the conversation. "Let's go."

They left the churchyard. Trinity's spire watched and judged. And back in his office, laser printer spitting out his report, Flanagan slumped in his chair and stared at his computer screen. He wasn't seeing the words, though. He was replaying his conversation with Harland, trying to sand down the little rough edges of guilt that were snagging at his gut. Easy, he told himself. Easy. You gave her excellent advice, and not a word of a lie. Did he believe that? Yes. You want the American Dream, you don't turn away when someone hands it to you. It would have been criminal to suggest Harland do anything else but kiss the ring on Chatman's finger. All right, then. This was all true. So what was the problem? Why this sharp little tooth gnawing at him where he couldn't reach? Why was he glad that Holly hadn't been there, and that he wouldn't have to tell her what he'd said? When he thought of Holly, the tooth sank in a little deeper, and that gave him a clue as to what was up. "Damn you to hell, Big Sister," he muttered. Her and her bloody liberal guilt. It was contagious, and it was free floating. Here he was, infected, and on a rational level he couldn't think of a single reason why Holly would have objected to his advice. Did she feel like this all the time? What kind of a life was that? And what the hell use was the guilt if it wasn't even applicable to anything? Unbelievable. But at least now that he had diagnosed the problem he was able to start prying the little jaws loose.

"Hello-ello-ello," said a voice.

Flanagan jumped, spooked back to earth by the trade-marked greeting of the one, the only, Johnathan W. Smith III. Flanagan grinned, sheepish. "Sorry. A little spaced there, for a minute."

A hand up: no problem, no worries. "I just wanted to check and see if, perchance, you could give me a projection on the completion of that little fleet report you were work-ing on? Hmmm?"

"Absolutely. In fact. . . ." Flanagan turned to his printer, which was just spitting out the last page. He snatched up the manuscript. "Here it is." He started to pass it over.

Both hands up, palms out: no no, not for me. "My dear boy, how superb. But you misunderstand me. I ask not for my benefit. That you are finished is most excellent. That means you can accompany me now, rather than later."

"Uh, where to?"

"Why, upstairs, of course. Oh, didn't I mention? Our munificent employer himself would like you to make a presentation of your report. In person, as it were."

Flanagan sat still for a moment, sorting it out. But no, no mistake. Opportunity was at the door. Knock knock knock. Better let it in.

2

Johnathan W. Smith III, head of InSec's Shipping department, encouraged one and all to refer to him by his full
name, complete with all accessories. "III" because he was
the third child born to Fred and Wendy Smith. The "W"
didn't stand for anything at all, but he thought it jazzed up
his name. Born and raised in Hoboken, but he flitted over
to England every summer to brush up on his phony accent.
Where he thought his diction was coming from was anybody's guess. He walked the high wire, netless, between
"character" and "pompous shit." He got away with it
because he buzzed self-irony. You wanted to hate him. You
wanted him to be insufferable. You wound up hanging out
with him.

Flanagan liked him. Here was a guy whose sense of the-
ater and routine not only was so consistent, it went light-
years beyond the poor shtick Flanagan and Harland came

up with. And as a boss, he couldn't be faulted. The captain of Shipping kept his own ship tight, and morale fairly crackled. Now they were going up to meet the admiral. Flanagan's mouth was dry as they stepped into the elevator. Johnathan W. Smith III stuck a key in the control panel, turned it, then hit the button for the sixtieth floor. Flanagan's grip on his report tightened as the elevator shot up. He glanced down at the papers, worried he was going to stain them with sweat.

A pat on the shoulder. "Relax, faithful lackey. All will be well."

The elevator doors opened. Smith III stepped out and Flanagan followed, skin tingling as he found himself, for the very first time, in the home of power. No cubicles on the sixtieth floor. Up here were only the gods, and they all had windows in their offices. The corridor from the elevators to Pembroke's sanctum was wide and sanitized. The pink marble of the floor and walls gleamed. Oak doors led off it on either side. Ahead, an even bigger set of doors. Above them, InSec's name in monolithic bronze. In front of the doors, a circular desk for Pembroke's receptionist. No Moneypenny here. His shoulders were much too broad, his stare much too bland and evaluating. Smith III bowed to him, and the receptionist jerked his chin: go in. Through the doors was an office three times the size of Flanagan's, and this just for Pembroke's secretary. She didn't look up from her computer as they passed by, through another set of doors, and finally into the lion's den.

Flanagan's initial impression was of space. Pembroke's office took up half of the sixtieth storey's floor space. A huge expanse of muted gray carpeting stretched out to floor-to-ceiling panoramic windows. The view was a half-horizon embrace of the Financial District, high enough up that Pembroke could look down at the narrow canyon of Wall Street. The effect was of the outside world as an extension of Pembroke's domain. His desk was a monster, but it was a tiny island in the office's immensity. Pembroke was seated at the desk, flanked by another man. The doors snicked closed behind Flanagan. He tried to generate enough saliva to swallow. Smith III ushered him forward, arms out to either side as if both welcoming and presenting. Pembroke got up from his chair and came around to the front of the desk.

"Mike Flanagan," Johnathan W. Smith III said, "Arthur Pembroke."

So this, Flanagan thought, is my boss of bosses. He wasn't sure what he had expected, but Pembroke wasn't it. Flanagan placed him in his early sixties. Short gray hair. Trim. Nice face, but nondescript. If Flanagan had seen him in the street, he would have pegged him as a mid-level civil servant, not the god of a transnational. Pembroke's hand-shake was almost disappointingly ordinary. Neither the crushing alpha male grip nor the dead fish avoidance of the lowly. "Thanks for coming up, Mike," Pembroke said, regular guy with a couple extra dollops of dignity. "This is Karl Noonan," he added, introducing the other man. Flanagan noticed that Pembroke didn't mention Noonan's title. If he was here, he was probably pretty high up in the pantheon. Noonan was a little guy, five six, maybe five seven, and Flanagan got the sense that there was a hell of a lot packed into that frame. When Noonan walked, he almost bounced, as if he had so much energy contained that it was all he could do to stay earthbound. His handshake had a studied ordinariness to it. It felt like a pulled punch. His eyes were wide and amused. Flanagan caught himself thinking of both stand-up comics and radars. "Have a seat." Pembroke's gesture took everyone in. They sat down in the three low arm-chairs that faced the desk. Noonan's foot started tapping immediately, but stopped when Pembroke shot him a look. Pembroke perched on the edge of the desk. "I realize you haven't had time to put together a formal oral report," he said to Flanagan. "So don't worry. Just give the salient points, if you will."

Flanagan nodded. Pembroke's manner had eased some of the pressure on his heart. He could swallow again. He could handle this. "In a nutshell, I think the new fleet is something we can't do without, if we're working from a long-term perspective here. And the bigger the ships, the better. They'll cost, but they'll also pay off." Pembroke nodded, waited for him to go on. Flanagan started to flip through his report for a graph, then stopped. Keep it concise, he told himself. Pembroke will ask for the figures if he wants them. Flanagan looked up and spoke without looking down at his pages. He explained that InSec's shipping patterns tended to concentrate first on one geographical focal point, then another. InSec needed to meet the demand of the focal points where and when they formed. It needed to move large cargoes, and it needed mobility. Big ships would meet that need with the greatest economy. Not only that, but the bigger and more imposing the individual cargo, the less time it tended to be held up in Customs. Particularly in the more corrupt regions, the amount of baksheesh InSec would have to budget for would be much less for one big shipment than for several smaller ones. "I did some rough calculations based on the cost of the average large freighter," Flanagan concluded, "and I think the new fleet will have paid for itself in less than ten years."

Pembroke took the report, rifled the pages, then put it down on the desk. "I'll go over this in detail later," he said, "but what you've told me already essentially confirms my own thinking."

Jackpot, Flanagan thought. Jesus loves me, this I know.

"There's another reason why I wanted to talk to you." Pembroke leaned forward slightly, serious business. Flanagan felt a quick twinge of *oh shit,* but then realized that no way would Pembroke take the time to tear a strip off someone as far down the ladder as he was. "I've noticed the same trends you have," Pembroke went on, "along with something else that you might or might not have specifically picked up on: political volatility. A change in the political weather, a coup at just the wrong time, and a shipment can be held up in port for months. Or it can be destroyed altogether. It has happened."

"All the more reason for mobility."

"Yes, but that's also one of the drawbacks of a big ship. If something goes wrong, we lose a lot more."

Flanagan saw a gaping hole open up in his report. "I'm afraid I haven't covered that eventuality," he admitted.

Pembroke smiled. "Don't worry about it. You couldn't be expected to cover everything. You don't have all the information."

This was true. InSec was unbelievably compartmentalized. Each section only received information on a need-to-know basis. On the whole, that didn't bother Flanagan. The hard and fast divisions made the organization clear, and he liked to know that everything was in its place. He suspected that Pembroke did too, and that the man was a control freak of the first order. But hell, it was his company, he could run it the way he wanted. And it seemed to be working.

"Did you know," said Pembroke, "that we have had at least six incidents of piracy in the last quarter?" When he saw Flanagan's eyes widen, he added, "It's not something we advertise. But this is the kind of loss I'd like to guard against."

Which has what to do with me? Flanagan wondered.

"This is what I think," said Pembroke, and Flanagan sensed that he was supposed to take what came next as the eleventh commandment. "Given the size that our shipments will be with the new fleet, the kind of pirates that will target us will not be interested in carting away a few crates, but in diverting the ship itself. I want to make that impossible."

Flanagan frowned. "I don't see how one can do that."

"We can do it if the captain's control over the ship can be overridden. Remote control navigation. When necessary, we take over the ship from here."

Weird, Flanagan thought. He turned the idea over in his mind, trying to imagine not the whys but the hows of the project. Weird, yes, but interesting, no doubt about it.

"Can it be done?" Pembroke asked.

Flanagan thought for a moment. "Yes. Yes, I think we could give it a shot. Access to Global Positioning Satellite information is completely public now, and if we slave that to some really first-class anti-hazard navigational equipment. . . ." He trailed off, routes to the project's realization beginning to open up before him. It began to seem cool instead of weird.

"Access to the override system would have to be strictly limited," said Pembroke.

"Of course, of course," Flanagan nodded, now only half in the meeting. The other half was already back downstairs, getting to work. "How many people will have authorization to use it?"

"Let's start with the assumption that only I will," said Pembroke.

Yup, Flanagan thought, control freak. "What kind of a time frame do I have?"

"I want the system installed and operational by July."

Flanagan was a hundred percent back in the room. He felt dizzy. "Of this year? But the ships—"

"—are already built. The decision that needed making was whether we bought them, or we let someone else pick them up."

Flanagan considered. July. It was on the tip of his tongue to ask why the rush, but he held back. Need-to-know basis, and Pembroke will tell you if you need to know. "That's not a lot of time." He tried to laugh. "Well, it's a challenge, I'll give it that."

Pembroke's mouth smiled, but his eyes were doing something else. Evaluating. "I'm sure you're up to it. We would, of course, give you every assistance. And you'd be granted relief from all your other duties for the duration of the project."

Flanagan looked at Pembroke straight on and smiled. "I'm going to give you a system that will knock your socks off," he said.

This time Pembroke's smile reached his eyes.

Johnathan W. Smith III was beaming as they rode the elevator back down to the fortieth floor. "My boy," he said, over and over, the proud father, "my boy." It was the first time he had spoken since he'd made the introductions. "You have a rare gift. You presented an argument that was in perfect accord with Our Fearless Leader's opinions *before* you knew what those opinions were. Is there anyone more blessed than the precognitive yes-man? I doubt it heartily."

Good old Smith III, Over The Top, and wasn't it grand? Flanagan's chest was swollen fit to tear his shirt. Massively in love with himself at this moment, but hey, he was entitled. He'd pulled it off. That loud blast was the horn of his ship coming in, and it was a luxury liner.

3

Ronald Hooks asked, "How long would it be for?"

"That's just it," Harland said. "I don't know. Several months, at the very least."

It was after dinner. Outside, freed of a properly elegant winter, Park Slope geared up for a properly elegant spring. Inside, Faith and Julie, nine and six, were sprawled on the living room floor in front of the television. Harland sat with her husband on the sofa. They spoke quietly, camouflaging their conversation under the cover of the whiz-bangs of *Sailor Moon*.

Hooks was silent for a bit. Finally: "The place is going to seem awfully empty," he said.

Harland sighed. "I know." They'd agreed on the principles the marriage would follow a year before the actual wedding, when they were both finishing their degrees, and they'd managed to stick to them. The agreement: whoever was making enough money to support the family on a single income would continue to work. That turned out to be Harland. Hooks had been true to his word, and had set about transforming himself into househusband. But still. Traditions were ancient ghosts with long shadows. Harland fought a constant struggle against the irrational voice, sometimes in her head, sometimes in other people's tones, that denounced the unfit, selfish mother. Hooks reassured her that there was no problem from his side. He certainly never acted as if there was. But still.

"I'm not saying it's going to be easy," Hooks said. He gave a short laugh. "Or even that I'm going to like it. But I really don't see how you can say no." A pause. Spaceships zoomed by on the TV. Hooks said, "Heck, I've always wanted to see Paris."

They smiled at each other, but Harland could still feel the strain. She reached out, touched her husband's face, then dropped her hand to his thigh. "We're going to have to make this week count." She moved her hand, just a bit. "I think the girls might need an early night, don't you?"

Flanagan turned up for Saturday dinner at Holly's Elmhurst apartment bearing gifts. Cowboy hat for Eddie, champagne for Holly, celebratory mood for himself. He wore the hat. Eddie answered the door. He was bobbing up and down. He was always bobbing. Flanagan figured he bounced off the walls even when he was asleep. Eyes a startling blue, face strangely serious even in the bobbing, Eddie looked up at Flanagan, and the blue eyes went neon when he saw the hat. "I think this is too small for me," Flanagan said. "You want it?"

"Yes!" Eddie exclaimed. "Thank you, Uncle Mike, thank you!" He put the hat on and raced off, galloping now instead of bouncing.

Flanagan closed the door behind him and sauntered

through the apartment. The place was a weird mix of the messy and the regimented. Eddie's toys and storybooks littered the floor, but always against the walls, leaving the center of the floor clear for Holly's wheelchair. The lower shelves of wall unit and bookcases overflowed with papers and stacked books. The upper shelves were empty. Flanagan found Holly at the kitchen table, slicing vegetables. She wore a brown cardigan that matched her eyes and her short hair. Her face, pale with high cheekbones, showed the delicate, easily broken side of the family looks. Holly looked up from the carrots. "A cowboy hat?" She cocked her head. "Going for most typical uncle gift of the year?"

"Well, I would have brought him a—" —*gun*, he'd been about to say, followed by some crack about knee-jerk anti-NRA liberals. And wouldn't that have been funny to the woman with the bullet-shattered spine. He hadn't stopped himself in time. He saw it in Holly's face as she completed his sentence for herself. Her eyes flinted briefly. She said nothing, cut carrots just a bit harder. "Sorry." He presented the champagne, flourish nixed now. "Brought this," he said, as Eddie barreled through the kitchen in hot pursuit of something. "After rustlers?" Flanagan called after him.

Eddie stopped, turned around. "Rustlers?" Puzzled at the new word.

"Rustlers," Flanagan repeated, as if that were an explanation. He put the pots on the stove. "Bad guys who steal cows."

"Nooooo," said Eddie, dismayed at adult naïveté. "Crack dealers." He took off again.

Flanagan stared at the spot where Eddie had been. "*Crack dealers?*" he echoed.

"What do you want?" said Holly. "He's an urban cowboy. It's called growing up in the big city." Her eyes were taking no shit again. "And enough delaying tactics. What's your news?"

Flanagan popped the cork on the champagne. "I met

Pembroke on Friday, and God Almighty Himself has given me a task to perform." He grinned. "Career jackpot." He got a couple of glasses from the cupboard and poured the champagne. "So?" he asked, handing Holly a glass. "Impressed?"

"Mm," said Holly. She sipped at her champagne. She looked more pensive than impressed. "Well done, brother mine." The words were mere motions gone through. Flanagan knew the signs. She was going to have to think things through for a while. And only then would she really congratulate him. Or tear a strip off him and ruin his day. Even money on either option. "Could you set the table?" Holly asked, subject closed for the moment. Flanagan scooped up knives and forks. As he headed for the dining room, a bouquet on the windowsill caught his eye. Holly never bought flowers for herself. He looked back at her, saw her turn away quickly and become absorbed in the vegetables. He pursed his lips, amused. If she was going to be coy, fine, but she was going to know he knew.

Dinner was roast chicken, roast potatoes, boiled vegetables, Flanagan clan Saturday fare since time immemorial. Flanagan kept catching Holly's eye and shifting an arch gaze at the flowers. She blushed all the way through the meal. By dessert, Eddie was getting restless, bored with the opaque adult game. Coffee time rolled around, the signal that child attendance at the table was no longer compulsory, and Eddie excused himself and took off after more crack dealers. Flanagan and Holly stayed at the dining room table, sipping decaf.

"This task of yours," Holly said, "whatever it is, will, I suppose, hugely aid in the shipping of all that wonderful Integrated Security."

Flanagan groaned. "Do we have to do this again? Goddammit, why is that I'm never allowed to turn a profit without being made to feel dirty? There's nothing wrong with making a buck, you know. I have it on good authority that there are quite a few CEOs in the country who have never contemplated genocide."

"I never said that making a profit was evil."

Flanagan rolled his eyes. "Well, excuse me for misunderstanding you most of my life. And here all this time I thought you were mounting rearguard action for the oppressed working classes."

"I wasn't finished."

Holly was going to say more, but Flanagan cut her off: "It's not like I'm laundering money and moving cocaine from port to port."

"No, you're shipping guns. That's so much better."

Yes, guns were better, because they were legal. But it didn't matter what he believed, or how firmly he made himself believe it, because Holly's questions nagged at him. They always did. Nasty, itchy, scratchy questions that sank needles into his marrow and niggled and wiggled and worried at his beliefs. The story of his relationship with his sister, going back as far as his first discovery of politics, a couple of years before he discovered sex. Big Sister with her ten-year head start, that much longer to marshal her arguments and firm up her views. They had had more sparring matches over this issue or that than he cared to count, and he couldn't remember ever having felt he'd won a round. Maybe his questions stabbed at Holly the way hers did at him, but if they did, she didn't let on. She hadn't budged an inch when he told her this was the big score, his ticket out of InSec. So he lay awake fuming far into Saturday night, imaginary arguments raging in his head. And even in his fantasies he wasn't necessarily getting the upper hand.

The internal dialogue kept up, unresolved, through Sunday, while he was trying to finish the project outline. It slowed him down, and he didn't get to bed until late. On Monday he was grumpy, and he wasn't looking forward to the initial meeting of his team for the nav control. Fortunately, the meeting wasn't until three. By that time, Holly's questions were mostly smothered under work, and he had his enthusiasm back when he walked into the conference room and made Project NAVCON big-time official. He barnstormed. He rock'n'rolled. He charged up his team of computer engineers with the god-fire of inspiration and promised bonuses. He didn't lose stride once, not even when Chris Grant asked how they were supposed to beta test the system. Flanagan promised a quick answer, and as soon as the briefing was over he charged off, spring in his step, flying high once again on the buzz of a job well nailed, to find the man with the answers.

"Hello-ello-ello, my favorite lackey!" Johnathan W. Smith III welcomed, arms outstretched. "Enter, enter."

Flanagan stepped into the office. The furniture was all standard issue InSec Exec, but Union Jacks and portraits of the Queen covered the walls. It wasn't so much an exercise in poor taste as mindbending wallpaper. Flanagan said, "I have a couple of questions about NAVCON."

"'NAVCON'?" Baffled. Not a good sign. Flanagan had sent him a memo summarizing his initial steps. If Smith III wasn't up to speed there, he might not be in other areas, either.

"The navigation project," Flanagan explained.

"Hold, hold." Palm up, traffic cop. "Do you observe the time?"

Flanagan dutifully turned and looked at the clock over the doorway. "Yes." Resigned. It was only just past four-thirty.

"I strongly suggest we take this discussion and retire with it to a congenial tavern. At which point we may talk necessary shop without the added pain of actually being *in* the aforementioned shop." He took Flanagan by the arm and led him from the office. Flanagan smelled liquor on his breath.

The Baying Hound was on the north side of Pine, just east of William, a five-minute wind through the streets from

InSec. It showed every sign of having been specifically tailored for Johnathan W. Smith III. Three blocks from InSec, the fact that it wasn't actually part of a skyscraper was about the only thing in its favor, as far as Flanagan was concerned. Faux English to the bone, but not working as a pub since there was a deli at the entrance, followed by a few steps up and then a long salad bar. Only then came the seating area, and the Brit show kicked in. All the dark wood was plastic. A huge painting of a hunting scene hung on the east wall. It had suspicious snow-capped peaks in the background. The Bodington's was in cans, though the Bud was on tap. Smith III's grin as they walked in told him that it was tongue-in-cheek time again, but Flanagan wasn't into kitsch appreciation. He wanted to work. Smith III chose one of the tables next to the big windows that looked out onto Cedar. What with the stairs to the salad bar and the slope of the streets, they were now a floor up from the sidewalk, and the view was a salving dose of New York, authentic throb come to cleanse the fakery. "This is a blessed establishment," Smith III confided. "It attracts a most comely clientele." He was looking to Flanagan's left, back toward the buffet. He tipped an imaginary hat. "Most comely," he repeated, and gave Flanagan the grin of the gentleman wolf.

Flanagan turned his head and caught a glimpse of a woman as she headed for the washrooms. Yes, yes, very attractive. Gesture made, he turned back to Smith III, hoping the man would finally let him talk business. No such luck. First, drinks had to be ordered. And when they arrived, a toast had to be made. "To you, faithful lackey," Smith III said, glass high, "and to your future. Once you enter the loop, may you never leave it." Down the hatch. "You can't see it now," Smith III went on, "because you haven't quite reached the loop yet. But once there, there is nothing more painful than being removed from it. Better never to have been an angel than to be a fallen one. Do not, I say, *do not* let this happen to you."

What the hell? Flanagan thought. What's going on here? Was Smith III on his way out? That didn't seem likely. And the pain in his tone was old, a nursed grievance, not a fresh wound. "I'll do my best," Flanagan said.

Smith III nodded, satisfied. "Good. Now unveil your difficulty for me."

"The beta testing. How are we going to do that? We aren't exactly going to have a freighter to play around with, are we?"

Smith III pursed his lips, attention focused in the right spot at last. "Hmm. Yes. Well, we will be able to transport a test unit on board a ship to check that the signals are indeed being passed back and forth, and that the position mapping is performing agreeably."

"But what about the navigation override?"

"Trickier," Smith III conceded. "But I expect some testing in port will be possible."

"I guess that will have to do, given the time we've got. I wish it wasn't such a rush. So many things could go wrong."

Smith III smiled wisely. "Then you'll just have to avoid them, won't you now? The accomplishment will be all the more—" He stopped. He was looking left again. His mouth was half-open, confused. Flanagan followed his gaze. There was a figure standing next to their table. Loose-fitting black clothes, balaclava, sunglasses. The figure pulled out a gun, and shot Smith III five times in the face.

4

Detective Ed Kroker could sense a shitstorm coming two days in advance. He would feel it in his knee, destroyed by college football thirty years ago and overhauled by surgery. Forty-eight hours before the storm hit, he would feel a weird, buzzing twitch in the tendons. And he'd been feeling the buzz big time since Saturday. It had screwed with his beauty sleep. Now he heaved his bulk out of his car and stood for a minute outside the Baying Hound. The buzz had stopped. Bad sign. That meant the storm was about to hit. But he didn't need his knee to tell him that. The street was barricaded, a 187 had been called in at dinnertime, and traffic had held him up. The week was off to a killer start, and it got even better when he stepped into the bar. It looked like he was practically the last one on the scene. The ident section was there in force, flashbulbing and dusting corner to corner. Paul Beckson, the ME, was bending over a booth at the back. Kroker's partner, Dyanne Lutz, fifty and still lanky as a sharp retort, sauntered over to meet him, saying, "The pool is already two-to-one this is going to be a shit-can." Kroker sighed. His stomach decided it was time to roil some gas. He didn't like hearing the case was going to go unsolved before he'd even begun work. Lutz went on: "Perp was covered head to toe and didn't say a word. The only description so far is that he was under six feet." She held up a notebook opened to a depressingly empty page.

"Build?" Kroker asked.

"Average, but that's a guess. The clothing was loose."

"Great."

"Oh, the joy's just getting started. You haven't seen the stiff yet. Come on."

They walked over to the rear of the café. Beckson saw them and stood back from the corpse. It had no face. None. It barely had a head. Kroker tried to remember when he had last seen cavitation this extreme. He couldn't. The entire front of the skull had been blasted to shrapnel. Little bits of flesh added consistency to the blood stew that slicked the table and the chairs. The body was wearing a suit that had turned into a sponge. "No shell casings," Lutz said. "No exit wounds. And every shot hit. No impacts any-where else."

Kroker began to think he'd take the pool's odds on the shitcan. The chances of recovering any kind of identifiable bullet were lousy. The killer had obviously used soft points, at the very least, and the deformation would be extreme. "What else?" he asked.

"This is a guess," said Beckson. "Don't quote me on this until I've had a chance to look at the body back in the lab, but I see some specks that look like shot to me."

Kroker frowned. "Shotgun?"

Lutz shook her head. "Witnesses say a handgun. And five shots."

Kroker paused, putting this together. The pieces didn't

want to fit at first, but when they did, he felt his eyes widen. "Glasers?"

"I'm leaning that way," said Beckson. "Like I said, I'm still guessing. It's a bit of a leap, but. . . ." He shrugged.

"*Five* Glasers?" Kroker demanded.

Beckson grimaced.

"Point blank," Lutz added.

"Unbelievable." Kroker was morbidly impressed. The Glaser Safety Slug was in the high aristocracy of manstoppers. Shot pellets floated in liquid Teflon, and when the slug hit, it exploded. As a touch of overkill, the Teflon had a habit of stopping the heart once it entered the bloodstream. In police use, the slug had almost always meant a one-hit kill. To shoot someone five times, point blank, in the face, with Glasers wasn't just murder. It was erasure.

"Execution?" Beckson suggested.

Kroker thought about this. "Not by the mob. Not their style. Glasers?" He shook his head. "Do we know who he is?"

"Johnathan W. Smith III, head of Shipping at Integrated Security," said Lutz.

"And he was ID'ed by . . . ?"

"An employee of his." Lutz flipped through her notes. "Michael Flanagan. They were having drinks together."

Kroker looked around the pub. Officers were speaking to witnesses, getting names and addresses. "Which one's Flanagan?" he asked.

"He's in the manager's office," said Lutz. "I thought you might want to take a crack at him early and without the crowd scene."

Kroker made his way to the back rooms of the Baying Hound. The office was down a little corridor that led off the west side, a little bit of darkness between the buffet and the dining area. Washrooms on the left, exit straight ahead, office on the right. Kroker pushed the door open. Flanagan was sitting in a chair facing the desk. Kroker noted the choice of seat: Flanagan had respect for the symbols of authority. He was hunched up, and Kroker detected a very slight back-and-forth rocking. His right leg drummed up and down. Blood spattered his suit. Kroker said, "I'm Detective Ed Kroker, NYPD Homicide." Flanagan stood, precarious, and shook his hand. Good, Kroker thought, he's still functioning. Kroker took the chair behind the desk. "I realize this is difficult for you, but the more information we can glean while events are still fresh for you, the better off we'll be for catching the killer."

"I'm not likely to forget anything," said Flanagan, green.

Kroker put on his understanding smile. "Trust me, Mr. Flanagan, you will. That's one of the beauties of the human ability to cope. This will fade." Flanagan looked unconvinced, but slightly calmer. "Now, is there anything you can tell me about the assailant?"

Flanagan shook his head. "No. Like I told the other officers, he was completely covered."

"And he said nothing."

"That's right."

"Can you remember anything about the clothing? Were there any labels visible?"

"No."

"Tell me about Mr. Smith. Can you think of any reason why anyone would want to kill him? Enemies? Was he in any trouble?"

Flanagan was looking both confused and thoughtful. "I got the feeling he was unhappy about something at work. He was sort of hinting that way just before ... just before."

Kroker's antennae didn't twitch. He sensed a dead-end lead. Still, follow it up. Follow everything up. "What do you think was bothering him?"

Flanagan grimaced. "I think he was feeling left out of something, or maybe he thought that he was being eased out. I'm really not sure. But nothing ... no reason anyone would want to.... Oh Jesus." His face paled to pure white and he started rocking harder. "Jesus Jesus Jesus."

"How well did you know him?" Kroker asked, trying to break through Flanagan's horror spiral.

Flanagan looked up and blinked a couple of times before Kroker's question got through. "Not that well. We've gone for a drink a couple of times."

"He was your immediate superior, I understand."

"Yeah."

"A good boss?"

"Yeah. A bit odd. But he treated you well."

Shitcan, Kroker thought, shitcan. Nice-guy boss gets whacked by killer with no visible characteristics and no apparent motive, using virtually untraceable weaponry. So they could try to trace all recent purchases of Glasers, if that's what the ammo turned out to be. That would generate a fair haul of paperwork, but most likely would end there. They'd do a background check on Smith, and maybe that would produce something. Maybe. And now Kroker's antennae twitched, because he remembered what his knee had been telling him. A shitcan was a shitcan, but a shitstorm was something else again. He was suddenly convinced that he had only seen the gathering of the clouds.

The police finished with Flanagan sooner than he had expected. Now he was sorry that they had. He was standing in the kitchen of his Hudson Tower apartment in Battery Park City. He couldn't remember why he was there. He hadn't come for food, he knew that. It was eleven o'clock, he was completely freaked, sleep was a very distant option, and he didn't want to be alone. He walked to the entrance hall and stared at his coat. Go out? Go out where? Call Holly? Call Harland? Again? No. They'd already done their time on the phone with him this evening. They were probably asleep now, and how much further could he justify bringing murder into their homes?

Okay, so go out. Just go where there are people. There

was a bar a block up at the corner of Albany and South End. He didn't go there often. It was called Characters, but that was a lie. It was about as generic as you could get, but that was probably for the best right now. Tonight the bar was practically deserted. Flanagan had hoped for more people. He counted six. Still, better than nothing. And now that he was here, he wasn't interested in socializing. He just wanted evidence of other lives, of the world continuing on as usual. He sat at the bar and ordered a boilermaker. He would deal with the hangover tomorrow. If he had to, he'd even call in sick.

Two drinks in, the buzz wasn't happening right. It was as if the adrenalin from earlier was still hanging around, burning off the alcohol almost as fast as he could down it. He could feel his body begin to lose precision, but his mind wasn't getting any of the benefit. Solution: order a third drink.

"Hard day at the office?"

Flanagan turned his head to the right. A woman had come in and was sitting two stools over. She was smiling, and she had a nice smile, but her eyes almost made him look away. Dark eyes, very dark, matching the raven of her short hair. They were deep, dangerously so, glittering, and he could feel targeting lasers coming from them, painting the terrain, evaluating and moving on. Caught in their search, he felt a scan take him in, size him up, and download everything worth knowing. Already vulnerable enough, he broke gaze. But when he looked again, the eyes had accomplished their mission, and there was only the smile. He smiled back, trying to place the other thing that was striking him about her. He couldn't put his finger on it. She was dressed in a black wool pantsuit and a white cotton blouse, pumps. The Career Woman, courtesy *Vogue*. And that was part of it: the clothes were perfect, but sat on her as if they weren't quite sure what they were doing there. But there was more. What, what? He could see the faint trace of a scar running a diagonal from her hairline, over her left eye, to her cheek. But still, so what, none of his business. Something else was hitting an off key, though, something else. . . . And yet there was that smile. It said, Talk to me. It said, Relax. It said, No fear. It said things he really needed to hear. "You don't want to know about my day," Flanagan said, now very much hoping that she would disagree, that she would get it out of him, that he could spill his guts yet again tonight.

"Why don't I be the judge of that?"

"You always this sympathetic with strange men, Ms . . . ?"

"Baylor. Jen Baylor." She shifted over to the stool next to his. "And you are?"

"Mike Flanagan." They shook, and the off-key something now rang home. Those were not Career Woman hands. Strong, calloused, strangers to manicures. Weird. But the grip was firm, and had the same Trust Me message as the smile. Flanagan decided to go with the good instincts.

"Pleased to meet you, Mike," said Baylor. "And to answer your question, let's say I feel pulled to tend wounded animals. And you look hurt."

Flanagan didn't object. He hadn't wanted to in the first place. "I saw my boss get shot and killed today," he said, and out the story all came again, but this time with none of the shakes and the hesitancies and cries of Jesus and God that had punctuated his monologues to Holly and Harland. Each sentence was as flat, calm and simple as the first. Each sentence went out for the last time, the desperate need to repeat and relive winding down. And it was all thanks to Baylor. He had no idea how she was doing this, but he was sure she was. As he tried to describe the chaos of his emotions as he saw someone he knew and (well, yes) liked blown to meat, he felt an understanding deep and absolute radiating from her, and he plunged into it, a balm. When he finished, he felt so calm he wanted to curl up and sleep on the bar floor. He didn't, though. Instead, soothed by a temporary closure, he waited through a brief but comfortable silence, and changed the subject. "And what about you?" he asked. "When you're not playing ministering angel to complete strangers, what do you do?"

"I write freelance."

Bang, the tension started ratcheting up again. He had sudden visions, dark and tabloid-red. Baylor must have noticed. "Relax." She laughed. "I wasn't pumping you for a scoop. I don't do that kind of writing. I do corporate stuff: copy, pamphlets, manuals, speeches, annual reports. That kind of thing. Most thrilling. Anyway, you're not interested. No," she shushed when Flangan started to protest. "What you are is exhausted. Go home. Sleep."

Flanagan surrendered. "Can I see you again?"

She gave him an appraising look that turned stern. "Depends. If I say yes, and you turn up looking hangdog again, then I might come to the conclusion that you like feeling sorry for yourself. And then I'd have to cross the street to avoid you." She gave him a quick, tight grin: joking but not really.

Flanagan nodded. Message received. "Stiff upper lip. I promise."

She appeared to think about it for another moment or two. "Well, you might be worth one shot, anyway." Sharp twinkle in those black eyes. She got a pen and a scrap of paper out of her purse. "Give me your number."

Flanagan did. "Can I have yours?"

"Not yet." Twinkle again, diamond hard and sharp as wit.

Flanagan stood up. "In that case, it's been a pleasure, Jen. Thanks again." They shook hands again, and he caught himself hoping she wouldn't squeeze too hard. "I hope you do call."

Jen Blaylock watched Flanagan leave the bar, and felt no guilt. Assessment: mixed. The pick-up couldn't have gone more smoothly. She had the man hooked, and could reel him in at her leisure. She had to be careful, though. He didn't seem dumb, and if he felt the tug of the line at any point, the game would be up. The big problem was his value: how much did he know? Was she wasting her time and putting the operation in jeopardy for nothing? Hard to say. But he'd been having drinks with Smith, and that had to be worth something. Flanagan might have access to things he couldn't imagine yet. If so, she'd have to help him rise to his full potential.

After she'd shot Smith, she had ducked back down the corridor to the washroom and out the fire door. It opened into the stairwell of another part of the building. No one around, so she'd doffed the dark clothes she'd worn over her civilian outfit, stuffed them into the gym bag, and sauntered outside. Across the way from the Baying Hound was an atrium. White pillars, twice the height of the potted trees, held the ceiling high over a big space. The white walls and white ceiling were delicate steel grids, and made the space seem even bigger. White metal tables and chairs were arranged along the periphery. People ate lunch at the tables or sat taking catnaps on the raised bases of the pillars. Blaylock had sat down on a base. She could watch the entrance to the Baying Hound from here, and she did, taking in the parade of sirens she'd triggered. She had wanted to see where Smith III's friend went. She wanted to get to know this guy. If she was going after Pembroke next, she needed a conduit to get information out of InSec, and to let her poison in. She waited until she saw Flanagan totter out, face pale, knees soft rubber. Then she followed him back to his apartment and staked it out again from the Battery Park City promenade until she saw him leave for the bar. After that, it had been easy-breezy. Problem: he seemed nice. He wasn't hurting for money, not if he was living in a riverfront building. But he gave all the signs of the genuine innocent, and she hadn't counted on Smith keeping such company. A lesson learned on the dangers of assumptions. Too late now, as far as

Flanagan was concerned. She was committed to this course of action, and determined to make it work. She felt no guilt. Some regret, maybe, but limited and contained. She could allow herself that, but no more. Especially now that the war had begun.

5

Bang. Five times. Johnathan W. Smith III's face sledgeham-
mered to compote. And did it feel good? Did it feel great,
seeing the blood spray and the bone chips fly? Did it feel
better with every pull of the trigger, every Glaser blast
knocking the corpse further into unrecognizable death?
Damn straight. The orgiastic thrill of overkill revenge.
Justice delayed too long, but oh so good in its summary.
Enough to make a non-smoker light up. Only it wasn't over
yet. Not in a fairy's dream. Good as Smith's execution had
been, she knew it had been too easy, and she felt the incom-
pleteness of a job barely begun. But at least the first real step
had been taken. First blood of vengeance charging her system with endorphins after years of first ignorance, and then
rage, impotence, research, planning. So long, so long. Her
wound was scabbed over on the surface, but was gangrene
and cancer underneath. Boom. Explosion. House and

family cremated. Blaylock concussed, glass slash in her face. But no burns, no broken bones, body bruised and shaken and cut but nothing serious. Lucky, the papers called her. They had that nerve. A miracle, they said, her stroll out to the back yard the miracle that had saved her from the gas-line explosion, the miracle out of tragedy.

Miracle. Bullshit. Miracle only for a God that liked sticking it to you up the ass.

A few days then in hospital, a wealth of stitches in her face, holding the blood and the pain and the bile in. Afterwards: the edges of flesh knitting together, the red ridge gradually fading, flattening out. But the trace remaining. The scar a point of pride, the sign of the broken inside, a riposte to the papers, screw you and your miracle.

Still, she bought the gas explosion. Her father's last phone conversation shunted to the far back of her memory by the deafening shout of the blast, she had no reason not to believe the official explanation. And why wouldn't she? The investigation had been thorough enough, or at least dressed itself up that way. Just plain bad luck, what it all came down to. Ain't it a bitch. Nice miracle, God, got to hand it to you, class act through and through. I hope Celia turned up at your doorstep with her skin flamed off, and you have to look at her every day.

The funeral, the mourning. Friends and relations doing their best, giving her a place to stay, shielding her from the media who were coming all over the death of one of their favorite pundits. One of her father's lawyer friends stepped in and smoothed out the knots of probate, slick as you please. And for that, she was grateful. Something else to be grateful for, if you liked sick jokes: no heartbreaking sorting through of belongings, or rattling around an echoing, bereaved house. Nothing like an explosion to tie up loose ends. No fuss, no muss, everything taken care of at once. Well done. And then? What next? Back to the army, that's what next. The home that survived. But restless, the throb of the scar not on the surface but deep, a rift in the heart. Peacetime awkward, empty. Get me to where the action is. Agitating for a peacekeeping mission, anywhere, anywhere.

The Balkans obliged. Unfinished business from World War I and before reared its head, and rage interminable stalked the land. A cornucopia of atrocities, incestuous genocide, screams of pain and of the kill reverberated through Europe as Yugoslavia found no rest but many pieces. No massive intervention this time, no Alliance stepping in with the firepower of the gods to set things straight, put on a show, and provide the backdrop for techno-thrillers yet unborn. Situation too complicated, percentages non-existent.

But the blood and the agony piled up too high to be swept under the carpet. Something had to be done. And so the thankless were sent off, underfunded, underequipped, undernumbered, and under strictly enforced Rules of Engagement as they stood between players who had discarded the rules long since. No video games, no Stealth magic, just the poor bloody infantry against the fist of history. And not even enough of them. No army, half a million strong, to slam the door shut on the war before it even gathered momentum. But just enough meddling and dithering on the part of the Powers to make sure everything really went to shit. Blaylock watched the news, read the reports, drank the evil down so she could know it and fight it, and begged, and begged, to be sent over.

In October 1992, she got her wish, shipping out as part of CANBAT 2 to Bosnia-Herzegovina. In Sarajevo she found work that needed doing. She found pain and loss to dwarf her own. She found explosions that had nothing to do with gas and bad luck. She found a dearth, absolute and complete, of miracles. She dug into the filth and the muck, total immersion with the prayer that she might be able to help others to the surface. Some nights, toward the beginning of her tour, she liked to think that she was being constructive, that she could see evidence of her ability to make a difference. But the hubris didn't last long. It only took a couple of incidents. A child she had saved from rubble on Saturday nailed by a sniper on Sunday. A family convinced to lay down weapons slaughtered by neighbors. Blaylock learned quickly. She stopped taking Good Samaritan pride, which had never really soothed the scar anyway. Need and duty fused. You did the work. You did what had to be done. And, as all too often, if the result was nothing, well then, you simply did it again. And again. And again. If she hadn't been able to hold her house together, what could she do for an entire country whose explosion was just as savage? She could do her best. And she did, becoming, in the process, one of the best. She never rotated out except when forced to, and was always back as soon as she was allowed.

The moonlighting started in her second year. RadOps wasn't enough. She had to be on the front lines. Problem: orders were orders, and she knew the reasons for discipline. Duty and need experienced a schism. She tried every legit channel first, volunteering for everything as a matter of course, and just as routinely being told no.

Because I don't have a dick?

No, because you are needed at your post.

Yeah, right, whatever. True or not, she wasn't having any of it. So how do you fulfil both duty and need? You go with the need in the cracks. And so she moonlighted whenever she could get away from her post without being AWOL. Moonlighting: mostly freelance mine removal. Utter insanity. But there she was, mucking about with her sketchy knowledge, daring the blast. Which never came. It was as if the explosion in Winnipeg had inoculated her, and she was immune from any further breath of flame. Other people noticed the charm. She had at least five near misses, and walked away without a scratch from each. Her luck became her reputation. In the hope that the luck was contagious, blind eyes were turned to regulations so she could be part of de-mining teams. Jen Blaylock, the anti-Jonah: stick with her and you'll be okay. That was a laugh. Proximity hadn't done her family a damned bit of good. But the myth held on, even when disproved. When one of the engineers she was helping stepped wrong and turned into red mist, he was blamed for having been careless. Believe that or give up.

November 1994. Two things: Bihac and a newspaper article. Bihac was a UN safe zone, a term which, for the Serbian army, seemed to translate as "target." The shells came down on the refugees, a hard rain. The Canadians watched, helpless, hands tied. Rules of Engagement: you fire if, and only if, fired upon. And they weren't being fired upon. So they watched, curses mounting to the deaf ears of distant but officious bureaucrats, as Hell came to the refugees. Blaylock's scar throbbed livid. Then Kelly Grimson, another RadOp, received a package from home. In with the cookies and the paperbacks were some recent issues of *The Globe and Mail*. "Rammer," she said to Blaylock, "there's an article here by your dad."

For a couple of seconds, the world spun backward on its axis. Blaylock fumbled with time, trying to remember the year, how old she was, and who was dead. She took the paper. Front page of the Focus section. "Howard Blaylock's Final Story." Buried for years, now found, here it was: an exposé of Protection Electronics, Inc. Proudly Canadian, Protection Electronics had a secret specialty in the completely illegal production and sale of electroshock batons. The clients were governments, police forces, paramilitary outfits and other groups who had substantive disagreements with Amnesty International. Canada part of the torture trade? Scandal! Or it would have been, had the article appeared in 1991. Now it was old news, no longer relevant, and an addendum to the article mentioned that Protection Electronics had shut down operations and evaporated in June of '91. They had never been prosecuted, and now it was too late. The former head of Protection Electronics, one Johnathan W. Smith III, had long since left the country.

Blaylock read, saw crimson. Her father's last phone call, his need for her advice, and his ashen face rushed together and made new meaning. The gas explosion became a lie. The evidence might have been circumstantial, only it didn't seem so here, surrounded as she was by the commonplace of savagery. The core-deep wound that had refused to heal and the long-troubling instinct fused and made themselves known for what they were at last: the cry for vengeance.

That night, first by stolen jeep and then on foot, she shadowflitted into the hills toward the nearest Serb gun emplacement. Closing in, heat-seeker, on her target, she saw a sentry and hid before he spotted her. He had chosen a good spot, giving him a good line of sight down the road. His machine gun had an excellent field of fire. But the PK was on top of a boulder by the side of the road, and was visible in silhouette when the sky flashed. Blaylock saw the post through a gap in the trees, a good ten paces before she reached the bend in the road that would have placed her dead in the sentry's sights. She went back down the road, about a hundred yards, then crossed. She moved uphill, deep into the woods. After ten minutes she was level with the sentry post, and she inched her way down the slope. Five yards from the post, her tree cover ended.

The sentry had his back to her, eyes fixed on the road. Blaylock drew her knife. Crouching, quiet as sin, moving with the rumbles of the guns, she scuttled up behind the sentry. She pulled her arm back, blade pointing forward. She coughed for attention, and drove her arm in. The sentry, startled by the cough, whirled around, off balance and awkward, and caught the knife deep in his trachea. He made a faint noise like the gurgling of phlegm, and fell back against the boulder. She pulled the sentry's jacket off and put it on over her own. She took his helmet, grabbing every strategic edge and to hell with the rules. She was playing dirty now, one with the animals. She unshouldered her C-7 and walked up the road, quiet, careful, but not obviously stalking. If she was spotted, she'd have a few seconds of knowing something the enemy didn't. She came around a curve and saw a clearing overlooking the steep hillside. A clear field of fire to Bihac. In the clearing was not a gun, but a Russian-made BM-21 rocket launcher.

Situational awareness: the total picture of a combat scene clicking in instantly, all variables calculated, strategy moving at the speed of instinct. Blaylock saw the possibilities and acted on them simultaneously. Six soldiers in the clearing: two to the left, three climbing down from the launcher, reload done, one in the cab. She pulled out a low-fragmentation offensive grenade, pulled the pin, counted, and lobbed it to the left. Even less than ten yards away, she was fairly safe from her own weapon. There was a nice big blast, but she didn't bother with cover. She had ridden explosions before. She stood her ground and was already firing before the grenade went off, strafing right to left along the launcher. Five men went down instantly, grenade-torn or gutted by her bullets. The man in the cab tried to get out on the side away from her, and she brought the gun back. Raking fire nailed him through the windshields, glass flying with metal, slash and penetrate. She saw the driver jerk up and down as if he liked the music.

Blaylock stopped firing, ran over to the BM-21, yanked open the door, hauled the driver out and climbed in. She looked towards the other hills, and waited until she spotted the flash of a gun. Then she started the launcher up and changed its orientation. Her artillery knowledge was limited, but she wasn't looking for a surgical hit. The joy of the BM-21: it was crude, it was simple, and it worked. It had forty tubes, each loaded with a 122 mm rocket. All you needed to target was the general area, since after the rockets hit, there would be no more general area. Blaylock launched. Seconds later, the hill opposite rocked and danced. When the echoes faded, the guns everywhere had stopped. Blaylock smirked. Confused, assholes? she thought. Something bite you?

As she climbed out of the BM-21, she noticed the holster that the driver was wearing. It was unusually large. She knelt and pulled out the pistol. Her eyes widened. It was a Heckler & Koch MK23 MOD O. Complete with silencer. She recognized it only from having read about it. It was a US Special Operations weapon. What the hell was a Serb artilleryman doing with one? She examined the body again. The man was a sergeant, and his boots were much newer-looking than those of the other soldiers. Good leather too. Someone with money? Maybe. Maybe he'd made a good black market score. It would have had to be damn good, though. A gun like this would cost. She grabbed the holster and gun, tossed a fragmentation grenade down a tube of the rocket launcher and ran like hell. At her back, light bloomed and the night suddenly warmed.

She took stock the following night. She had killed seven men. And how many had been erased by her rocket volley? Interesting to speculate. So how did she feel? Any regrets? No. Regret, perhaps, that she felt no regrets. Regret also that she hadn't been able to do more. The artillery attack on Bihac had stopped for three hours after she had fired off the missiles, but then boom, business as usual. A temporary, limited effect at best. Still, not bad for one person, not bad for an improvisation. There was a lesson here. It was possible for the individual to cast a long shadow. You needed leverage. You needed a big stick. But it was possible.

Last night, though, she had fought someone else's war. The side she had chosen was a circumstantial fluke. She didn't believe in any of the causes here. It was just a question of whose turn it was to be on the receiving end of the atrocities. Some months or miles' difference, and she could have been slaughtering Croats or Muslims instead of Serbs. True, the anger she felt about Bihac was genuine. She'd launch those missiles all over again, but that wasn't what she wanted. She had her own war now, and it wasn't here. Johnathan W. Smith III, Protection Electronics: now those were targets. But Protection Electronics was dead, and Smith had disappeared. So find him.

December 1995. Home. Or at least back to Canada where home had been. Dealing with the surprising amount of money that had come her way via life insurance and inheritance. Seed for the war. Put aside, tended carefully, it bore fruit. The arsenal slowly building, little bits of death one at a time. But lacking direction. She didn't know what she was preparing for. She didn't know the nature of the campaign. Meanwhile, staying with the forces for now, the false pretences gnawing at her, Blaylock the quisling. She knew that her destination, sooner or later, was underground. But the forces were perfect for training. Research. Intelligence. And so she used them, conscience long since damned.

No repercussions ever from her guerilla strike in Bosnia. At first, she had put it down to luck, pure and dumb. She should be in jail, she should be dead. But as she trained, gathering skills and knowledge faster and faster, her edge honing to the quick, she realized that the only luck had been her opponents' bad decisions. Everyone made mistakes. She just had to be there to exploit them. Epiphany: she wasn't lucky, she was good.

And where was the peacekeeper? Where were the eyes that had been shocked into disillusion by the Highway of Death? Buried. Maybe alive, maybe dead, it didn't matter. The peacekeeper would get in the way of justice, would try to prevent the snarling instinct from strutting the blossoming skills. Look what I can do, the warrior said. You can't do war and peace at the same time. One or the other, Churchill or Chamberlain, kill or slink away.

July 1997. The trail picked up. Endless searches on the Net, going through one corporate roll call after another, at last produced Johnathan W. Smith III, working in New York as head of Shipping for Integrated Security. Shipping? What the hell? Hiding in ignominy, now harmless? It didn't seem likely. She had to be wary of benign names (Protection Electronics and its torture batons). So now she knew where her target was. There was still more digging to be done. She wanted to make absolutely sure she waged war on the right parties. She would have liked to have whoever had actually rigged her parents' house in her sights, but she didn't have any illusions that way. If the actual bomber fell in her way, that would be luck. But it was the commanders, not the soldiers, that she wanted. If the trail ended with Smith, good. But make sure.

February 1998. England. Surrey. The suburb of Esher. Sandown Park. A racing complex the location for that year's IMTEX: the Incident Management Technologies Exhibition. Translation: arms a-go-go. Everything for your military, your police force, your militia, your special forces, your intelligence agency, your death squad. Officially sanctioned illegal sales. Blaylock, already mastering the false identity, already halfway underground, mingling with NATO buyers, pariah state reps and Amnesty International's Top 100 Most Wanted. Easy to get in, because one of her selves was making friends by buying all the right weapons. Here for two reasons. One: see the new toys, maybe pick some up. Two: observe the enemy, find out about the people who sold and bartered death. She felt no hypocrisy. She walked the aisles, and wanted the weapons, and wanted to use them to blow the entire exhibition to hell. Every eye she met deserved to be blinded. These were the people her father had been fighting. She knew now that Smith would not be enough. Smith would just be tit-for-tat. Her strike had to be deep. It had to be felt. Her father had fought the good fight, but his tactics were wrong. Fire with fire, the only way. Hoist them with their own petards.

And down one aisle, what did we have here? A demo model of the Heckler & Koch she had picked up in Bosnia.

She stopped and stared at the gun. Then she looked at her program, combing through the fine print. The joy of IMTEX, as far as the weapons manufacturers were concerned, was that they themselves were not officially present. Their products were there, but with no attendant responsibility. The actual dealer, the distributor, was someone else. She scanned the legalese until she found the entity under whose auspices IMTEX happened. She found the name. She found the target: InSec. She spent another few years bearing down on that target, until now, a decade late, not the beginning of hostilities after all, but returned fire. Bang. Five times.

6

Pembroke was pacing. That was bad. Karl Noonan knew to keep himself sitting still when Pembroke was restless. The man's mood was dangerous, looking for a target. No point in giving him one. It wasn't that Pembroke frightened Noonan. Not exactly. Certainly not physically. Special Operations Forces had taught Noonan at least a dozen ways to drop Pembroke, starting from his own sitting position. But there were other forms of power, and Pembroke had them in spades. He knew it too, and it all came through in his eyes. Not often, though. Pembroke kept things under wraps, and Noonan saluted him for that. But every so often, someone would do something that would make Pembroke lose his cool. He wouldn't shout or turn purple or threaten. His tone might drop a few degrees. But the big thing was his eyes. They went distant, not quite looking through you, but looking through time to your removal. Spooky. In the five years he'd worked for Pembroke, Noonan had seen the look happen maybe six or seven times, usually in negotiations with people who didn't know better. Whoever got the look either smartened up sharp, or took a long, plummeting fall. Either way, the look was the only warning. Noonan had never been on the receiving end of the look. He wanted to keep it that way. He liked his job. He liked his life. Pembroke wouldn't hesitate to relieve him of either. And he knew that Pembroke could too. So he behaved himself.

Pembroke stopped pacing and stood looking out the window. "I imagine the police will be in touch shortly."

"Yeah." It was just after nine. Flanagan had called, terrified and halting, to let them know what had happened at the Baying Hound. He thought he should be the one to tell them, he'd said.

"Good judgment on Flanagan's part," Pembroke commented, almost absently.

"Like I said before, he's a team player all the way."

Pembroke nodded. "That's the one good thing to come out of this so far. You were right to recommend him." He turned around to face Noonan. "Any theories on who and why?"

Noonan shook his head. Smith III getting himself whacked was major-league strange. "I haven't heard of him pissing anyone off. He's been careful. Either he was doing something on the side, or this is old blood."

Pembroke stood very still. Noonan watched his eyes take on another specialized gaze. This one looked into the abstract and calculated angles, percentages, risks. Noonan knew Pembroke had settled on a strategy when his eyes cleared. "Call the police," he said.

"You sure?"

"Yes. Tell them the truth." Twitch-smile: the truth as long as it is useful and harmless. "Tell them that Flanagan spoke to us, and that we're anxious to help out in the investigation. Invite them over. I'll meet with them. And you," flash of significant humor in the eyes, "get cosy. I want all the information we can get. If the hit turns out to be some settling of old scores, then I don't think we need to worry much. But if Smith was up to some kind of side deal that turned sour, we need to know about it. I'm a little worried about the timing."

"IMTEX?" New York was home to the exhibition this year. It was coming up on the weekend.

Pembroke waved a hand, dismissive. "No. What's to worry there? The worst we get is a nasty *60 Minutes* segment. Who cares? But MAI and the Russian deal are getting close to the boil. I don't want anything to screw them up."

"How much time do you want me to put into this?"

"Don't let it affect the timetable unless there's just cause. I still want you in Russia and everything sorted out for when the freighters get there."

"Right." Noonan got to his feet. "I'd better make that call before the cops beat us to it."

"Yes," said Pembroke. "And Karl?"

"Yeah?"

"Keep a close eye on Flanagan. He looks like a good man, but he's under a lot of stress right now. That's an invitation to chaos. We don't want that."

"Not yet, anyway," Noonan joked.

The first precinct station house, 16 Ericsson Place. The Tuesday morning dive into the city's grime. But so far, it was getting off to a not-bad start. Ed Kroker put down the phone and wondered if his knee had been wrong after all. He looked up at Dyanne Lutz, who was hovering over his desk. "That," he said, "was Johnathan W. Smith III's employers, offering any and all assistance and inviting us over."

"How very civic." Tone dry, dry, a twig that gave off dust when it snapped. Lutz perched on the edge of Kroker's desk. She opened the file she was holding. "Our boy," she said.

"No criminal record. Lived in Canada from 1988 to 1991. And," she held up a finger, "one point of interest: there was an INTERPOL request for his record from the RCMP in 1994."

"Really. Any indication why?"

Lutz shook her head. "I've filed a request going the other way now, asking why they were looking into him."

"Do we know what he was doing in Canada?"

"No."

Kroker thought for a minute. "I want to see this guy's personnel record."

"Follow the gaps," said Lutz.

"Yeah." Smith had to have something interesting and dark in one of those gaps. Nobody took five Glasers to the face for an overdue library book. "So what do you say?" he asked Lutz. "The good folks at InSec just rolled out the welcome mat. Shall we take advantage?"

Pembroke watched Noonan see the two detectives out. He wondered how long it would take them to connect the dots and link up InSec and Protection Electronics. Not long, he thought. By tomorrow? Probably. If not sooner. But that was all right. An unavoidable consequence of having one of his employees murdered was that as soon as the police realized the nature of InSec's trade, their eyes would light up. The trick was to direct their energies down paths that would lead to the least amount of damage and publicity. And when they came back, what would he say? Why yes, Integrated Security *did* deal in weapons. So? If Johnathan W. Smith III had been involved in something illegal, and been killed because of his game, that had nothing to do with InSec. Admitting InSec was in the arms trade was only a half truth, though. The full truth: InSec was the arms trade. Arthur Pembroke's dream, born as the Cold War crumbled and melted away. The idea was inevitable. Pembroke simply got there first.

1986. Reagan in the White House. Thatcher in 10 Downing Street. The neo-con revolution gathering steam, the hawks triumphant. Pembroke was running Deliveries Unlimited, a middling-large arms dealership, doing nicely off superpower squabble zones like Angola, El Salvador, Nicaragua. But he, if no one else, could see what was coming. Gorbachev had been General Secretary for a year. Just enough changes had begun for Pembroke to gauge the health of the old order, and the prognosis was not good. He extrapolated a worst-case scenario. If the Cold War ended, world conflict would not, but the intensities would drop, and so would the demand for arms. Deliveries Unlimited and its competitors would be fighting for pieces of a much smaller pie. Two options. One: stir the pot and keep the demand up. Good, but tricky. A lot of clout needed for that. Two: eliminate the competition. Better. InSec wailed its first cry.

Over the next two years, Pembroke negotiated, cajoled, promised, threatened, executed. Mergers, acquisitions, alliances, takeovers. The more InSec grew, the greater its momentum, as other dealers realized the advantages of a monopoly and signed on for the ride. The price of arms stabilized. By the early nineties, with Pembroke's dream almost completely realized, the price, now centrally regulated, started going up again. There were still a few independent operators out there, but strictly small fry, only worth squashing if they actually got in the way. Few of them did.

Pembroke liked to think of InSec as the ultimate transnational. It covered the globe, but less than half of its subsidiaries were on paper and could be traced back to a headquarters that was American only in a geographic sense. The other branches were connected through feudal servitude, a model Pembroke had borrowed from the Mafia. The result was beautiful. InSec represented access, egalitarianism, flexibility. Access: One Stop Shopping. You wanted it, InSec had it, or would get it for you. Contacts legal and otherwise made sure of that. Pembroke had done plenty of favors for intelligence agencies concerned with plausible deniability. He had friends there, and was so useful that it would take a lot for governmental blind eyes to open. Egalitarianism: no such thing as a pariah state, as far as InSec was concerned. All nations equal under the gun. American corporations were prohibited from trade with Libya? Fine, then France's Résultats (an unprovably wholly owned subsidiary of InSec) would handle the sale. InSec flourished. Once it got going, the monster couldn't be stopped. Flexibility: Pembroke had to diversify into freight companies just to keep up with the growth.

But there was still that niggling, nagging itch. One could always do better. And Pembroke had only exercised Option Two. Business must always grow, and Pembroke finally saw a way of deploying Option One. The MAI and Russia were the keys to that. As long as Smith III hadn't screwed things up.

Pembroke worked until seven. He could have gone on a few hours more, but he didn't want to make things too late for Nancy. He got up, grabbed his coat and left his office. Jack Lentricchia, suit jacket straining at the shoulders, stood up from behind the reception. The bulge of the shoulder-holstered gun was more visible when he was standing straight. Lentricchia opened his cell phone, called down for the car to be ready, then preceded Pembroke to the elevator. On the ground floor, the limo was pulling up to the Edgar entrance. Lentricchia stepped outside, scanned, then nodded an all-clear to Pembroke. The limo driver ceded his place to Lentricchia and held the rear door open for Pembroke. "Mount Sinai," Pembroke said as he settled himself against the embracing leather of the seat.

"Yes, sir." Lentricchia's tone carried no hint that he had known what Pembroke was going to say, that the pattern of

Pembroke's needs was so entrenched that Lentricchia would have driven him to the hospital without being told. Pembroke appreciated the bodyguard's attention to the small details of duty.

Pembroke said nothing during the ride. He watched evening settle on the city, bulletproof glass between him and New York. He tired of the precautions sometimes. There had only ever been one attempt on his life, back in the first year of InSec's formation, and a half-assed try it had been too. A competitor, unable to see the advantages of merger, had managed to sneak a Baby Browning into a meeting by taping it to his inner thigh, next to his testicles. The concealment had been clever, but all tactical thought had stopped there. To get at the gun, the idiot stood up suddenly mid-conference and jammed his hand down the front of his pants. The thumb safety on the pistol was so small that it was a snag waiting to happen, and it happened. He shot the end of his penis off on the draw. Since then, nothing. But it only took once, so Pembroke kept up the defenses. If he ever went down, it would not be due to stupidity.

Lentricchia made the Upper East Side in good time. It was not quite seven-thirty when Pembroke walked into his daughter's private room. She had her eyes closed. The bowl that had held her dinner was next to her bed. Pembroke moved quietly, not wanting to wake her, but she opened her eyes when he sat down beside her. "Hey Dad." Voice the thinnest of brittle papers.

"Hey there, Nancy." He put his hand on top of hers, but didn't hold it, scared of breaking her if he squeezed. His little girl, who had inherited the wrong set of genes from her mother, and was following the same path. Spending her thirties enjoying the best palliative care money could buy. Oh, it was still called treatment at this point, but Pembroke had played the game before, and he knew it well. The chemo, the chemicals, the false hopes and fading body. The vanishing weight, the bone-cold hands, the wisping away of hair, the skin bleaching to sheet-white and thinning taut with age too soon arrived. He knew the game. He had barely seen Sylvia through to the end of hers when Nancy had picked up the torch. He'd been doing this for so long now that he could barely imagine another way of life. Families were for dying. That was the way of things. "How are things today?" he asked.

Nancy spread her fingers slightly, her version of a shrug. "Oh, you know. The usual." The unspoken question: Does it hurt? The unnecessary answer: Yes, it does. "I was watching the news," Nancy said.

"Oh?" Playing dumb, but he knew where she was headed.

"They said Johnathan has been killed. Is that true?"

"Yes, it is." Sorry she had to learn it from the television, glad he didn't have to tell her himself. Smith III had been "Uncle" Johnathan, the family friend with the funny way of speaking and the great imagination in games. Nancy knew nothing of the corporate lieutenant who had had to be extracted from Canada and buried when he had bungled things so badly the one time he'd been given a company of his own to run. Smith III had met with a man posing as a buyer. Without doing a proper check, he'd allowed Protection Electronics to make an electroshock baton sale. One illegal sale made public would have been bad enough, but then it turned out that the man wrote for newspapers and had made the link between Protection and InSec, and a major arms sale to Iraq *during* the Gulf War. The kind of publicity that caught the attention of grand juries and politicians. Pembroke had ordered the writer taken out. And Smith III had done it in a spectacularly messy way. That the accident story had held was barely short of miraculous, even supported as it had been by generous and untraceable donations.

Nancy asked, "Why would anyone want to kill him?"

For Pembroke the better question was "who?" not

"why?" He could think of any number of likely blunders Smith III might have committed over the years to bring a contract down on his head. But he thought he'd managed to cover Smith's clumsy tracks. Why he'd done so was loyalty to a childhood friend. Pragmatically speaking, a lousy reason. But to date it had been the only instance of sentimentality Pembroke had permitted himself in the conduct of business. If he was honest, hanging on to Smith III was a mistake that had stretched over decades, and if the smoke cleared and his death didn't create more problems than his life, then Pembroke should track the assassin down and reward him. He was no longer trapped between common sense and obligation to Smith III's unwavering devotion. "I don't know why anyone would want to kill Johnathan," he told his daughter. "It doesn't make sense. Maybe he was mistaken for someone else." That was feeble. He could tell from Nancy's eyes that she thought so too. No one could possibly take Johnathan W. Smith III for anyone other than his own caricatured self. "Or maybe it was random," he hurried on. "Something gang-related. An initiation kill, that sort of thing. Did the TV suggest anything?"

"No."

"Well, the police spoke to me today. They'll find out what happened soon enough."

Nancy said nothing. Pembroke looked at her, and saw tears. They flowed gently, without resistance. She didn't have the strength for sobs. His right hand, the one that wasn't covering Nancy's brittleness, clenched in anger at Smith III. Trust the man to be clumsy and thoughtless even in death. Pembroke took a breath, calmed himself, and stroked Nancy's hair.

"Dad, the same thing isn't going to happen to you, is it?"

"Of course not. Don't be silly." Spoken just a tad too quickly, perhaps, but he was thrown by the question. He glanced at Nancy's face, and then away, not meeting her eyes. Worried: how much did Nancy know about InSec? He had always kept camouflage netting over Deliveries Unlimited and InSec, hiding the glint of gunmetal from his family. He thought he'd done it well. But now. . . . Had Nancy been protecting him from the truth of her own knowledge? No. He doubted she'd have kept quiet about it.

"Promise?"

"I promise." And now his tone was sure and calm. He had every intention of keeping that promise. There was not a doubt in his mind that Smith had brought himself down through terminal stupidity.

He stayed with Nancy for another half-hour. She fell asleep after ten minutes, the reassurance of the promise soothing like a lullaby. Pembroke watched her eyes close, her labored breathing deepen. He could see her pulse on her neck featherbeating through the parchment of her skin. He watched her until he felt sure that she had at least another night in her, that he could leave her to breathe unsupervised. Then he left the room. Lentricchia was waiting for him in the corridor. He asked, "Local or home, sir?" Again, every appearance that the question was an honest one, that he wasn't anticipating Pembroke's answer.

"Local." Home was the Greenwich, Connecticut, mansion he had shared with Sylvia. Where Nancy had grown up. Home was fully staffed and perfectly maintained. Home had immaculate grounds, dust-free interiors, restored antiques and shellacked memories. He hadn't spent more than an hour there in close to a year. Local was the Bedford on Central Park West at 81st. Before Sylvia's illness, Pembroke had used it as guest accommodation for the client or politico who needed pampering. But once he found himself in the shadow of Mount Sinai, Pembroke started using the apartment for himself. Lentricchia stopped the car in front of the building. There was a space reserved for Pembroke at the entrance. He had bought the entire building a few years ago, but permitted screened tenants. The doorman saluted as Pembroke made his way inside, into the realm of brown marble and brass, Lentricchia dogging his heels. The brass sun on the elevator doors parted and let them in.

They took the elevator to the penthouse. A luxury fortress, the Bedford had two squat turrets standing sentinel over the park. Pembroke's apartment took up one of them. He waited while Lentricchia unlocked the apartment, went inside and checked it out. It took him three minutes. Thorough to a fault every night. "Clean, sir," he announced as he stepped back out.

"Thank you, Jack," Pembroke said. Lentricchia stood guard in the doorway until Pembroke closed the door and locked it.

Local: goodby art deco, hello chrome and glass. Black leather and steel. No memories here to ambush him. Local was all function, an office once-removed. Places to sit, level surfaces for work or meals, television for news, bed for sleeping, computer for more work. No prints on the walls, no plants, no books that weren't industry reports from *Jane's*. Comfort in the sterile.

There was a prepared dinner waiting for Pembroke in the microwave. He glanced at the instructions the housekeeper had left for him, hit the right buttons, then poured himself a glass of Macallan. He walked through the apartment, turning off most of the lights Lentricchia had turned on. He left the kitchen light on. While he waited for his dinner to nuke, he stood at the living room window, sipping his bourbon. He looked out over the night mass of the park. He tracked his gaze north. Constant practice, siamese-twinned to obsession, let him pick out the lights of Mount Sinai. He couldn't see Nancy's east-side room, but standing guard on the hospital itself would do.

He stood and watched. The bulletproof window, traitor, let the pain through.

7

On Friday evening, Blaylock entered the belly of the beast.

She had given Flanagan a day to wonder, and then phoned him Wednesday night. They were barely three sentences into the conversation before he asked her to dinner. Feeling every inch the first-class, game-playing hell-bitch, she pretended to think it over, keeping Flanagan twisting in the wind for a good fifteen seconds before she agreed. What time and where should they meet? He would likely have to work a bit late. Why didn't she drop by his office around seven? He said this with a shy little tightness in his voice—a man wanting to show off his workplace. Sure, she said, mind almost blown by luck unbelievable. She hadn't expected to get inside InSec so soon or so easily. She'd been prepared to squeeze some sort of invitation out of Flanagan over the next week or so. But this was unlooked-for, a strategic gift.

She could get her first look in without having to worry about raising any suspicions.

The InSec building did not hiss as she approached it. It did not uncoil and rattle a tail in warning. It did not growl a menace, raise its hackles and back off, claws extended, when she reached the entrance. If it recognized her as dangerous, it gave no sign. Even when she passed through the revolving doors and stood inside, the virus penetrating the host, there was nothing. Perhaps it was complacent, so confident of its invulnerability that it dismissed her as insignificant. (If so, then it was in for a surprise.) Perhaps it thought that it could and would squash her in its own time. (If so, she would prove it wrong, dragging it down into the blood with her.) Or perhaps it knew that it wasn't going to be her target after all. (If so, it was probably right. Pembroke and his lackeys were who she wanted, the soft humans who gave the building life and meaning. She was looking for the surgical strike. No Oklahoma City for her. No Highway of Death. No Ground Zero.)

The building welcomed her. It took her past the reptile-eyed security guard, through the turnstile, up to Shipping. And it *was* a nice building, Blaylock admitted as she walked down the corridor, hunting for Flanagan's office. Nicely laid out, colors and lighting quite humane. A model work environment. Every ceiling tile oozed sober respectability. She hadn't expected hydraulically powered steel doors thick as walls, gun barrels poking down out of corners to cover approaches, or maps of hollowed-out volcanoes (though that would have been cool). InSec was not set on world domination. Merely good business.

Sometimes the nuance was very subtle.

She heard laughter echo across the cubicles as she drew near Flanagan's office. Not alone? Possibly interesting. She reached 4023 and poked her head around the door. There was another man with Flanagan. Small, bouncing, laughing like machine-gun fire. "So then—" Flanagan started to say, but the other man spotted her. Instantly.

"Heyheyhey," he said, words a staccato streak. "Checkitout: company."

Flanagan looked up. "Jen," he said, pleased, so pleased, and Blaylock felt a tickle of something that, if she didn't know better, she would have tagged as guilt. "Come in, come in."

She stepped inside. Flanagan's eyes grew wide, so the outfit was doing its job. The other man seemed to be enjoying the view too, perhaps more than she would have liked. Until she knew who he was, though, friend or foe, peon or kingpin, she preferred to have him horny and distracted. She was wearing black pumps, seamed black nylons and a short, bruised aubergine dress. The dress's design was simple—no frills, form-hugging, square cut. She'd bought it because she needed something that wouldn't go out of style, and the women's magazines all assured her that this number was basic to any wardrobe. She accepted this on faith, taking the untested dress into the field as she would never consider doing for any other weapon. Her concession to personal whim was going for the aubergine instead of outright black. Depending on the way the light hit, the microfibers sheened from purple to black. "Hello, Mike," she said, after the silence verged to within a hair of uncomfortable. She looked significantly from Flanagan to the other man, waiting for the introduction, and claiming the social high ground.

"I'm so glad you made it," Flanagan said, both genuine and trying to recover himself. "Um, Jen Baylor, Karl Noonan."

Noonan bounced forward, eyes sparkling over killer grin. His expression: eat you up, little missy. His walk: prowling carnivore. Watch this guy, Blaylock thought. Dangerous. They shook hands. She felt power in his grip that ran all the way to his core. Very dangerous. It was an effort not to respond in kind, but she held her own strength back as far as she could. But either some got through, or her pretence showed, because Noonan's eyes shifted. Some of the hunger left, to be replaced by the lightest of frowns, the slightest wariness, the gentlest questioning. It was inevitable, Blaylock supposed: the mutual recognition of predators. "New to New York, heyhey?" said Noonan.

"How did you know?" She didn't have to fake her surprise.

He laughed, rapid-high, tickled pink with himself. The laugh was virulent, impossible to fight off, even though Blaylock missed the joke completely. "It's your accent." He winked at her, enigmatic clown with teeth. "Gotta go." A blink, and he was at the office door. "Be good, you crazy kids. Don't do anything illegal without calling me first." He disappeared.

Blaylock stared at the spot where he had been. Flanagan chuckled. "He's a character, isn't he? He has to hold himself in so much around Pembroke that he explodes when the Old Man's not around."

"Pembroke? You know Arthur Pembroke?" It was, Blaylock knew, exactly what Flanagan wanted her to ask, and she could have kissed him for handing her that line on a silver platter.

Self-deprecating snort. "We're not golfing buddies, if that's what you mean." The obligatory backing down: not good form to be too much of a show-off. "But we've met a couple of times. Karl's some kind of personal assistant. I think."

Hatchet man, you mean, you naïve little twit, Blaylock thought. But she kept up the role of the impressed date. "Even so, how come you've met Pembroke at all? Does he come down to each department to hand out the Christmas bonus checks personally?" Calculated doubt to keep Flanagan's pride on the boil.

"He's had me in his office a couple of times. I'm working on a project for him."

"And I don't suppose you can tell me what it is."

Flanagan grinned. "You did say you were a corporate writer, not a journalist?"

Blaylock pulled a face. "I like to keep my options open."

"That's reassuring," Flanagan said. He slipped on his suit jacket and led the way back to the elevators. He was wearing dark Armani. Très chic, Blaylock thought, good angles and lines. And she did not believe for a moment that he dressed semi-formal for work. He must have brought the suit with him and changed a little while ago. Maybe Noonan had been giving him a hard time for the date contortions. Her lips twitched. It was sort of cute, though.

Flanagan called the elevator, then turned to Blaylock with a frown. He looked for all the world like a man who has just heard a penny drop. "Never mind how I know Pembroke," Flanagan said. "How do you know about him?"

"What kind of corporate writer would I be if I didn't keep up with the CEO roll call?"

"Fair enough, but he isn't one of the most visible. I didn't know who ran InSec until I'd been here four months."

"And because you're slow, I should be too?"

Flanagan shook his head. "Sorry. You're right." The elevator doors opened.

Blaylock decided that she didn't want him to drop the line of questioning just yet. It was time to dangle the first bit of bait. "Pembroke's better known than you know," she said. "Move in the right circles, and InSec's almost mythic."

"Really." Flanagan sounded uncomfortable. Blaylock watched him closely, and it took her a moment to notice that the elevator was going up, not down. She raised an eyebrow. Flanagan said, "You'll see."

The elevator stopped two floors from the top. The doors opened, and Flanagan ushered Blaylock into Le Céleste. The restaurant was blue. Floor, walls and ceiling were a deep, deep blue, dotted with constellations. The decor conveyed the depth and weightlessness of space but none of its cold. When the maitre d' brought Blaylock and Flanagan to their table next to the south-facing, floor-to-ceiling windows,

Blaylock felt as if she were hovering, and could fly an effortless orbit over the Manhattan skyline.

"This," she said as she sat down, "is spectacular."

Flanagan nodded, too impressed himself to act pleased at Blaylock's reaction.

They spoke quietly. The setting demanded it. When the food arrived, it did so with the pomp of full-out pretension. French cuisine staged an expensive waltz of snobbery. Her steps: asparagus in truffle broth, duck breasts with comice pears and radiccio. His steps: foie gras with raspberry sauce, and cod with chanterelles and beef marrow. They came together for dandelion salad, then danced apart for dessert. She had sorbet au Marc; he had white chocolate and blueberry mousse. Flanagan insisted they drink InSec's house wine with the meal. Blaylock had doubts, but they died on her first sip. The finale: Williams pale brandy. Blaylock enjoyed herself. Hugely. She hadn't counted on the fringe benefits of her mission. And then, as she thought this, and glanced over at Flanagan, there it was: the throb throb throb of guilt, no mistake and no escape. Shit.

No backing down, though, not for anything, not for anyone. But as they talked, as she learned about Flanagan, it was getting harder and harder not to back off from the iron. He was no corporate shark. He'd moved to the city only a year before, had never known New York with a World Trade Center, had never seen dust blanket Battery Park City. He knew the city fairly well, and traveled to his sister's place in Queens pretty regularly, but he still had a lot of the Small Town Connecticut in him. Blaylock had the sense that each time he set down roots, he staked out a territory and did not budge from it. The more she learned, the more he had Harmless and Vulnerable written all over. And so she made a concession to the guilt: if she could at all avoid it, Flanagan would not be hurt. (Oh, big deal, she thought. What largesse.) Then Flanagan asked just the right question, unconsciously greasing the gears of Blaylock's machine, cheerfully putting himself in harm's way: "So really, why are you in town?"

Here we go, Blaylock thought. "For IMTEX."

"Oh." Flanagan visibly tensed, caution walls going up all around.

"You going?"

"No. I don't like guns." When Blaylock choked on her brandy, he said, "Don't look at me like that. I have nothing to do with the weapon side of things. I do shipping, and we could be marketing joy buzzers for all that I have to do with product."

Blaylock eyed him. Then she said, "In that case, you're coming with me to IMTEX on Sunday." He opened his mouth, but she cut him off with steel: "Yes."

After dinner. Wrapping the evening.

She let Flanagan hail her a cab, conceding that much to him and his expectations of how the male and female roles of the date should play out. She thanked him for dinner, and even gave him a quick peck on the cheek before getting into the back seat of the car. She let him hear her give the cabbie the name of a Chinatown Holiday Inn.

Home, then, taking precautions. Was she being followed? She doubted it very much. But she assumed she was. The InSec building was a half-dozen blocks behind when she told the cabbie she'd changed her mind. She had him drop her off at Penn Station, where the night life was out, screaming the laws of a Biblical Jesus and buying the bliss of a chemical one. Blaylock made her way inside to a wall of lockers, pulled out a key, opened a locker and removed a gym bag. She ducked into a women's washroom, scanned for trouble, saw none, and changed into jeans, T-shirt, leather jacket and runners. Then she left the station for a roundabout route back to home base. She started by walking west on 33rd, the wrong way. Once she'd left behind the ruckus of 8th Avenue, she realized she had company. It was a man, dressed in camouflage fatigues. He kept a block behind her, and his route *might* have been a coincidence until, two turns later, he was still there. Fine, Blaylock thought, be that way. What she wanted now was the quiet and the dark. She started to zig and zag, gradually heading back north and east into Clinton, not wanting to have too far left to walk once she got this sorted out. 40th was almost deserted, and she slowed down. Now she could hear Camouflage's footsteps. He wasn't being subtle. Boot heels clopped down for the echo effect. He was playing for intimidation before he closed in. So he wasn't a tail, then. Most likely out for some.

Just before the intersection of 40th and 10th, Blaylock glanced over her shoulder, quickly, made the ohmigod sound of a sudden gasp, and then began to trot, the frightened prey. She heard him start to run. She had maybe thirty seconds before he caught up. She whipped around the corner. At the first ink pool of shadows, she dropped her gym bag, turned and waited.

Training. Ten years ago, when she first became aware of something called tai chi, she'd dismissed it as middle-aged women slow-dancing in the park. Kelly Grimson had set her straight on the difference between Yang style and Taoist. Taoist was dancing. Yang style broke bones and killed. And so Blaylock had worked it into the program. Any soldier who went into war depending solely on hardware was asking for it.

Camouflage burst around the corner. He didn't see her right away, and he still had forward momentum when Blaylock lunged. Almost in Camouflage's face, she rooted on her forward right leg, swung her arms out, and snapped her wrists, slamming the backs of her hands against Camouflage's ears. Blood exploded from his mouth. Inner ear cluster-bombed, he fell down. Blaylock stomped on his left ankle, breaking it. Camouflage passed out from the shock. Blaylock dragged him into the light for a better look. He was less heavy than she had expected. The fatigues hung loose. His face was coke-white, pitted, sheened with bad sweat. She rolled up a sleeve and found an arm roadmapped by needles. She noticed that he'd undone his fly, getting way ahead of himself, but she would have been surprised if he'd actually managed to get hard. She straightened up. She was satisfied that Camouflage had picked her at random. He wasn't a pro tailing her, that was for sure. And even if he had been hired, he wasn't going to tell anyone anything useful. So now what? Kill him? She shut her eyes against the thought. It had come far too easily, a reflex, the brush of a tentacle reaching out of Nietzsche's abyss. No. She opened her eyes and looked down at Camouflage, a screwed-up, vicious little animal. With that ankle pointing wrong, he wasn't going to be hurting anyone right away. No, she thought again, and made herself walk away. No killing, not tonight. For her sake, if not for his.

One more block and home. A hotel, yes, but a single-room-occupancy fleabag. Her room was on the fourth floor. The bare necessities: bed, chair, table, stains, insects, weapons chest. The window looked at a wall. No exit there, but from the roof she could get to the tops of other buildings. So she had her back door. It was an acceptable defensive position. And the anonymity was the main attraction. Her presence in the city was absolutely unregistered. Blaylock didn't bother to turn on the lights. She dropped her gym bag to the floor and threw herself onto the bed.

There was a stool beside the bed. On the stool was a picture frame. The frame was a bit of salvage, a survivor of the Winnipeg explosion. The frame had held a family portrait, taken the fall before Blaylock had left for the Gulf. The military storm had been gathering, and Blaylock's mother, nervous, had cajoled husband and daughters into sitting for the picture. Celia had resisted at first. Blaylock had taken her aside and explained how important this was to their mother.

"This will be a record of us," she had said, "of the whole family. It looks like there's a war coming, Cee. Things can happen." Celia, solemn, had agreed, and then had been delighted when she saw the result. Blaylock didn't enjoy having her picture taken, but she'd liked this one. It was a good picture. The photographer had cracked a joke and taken the shot the instant before they all laughed. He caught them in the instant of dawning hilarity. A good picture. Framed, it had been mounted on the wall near the front door. When Blaylock got back from the Gulf, the picture had been the first thing she'd seen when she'd stepped into the house. It was the sign of Home. And then boom. The frame fine, barring some slight discoloration and a few scratches. The picture burned, memory flaked to ash.

Blaylock had kept the frame. She wasn't sure why, at first. She could have had the picture replaced. Both of her grandmothers had still been alive in '91, and they had copies of the shot. But she didn't ask for one. It wasn't until Bosnia, when her war had begun, that she had realized why she needed the frame without picture. It was a reminder. The talisman of loss. It broadcast absence every time her eye fell on it, and acted as a spur if the convolutions and slug pace of her campaign wore her down. It was also a shield. She wouldn't be able to bear the actual faces of her parents and Celia staring at her, holding her accountable. Her war was not for them. It was selfish, the luxury of vendetta, and she knew it. But she could keep the worst doubts at bay as long as the frame showed only wood.

Sometimes, though, the doubts came through anyway. She turned her head. She could just make out the shape of the frame, a darker rectangle in the urban night gray of the room. What would you think, Mum? The thought unwanted but inescapable. What would you think about tonight? What would you think about Johnathan W. Smith III? And there it came again: her last memory of her mother. "I'm not sure what upsets me more: that you feel some people need killing, or that you believe you're one of those chosen to do the killing."

Blaylock closed her eyes, tight, tight, and reached inside for her strength. She found it: a cold stone, round and hard and strong as the rage it was. She gripped it, and didn't let go, not even in sleep.

8

Blaylock arrived at Flanagan's building just after seven Saturday evening. This is not a good idea, she thought as she walked down the corridor to his apartment. Flanagan had already agreed to come to IMTEX tomorrow. She didn't have to do any more fraternizing. Once she got him to IMTEX, she was pretty sure she could turn him and that she'd have her mole in InSec. So this was extra, this was superfluous, this was stupid. She was risking her detachment by coming here. If she wasn't careful, she might actually start to like the guy. But he'd insisted. He wanted her to meet his sister and her kid. She'd resisted. But not very hard, and not very well. Because here she was, knocking on the door. And here was Flanagan, beaming, ushering her inside. The apartment was furnished in Executive Bachelor. The armchair and the sofa matched, but looked as if they'd been reupholstered. Relics from the family home, Blaylock suspected, retained for the sake of both comfort and nostalgia. The couch was arranged for comfortable prone viewing of an enormous television. There were dry-mounted movie posters for *Double Indemnity* and *The Sweet Smell of Success*. There were no plants—they would have required watering and died. The place was spotless, and Blaylock assumed he had a cleaner come in once a week. The living room window looked east, back into the Financial District.

There was a boy on the sofa, watching the TV. He got up, proper little gentleman, to meet her. His mother wheeled her chair forward. Blaylock saw Holly as a war comrade, wounded in battle. She was one of the people for whom Pembroke was going to take his fall.

Blaylock had made herself a bet: that Flanagan would serve them steak. She lost. She knew that when he handed her a glass of white wine instead of red. When they sat down around his dinner table, he served chicken breasts in a white wine and escargot sauce. It was pretty good. Dessert was an apple tart. It was even better.

As he served coffee, Flanagan asked Holly, "Did I tell you Rebecca's off to Paris?"

"What's she doing there?"

"Assisting Terry Chatman on the MAI."

Stone silence. Blaylock's interest was pricked. What was InSec's angle with the MAI?

Holly said, "You know what this bill of rights does, Mike? It'll let assets fly out of countries, and no one will be able to say boo about it. Your precious capital? Zing, flowing at lightspeed, no controls. You think the market is volatile now? You ain't seen nuthin'. Local development? Restricted. Or doesn't it bother you that the rules favor only the multinationals?"

"Don't forget the legal stuff," Blaylock chimed in. "That's my favorite part."

That really got Holly going. Blaylock sat back and watched as Holly launched into a litany of future environmental and labor catastrophes as corporations sued governments over any regulation that infringed on the ability to trade. She went on for almost five minutes. When she paused, Flanagan said, "Done?" and stalked off into the kitchen.

Blaylock followed him. "You don't like being ganged up on, do you?"

"No, I'm used to that." He ran water in the sink. "Holly would have probably had her rant without being prompted. It's the whole apocalyptic fantasy I get tired of. I haven't noticed NAFTA bringing about the end of the world. Did you?"

"Depends on who you ask."

Halfway through the dishes, Blaylock heard Holly scream and Eddie giggle. She moved to the kitchen doorway. Holly had turned the TV off, and Eddie was reading to her from a *Goosebumps*. Holly was pretending to be frightened.

"How old is he?" Blaylock asked Flanagan softly.

He came and looked too. "Eight."

"They're both great."

"Yeah."

Blaylock watched a moment more. It was like seeing a documentary on a foreign culture. There was the world Holly and Eddie inhabited, and there was hers. Between them were doors, steel-plated and locked tight.

Sunday morning.

The Jacob K. Javits Convention Center sprawled a glass-fronted immensity over five blocks, claiming the view of the Hudson for its own from 34th Street to 39th. The cab dropped Blaylock and Flanagan off at the main entrance. Blaylock opened the briefcase she had brought with her and pulled out two ID badges. Hers had a picture, and the name J. TAYLOR. Underneath the name, in smaller letters, LR INC. The letters of IMTEX lurked in a hologram in the lower corner. She handed Flanagan a badge that said GUEST OF LR INC. where there would have been a name and picture. "Put this on," she said. "The party's by invitation only."

Flanagan gave his ID a long stare, then favored Blaylock's with an even longer one.

Blaylock said, "Joan Taylor and the organization she represents have been, via IMTEX, very good customers for InSec. They get invited every year."

"And who is Joan Taylor?" When Blaylock just smiled, Flanagan's face twitched as if his next question tasted awful. "So how do I know if your name is Baylor?"

Blaylock blinked as if surprised. "Whatever made you think it was?" she asked, all puzzled ingenuousness. "Come on," she said, as Flanagan began to stammer. She took him by the arm and dragged him inside.

The Javits Center was another of I.M. Pei's exercises in the architecturally sound and the esthetically eccentric. The main hall was the building's pride of the unusual. It was an exposed-steel space frame, God's own tinkertoys painted black and linking up to form walls and ceiling, airy strength supporting glass that reflected black outside, but poured in filtered light inside. Tan stone separated the different exhibition halls. Blaylock led Flanagan along the ground floor until they reached the escalator leading to the upper-level hall. They saw their first guard at the top of the escalator. He was a friendly, generic rent-a-cop. He barely glanced at the badges before waving them on. Blaylock was familiar with the pattern of defense by now. Rent-a-cop was there to make sure anyone taking a wrong turn was redirected without being made nervous or curious. The stage two barrier was a pair of guards with holstered side arms. They stood at the entrance to the exhibit proper. The glass walls had been hung with black curtains, blocking view and bullets from the displays. The guards looked at the badges carefully. One of them spoke Joan Taylor's name into a cell phone. While he waited for a response, his buddy watched them, hands on hips, fingers a twitch away from his holster. The right answer came back on the cell phone, and Blaylock and Flanagan were waved on.

Flanagan paled when they got to stage three, which they hit the instant they stepped inside. A large IMTEX sign still blocked the way in case someone failed the final checkpoint. There was a line of guards here, all in Gestapo-black, every other one cradling an M-16. Flanagan gave Blaylock hard and frightened looks. She kept her hand at his back in case he needed support, and they stepped into the hall. "Welcome to IMTEX," said Blaylock. She watched Flanagan's face as he took in the show. There were almost as many metal cylinders on the show floor as there were holding up the ceiling. The gun barrels turned the space frame's 76,000 tubes into a skyward rush of dancing artillery. Flanagan's eyes got very wide. Then a shutter seemed to fall over them, and he turned around. He took a step to go. "I told you, I don't like guns," he said.

Blaylock stopped him. "Tough. Get to know your business." And she led him down into the valley of steel. She watched him get an education, the shelter of his life stripped away by a force of hail. She guided him gently, giving him a build-up from concealed pistols, to semi-automatics, to submachine guns, and from thence to the missiles.

In a forest of Stingers, he stopped and spoke for the first time in half an hour. "I don't know why I should feel bad about being involved in a completely legal and above-board enterprise."

"I don't see why, either." Blaylock kept her tone deadpan. Flanagan looked at her warily. "Let me show you something," she said. He didn't seem keen on being shown anything else, but too bad. She wasn't about to pull the hook. She was going to sink it deeper in, and then twist. She brought him over to a series of booths that were off-side from the heavy metal. They were lined up under a banner that read INFORMATIONAL PURPOSES ONLY. Blaylock scooped up some pamphlets. The first one had glossy photos of an old and treasured enemy. "Check this out," she said, handing Flanagan the ad for electric batons. He held it gingerly, as if afraid it might bite. "Everything legal," Blaylock threw back at him. "Everything above-board. So's this." A prospectus for informational courses on torture techniques. Purely for preventative uses, naturally. "All part of the same show, Mike. Now look at this." She put her briefcase on the table, and pulled out a photo album. "The fruit of your labor," she said, and began to turn the pages for him. She showed him picture after picture of exit wounds, of legs blown off by land mines, of jaws torn away, of genitals marked with electrical burns. A lot of the pictures were of children. "This is your business. This is what you sell."

Flanagan shook his head and tossed the pamphlets back onto the table. He walked away, but not toward the exit. Blaylock shoved the album back into her briefcase and kept pace, and knew she had him. She'd connected him to the reality of InSec. The fascination was there on his face, and even stronger was the revulsion. He stopped in the middle of an aisle and watched a salesman, speaking fractured Italian, trying to sell a prospect on the benefits of the latest variant on the Vektor CR21 bullpup infantry rifle. Blaylock watched Flanagan's eyes, saw them slide over the bullpup's compact, elegant curves, saw them register the fetish and eroticism of the arm, saw them wince in horror at their own pleasure. He looked up, focused on something in the crowd behind Blaylock, and his eyes shifted from horror to fear. "Oh shit," Flanagan whispered. "Pembroke and Noonan are here."

Blaylock hauled Flanagan down to the other end of the aisle. She looked back as she shoved him toward the Stingers. She spotted Noonan right away, and beside him, at long last, she saw the Enemy. He was holding a palm-sized anti-personnel mine, looking it over and grinning. Blaylock memorized his features. She felt a pang of deep and frustrated hunger. There he was, InSec's avatar, and here she was, surrounded by enough ordnance to wage a good war, and she couldn't touch a single round. Blaylock stared, feeling her hate and feeding it, but also fighting a grin at the thought of Pembroke coming so close to his death and not even knowing it. Neither he nor Noonan was paying attention to anything other than the weapons.

She caught up to Flanagan. He was cowering in the shadow of the Stingers. The display was unattended for the moment. "They haven't seen us," she said. "And you're right not to want them to." It was time to get Flanagan out of here, but she had to know something first. "Last night Holly mentioned something about you and a big project." She stepped closer, backing him into the missiles, and made sure Flanagan could see what was in her eyes. "You tell me what that project is, or I'm going to march right over and high five Noonan."

Flanagan asked, "Who *are* you?" When she didn't answer, he closed his eyes for a moment, as if calculating the balance of evils. Blaylock won. "A remote guidance system for freighters," he said.

Blaylock blinked. What the hell? And even with the confusion came the sense of a horizon both terrible and liberating opening up. She had the intuition that the war was not just hers, that something infinitely bigger than her own vengeance was in the process of mobilization. All the more reason to avoid compromising Flanagan. She smiled at him, gently. "Wait till I say," she said, "then get out of here." She ducked back to the aisle they had left, took a peek around the corner. Pembroke and Noonan had moved further down, closer to her. Noonan appeared to be browbeating a sales rep while Pembroke looked on. Blaylock looked back and mouthed, "Go."

Flanagan went. He disappeared into the rows of weapons, heading for the exit. Blaylock glanced back. The enemy hadn't moved. She took a step back, waited out of sight for thirty seconds, giving Flanagan time to be gone, then checked again. Pembroke and Noonan were gone. Shit. But then some luck as a cluster of suits walked past, chatting rates of fire. They were going her way. Blaylock stepped in behind them and moved to the outside of the group, close to the wall, keeping them between her and the main activity of the hall. She stayed just far enough that she wasn't intruding on the group's space, but close enough that from a distance she might blend in. The instinct was to look over shoulders, to hunch and run, evading fire. But she kept her movements to her role: the pro on a shopping trip. When she turned her head, it was the gesture of casual interest, a sexy RPG catching her eye. A good act, but the searches were useless. She couldn't find Pembroke and Noonan anywhere. What a mess. She could feel the shit just waiting to rain down.

The exit came closer. She began to wonder if her group shield was actually planning on leaving. That would be too good to be true. It was. Even with the exit, the suits turned up an aisle. And there was Noonan, wouldn't you know it. Right in front of her. They almost collided. Too perfect to be a coincidence. No, it was the joke of lame-ass God. Noonan took a step backward, startled speechless. So he didn't know. She'd come this close to clean escape. Blaylock laughed. A short, sharp bark: "Hunh!" She held out her hands: what can I say? Then she shrugged, and danced sideways out of the hall, waving. Noonan waved back.

9

Bossman circling. Enemies on the ramparts. Time for Noonan to earn his keep. He stood behind Bill Jancovich and enforced productivity through terror. Jancovich: big with middle-age spread. Wife long gone, now in a monogamous relationship with VDT radiation. Jancovich: Noonan's pet hacker. No industrial espionage or rival sabotage this evening, though. Hauled up to the computer room next to Noonan's top-floor office, he was doing a simple search, strictly legit. Jancovich accessed the database of registered IMTEX attendees. "She had a badge?" he asked.

"I told you that, didn't I? Didn't I already tell you that?" Noonan watched Jancovich twitch and liked it. He was on edge today, and would hurt someone, given a chance. That woman was maybe nothing, but as long as she was unexplained, she was a thorn in the side of his peace. Worse yet, she bothered Pembroke.

Jancovich started the search. Noonan watched. Jancovich began by cutting the pool down to women only. That shrank the numbers big time. He shrank them further by hair color and age, then called up identification photos, a digital slide show, one at a time. And there, easy as pie, six faces in, was the woman: Joan Taylor, 33, purchasing agent on behalf of LR INC.

Noonan shook his head. "Last time I saw her, her name was Jen Baylor. Who's LR?"

Jancovich keyed in the query. "Not sure. Doesn't say what the letters stand for." He scrolled down the screen. "They've been a steady purchaser. Mostly small arms and ammunition, some explosives, the odd mortar and anti-tank order. Nothing big time."

Noonan looked at the list of orders. They started two years ago. Jancovich was right, the arsenal wasn't huge, but it would equip a small force very nicely. The range of weapons was too precise, too carefully thought out to be the work of amateurs. He noticed the orders went to a warehouse in Miami. Noonan turned this over in his mind. A vague corporation, no doubt a dummy. That wasn't unusual—half of InSec's clients either couldn't or didn't want their real identities known. That was fine. InSec was Swiss in its discretion. But sending the weapons to Miami, that set up an equation that combined a port and the drug trade, and led back down the white crystal road to Colombia. And that made sense. This was just the right kind of material for drug-war soldiers, whatever side they happened to be on. But that still didn't clear up what kind of game this Baylor or Taylor or whatever was playing.

Noonan's cell phone trilled. He patted Jancovich's shoulder, just a bit too hard. "See what else you can find. Dig dig dig." He stepped into the next office to take the call.

It was Pembroke, and Pembroke didn't care about Colombia. "Is Flanagan working with her?"

Noonan laughed. "Not a chance. That chump couldn't

bluff his way through a poker hand with Helen Keller. Checkitout, he was practically coming all over himself when he was going to take her out Friday night. He couldn't stop yammering about this hot piece he'd picked up. He's clean."

"Even so, tighten up the surveillance on him. I want to be sure."

"And if she turns up again?"

"Kill her. She might be harmless, but I'd rather lose a couple of clients than take any risks. If Flanagan knows she's around, make it an accident. I want him happy until the work is done." Pembroke hung up.

Noonan folded his phone shut and smiled. Wet work. It had been a while. And he loved to get wet. That was what had made him such an asset for Special Ops in Nicaragua and during the Gulf War. It was also, he knew, why they had eased him out afterwards. Enthusiasm made them nervous. But then InSec had been looking for a few good men, and Pembroke had promised him creative freedom, provided all the targets were authorized.

Before the wet work: send feelers out. Monday lunch, Noonan stopped by the 1st Precinct to visit his new friend. "Ed Ed Ed," he said, all bouncing grin as Kroker, wafting fatigue, came out front to greet him. Noonan held up a large brown bag. He took a step toward the precinct door and gestured for Kroker to follow. "It's lunchtime, you need to eat, I got info, and the air in here stinks like a chain-smoking whore."

They went outside and sat on the precinct's tiny two-step porch. Noonan handed Kroker a carton of Chinese food. "So checkitout," he said, "there's this broad who's been hanging around Mike Flanagan. As far as he knows, she's Jen Baylor, but our records have her as Joan Taylor. And Mike first mentioned her a couple of days after Johnathan got whacked."

Kroker raised his eyebrows. "You think she killed Smith?"

Noonan roared. "Hell no. I mean, the coincidence reeks a bit, that's all. Maybe there's something there. Maybe she's working for someone who has someone working for them who did the hit." But at the back of his mind, he felt a slight tickle. The woman was dangerous. He should have recognized that when he'd first met her.

Kroker was silent for a moment. Noonan chewed on a spring roll, waiting to see what the cop did with the bait. There was a risk he might slip it right off the hook without biting down. Finally, Kroker asked, "Industrial espionage?"

"Could be."

Kroker stuffed his empty container into the paper bag and stood up. "Okay. Thanks for the tip. I'll look into it. You tell us if and when she turns up again." He tossed the bag into a bin.

"You will too?"

Kroker had his hand against the precinct door, half pushing it open. But now he let go and turned around, an I-knew-it grin twisting his lips. "Why? What do you want with her?"

"We're going to sue her to hell. She was digging for proprietary technologies."

"Why didn't you just come out and say so? Jesus, what a stupid game for nothing." Chomp. Kroker went back inside the station, Noonan's hook sticking out of his cheek.

Noonan began to saunter back in the direction of InSec. It was a twenty-minute walk, but he didn't mind. He thought well when he was in motion.

Handing Kroker the Baylor/Taylor tip had been a hard eight dice roll. There were avenues of InSec business that Pembroke would not want Kroker walking, and that woman was close enough to some of them that there was a real risk that she might lure the police down those roads. But Kroker was a well-defined variable. The police could be contained. If Kroker took a few too many undesirable turns down his road, then he could be taken out. That was not a problem. That was Noonan's job. The payoff for the gamble, however, made it worth it. There was now a whole other network that would be looking for Baylor/Taylor. Noonan wasn't even that worried if she found out that the police were interested in her. Even that mere knowledge was likely to cramp her style. Noonan started to whistle.

Holly asked, "And you haven't heard from her since?"

Flanagan shook his head. It was Sunday again, afternoon again, the beautiful weather still holding, but this time no guns in sight. They were sitting on the patio of the Bean Supreme, a coffee bar two blocks from Holly's apartment. Flanagan had made it through the week with his mouth sealed shut against any mention of Jen Baylor or IMTEX, terrified that the least word would summon an army of balaclavaed goons through the door. The week had passed, no one had taken a potshot at him, his car hadn't exploded, Karl Noonan wasn't looking at him sideways, there had been no strange clicking noises on his phone, and he still had his job. That was good. But Baylor had disappeared.

He'd needed to talk to Holly. The few secrets they had kept from each other throughout their lives had always been short-term, rarely staying locked inside for more than a couple of weeks. His secret this time was too much of a bulge in his chest to be kept in for another week, so he'd called Holly. And she'd said of course she would meet him for coffee. Of course she did. She could read the signs of something up in his voice as easily as he could in hers. They'd met. The sun had warmed. He'd spoken. Of Baylor, of InSec, of IMTEX, of finally confronting the bloody realities of his profession. And now the bulge, while not excised, had lost some of its sharper edges.

Holly shook her head sympathetically. "Quit, Mike. For God's sake, quit. You say you want out. What have you got to lose?"

"My life."

Silence. Then Holly asked, "We're just talking worst cases here, right?"

"Right." But that didn't feel like the truth. People died in this business. He'd seen it happen. He had no idea who Smith III had pissed off, but whoever it was didn't believe in pink slips or slaps on the wrist. Smith III had been moaning about having been cut out of the loop just before he'd been shot. What did that mean? That Pembroke was the one who got mad? That when InSec said termination, they really meant it?

A couple walked by, golden lab on leash. The dog wore a red bandana around his neck, and was grinning big. Flanagan eyed the grin, feeling a huge envy. Trade places, he begged the dog. You be me. I'll be you. But the lab was on a walk, all was well in the universe, and he wasn't buying what Flanagan was selling. Flanagan shifted his gaze to the couple, and felt the same envy, this time pleading for their problems. Financial straits? Loud neighbors? Impotence? Throw it my way, all of it. And you take the rocket-propelled grenades and mortar shells. They ignored him too. Couple and dog disappeared around the corner.

"Your tanker project," said Holly, pulling him out of inane escape fantasies, "what do you think it's really about?"

Now, he hadn't thought of that, had he? Hadn't thought about how he, Mike Flanagan, was doing his bit for the global arms trade. "What an absolutely superb question," he said. He thought about Pembroke's rationale for the NAV-CON, and about the camouflage legalese of IMTEX, and the whole story stank of the primest bullshit. "I doubt I'd like the answer. But don't worry. I'm not going to do anything stupid. I'm not going to walk up to Pembroke and say, Hey, what am I really doing here?"

"But what are you going to do?" Holly put her hand on his wrist. It was the touch of a sister worried about a brother's sudden and final absence.

Flanagan put his other hand over Holly's. "No worries. I'm a coward. I'm just going to keep my eyes open for now. I should know soon enough if they're sniffing around me." Silence for a bit. Flanagan felt commitment settle like ice around his heart. It beat frantic in protest. "And at the first opportunity," he said, throat dry, "I'm blowing the whistle."

"To Jen?" Holly asked. "Do you think she's FBI or Agency or something?"

"She isn't a freelance writer, I can tell you that."

10

Paris in the springtime, and how much was she seeing of it? It was May, lovertime, the trees unfolding full green, the city in pre-heat and pre-tourist splendor, and Rebecca Harland's view was limited to a few postcard scenes. She had a night shot and a dawn shot of St. Sulpice church and its square from the living room window of her tiny fourth-floor bachelor apartment on the rue Bonaparte in the 6th Arrondissement. The church, proud in its eighteenth-century serenity, invited her to step in and rest. She hoped she would before she left. But for now it was nothing more than the sight that preceded the collapse into bed and followed the bleary rise.

The other view was of the city hall as she emerged from or sank down into the Hôtel de Ville metro stop. From that point, it was a quick walk deeper into the Marais district to the rue de la Verrerie and the building that quartered the

MAI negotiations. And there, the only windows she had access to for the day looked down into a courtyard. The first few days it had been picturesque, so utterly un-New York. Now the courtyard was drawing the claustrophobic robe of a stone prison about itself.

Harland hadn't had a precise image of her workplace in mind before arriving. But whatever she was imagining, she knew this wasn't it. She'd thought vaguely in terms of either European-brand ultra-modernism, or history-soaked governmental buildings. The city hall, for instance, vast, turreted and multi-sculpted, would have been just the thing. The actual headquarters of the Organization for Economic Cooperation and Development were in an impressive palace on the rue André Pascal on the other side of the city. She'd been expecting to work either there or in the office block opposite. Instead, she was in a five-storey heap of dankness on Verrerie. The building was old all right, but lived creakingly on only for function, not the picturesque. Wooden floors and staircases scuffed and polished pale by centuries of shoe leather, walls always about to become damp, windows thick and clouded with lead and grime. The light was never good enough, even the fluorescent and halogen bulbs barely managing to shift the brown in the air. The offices were many and scattered, heavy doors leading to antechambers and more heavy doors, hallways and stairs getting in the way of the shortest distance between two points. She wasn't sure why the talks were going on here. There was something clandestine about the unmarked locale. But the building did its job, even though it insisted on doing it in its own way. It had the conference rooms. It had the offices. It had the means. Harland worked in a room three times the size of her office back home. But it was not her room. It had seen too many people through time to admit to any kind of ownership. It permitted her occupancy, no more, and that only as long as she didn't get ideas above her station.

Her resources: latest generation Pentium workstation with multigig RAM and a hard drive big enough to contain the known universe, cable link to the Net and to the InSec mainframe. Her mission: provide Terry Chatman with whatever data he required in the negotiations. Specifically: come up with financial figures to support the argument that the MAI would be a Good Thing. More specifically: massage those figures as necessary.

The massage. She'd pulled this kind of shit duty before. It came with the territory. Chatman had a laptop that he used upstairs in the conference rooms. If he hit a data gap, he would type a query and spur Harland into a search. Harland had to explain why the MAI would not be a licence to kill for the transnationals, why it would not wipe out first any remaining economic sovereignty of nations before moving on to political and cultural fronts, why it wouldn't steamroll any citizen not set up to roll with the market. She came up with the figures. She made them fit the explanations. It was her job. She did it well. It was May in Paris, lovertime, and Rebecca Harland was choking on the filth of her lies.

Still, there was nothing she could do, was there? The best that reluctant governments and citizens' groups had managed a few years before was to hiccup the process. The accord was supposed to have died, but here it was, phoenix with talons outstretched. The momentum was too huge for her even to contemplate fighting it. You don't wade into a tsunami. And anyway, this was her big score. Bag the bucks, then get out. So she kept doing her job, earning her money, doing her part for the world of business, which, after all, had everyone's interests at heart.

Lovertime spring in Paris, late afternoon on Friday, brief lull in the negotiations. Chatman turned up in Harland's office. "I need stats on gun control in North America," he said. "It's the Australian. All freaked out over nothing, as far as I can tell, but c'est la vie with the political types. Enough constituents get a bee in their bonnets and it turns into a burr up their rep's ass. Can I mix my metaphors like that?" Still cracking jokes as he stood, leaning one-handed on her doorframe, tie lost, shirtsleeves rolled, eyes fatigue-pouched. If he'd had any hair, it would have been messy beyond the art of the comb. He must have been averaging four hours tops of sleep a night, he was clearly exhausted, but he was still radiating out the charisma, the grin, and the *belief*. For Chatman, there were no doubts, no bad conscience or nasty second-guessing. If he needed lies for his cause, that was fine, because the cause itself was *right*, it was *good*, it was *just*. The MAI was prosperity's dream, the full and final flowering of unshackled and wealth-spreading business, capital in ecstasy-flight to the moon. Chatman had the faith.

Harland asked, "What kind of stats?"

"Stuff to show that NAFTA didn't do a damn thing to force Canadian gun laws to match up with ours. By tomorrow morning."

"All over it."

"Blessed art thou among women," he said, and swanned out of the office.

Harland turned back to her computer. She jumped into the InSec mainframe. She called up a search engine that checked both InSec and the Net, and got to work. At first, finding what she needed was easy. That was the first warning sign. She should have known this was going to be trouble. But initially she had visions of getting the job done in twenty minutes. Slick as shit, she had the NAFTA agreement, and she had the Canadian and US gun laws. Since the Canadian rules were stricter than those in the States, what she wanted to find for Chatman was either no change since NAFTA, or signs of the gap widening. No problem. There weren't a lot of significant changes in the Canadian laws in the first few post-NAFTA years. A couple of strategic cross-checks with Texas and other points south gave her the widening gap she needed. Perfect. All done. That's that.

Only it wasn't. The NAFTA stuff was easy, but they weren't here for NAFTA. Out of curiosity, she cross-referenced "MAI" and "guns," and she landed on some old websites dating back to the initial run at the accord. Shortly before the collapse, it had seemed like a done deal, and somebody had jumped the gun. She found references to court challenges to the Canadian laws, all of them launched by gun manufacturers and distributors, all of them using the MAI as basis for challenge, all of them under the auspices of the WTO, all of them with resolutions still pending because of the freeze on negotiations. She was also referred to a colossal number of InSec files, all of them declaring themselves off-limits to anyone with such pitiful clearance as herself.

Harland sat back and stared at the screen. Bad feeling in her gut. Danger lights flashing. Don't dig any deeper. If she did, she'd hit the last thing she wanted: a revelation. One she couldn't shunt to the dark vaults in her mind and seal off. Her screen saver came up. Escher birds flew into and out of each other, wiping out the bad data and worse speculations. Harland took the hint. She sat up straight and got back into WordPerfect. She marshaled the information she'd found, the good stuff, the figures that would make Chatman grin, and worked it up into a quick report. She bolded the elements that would make Chatman's case most strongly. When she was done, she printed it out, four pages of data cooked to well-done perfection. She glanced at her watch. Six. Today's round of negotiations would be over, but Chatman might still be in his office. Harland picked up the papers and went to see.

Chatman's office was one floor up. Harland didn't see anyone on her way there. Most of the crew had gone home. Even in this snake pit of workaholics, the weekend beckoned. But she could see light coming from the open door of Chatman's office. She had taken two steps down the corridor when she heard Chatman laugh. Laugh long, loud and mean. And then: "*Christ* no!" A pause, then another laugh. Chatman on the phone.

Listen, said a voice. Bad voice, wrong voice, but she did what it said anyway. She put her feet down slowly so her heels wouldn't click on the wood. She got closer, Chatman's voice growing clearer. She stopped ten paces down from his door, wondering how the hell she would disappear if she had to, but nailed to the spot by the Medusa call of the conversation.

". . . Brit's still making trouble," Chatman was saying. "That PR bonanza gun law and all, you know. . . . Well, yeah, exactly. That's what I told him. Look, I said, the WTO hasn't given you guys the slightest bit of grief for that law, now, have they? So why would they start now? . . . Yeah. . . . Yeah. . . . I've got Harland looking into it, getting some NAFTA ammo. . . . What? . . . No, I can't see what harm it could do. She has no motive, she has no stakes, she has no pieces, so what the hey?" A long pause. Then serious: "You want to know the truth, Arthur? I think we're going to run into the same problems as last time. I can surround the key points with all the chaff in the world and some officious little dickwad is still going to hit the target, even if it's a fluke. I'm going to get us as close to word-for-word as I can, but you know it's not looking good. If they're already starting to yammer on about arms. . . . Yes, I think so too. If you're going to have the goods anyway, might as well put them to good use. Karl's ready to roll? . . . What? . . . That's weird. Any idea who she's working for? . . . Oh. But nothing since? . . . Oh, good. And Flanagan's behaving himself? . . . Good. All right, what do you want me to do right now? If I know Harland, she'll give me what I need for most of these assholes, but I'm sure the Brit is going to stick just to stick. . . . Oh really? Holy shit. Okay, hang on, let me see." Harland heard a chair squeak, and then the clicking of Chatman's keyboard. "I'm in. What's the directory? . . . PRODS, okay. Password? . . . Small-s-p-u-n-k-big-H-i-t. Got it. Pretty rude, boss. . . . Yeah, I bet it was Karl's idea. Oookayyy, let's see what—" Louder, longer, meaner laughter. "Oh, beauty! Is it real? . . .

No, I can't tell. Doubt the papers would either. . . . Yes . . . yes. . . . Right. Later." Clatter of phone going back into cradle.

Harland backed up down the corridor. Slow, slow, quiet, head ringing and stomach twisting from having heard too much and too little. She tried each door handle as she retreated, hoping she would find an unlocked office, and hoping she wouldn't. Three doors down, she found one. Quiet, quiet, slow, she opened the door, stepped into the dark office and pushed the door to, leaving the tiniest crack for her to watch the corridor. She waited. Her mouth was dry. She could taste tendrils of bile in the back of her throat. She was being stupid on a cosmic scale, she knew that. The risks she was taking didn't bear thinking about. But pushing her on, nailing her to the course, was the sense, unshakable and granite, that she was doing the right thing. So she waited. After twenty minutes, she was beginning to think the gods of Fate were going to smile on her. Chatman was going to lock up, go home, and that would be that. Nothing more she could do. At least for today.

But oh no, no wriggling off the hook. She heard Chatman get up and start walking. She heard him pull his door closed. Then he walked past her, and in the flash snapshot she had of him, she saw that he had a newspaper in his hand. His footsteps went down the hall. The stairwell door opened and closed. Off to the can for a patented Chatman dump. Patented because of its predictability. Great guy to work for, lovely boss, but he did have those necessary targets for the office caricaturist. The Chatman dump was the easiest. If he went to the can empty-handed, then it was just for a whiz, and he'd be back in thirty seconds. But a newspaper meant a matter of some moment. Eleven minutes, set your watches. Harland decided to allow herself six. Less if she could.

Locked in, girl, here we go. She opened the door, stepped out, closed the door, tiptoed down to Chatman's office. Let herself in, and went straight to the computer. She didn't sit, she didn't touch anything except the keyboard. She logged onto the InSec mainframe, and requested directory PRODS. The computer asked her for a password. She typed "spunkHit." A list of subdirectories came up, each with the name of one of the MAI negotiators. Harland clicked on "Reginald Harmsworth," the British representative, and got a slide show: Harmsworth and two little boys. Naked. Ten pictures, all good, solid, NAMBLA jerk-off material. Harland logged out in a hurry. Fakes, she guessed, from what Chatman had said. Good fakes, though. Excellent blackmail material. She couldn't imagine too many people being able to stand up to that kind of assault. But Chatman didn't seem to think this was enough. Why not? Because Harmsworth didn't have enough clout on his own? Because he could always be replaced and the game would have to start all over again? What game, though? And why was it so necessary to win? Chatman's words: "I'm going to get us as close to word-for-word as I can." Close to what?

Harland glanced at her watch. Three minutes to go. She jumped into Chatman's file manager and scanned directories. She chose "MAI." Dozens of file names popped up. She ran her eyes over them. Nothing was labeled "EVIL PLAN." She reread the file names. One last look and then she would give up. The last look did it. There was a WordPerfect file called "CORE." She opened it. One minute to go, and the bitter fruit of her efforts was on the screen. Two provisions for the MAI, couched in diplomatic excelsior, but clear enough once she put them together with Chatman's conversation and what she'd found on the Net. Harland felt her blood retreat deep inside. She pulled out of the file, got back to the Windows screen she'd started from, and stood back from the computer. Quick look around. Anything moved? No. Anything dropped? No. Time to leave? Yes.

Silent to the door, all she could do not to break into a

panic run. Peek into the corridor. All clear. Last scan over the office. Still no mistakes. All right. Go. Quiet and quick, down the corridor, to the stairs. Now time to hold her breath, because the can was the first door off the stairs on her floor. No choice but to go past it. She slipped her heels off and padded down. She stopped just shy of the washroom door, ears straining for the sound of Chatman about to exit. Nothing.

Moment of truth. She dashed past the door. Kept going, shoulders hunched against the doomsound of Chatman's steps. But nothing happened, and nothing happened, and she got back to her office. Lickety split, turning off her computer, putting shoes back on, grabbing the work she needed and shoving it into her briefcase. She took the notes she had printed off too. Chatman would get them when he expected: tomorrow morning. Harland picked up her coat, turned out the lights, and left the building.

Satisfyingly crapped out, Terry Chatman tossed the *Financial Times* onto his desk and sat down. He cracked his knuckles and rotated his chair to face his computer. His hands froze over the keyboard. Instinct flashed a warning sign. Something wrong, what what what? Everything looked fine, yes. So....Ah. He had it: a break in the routine. He had his screen saver set to kick in after ten minutes. Whenever he had his newspaper break in the can, he always had to chase the saver away when he got back to work. This time he didn't. He looked at his watch, then waited, keeping track.

It was almost five minutes before the saver came on. His armpits started to sweat. He had to find the leak and plug it, or Pembroke would have his hide. He took hold of the mouse, called up the TRACE software and set it loose. TRACE was an InSec in-house security program. It tracked and recorded all commands made on a given terminal. Chatman asked for the journal of the last fifteen minutes. The reconstruction took five seconds. Chatman stared at Harland's journey and her logon user ID. Then he reached for the phone.

11

Springtime in Paris. Hard as glass. Harland sat nursing a coffee in a dark corner of a café a half-dozen blocks from the negotiations center. She had picked her direction at random, keeping off her usual route, staying away from her apartment. This was sanctuary. She had the time and space to think, to choose a next move that would not be stupid. If Chatman and Pembroke were into blackmail and God knew what else, she didn't want them pissed at her. Safety required anonymity. Whatever she did, no one could know. A media leak, then? Harland sipped, considering. Possibilities here. The information she would pass on would not be anything she was supposed to have access to in the first place. Nothing would point to her. As long as she continued to behave normally, that is.

She finished her coffee. Go home, she thought. Go to where you're supposed to be. Turn up for work, do your job, act normal, wait for the sky to start falling. She stood up, paid and left. Outside, straight to the nearest phone booth. She wasn't going to call from home, no thank you. That would be asking for it, in neon. She pulled out her Télécarte, and started dialing. A quick bit of business first with the directory assistance, which got her the number of the *Guardian*'s Paris office. She dialed, but paused before hitting the tenth digit. Rubicon coming up. One more beep and she was crossing. She closed her eyes, trying to find the courage. She didn't find it. But she found a need and an anger instead. Good enough. She pushed the button, and half-hoped there would be no one working late in the offices. She was answered after only two rings.

She walked out of the booth ten minutes later. A weird euphoria was dancing in her gut. She'd never started an avalanche before. It felt good. It felt like power. It felt like the first hard blow in a fight for something big. It felt right. And it felt right all the way back to her apartment. But when she stepped in, she saw the message light flashing on her phone, and she had to run to the bathroom and puke. She clutched the sides of the toilet bowl, breathing hard, little child wanting to start the day over and take back her actions, this time I'll be good, I promise. But the day kept going. She could hear the distant rumble of the gathering rockslide, momentum irrevocable. She stood up, took a breath and swallowed, trace vomit stinging her throat. She went to face the phone, which was still flashing, inexorable, just one of the falling rocks come to take her down too. She picked up the receiver. Dialed for her message.

Chatman's voice, friendly, concerned, worried: "Hey there, Rebecca, Terry here. Listen, I know you've had to face some hard choices today, and I want you to know that whichever way you decide to go, we'll be right behind you all the way. I think you know where I stand, and I don't want to belabor the point. I know that there's no way for me to understand completely how it is for you, your being a mother and all. But I'm thinking of you. See you tomorrow. Bye." Click.

Clatter of the phone hitting the table, and Harland down on her knees, the dry heaves coming hard but she'd already had her chance and nothing came up. When the heaves passed, Harland made herself stand. Get vertical. Fight. And think. The *Guardian* phone call was something she couldn't take back now even though she wanted to. Pleading with Chatman would be useless. And he would assume she had ignored his warning when the story hit. So she had to act first. Get her family out of the firing line. She dialed home. Her own voice came down the line. "Hi, this is the home of Harland and Hooks. Please leave your message after the——"

She hung up, looked at her watch, and counted backwards. It was early afternoon in New York. Plenty of reasons for no one to be home. Pembroke wouldn't have sent out the stormtroopers yet, would he? She phoned back, waited for the machine to stop speaking. "Ronald, you and the kids have to get out of the house *right now*. Leave town. Don't phone here. I love you." That should be scary enough. Better too if she didn't know where they were going. What she didn't know, she couldn't tell.

She thought again. Leaving the message wasn't enough. Ronald might not get it until it was too late. Might need help. She needed someone in New York she could trust to help. She called Flanagan's office, knowing that she might as well send a personal message to Pembroke, hating that she was going to expose Flanagan to risks he shouldn't have to face, but her family needed saving, and she wasn't there, and she had put them in danger, and she had to get them out. When Flanagan answered, she said only this: "InSec's going to hurt my family. Warn them." Harland slammed the receiver down and took a breath. Time she was gone too. She had to try to keep ahead of the rockslide. She sprinted to the bedroom to pack.

Chatman was still at the office. He was pissed off, he was hungry, he was tired, and all signs were pointing to an all-nighter. Given the chance, he would strangle Harland himself. No fobbing her off to Noonan and his team. Then his phone trilled. He hit the speaker button, and Noonan's voice growled. "What the hell is that bitch doing calling Flanagan?"

"I think she's trying to fight," Chatman said.

"Good." Noonan sounded eager.

Chatman thought for a moment. "I wouldn't be too rough yet. If she loses her family, we also lose our best leverage over her."

"I know it. Trust me, Terry, I know how to play this."

"What's next, then?" Chatman asked, deferring to Noonan. Chatman knew the rules for the MAI negotiations game, but as soon as things threatened to get wet, the plays were Noonan's all the way.

"Start with containment. She doesn't want to take a hint, fine. You've got a strike team out there, yes?"

"Small one."

"Don't need a big one. You know where she lives. Pick her up."

"On it," said Chatman, and punched up another phone line.

Jean Felouse had professional pride. A strike team wasn't just about hitting, it was about hitting fast. He believed in speed, and in his ability to deliver InSec's France operatives to the scene before the target of the blow even knew the order had been sent. He had met Karl Noonan a couple of times, and knew that he was still several volts down from Noonan's electric kill current. Even so, he knew about shocks, and how to administer them.

He and Alain Bompais pulled up a block from Harland's apartment building fifteen minutes after getting the order.

They got out of the car, a Twingo battered and dirty enough to be hard to notice, engine beefed up to hunter-killer speeds. Felouse moved toward the building door, feeling circuits close and juice flow. Bompais tapped the entry code into the keypad in the recessed wall. Buzz-click from the door and they were in. They took the stairs quietly, favoring surprise over speed. No rush now: there was no back way. Neither drew their shoulder-holstered SIG-Sauer P228s. The weapons were last resorts, measures of desperate contingency. Harland had no gun, and this wasn't a wet job yet. If size wasn't intimidation enough, strength would tilt the scales the rest of the way, so recourse to ballistics would be unprofessional.

They reached the fourth floor and padded to Harland's door. Felouse leaned an ear against it. Dead quiet on the other side. He frowned, antennae picking up trouble. He pulled the spare key Chatman had given him out of his pocket. Quickshove into the deadbolt lock, sharp twist of the wrist, simultaneous with a hard turn of the doorknob. Inside, Felouse knew immediately that they were too late. Empty apartments had a thick stillness to the air, the silence of vanished movement. He and Bompais exchanged looks, shrugs, and searched the place anyway. There wasn't a lot to say that Harland hadn't just stepped out. There were plenty of clothes, and one suitcase, in the bedroom closet. There were papers all over the coffee table. But there were a few empty hangers, no purse, and some of the papers were on the floor in the scattered disarray of hurry. Felouse grimaced. He hated missing.

Chatman chewed his thumbnail while he did two kinds of waiting. He waited for the phone to ring, willing it to bring him the news that Felouse and Bompais had fluked out and found Harland before she got on a plane. He'd sent them to Charles de Gaulle airport on a likelihood gamble, but he knew he was rolling against luck. He also waited for the computer to spit out a lead. Multi-tasking, one program wormed its way into the passenger manifests of, first, all planes departing Paris for New York, then all bound for the States, then for North America, then for anywhere. So far nothing. But Harland couldn't be flying out under an assumed name. She had to use her passport. The other program was watching for any credit card transactions she made. That was the mistake Chatman was counting on, the big-ticket purchase that would hook him a meddling nigger.

The computer beeped. Chatman jumped, biting through the nail and swallowing. He choked on the cuticle, eyes tearing. He wiped them clear, stared at the screen. And there it was: a major credit card move to the tune of ten thousand dollars. Cash advance on a company no-limit card. Withdrawn from a bank machine in the south of the city. Nowhere near any team Chatman could field in time.

"*Shit!*" Chatman roared. "*Bitch!*" He rocked the computer screen back and forth.

Flight. On the run, trying to outdistance the avalanche. Flight was trying to stay two guesses ahead of Chatman and the digital web and bulletwound tactics of InSec. Flight was assuming near omniscience, and avoiding computers. All transactions cash. She would likely have to use her passport and let her name enter the dataflow at some point if she was going to get a flight. But there might be a way around that. She could take detours. Stay off the main path of the slide. And so? And so flight was the gray blur of countryside and speed, and Harland sitting, face turned to the window, watching late-evening France rush past the TGV on its rocket-run to Belgium. Paris-Gare du Nord to Brussels-Midi in an hour and a half. Flight was taking the routes that weren't obvious. Paris to Brussels by train. Brussels to Montreal by plane, but buy a ticket for Toronto. After that she'd improvise.

That was the plan. And its length ate at her. She wanted lightning, she wanted teleportation, she wanted back in New York *now*. But to do what? What real use speed? Her husband and children were safe or they were not, and her arrival now or tomorrow would have all the effect of trying to hold back the avalanche with her hands.

Ninety-two minutes to Brussels. She arrived at 11 pm. Twenty-minute wait for the Airport City Express, then fifteen minutes to the terminal. 11:35. A rush to the ticket counters, and the first flight to Toronto via Montreal was Air Canada 333. In just under twelve hours.

"Calm down," Noonan told Chatman.

"How? She's out of the city, I have no idea where to. She's uncontained!"

"She's coming back here."

"How do you know?"

"Checkitout: where else is she going to go? She's a family woman."

"And how is the family?"

"Just fine."

Chatman could hear Noonan's smile, could feel the smile. He made himself a promise never to have the smile aimed his way.

Noonan folded the cell phone and shoved it back in his pocket, thinking sad and dark thoughts about bureaucrats trying to play war. Chatman liked to think he was a shark, drawing blood in negotiations and blackmail, but he didn't know the first thing about a real feed. Noonan reached into the bag on the car seat beside him and grabbed a handful of fries. They were cold now, floppy cardboard. He poured some more salt on to simulate flavor. He watched as, a block away, Ronald Hooks organized Faith and Julie. The girls had their arms full of stuffed animals. Snoopy fell into the street as they struggled to shove all their friends at once into the back of an InSec minivan. Two of Noonan's operatives stood by, working hard at not being sinister. Noonan glanced at his watch, wondering why God thought so highly of him. Flanagan hadn't shown up yet, and it had been over an hour since Harland had made the call. Noonan couldn't imagine where Flanagan was spending the time. True, the idiot didn't own a car: New York traffic freaked him out so much he didn't have the nerve to tackle it on his own. But still, a cab should have had him here in thirty minutes at worst. Subway ditto. He wasn't taking the bus, was he? Noonan chuckled. Some friend. Urgent call, go at once, yes'm right away, by which I mean eventually. Noonan had been able to get all his ducks lined up without even breaking a sweat.

A bright red Tercel pulled up across the street from the minivan. Noonan saw the Budget rental plate on the front. Don't kid me now, he thought. The driver's door opened and Flanagan stepped out. Noonan laughed at the sight of the game being played with such appealing naïveté. He wanted to shake Flanagan's hand, then beat some sense into his head. Noonan choked down his laughter before it turned into a fit, got out of his car, and strolled down the block. No wet work now, not here anyway. Flanagan was doing good work on NAVCON, and Pembroke didn't want to have to go through the trouble of finding a new project leader if it wasn't necessary. Keep Flanagan onside, that was the game rule for the time being. Well, all right then. There was fun to be had in these moves too. Checkitout Chatman, this is how we do our job. "Mike!" Noonan called. Flanagan jumped, rabbit ready to bolt. Noonan fought to keep his face straight. Some getaway driver. What a guy. The day shone brighter by the second.

Flanagan wondered if there was a limit on how many stupid things you could pile up in a day. He stood, waiting for Noonan to reach him, his eyes flicking back and forth between the subcompact he'd rented and the minivan, its cargo space filling up with the vital treasures of children, the toys and the books and blankets that simply could not be left behind.

"Karl," he said as Noonan came up. "Hey." Noonan was good: his eyebrows were raised in surprise, and his smile was wide in welcome. Flanagan only had the thumping of his heart to remind him that Noonan knew damn well why he was here. Had to. And if Noonan was here, that meant Flanagan's phone was bugged, which meant they knew exactly what Harland had said, and she had explicitly said InSec was the danger here. He glanced over at the brownstone, and saw Hooks come out, a box in his arms.

Noonan followed his look. "Hey, Ronald," he said, "look who's here."

Hooks nodded a greeting, dumped the box in the van and crossed the street, wiping his hands on his jeans. "Mike," he said, "did Rebecca call you too? What's with the car?"

Noonan laughed, clapped Flanagan on the shoulder. "He came to rescue you from me," he told Hooks.

Hooks blinked, then laughed. "He kidding?" he asked Flanagan.

Flanagan shook his head. Through his hammering pulse, he could feel himself blushing, blushing.

Noonan's smile eased up, and when he spoke again his tone was serious, patient, calming. "It's all right, Mike. Yes, your office line is monitored." He shrugged, arms out in so-sue-me ingratiation. "Checkitout: you're working on a sensitive project. It's Standard Operating Procedure to keep tabs. Kinda sleazy, but. . . ." He shrugged again. "Anyway, we've been expecting something like this."

"Like what?"

"This is part of what happened to Smith," said Noonan.

He was quiet for a moment while Flanagan felt something wobble beneath his feet. Then Noonan jerked his head for them to follow him into the back of the van. Once there, he gave each of them a hard I'm-not-kidding-here look. "Listen. The only reason I'm telling you both this is that I don't want somebody running off half-cocked, which might happen if you've got the story back asswards. But this goes no further. Got it?" Hooks nodded, his trust complete. Flanagan made a noise in his throat. "All right. We've got something. Someone else wants it. They want to get it and screw us over at the same time. Industrial espionage plus sabotage. See?"

Flanagan felt unwelcome wheels turn in his head. Noonan kept looking at him. Finally, he had to speak, had to give the answer, had to get it into the air as if that would get it out of his mouth, out of his mind, and stop leading him down a path whose twists and thorns he couldn't navigate. "My project?" he said, almost a whisper, utterly a plea for Noonan to tell him he was wrong. But Noonan nodded. "Who?" Flanagan said. He didn't want to, but Noonan had him on the hook now.

"We're not sure. Personally, my money is on Colombians."

Colombians. Right. Flanagan felt the ground underfoot become a little surer. Noonan's bad guys were too stock, too all-purpose. As long as he could be sure that Noonan was lying, then he had something to cling to. His disbelief must have showed. "I'm not saying it is them," said Noonan. "But think about it. We've got the kind of distribution and transportation system a drug baron would cream his pants for. Think about the kind of problems that NAVCON is supposed to solve. Who else has those kinds of difficulties? What do you think that kind of technology would be worth in Medellín or Cali?"

A lot, Flanagan admitted to himself, starting to worry again. Was he being too glib, laughing off Noonan's story? The cartels *did* exist, yes? People did run into problems with them, yes? He wasn't immune, yes? Yes. But.

Crown Fire

"I can't figure out what all this has to do with Rebecca," said Hooks. "Why the hell would the Colombians be at all concerned with international trade negotiations?"

Exactly, Flanagan thought. And there, was that the cobra glint in Noonan's eyes?

Noonan grimaced. "You gotta remember, we're doing a lot of guessing here. I don't think they give a rat's ass what Rebecca is doing in Paris. But if they've been doing their homework, and you better believe they have, they know you guys are friends with Mike here."

There was silence. The idea sank in like slow poison. Hooks turned his head, quickly, as his daughters chased each other past the van. Noonan's men watched them. "Faith! Julie!" he called. "Stay out of the street!" He turned back to Noonan. "You mean those bastards would use us as leverage against Mike?"

"It's just a guess."

"But why them?" Flanagan demanded. "Why not Holly and Eddie?"

"Did I say not them?" Noonan asked, harsh. "Did I say they weren't targets?"

The day turned to hard metal, sharp with frost. Flanagan swallowed the warning and it tore his throat as it went down. He was going to bleed, no matter what now. If Noonan was telling the truth, that was already very, very bad. If Noonan was lying, he'd just been put on notice: behave.

"But why us first?" Hooks insisted. Flanagan barely heard him.

"Because it shafts us better," said Noonan. "Two birds with one stone: Mike's under pressure, and even better if the threat looks like it's coming from us. If Rebecca really thinks we're after her for some reason, the damage is that much more extensive. Pretty nifty, huh?"

Flanagan closed his eyes. If he kept them closed, he wouldn't have to see the quicksand as it rose to cover his head.

"It gets better," said Noonan. Flanagan opened his eyes. Noonan was staring at him. "And you're really not going to like this bit, Mike. You want to know how to work a really good con? You give the mark someone to trust. Someone he's going to turn to when all the bad shit starts happening. It's beautiful, when you do it right. The mark just throws himself into the trap and thanks you for it. You see what I'm saying, don't you? She's got more than one name, Mike."

Suddenly, all Flanagan wanted to do was curl up in a ball and go to sleep. Right here. Right now. On the road beside the car. A chorus started in his head: leave me alone, leave me alone, leave me alone. "So where are you guys going?" he whispered.

"Safer if you don't know," Noonan said. And he smiled. Cobraflash.

12

Brussels has guns. Brussels makes guns. Fabrique Nationale is one of the top manufacturers in the world. Brussels makes ammunition. Brussels exports what it makes. Brussels makes a lot of money doing this. Bad knowledge to have, even worse to remember it now. But there it was, tick-tocking through Harland's head as she sat in the Brussels Café, waiting for the hours to free her, waiting for the flight to start again.

The Brussels Café was an attempt to help travelers break with the streamlined sterility of airport architecture. The idea was that you sat here and were back in the center of Brussels: big bar, beer from barrels, art-nouveau buildings illustrating the walls, so never mind the 747s lifting up past the window. Harland didn't care about the atmosphere. The place had booths, though, booths with corners where she could curl up with protective shadows.

It was the puppets that bothered her. Huge marionettes dangled from the ceiling, bonus cultural kitsch for the tourists. And every time Harland looked up, every time she saw the strings, she felt the sharp, stabbing tug of her own. The strings, to her, looked like a razor web, not the means of granting movement but the unforgiving tools of terminal constriction. Movement arrested or movement controlled, it was all the same. To step out of line was to be broken. And she was well out of line.

She wanted to phone home. If no one answered, she could pretend that Ronald and the kids were safe. She wanted to phone Flanagan. She wanted to hear him say that his mission was accomplished. She wanted. She couldn't. She knew when the fix was in. If she called, her call would be traced in zero flat and the hounds would be on to her. Her shiniest hope now was that even if Pembroke's stormtroopers figured her route, they didn't actually *know*.

But they would know if Rebecca Harland bought a ticket. The instant her name entered the computer network she would stumble over an InSec tripwire and boom, game over. So instead, two tickets for Mr. and Mrs. Ronald Hooks were bought. Mr. Hooks was due on the next train, Harland had told the ticket agent. He would be here on time, yes he would. The agent had glanced at Harland's passport, saw Hooks there as next-of-kin, and printed up the tickets.

Now she looked at her watch. Another two hours to go. Getting onto the home stretch of the wait, this eternity of hopping from one plastic bar and cafeteria to another. Her stomach bubbled, but she wasn't hungry.

Two men came into the bar. Harland sank into the booth's shadows and gave the men the hard scan, as she had every new arrival. The details piled up bad. The men were big. They wore suit jackets that looked just a shade loose, perfect for concealing. They carried no luggage. Assume the worst. They blocked the entrance and looked around. Know the worst. Harland tried to shrink further yet. Her booth was at a bad angle for people stepping into the bar, and the lighting worked to her advantage. Suit One walked into the bar, strolling past the booths on the other side of the room from her. The search was going to be systematic. Suit Two stayed where he was and watched his partner. No exit. The moves were professional, but the Suits were bored. They weren't expecting to find her here, otherwise Suit Two would be more alert to the rest of the bar. Just going through the motions. But that would be enough if she stayed where she was. She had a few seconds left to make a move. She stood, grabbed her bags, and walked to the washroom. She kept her pace normal, tried not to jerk, did not look back. The lighting was dim, other people were moving around. She might blend. She stepped into the washroom. It was empty. She shut herself into the far cubicle, put her overnight bag on top of the tank, and climbed up on the seat. She almost lost her footing on the plastic. She heard the washroom door swing open. Someone took a couple of steps, then banged a cubicle door. A couple more steps, and bang again. She stared at the little rectangle of floor visible underneath the door of her cubicle, and waited, options all used up. If they came, she'd try to fight. The washroom door opened again. Harland heard high heels click on tiling, and then a woman began to yell.

"*Ça n'va pas, non? Mais il se croit où, celui-là?*"

"*Pardon, madame—*" the man began, voice a deep rumble, placating, condescending.

Mistake. The woman's voice got louder. "*Mais vous sortez, oui ou merde?*"

The fury of descending management would be the next step. The man grunted. Harland heard him walk out. She breathed. The woman went into a cubicle. Harland waited her out, wondering whether to leave with her. No. Then the Suits would know for sure she was here, and she would only buy minutes at best. She had to keep their uncertainty if she could.

The woman finished and washed her hands. Harland waited. The woman ran the hot-air dryer. Harland tensed, worried she wouldn't be able to hear the door. But the woman was fastidious. The dryer finished and she started it up again. Harland got down off the toilet seat. She picked up her bag and waited again. She was about to step out of the cubicle anyway, risk the other woman seeing her and being able to answer questions later, when the dryer shut off and she heard the woman leave. Harland burst from her cubicle and ran to the one nearest the entrance. She was counting seconds. She jumped up on the toilet there, bag on the tank again, and pushed the door until it was almost, but not quite, closed. Then she waited for the odds to play out. She didn't wait long. It had taken her under ten seconds to change cubicles. She was on her perch less than five when she heard the Suit walk back in.

She forced herself not to hold her breath. She breathed through her mouth, slow and shallow. She saw a man's shadow move past on the floor. You've already looked in here, she thought. The door is still open. Nobody's hiding. The footsteps moved down to the end of the washroom. The last two doors banged. The footsteps moved to the center of the room and stopped. Harland couldn't help it. She held her breath. The Suit snorted and walked out. Harland breathed. She climbed down and sat on the toilet seat, ready to hop back up if the door opened again. Four minutes had passed since the Suits arrived. Still at least an hour and a half before her plane boarded. Then that's how long she would wait.

A minute went by. Another. Then five. The washroom door opened and she jumped up on the seat. The cubicle door flew open.

"*Oh, pardon,*" the woman apologized and ducked away, too embarrassed to notice Harland's vulture crouch. Harland got down, locked the cubicle door and sat down again, sagging. Adrenalin leaked out. She felt the first shakes of shock set in, and she had to fight the sobs that were coming on strong. She stared at the gray metal walls of her prison, and willed the time to pass. It passed. But it passed at its own pace, measured ticks of tedium death broken up by tocks of jumping on the seat and cold-sweat panic speculation over what might be outside. Yeah, it passed.

Thirty minutes before take-off. Time to go. She stood up. Her knees cracked, not big on moving now. She took her bag and stepped out of the cubicle. No one jumped up and shot her. She steadied her breathing and marched to the door. Her hand froze solid on the handle. Her body tensed, fight-or-flight. It wanted another exit. But there wasn't any, and the choices were all used up, so she opened the door and walked out.

The Suits were gone. A couple was sitting in her booth, and she was glad that she had been settling up after each order. Irate management after her ass would have been the dumbest way to go down.

She left the Brussels Café behind. There were no Suits in sight. Tensed against a grab on her arm, she made her way to her gate. No one stopped her. She boarded the plane. The luck run still didn't sour. She sat in the window seat and waited. With ten minutes to go, she knew that Ronald Hooks was being paged on the airport PA system. The big hope: that all the Suits had were her name and photo. No reason for them to connect a man's name to her.

Five minutes left. An attendant walked down the aisle to her row. There was a man in a business suit right behind him. The attendant glanced quickly at the empty seat next to her before he spoke. "Mrs. Hooks?"

"Yes," said Harland. Her voice was a croak. But the other man didn't look like a Suit. His jacket fit properly.

"Your husband still hasn't checked in. We can't delay the flight. I'm afraid your husband will have to catch another one."

Phony panic and outrage: "But I've already paid for his ticket!"

"We'll see if any arrangements can be made. But I'm afraid it's too late now. This gentleman was on standby, and we've given him your husband's seat."

"I see." Harland slumped, pouting, defeated. The man sat down. The attendant walked back toward the front of the cabin. And then the plane took off, and Harland felt her lead grow that much more, and she had almost eight hours to let her guard down, and so she let the sobs come. They hurt.

"Christ, lady," said the man. "It's not the end of the world."

"Got her again," said Chatman. He didn't sound triumphant. "She used her husband's name to buy her tickets. It never occurred to us that—"

"I guess it didn't," Noonan said. "Where is she?"

"She booked a flight from Brussels to Toronto."

Noonan laughed. "Niggerbitch is ahead of you all the way, isn't she? When does it get in?" Noonan checked his watch. Quarter past four.

Pause. "It landed ten minutes ago."

Typical. "We'll take it from here," Noonan said and killed the connection. All right, no more screwing around with jerk-offs like Chatman. Now Noonan could play with minions who knew what shit was up. He dialed Bill Jancovich, who answered after the first ring. "Kill what you're doing," Noonan told him. "Locate Rebecca Harland, possibly traveling under the name Hooks. Last tracked to Toronto. Don't know what flight, but it just got in. Probable final destination New York. I want a flag to go up if she books another flight, if she rents a car, if she crosses Customs, if she takes a shit. Got it?" Noonan hung up. His phone trilled immediately. He sighed, almost didn't answer, tired of the telemarketer life. He wanted to be moving. He answered anyway, thinking that it had better not be Chatman pulling a girlie-fit.

Pembroke asked, "Do you read the international papers?"
Noonan sniffed sulfur in the air.

There was one more person in front of her at the Avis
counter when Harland changed her mind. It was the sight
of the computer terminals that did it. She didn't need a
clerk injecting her fatal stats into the system for InSec
trollers to snag. Stupid to have forgotten minor details like
computer death traps. She was getting tired. She walked
away from the rental counter. Now what? Take a bus?
Downside there too: the New Normal had led to tighter
controls at the US-Canada border. The wait to cross was
multiple hours, Mexico without the barbed wire, and computers crunched everybody's name there too. An hour later
she was standing by the side of Highway 138, thumb out.

How do you beat the computers? How do you cross bor-
ders and pass through the digital mesh? It was easier than
Harland thought. It was long and exhausting, but it was easy.
She hitchhiked to Hemmingford, a zigzag off the beaten
path route that landed her a few miles north of the border.
Then she walked. She waited for night, then stepped off the
road into the woods. She kept the road just in sight, her tar-
mac guide. The States waited for her on the other side of a
scythed line cleared through the forest. She waited, looking
for guards, dogs, helicopters, anything that might spring
from paranoia's fever dreams into reality. Then she ran across
the clearing.

Nobody cared. The anticlimax almost killed her. She was
shaking hard as she made her way back to the road. She was
close to pain. It wasn't tears this time, like on the plane from
Brussels. It was the giggles, it was laughs, it was roars. She
finally got herself under control in time to hitch another
ride to Plattsburgh. The bus from there brought her to
Newark for late Sunday evening. She had plenty of money
left for the long cab ride home.

Sunday late. Flanagan shuffled down Albany towards the Hudson Tower. He felt every shade of exhausted. NAVCON had turned into a seven-day-a-week-doubleplus-overtime marathon. Noonan was breathing down his neck, and the deadline was showing all the characteristics of a locomotive steaming straight for his head. Damned if he was going to let it hit, though.

The voice snaked out, a low whisper-purr, from his right. "Hey, Mike, been a while."

Flanagan froze. He turned. Next to the building was a large sculpture called *Upper Room*. It looked like a chess set made of pink stone, each pillar-piece twice the height of a man. Flanagan squinted at the shadows. Baylor stepped out from behind a pillar. She was dressed in a black turtleneck and black jeans. Still elegant enough to pass for street clothes, but Flanagan wasn't buying this time. Flanagan took a step back. She stopped, held up her hands. Nothing up her sleeves. "For God's sake, don't be scared."

"Why shouldn't I be? On top of your aliases, I start hearing about South American links I'd rather not think about." Silence. "So?" Flanagan continued. "Should I run? Should I call the police? I don't know. What do you think?"

"You're right. You don't have much reason to trust me."

"Make that *any*. You pick me up, pretend to be some harmless freelance, and then, having dropped me into scary shit, you and your names go poof off the map. And now you're back. Hurray."

She shrugged. "Who do you know on your MAI negotiation team in Paris?" When Flanagan didn't answer, she asked, "Have you read today's paper?"

"No." He'd been manacled to his screen.

"Someone ratted out InSec to the media. I need to get in touch with the leak. If you don't know who this is, forget it. If you do, get in touch. You don't have to tell me how you do it. I just need you to relay a message for me. I want to talk to whoever this is."

Flanagan felt the decision squeeze hard in his gut. Which liar to believe? Baylor-Taylor-Whatever or Noonan? The solution: Who scares you most? "I can't," he said, very quiet.

"Why not?"

"She's not in Paris anymore. I've tried to call her but no luck. She's scared InSec's after her and her family. And Noonan took her family to. . . ."

"To?"

"A safe house."

It sounded lame even before she laughed. The laugh was hard, despair barking. "Oh Jesus," she said. "I wonder if we can really screw up any worse. Tell me where she lives, Mike."

"How do you know she's there?"

"I don't. But if she shows up, I want to leave a message so she can get hold of me."

"I'll take you there," Flanagan said. "I have her spare key."

Harland stood across the street from her brownstone. She watched the windows. They were black, blind from the emptiness within. She had walked up and down a three-block length four times. She'd stuck to the shadows, and looked in every car parked on the street. She saw no one. Now she'd been watching the apartment for half an hour. No flashlight beams moving past the windows. Nothing. She might still have a few minutes' grace.

She looked both ways for Suits and crossed the street. She already had her key out, and she was in the building like boom. Then she was at her apartment door. Five minutes, she told herself. Five minutes and then you're out, and you start the race again. Destination random. That should throw the bastards off. She slid the key in the lock, turned, click-clock, and got inside. She shut the door. She started counting while she waited for her eyes to adjust. At 300, she had to be gone.

Light from the street filtered pale gray through the curtains. She could make out faint humps of furniture, but that was it. She would have to turn on a light at some point, if she was going find out anything useful. She held her breath and listened. Heard nothing. She moved forward, one step at a time through the familiar dark. She'd already counted up to sixty.

She decided to start with the bedroom. She and Ronald kept their suitcase in the closet. She'd be able to feel if it was gone. She could see the doorway ahead, darker black against black. She felt her way in. Three steps and her knee bumped against the bed. She edged around it. In the wall opposite was the closet. It was open. She got down on her hands and knees and reached out to where the suitcase should be. Gone. She stood up, stepped back until she felt the bed against her legs, and sat down. Her count was up to 150, but she needed a moment. Relief was tangible, a warm embrace that leached the strength from her legs. She rested for a count of fifty. The pause before the pendulum swung again, and it was time to run once more. Staying in New York was mortally foolish. 200. Time to go. She stood, moved around the bed to the doorway.

The door was closed. Her fingers froze cold against the wood. She hadn't closed it, hadn't heard it close. It wasn't a door that shut by itself. Her mouth opened, and something very like a whimper crept out of her throat. Then there was light. Light and the voice of God: "Stupid bitch." Harland whirled.

Karl Noonan stood by the bedside lamp. He must have been there the whole time, the silent joker playing with the door, sadist at the organ of fear, flicking switches and pushing buttons. A man who loved his work. He held a gun in one hand, a newspaper in the other. The gun was pointing at Harland's face. Noonan was grinning. "Checkitout: a goddamn moron." He held up the newspaper so she could read the first page. It was the *Times*. INSEC ACCUSED OF

EXTORTION IN MAI NEGOTIATIONS, one of the headlines read. "Do you know what this means?" he asked. "It means the damage is done. It means you couldn't keep your yap shut. It means there really isn't any point in threatening you, is there?"

Finally, she spoke the thought that had driven her entire run home. "My family?"

"Ah," said Noonan. He tossed the newspaper onto the bed. "See, that's the difference between you and me." He tapped a finger against his forehead. "Always thinking, that's me. Always thinking." He pulled the trigger.

13

"There's a light on," said Flanagan. He pointed up at the second-floor window. "But there shouldn't be anyone there unless Noonan left somebody to watch over the place."

"Right. Give me the key." Her hiss sounded harsh and loud as a sandblaster in the night-quiet of the street. "Wait here." She moved off.

Flanagan waited. He shifted from foot to foot. Here are the facts, Jack: there's some kind of war going on, and you're involved, like it or not. You're going to have to take a stand, or the crossfire is going to take you out. He wished he could speak to Harland. He wanted to know what her side of the nightmare was. But even that was an excuse, a delay to making a decision. His bones knew: line up with InSec and all will be well, but kiss ethics goodbye. Stick with Baylor and probably get killed, but feel good about it.

He started to feel weird standing there, a motionless

target. Go for a stroll, he thought, local resident on his nightly constitutional. He started to walk, but he kept his eyes on Harland's lit window. He listened for the sound of gunshots and breaking glass, screams and thuds, the sounds of a war about to reach out and take him down, but heard nothing. He made it to the end of the block and turned back. Now he didn't have to twist his head to watch the building. He was almost level with it again when Baylor walked out of the front entrance. Flanagan stopped and waited for her. "Keep walking," she said as she came up. She lengthened her stride as they left the apartment behind. Flanagan began to have trouble keeping up. They turned left at the corner, and Baylor broke into a jog. She took a zig-zag route for a half-dozen blocks. Flanagan was completely turned around by the time they slowed down. His breath was coming in gasps. "Describe Rebecca Harland," Baylor said.

"Black, high cheekbones, mole about here."

"Don't describe her face," Baylor interrupted.

"Short hair, pretty close crop, average build. . . ."

"Thought so."

Sunday evening in Mount Sinai. Nancy's eyes were closed when Pembroke looked in. He'd sit beside her for a few minutes, he decided, then leave. He didn't want to wake her. He put this week's flowers down on her bedside table and started to clean up the clutter of the new batch of get-well cards and their envelopes. He tossed the envelopes, then stacked the cards on a corner of the dresser. He would leave the Sue Grafton where it was on the table. But he did pick it up to check where the bookmark was. Page 56. Four pages further than last week.

"Dad?" Awake, and there was something wrong with her tone. Through its dry-parchment weakness, Pembroke could make out an edge. She was looking hard at him, more sharply focused than he'd seen in months. "I watched a lot of TV today."

He saw where this was going. He would be giving orders for executions before the night was out. But he tried to pretend he didn't know. "Calm down, Nancy. You shouldn't let the damn box get you worked up. You know how much that takes out of you."

"Yeah, Dad, yeah. I do." Her voice was louder. Pembroke glanced at her monitor, terrified he'd see lines spiking danger. "You're right. I shouldn't let myself get worked up. But the funny thing is, it's really, *really* hard not to get worked up when my father's business is suddenly big, big news. And not just for CNN. It was even bigger news to me."

Pembroke had to look away from the force of her glare. "I was hoping you wouldn't see that stuff," he said quietly.

"It's not quite like trying to avoid Lewinsky or Enron," Nancy grated, "but it's getting there."

"Nancy." He looked at her again, but not at her eyes. "Nancy, it isn't true. There's an employee, you see. We let her go. Turns out she's not only incompetent, but unstable to boot. The story's nothing more than the fabrication of one disgruntled nut." He wanted to sound firm. He wanted to sound sincere.

"Right." Nancy glared at him, her face a mix of hurt, anger, outrage and insipient hatred. "I'd like you to go now," she said. "And Dad?"

He paused at the doorway. "Yes?"

"Don't come tomorrow."

Sunday evening in Washington, where the gray men never rest.

President Walter Campbell knew he was a gray man. Tall but with a stoop that made him look like he was always about to duck, gray hair refusing any look but the functional, he knew that he had not won the election on personal charisma. He'd won it because, as a gray man, he knew the game, and played it better than his opponent. He knew who to know, who to stroke, who to placate, who to unleash. He knew that the business of the game never ended, and he enjoyed it. And he took it seriously. The game only tolerated players; it did not like them. It would bite if given half a chance.

He glanced over the front page of the *Washington Post,* then added the paper to the stack of others that Martin Jordan had brought in. The MAI and InSec were page one on them all. Maybe not always the lead story, but so what. The coverage was there. It was wide. It was sexy. It did damage. "Ouch," Campbell said to Jordan. The campaign advisor nodded in agreement.

They were sitting on facing couches in the Oval Office. The couches were the same white as the walls, just bright enough that the eye couldn't relax. Their lines were emphatic, no nonsense, begrudging of curves. They were comfortable only in the broadest definition of the word. There were other offices, other sitting rooms that knew how to make their occupants relax. But Campbell liked this room. He liked spending as much time here as he could. This was the nodal point of the world's power. He felt the vibe in the air he breathed here. He had had his career crosshairs centered on this particular location for his entire adult life. The gray business of politics, as far as he was concerned, had this room as goal. Once here, the business consisted in remaining here for as long as possible. Successfully doing so meant doing right by the country. Right now, official business was taking a break. That meant time for the real application of the room's power. Time to work on the real meat. Campbell asked, "Is this hurting us yet?"

"No," said Jordan. "All the mud is on InSec and the accord for the moment. But I wouldn't wait past tomorrow to issue a statement."

Campbell traced patterns in the material of the couch.

The fabric was soft Braille under his fingers. "So how do you call it?"

Jordan sighed. "I say we pull out and let the agreement hibernate again." When Campbell nodded, he continued, "The taint is bad. I don't know how far it's going to spread. I don't know what kind of damage control InSec is doing. But this will give the MAI opposition groups a huge shot in the arm."

"Not to mention the protectionists in Congress in both parties," Campbell added. "And if we stay in, it looks like we deal with extortionist gun-runners." So here we go again, he thought. The negotiations had collapsed in '98 because the bad press had frightened the right people. Same again. The plan had been to announce the signed accord at the G8 summit in August, but now with the MAI growing horns again, he couldn't see any of the other gray men wanting to promote it, either. Campbell knew some megacorp execs who were going to be pissed, but he'd find some other way of unruffling the feathers. And they could be patient. A couple of years and the public memory would be wiped, and the dance could start up again. "Okay. We pull out."

"Weakened or not, Pembroke is going to lose it," Jordan cautioned.

Campbell stood up and picked up the *Post* again. "You see this? I want you to imagine all the words in here as all the things Pembroke could say, privately or publicly. Especially publicly. They are his. They are the sum total of his markers. The paper the words are on is his credibility. The credibility is what gives his words backing." Campbell tossed the paper into the fireplace. The flames leapt. "Credibility, up in smoke. Pembroke out of the game." Campbell smiled and sat back down.

Jordan nodded, conceding the point. "How do you want the speech?"

Campbell thought for a moment. "Lots of principle. Don't make it anti-business, but punch up the ethics. Maybe something about how the agreement itself is a laudable concept, in theory, but how corruption can cripple even the most worthy endeavor, blah blah et cetera. That should fly."

Monday morning at the 1st Precinct. It had taken a while, but Ed Kroker was seeing his bones proven right again. The InSec case was turning into a shitstorm. The Smith job was bad enough because it was a mess to start with, and because there were no leads, or else they spiraled into absurdity. He still didn't buy Noonan's Colombian theory. But now they had another stiff, called in anonymously. One Rebecca Harland. Another InSec employee. Another Glaser kill. And now he had to talk to that clown Noonan. Bane of his existence with all that phony howzitgoingbuddy checkitout bullshit.

"What was she doing back in the country?" Noonan was saying. "She's supposed to be in Paris. I don't get this."

"What was she doing in Paris?"

The minutest uncertainty in Noonan's voice. "Working on the MAI. Checkitout: turned out not to be quite the plum assignment after all." The humor sounded forced.

"Is she involved in the scandal?"

"Not a chance." Quick-draw. "Pretty low down on the totem pole."

"I see." In a pig's eye, I do. I can read you, Karl old buddy old pal. I don't know what kind of shit it is you're trying to pull on me, but the surprise Chinese lunch was a big mistake.

"Hey hey hey, I just realized," said Noonan. "How is her family taking it?"

"We can't locate them. Is there anyone you can think of who was close to her?"

There was a tiny hesitation. "No," said Noonan. "Not off the top of my head."

Liar, Kroker thought. But how come? What's the angle?

"Will you come down to the morgue and identify the body?"

"Absolutely, Ed. Always happy to help. Noon okay?"

"Noon is fine. See you then." He hung up before Noonan could get friendly again. He looked over at Dyanne Lutz. She was sitting in a chair on the other side of his desk. She'd been listening to the conversation over the speakerphone. Kroker raised an eyebrow at her.

"He's hiding something," Lutz said. "Has been from the start. I mean, Christ, what the hell has all that corporate benevolence and cooperation been about? This has got diversion written all over it."

"Yeah, but from what?"

Lutz blew smoke. Her cigarette, overdue for an ashtray, dangled ash. "Let's see. Johnathan W. Smith III gets whacked. Smith works for InSec. Smith used to work in Canada for Protection Electronics. The RCMP put in some kind of query about Smith with INTERPOL a few years back after a newspaper article gets the wind up briefly."

"Said request now gone without trace," Kroker put in.

"Significant." Lutz drew hard, exhaled. The smoke drifted into Kroker's face. He coughed once. Lutz shrugged and stubbed the cigarette out. It would be two minutes tops before she lit up again. Word was she was improving. Her word. "InSec is megahuge in the arms business. InSec is also megahuge, it turns out, in the MAI deal. Somebody blows the whistle on an extortion scam. Big boom in the papers. An employee who is supposed to be working on the MAI in Paris turns up here instead, also with a Glaser-erased face. And in all this we have Your Pal Karl."

Kroker put his hands behind his head and leaned back. "My Pal Karl. Mr. Civic Duty with his hot tip."

"Mr. Bullshit," said Lutz. She tapped another Lucky Strike out of her pack. "I love this. This is my favorite part. Let me do this. I want to see if I've got it right. There's this babe who's supposed to be some sort of industrial spy for the Colombian drug cartels. Right?" She lit up and blew smoke. The smell made Kroker think of a smoky-dry version of wet dog.

"Right."

"And she's been hanging around Michael Flanagan."

"Who's working on some hush-hush project vital to InSec."

"And who used to work under Smith, but whose name was not mentioned as an associate or friend of Rebecca Harland." Lutz smoked quietly for a minute, then asked, "You think there is a Flanagan link?"

Kroker rubbed his chin. "I like the Glaser coincidence. And we've been encouraged to leave poor Mikey alone from Day One."

"Worth talking to him. If he doesn't know her, he doesn't know her."

Lutz blew smoke again, up this time. Kroker coughed anyway. Lutz shot him the finger. She tapped the speakerphone. "And this guy. Something's unraveling. I think this is the first time Your Pal Karl's even broken a sweat, and not a big one at that. Let's make him sweat more. Let's do some digging."

14

Monday evening at InSec. Flanagan sat in front of his computer monitor. He had a schematic of NAVCON on the screen. He was looking at it. He wasn't seeing it. Sweat tickled and trickled down his armpits. His hand was wet but cold as it held the mouse. He didn't move the cursor. Cops, he thought. God damn the goddamn cops. They would have to call him at work. They *would* have to ask him if he knew Rebecca Harland. They *would* have to set him up in a lose-lose nutcracker. He'd answered, "She's a good friend of mine." And he'd heard it, right there, as clear and unmistakeable as opportunity's rap on the door had been: the crack of doom. Because here was the thing: he took it on faith that his line was bugged, that everything he said would be heard, sooner or later, by Noonan. The rest of the conversation had played out like a steel-trap farce.

Kroker, solicitous after a long pause: "I'm sorry to tell

you that she's been murdered." And then, after Flanagan's reaction: "Would it surprise you to learn she was killed in her home?"

"I thought she was in Paris."

Kroker: "Any idea why she would be back here?"

Million-dollar decision. Pretend ignorance, and help cover tracks? But Noonan would know then that he knew that something was up. That the cobra tales told while Hooks and kids packed up had not been swallowed whole. Option Two: pretend absolute belief in the tales, and that Noonan would want him to be free and open with the police. Flanagan, rolling the dice: "She was worried about her family. She thought someone was after her, and might use her family to get at her."

Kroker: "Why was that?"

Flanagan, thowing out his lies: "Something to do with industrial espionage." And then, as near as he remembered it, Noonan's story.

Kroker: "I see. Do you know where her family is now?"

Flanagan: "No. Mr. Noonan took them somewhere safe."

Big silence, letting Flanagan know that some lies had just imploded. Then Kroker, shifting gears: "Did Karl Noonan know about your friendship with Ms Harland?"

Flanagan, running toward doom: "Yes."

Kroker, sharp: "Do you have any idea why he wouldn't mention this friendship?"

Flanagan, desperate: "No."

Kroker, official to the core: "Mr. Flanagan, I'm going to have to ask you to come down to the station to give a formal statement. Tomorrow noon. In fairness, I should also tell you that we have reason to believe that Ms Harland was murdered by the same individual who killed Johnathan Smith. Given your connection to both these people, I suggest you exercise caution. Now, the killer could easily have shot you too at the Baying Hound. So I don't think you're likely to be a target. But we can't be completely sure. And if

... Mr. Noonan ... is right about industrial espionage, and your importance to certain people, well. ... Just be careful. That's all."

"That's all," Flanagan muttered now at his screen. Tickle trickle of sweat, and he was back to wondering just who wore the white hat in the game after all, or whether he should run screaming from them all. Problem was, he could run all he wanted, but someone would catch up. And there was nowhere to run to. So what did that leave? That left taking a stand. Take it and fight for it. A radical concept. He would have to make the decision himself. This wasn't an area where the *Wall Street Journal*, his eternal guru, would be able to provide guidance. Holly, the *Journal*'s opposite number, couldn't help, either. She might try, but she didn't know the full layout of the battlefield, or even as much as he did. She couldn't see, and shouldn't have to, the whole perspective of risk. And he couldn't draw her into this.

The screen saver came up again. Fractals spiraled. This time Flanagan didn't hit the space bar and call the schematic up again. No point in pretending here. He couldn't work, not while he knew he was a pawn in the war, but didn't even know which color he was supposed to be. He'd told Holly weeks ago that he would try to find out what was really going on, what NAVCON was really going to be used for. A fine job he'd done there. He'd kept his eyes open, all right. Eyes wide, ear to the ground, nose to the wind. Head in the sand. So enough. Time to stop reacting, time to stop cowering. Time to bring somebody down.

He stood up, shrugged into his suit jacket, and left. Outside, the evening was warm enough, even with the sun down, to change his sweat from fear to honest discomfort. June wasn't up to bat until next week, but summer was stealing home. The temperatures were already hitting the high seventies consistently. It was going to be a dog season. At least New York wasn't being singled out. The sun had staked a claim continent-wide. The weather was already becoming news, and was on its way to becoming a lead. Long-term predictions were all the rage. The heat was going to be a piledriver. Old people were going to die. Forest fires were going to set records.

Flanagan walked to Broadway, went up it until he found a phone booth. For the moment, he was playing by Baylor's rules: only use phones where there's lots of background noise, be it traffic or people. That messed with directional microphones. He let himself into the booth, and pulled a card out of his wallet. Did he count this as a gesture of trust, Baylor giving him the means to contact her? Only enough to keep the jury out for a little longer. He'd had to struggle to get it, after all. A concession under duress was not the same thing as a gift. She picked up after the third ring. "Not wise," she grunted when he demanded they meet.

He took a few breaths, made himself calm down. If he lost it and tantrumed, he'd never get anywhere, and any stand he took would be based only on the manipulative need-to-know morsels handed to a once-and-always-forever pawn. He kept his voice slow, clear, steady. An official grab at authority. "Listen, if I don't see you, and if I don't get the answers I want, then I'm going to give you to Noonan."

He thought he heard a snort. There was a long silence. He waited. And then she laughed. The laugh threw Flanagan completely. It wasn't a harsh bark. It wasn't loaded with contempt, bitter amusement or counterthreats. It certainly wasn't nervous or despairing. It was a good laugh, a genuine laugh, a roar of strength defined by relief. He'd never heard Baylor do more than chuckle. The laugh went on for a full minute. Flanagan didn't interrupt. It sounded too good. It sounded too necessary. He knew that it was important that he let the laugh be. When it ended, he had an idiot grin on his face. He didn't know why. It had no reason being there, because life was storming with evil, scary shit. But it felt good. Baylor took a breath that turned into a huge sigh.

Then she was okay again. "All right," she said. "Let's meet. Here's what you do."

Flanagan listened. He listened very carefully. When she was done, he hung up, and strolled off to the Baying Hound. He had thought he should zigzag a bit, randomize his route. But no, Baylor had said, that would tip off anyone who was following that he was on to them. So boom, straight to the bar. He ordered a Guinness, and sat down at a table that gave him a view of the entrance. No one he recognized came in, but that meant nothing. He tried to look like he was expecting someone. He made himself perk up expectantly and then appear disappointed whenever a woman walked in. He glanced at his watch a couple of times. He sighed. He drummed his fingers. He was sure he was overacting.

When the beer was half done, he got up and walked down the hall to the washrooms. He walked right past the men's. At the end of the corridor was a fire exit, just as Baylor had said. It worried him that she had told him to come to this bar. It worried him even more that she knew these details of layout and how to use them.

He pushed the door open and stepped. Into a stairwell, like she said. He walked down. This part of the building had two exits. He took the door that opened onto Cedar. He turned right and trotted down the slope of the street. He turned north on Pearl, walking briskly. He felt good. He felt chuffed. He was sure he'd shaken whatever half-assed team had been on his tail. He knew they'd be more careful from now on, and that his win was probably a one-time-only deal, and that it was pretty small beer. But it was action taken. It was a move. And even pawns could be strategic. Now he did have permission to go random, so he did. He walked for a few minutes, and hailed a cab at the corner on Fulton. Then he settled down in the back seat, and tried to make himself strong.

Baylor had warned him about the neighborhood. It wasn't the South Bronx, but it was about as low as the Lower East Side still got. Flanagan felt his sweat turn back to cold as the evening light dimmed and with it the hope on the streets. The comfort of the streetlights became bleak. Graffiti spread like a rank weed. Misery overdosed in the doorways. Buildings were the bruised overseers of poverty ungenteel and rotting. The taxi pulled up in front of the SRO Baylor had told Flanagan to go to. It was black with grime and apathy. Flanagan paid the cabbie before getting out of the car. His small-town-boy-in-the-big-city paranoia, never really shed, was up and high-revving, and he wanted his outside exposure kept to a minimum. He jumped out of the car and walked into the building as fast as he could without the giveaway of a run. He felt eyes on him. At least he knew they weren't corporate.

Bulbs were out in the staircase. The climb up to the third floor was through darkness and the bouncing echoes of his footsteps. The walls smelled of old urine. Flanagan was holding his breath by the time he knocked on the door to 323. He rapped three times, paused, two times, paused, and three again. Baylor opened the door, locked it behind him. The room was completely unfurnished except for a couple of crates on the floor. The bare bulb in the ceiling lit the place with a hundred-watt stare. There were thick blinds over the windows. The blinds looked new. Flanagan sat down on a crate and mopped his brow. "So this is your idea of a safe house?" he asked.

Baylor dragged the other crate over and sat down to face him. "It's cheap and no one asks for ID. But if we use this place more than a couple of times, we'll be asking for it."

"You've got other places?"

She shrugged. "Maybe. But I don't think that's why you wanted to see me. So give. What's with the blackmail?" She didn't seem angry at all. She still sounded cheerful, and there was something else in her tone that Flanagan wasn't sure he was reading properly.

"I want the truth," he said. "I want to know who you are. I want to know what's going on. I want to know why people are messing with me. *I want to know why my friends are getting killed.*"

"And why are you asking me?"

"Christ, I don't know." He stood up and started to pace. "I guess I want to trust you. I like you, though I sure don't have any reason to. I really, really hope that if someone is going to tell me the truth, if someone is going to turn out to be one of the good guys, that someone is you."

"Why not Noonan?"

"Because you at least have told me that you lie. He doesn't. He's too slick, too plausible by half, and he's lying to the police. And because Rebecca was freaked out about InSec too." Flanagan paused. "But here's the thing," he went on. He stopped pacing and faced Baylor. "My life at InSec is sweet rose and honey until you show up. The day I first see you, my boss is shot, and everything is downhill from there. You disappear for weeks, and when you show up again, my best friend is killed. You say you only wanted to help her. But I'm starting to need a little more convincing. I know I'm just a little peon who's getting too big for his britches, but too bad. You give me something or I bring you down."

Baylor didn't laugh again. But Flanagan saw her eyes shine. Her anticipation built to excitement and thrummed the air. He took a step back. "If you find out what's happening, what will you do?" she asked.

"Fight," he said, and meant it.

She looked at him, hard. He felt her eyes read his, scouring deep, sifting fine. He felt, mixed with her excitement and fueling it, a need. Her moment of decision was tangible. He almost heard a click. "Sit down," she said. Her voice was calm and firm. Flanagan sat. "My name is Jen Blaylock," she said. "I shot Johnathan W. Smith III." She pronounced each syllable of the dead man's name with the articulation of contempt. Then she was silent, waiting.

Baylor ... no, *Blaylock*'s words rang a pure note. They were truth: pure, uncompromising, vital. With what she had said, she had committed herself to trusting Flanagan. Unless she killed him, there was nothing to stop him from going straight to the police. But he didn't think he would. Right now, his responsibility was to ask the right questions. To ask what he wanted and needed to know so that he could see the battlefield, and fulfil his promise. Because he had made one when he had uttered the word "fight." He asked, "Did you kill Rebecca?"

"No."

Another pure note. "Why did you kill Smith III?"

"Because he killed my family."

Flanagan hadn't expected that. He tried to picture Smith III, harmlessly jovial pseudo-Brit, opening fire on a cowering group of Mom, Pop and the Kids. The image wouldn't gel. It was too strange. But it was true. He knew it was. "Tell me," Flanagan said, and she told him. She didn't embellish. She didn't rant. She spoke clearly, calmly, and with steel. When she was done, he felt tears of loss and anger constricting his throat. It hurt to swallow, and it was a moment before he could speak again. "So you want to kill Pembroke," he finally said.

"Yes," said Blaylock. "And until recently that would have been enough. But now it isn't. Because it isn't just Pembroke. Oh, he's a key piece of the machine, but taking him out isn't as important as *how* I take him out. If I walked into his office tomorrow and shot his brains out through the back of his head, what difference would that make? Do you think InSec would do more than stumble a bit before carrying on as usual? You think he hasn't got plenty of lieutenants who'd be more than happy to step in and pick up the torch? Your friend Rebecca has probably already caused more damage to the company than a simple assassination ever could, and that's going to blow over too, just watch. People's attention spans are much too short and their discomfort thresholds much too low for systemic change to happen."

Flanagan blinked. "Systemic ...?"

"I'm talking about the whole bloody corporate nightmare."

Oh Jesus. "Oh no, Jen. No. No. Listen to yourself. I can understand killing Smith III and Pembroke, I can understand wanting to wreck InSec. And I'm with you up to there. But be realistic. You're starting to sound like some sort of Marxist and next you're going to be extoling the virtues of the welfare st—"

This time her laugh was a harsh bark. "Oh, give me a break. I know where you're going and you can spare me the neo-con cant and the defense-of-the-market bullshit. Have you actually read your Adam Smith? I'll bet you haven't. Because what he had in mind was not a handful of nation-unto-themselves corporate Godzillas carving up the pie between high-end stockholders." She was hitting her stride now. She was leaning forward, stabbing the air with her finger as she made each point. Her voice built strength until it was a snarl. "Let me tell you something. The megacorps, they don't care about you. They don't care about your precious US of goddamn A. They just care about being big. That's what the MAI is really about. If anything, InSec is probably just a little more direct in its approach, that's all." She sat back. Flanagan stared at her. They read each other's eyes again. Flanagan saw some of the flame in hers damp down. She knew she'd pushed it. And he saw a completely new emotion cross her face. He almost didn't recognize it, because he never thought he'd see it. It was the fear of rejection. "Sorry," she said, calm again.

Flanagan tried to laugh, but he wasn't as good at getting it out as she was. "At least I know you're being honest."

She smiled. The smile was tired, but it was genuine. "Okay, look. You don't have to agree with me. But we're on the same page as far as InSec goes, yes?"

"Yes." Blaylock's outburst hadn't changed a thing there. There was one monster he was more than willing to bring down.

"Fine. I said Pembroke was a key piece of InSec. We can crash a lot of machinery if we take him out, but we have to be careful how and when we do that, or it won't matter. He's up to something with you and your NAVCON. But we don't know what that is."

"It's big, though," said Flanagan.

Blaylock laughed again, and the laugh was relaxed, closer to the genuine and happy amusement Flanagan had heard on the phone. "So it's big. And it's InSec. And so it's very, very bad." She was serious now. "And whatever this bad thing is, I want to stop it. Do you?"

"Yes." He was absolute in his loyalty to his oath.

"So what I think is that if this thing is big enough, if we wreck both it and Pembroke at the same time, we give InSec a serious screwing."

"But how do we do that?"

"That's just it. We can't trash *it* until we know what *it* is. Military intelligence fundamentals there."

Flanagan said, quietly, "Military intelligence." Scared again.

"Look at me, Mike. You said you were with me." Her eyes were the most serious and the most hopeful he had seen them yet, shimmering, on the brink of a colossal leap.

"I am," he said.

"And you understand what this is we're doing."

He nodded. "War," he said.

Her eyes took the leap. She leaned forward. She took his face between her hands. Her kiss was the softest of touches against his lips.

15

Tuesday.

Noonan rewound the tape and played it again. Flanagan and Kroker spoke to each other again. Their dialogue was just the same as it had been the last twenty times he'd listened. The news was just as bad. Noonan stood and walked over to the minigym that took up half of his office space. He hit the heavybag. Hard. "*Shit,*" he yelled. He hit the bag again. The tape was the enemy. His lies had interconnected into a beautiful tapestry, a goddamn work of art. And that tape was the sound, not of the fabric fraying at the edges, but of the whole thing unraveling.

The tape was the enemy. But he was the idiot. He was the one who couldn't keep his lies straight. And there was no excuse for that. That was plain, simple incompetence. That was failing his most basic job requirements. If anyone under his command had screwed up like this, had blundered with stupidity pure and neon-bright, he would have broken the bastard's neck. Only now he wanted to save his. He pounded the bag until his fists bled and his sweat had soaked all the way through his shirt. Exhausted, he stopped and stood still for a moment. Think, he told himself. He had to cut the dangling threads and stop any more unraveling.

He shrugged out of his shirt, balled it up and tossed it into a corner. A washroom with shower connected to his office, and he walked in. He turned the shower on full and cold and stuck his face into it. It hurt. It numbed. It calmed. When he felt ready to think again, he turned the water off, toweled his face and chest, then grabbed a new shirt out of the wardrobe next to the minigym. He sat back down at his desk, and played the tape again. But this time, he listened carefully, without freaking out. This time, the tape was not the enemy, trumpeting the news of his doom. This time it was a spy, giving him the heads up. All information is opportunity. All advance information is weaponry.

He finished listening. He crossed his arms on the desktop and thought. Here was the scoop. Fact: Kroker knew he'd lied. Consequences: all the work he'd been doing with Kroker was wasted; the cop wouldn't follow any lead Noonan suggested, or believe a word he said; so much for getting the police to do some legwork for him and chase after Baylor/Taylor; attention would be coming his way; his duties would become harder to accomplish; Kroker would be sniffing around him to find Hooks and family; shit would fly; Pembroke would be seriously pissed.

Noonan got nervous again. He made himself keep cool and finish working things out. Fact: Flanagan also knew he lied. Consequences: tons. And here he could only guess. Flanagan might assume more lies. Flanagan might start digging around too. Yet more shit would be in the air. Then there were the questions. Did Flanagan really believe the whole Colombian story? If not, why was he covering for Noonan? (And screwing him over at the same time. That was a neat trick.) So what was Flanagan up to? And everything came back to Pembroke being pissed. He was pissed about the MAI fiasco. He would be pissed about the screwup with Kroker. He'd be even more pissed if Flanagan, Noonan's choice, Noonan's recommendation, went rogue. Sure, Flanagan was replaceable. But so was Noonan.

All right. Sitrep concluded. What were the objectives? He had to redirect the cops. In particular, he had to stop Kroker from leaning on him before the detective even got started. And he had to frighten the Jesus out of Flanagan to keep him in check. Even if he wasn't thinking of stepping over the line, Noonan couldn't take the risk. Flanagan scared easy. Give him a really big scare, and he'd snivel into his hole and never budge again.

Noonan visualized the threads that were doing the unraveling. He knew where to cut.

Blaylock hit the streets. She had to. She'd been cooped up in her Hell's Kitchen room too long. She was going to pace her way right through the floor. So she might as well pace where there was space. It was a needless risk, yes. But a small one. She'd been lying low since IMTEX, venturing out rarely and only at night. Every day, the boredom and the frustration had grown. She bought a cheap TV and rabbit ears to track the news, but that only cut the tedium for a couple of days. She'd known she couldn't do anything immediately. She had to lull Pembroke and his goon back to sleep, or at least enough that they wouldn't worry too much about Flanagan. But the inactivity almost had her clawing the walls. It was the hurry-up-and-wait of Bosnia all over again. Then the MAI story blew up. Lying low became the coward's option. Only she'd moved too late.

But now? Now she felt good. She was waiting again, but she could give it a couple of days more. Now she knew the wait would have an end. Now she had an ally, a real one, one she wasn't bullying or manipulating into fighting her war. So she hit the streets in late afternoon, and if she bumped into Noonan himself around the corner, she'd smile at him. She felt that good. She'd also bite his throat out, which would make her feel even better, but she'd still smile at him first.

She hit the streets, but not without a disguise. She wore a scarf over her hair, sunglasses, and a Laura Ashley summer dress—all happy flowers in variations on a theme of pink. About as un-her as it was possible to get. If the InSec teams were still looking for her, and beat the odds so spectacularly as to find and recognize her, then they were that good and deserved to win. But she doubted it. She felt the luck flowing her way for now.

She hit the streets, and she did have a good reason to be out. She was on a preliminary recon before the next strike. She walked. It was a long walk, but she loved it. She went east until she hit Fifth Avenue, then took it south, and let New York jazz her hard. The city's engine pulsed, and she felt it grab hold of her heartbeat and slave it to the beat of megalopolis in full glory. Even when she was between the main throbs of midtown and the Financial District, moving through the relative calm of Greenwich Village, SoHo and TriBeCa, the power was there, generator huge and all around. In the Village, she stopped briefly in Washington Square. She followed the gravity of a crowd that stood watching a show in the center of the square. She stood with them, but her attention split into periphery and deep core. At the periphery, she watched a unicyclist juggle torches. She watched a man toss a ball to his bulldog. She watched the dog, standing on a low pillar, headbutt the ball back to the man. At the core, she looked north, and saw the Empire State. She looked south, and felt the throb of anger at the absence of the World Trade Center. But the ley line still ran between the two power centers, and she was plugged and welded into the current. She didn't know if she was taking

Manhattan or Manhattan was taking her. It didn't matter. Either was good. She could see the muscle of the city, and it was her ally.

She started walking again, kept going south until the island ended, then caught the Staten Island ferry. She knew she looked like a tourist. She felt like one too. The mission today was too much like fun. She had bounce, she had rhythm, she felt cheerful in a stupid and hilarious way. She couldn't remember when she had felt this good. The sun was a blast of sharp bright, and she felt she could blast right back at it with the grin inside.

She knew what was fueling the grin. It was more than just the city. Yes, it was her ally, but she had another one too. And there was more yet. An ally was for war. But as well as the power, she felt a lightness now, one that had nothing to do with being good at killing people. This had nothing to do with the blood satisfaction of putting bullets into Smith III's face. It had everything to do with the lifting of a weight. She wasn't alone. She hadn't realized how much the lone warrior campaign had been squeezing her. The difference between now and before Flanagan had called her was night and day, black and white, Old Testament and New. Trench warfare and aerial dogfight. She could take on the world, break it in half, and laugh and dance to the beat of the drums, to the roar of the guns.

The ferry pulled away from Manhattan, and Blaylock moved to the railing to look back at the East River. She stood next to a family. They were tourists, honest-to-God ones, no camouflaged guerillas here. Blaylock tilted her head slightly and took them in through her shades. Mum, Dad, big sister, little brother: the pure U-235 nuclear unit. And yes, each one of them had a camcorder. Blaylock suppressed a smile, looked at the sister more closely, and found herself thinking of Celia. The girl was a couple of years younger than Celia had been, and looked nothing like her. Sister's hair was a dirty blond, and Celia's had been dark brown. Sister's complexion was clear. Celia had been the Clearasil stockholder's best friend. Celia, idol-worshipping Wonder Woman Jen, had gone full-throttle into becoming a jock-of-all-trades. Sister, Blaylock thought, had a much too cosy relationship with the holy trinity of TV, chocolate and couch. No, no reason to think of Celia. But she did. She thought of Celia, and of how all her possibilities were taken out of her hands and reduced to the simple, single, final option of blast victim. The short, sharp, shock of the world making its arbitrary cruelty known. Blaylock thought about this, and about how to hurt back.

She turned away from the family and looked out over the water again. She saw what she was looking for. Big as a good-sized skyscraper, a world of steel, the ship moved slowly towards the Brooklyn side of the river, shepherded by tugboats. Flanagan had said that one of InSec's new freighters was supposed to be arriving today. NAVCON was almost ready for installation and preliminary tests. One ship was going to be the guinea pig, and the first trials were due to start next week. Blaylock wanted a look at what Flanagan's work was going to complete. So good, here it was, but wasn't it supposed to be new? This ship looked like one of the older workpigs going. She checked her watch. No, this was when the *Bhopal* was due. Maybe this was the wrong boat. She pulled a small pair of binoculars out of her purse and focused on the bow. There was the name: *Bhopal*. So this was it. There couldn't be two different ships with the same name showing up at the same time in the same place, could there now? No, there couldn't. The name was a problem too. She really had to look hard to make it out. Grime almost completely obscured it. Where did a new boat get that filthy? It looked like years of shit and rust covering the outside of the hull.

She lowered the binoculars so she could take in the whole ship. Leviathan in repose, its movement was barely perceptible. Blaylock thought about the immensity. She thought about a fleet of eight of these monsters. She thought about InSec's business. New superfreighters that look old, plus arms? The equation was bad, even though she couldn't make sense of it. What the hell do you guys need these things for, anyway? she wondered. And why the camouflage, if that's what it is? Flanagan was too right: whatever the game was, it was big.

Pembroke respected Nancy's wishes. He didn't go to the hospital. He didn't try to get in to see her. But he did call. Twice. She hung up both times. As soon as he spoke. She didn't say anything. He stood at his window, glaring at the skyline, fists balled. He heard the office door open and shut behind him. Noonan, on time. Pembroke turned around. "So," he said, "ready for Russia?" The timetable called for Noonan to leave Saturday. Business would likely take a couple of months. He wanted Noonan to have as much of a margin as possible.

"Oh, I'll be ready, no problem," Noonan said. "Just tying up some loose ends."

Pembroke frowned. There shouldn't be any ends that needed tying. But Noonan was competent. He let it go. "Do a good job over there, Karl. We're going to need that material."

"It's looking bad?"

"The MAI is dead," said Pembroke. "Again. They're still going through the motions in Paris, but there isn't a single head of state willing to go to bat for it. The publicity is poison. Chatman's flying back in tomorrow. No point in keeping him there anymore."

"So we're going with the leverage?"

"Yes." We're going to do a lot more than that, Pembroke thought. We're going to do some crushing. "What's the latest on the G8 summit?"

"No changes," said Noonan. He looked happy to be able to give some good news.

"No one's connected us with the lodge?"

"How could they?"

"Checkitout," Pembroke mimicked, anger and ice. "What were the odds of one bitch scuttling the MAI?"

"That will blow over—" Noonan began. Pembroke watched him realize his mistake and shut his mouth. "Sorry."

Pembroke didn't feel forgiving today. "Blow over," he said. "Blow over. Sure. And we have to wait, what, another two years? Three? Four? More? And we have to start over from scratch. No." He shook his head, once, short and quick. "I'm not playing that game anymore. We're going to have the cards to force a win this time, so we're going to use them." He waved Noonan out of the office.

Pembroke paced. Pembroke itched. Slapping Noonan down wasn't enough. It was too easy, too everyday. He still needed to crush. He stopped at his desk and stared at the phone. What the hell. Might as well set this wheel in motion. He picked up the receiver and dialed. Paul Kuhn answered. Kuhn was Secret Service. Kuhn was very close to the president. Pembroke said, "I'm making you active."

"Shit," said Kroker.

"Yeah," said Lutz.

They were standing outside the precinct garage, beside Kroker's car. His battered brown Continental was parked in the street. He'd been about to drive off to beard Noonan in his den. Speak to the man again, face-to-face this time, look for the twitches, poke away at that underbelly, see it soft and white. Lutz had caught up to him, waving a folder. It was the results of her dig into Noonan's background.

"Special Operations," Kroker said weakly.

Lutz nodded. "Some piece of work."

Kroker flipped through the folder again. "No criminal record, though."

"No," Lutz conceded, "but his name keeps turning up in cases, even if it gets ruled out. And frankly, when SOF goes into business for private sector, and private sector is InSec, you've got to wonder."

"Yeah." Kroker thumbed the pages, but he wasn't reading them. He thought about what Lutz had just said. He thought about Noonan as a frequent almost-suspect, and he got angry. When it came to recurring names, Kroker believed in once-accident, twice-coincidence, thrice-enemy-action as gospel. The more often you got ruled out, the guiltier you were. You, or somebody who liked you, had deep pockets and high connections. And if your luck was very, very good, then you were very, very bad. Noonan had the luck of the gods. Kroker decided an interview would be useless. But he was still going to nail the bastard to the wall, and then he was going to sit back and watch him bleed.

Phone sex. Foreplay before the plastique.

"And you want us to claim responsibility for that?"

"So don't claim responsibility for it. Get someone else to take credit, blame FARC. Whatever. It's up to you."

"Just as long as someone in Colombia takes the heat."

"Basically. Yeah."

"Why should I do this?"

"Checkitout: how much do you think your prestige would go up if the word went out that your organization had done this amazing thing?"

"You're still not saying what *you* are going to do for me."

"Well, let's see. You know those nasty Turbo Thrushes and OV-10 Broncos that keep dusting your crops with poison? Want to give them pause for thought?"

"What are you talking?"

"I'm talking fifty SAMs."

"I see. When exactly does this heinous act of terrorism,

for which we despicable Colombians are responsible, take place?"

Noonan hit the streets. Noonan had the vibe. He was juiced. He was rocking. Pembroke and Kroker and Flanagan and Taylor be damned, he had his fist around the whole electric current of events, and he was gulping the charge. He was snipping the loose ends so well he'd figured out how to do some pre-emptive cutting as well. He was going to come out this maneuver so far ahead it was obscene. God, he loved this. And he loved his job. Especially now, when it was time to get wet.

He'd spotted the police tail late in the afternoon. Bunch of ass-dragging amateurs, he could have shaken them by accident. He didn't want to, though. He wanted them on him tomorrow. He'd leave a trail of his own shit in the street if it was necessary. Tonight, though, he needed some personal space to get the party ready. He called Jack Lentricchia and told him he needed a driver at midnight. Discreet. Lentricchia suggested Shawna Layton. Noonan said yes, and to tell her to bring her own car, and to take it into the underground parkade of Noonan's building. He hung up, pleased with Lentricchia. Layton was deep enough into the Black Ops areas of InSec that she would have a vested interest in not screwing anything up. Plus Noonan thought she was hot. And he knew Lentricchia knew he did.

Noonan killed time. He made another phone call, then watched cable porn until it was time to go. He left the lights and television on in his apartment. A timer would switch everything off just after two. As far as an outside observer would be concerned, he was in. He lived in the Alden, across 82nd from the Beresford. Close enough to be on-hand in bang flat if called, but still in his own domain. Tonight he had let Bossman know that he was on a job and would be unreachable.

Noonan took the elevator down to the garage. When the doors opened, he stepped quickly out of the elevator and to his right. There was a pool of black here, where two of the building's walls met. Noonan kept the light in the corner out by regularly smashing the bulbs. They hadn't been replaced for almost a week now, and he was beginning to hope that management had given up. He scanned the parkade. He didn't think there'd be any cop presence here, but he never put anything past the enemy, even when they were as stupid as Kroker and pals. He couldn't see anyone waiting. Certainly not near enough to the elevators to make a difference.

Layton arrived five minutes later. She pulled up next to the elevators, per Noonan's instructions, and opened her passenger door. Noonan scuttled into the car and hunkered down. He got his head level with Layton's thighs. She was wearing a miniskirt. Sweet. Layton sighed. Her legs shifted slightly away from Noonan's face. He liked the sound her body made against the upholstery.

Noonan didn't say where to go at first. He didn't have to. He knew Layton would drive at random for a while, check-ing for any cars following. "Clear," she said ten minutes later.

Noonan sat up. He gave her thigh a lick as he did. She was smart enough not to say anything, but he caught the way she tensed and tried to shrink into her seat. He got hard. He grinned. He said, "Chelsea. 27th Street." Layton looked at him funny. "Don't worry about me, honey." He put a hand on her knee. "Just drive."

When they got to 27th, Noonan had Layton drop him off at the corner of 10th Avenue. "Scat," he told her. He watched her go, and shook his head over the sad exigencies of duty. Bye bye Layton. And there was going to be chance absolute zero of getting any where he was going. But that was okay. By the end of the night, he'd be having fun better than sex. He turned around and sauntered into Finland Tom's.

Noonan let himself be frisked at the entrance, but his flesh crawled at the touch of the bouncer's hands. It took a conscious effort not to take the asshole's head off. But then it was over and he was in. It was early in the week, but the night club was still close to packed. Noonan paused before stepping into the room. He looked at the crowd. Faggot central, he thought. He snarled. No one heard.

The lights pulsed. Barbra Streisand and Celine Dion, sampled, co-opted, and processed into industrial damage, stomped a digital goosestep out of the speakers. Go-go boys rattled the bars of their cages on a catwalk. The trade got rough on the dance floor. Noonan waded in. He felt himself ticking over into bash mode. He held it back. He was here on a mission, and a freak-out wouldn't help. He needed to find a man. Given the physical type he was looking for, a joint like this stood a good chance of providing him what he needed.

He worked the room. He danced, feeling clammy in the gut and angry in the head. But he did his job. He danced, and when someone copped a feel, he didn't hit and he didn't puke. He worked the room for an hour, and had almost reached the end of his tether when he saw what he needed. The guy was leaning against the bar, hard man in combat fatigues. Noonan checked him out as he made his way over. Height same as his, hair short and the right color. Beefy, ornamental muscles made the frame a touch big, but close e-goddamn-nough. That suck-me mustache would have to go, though.

The guy seemed to spot someone and pushed away from the bar just as Noonan got close. Noonan punched him on the shoulder before he got away. The guy turned. "The hell?" he asked.

"Up to you," said Noonan, and put on a show. He folded his arms. He flexed some fingers and the muscles on his arms rippled. The guy checked him up and down, looking interested. "What's your name?" Noonan asked.

"Buck."

"Right," said Noonan. "Right. Whatever you say, *Buck.* Well, the way I see it, this cock is leaving here. You want to be on it, you got thirty seconds."

Buck hesitated. He rubbed one of his biceps for Noonan's benefit. Noonan wasn't sure if this was a promise or a warning. He wanted to laugh either way. "How much can you take?" Buck finally asked.

Noonan nodded. "All right then. Let's go. My place." They left. Buck walked close. "Hands off until we get there," Noonan warned.

They had to walk three blocks before they found a cab. They piled in and Noonan gave an address in Queens. Buck frowned. "Isn't that Corona?"

"You a snob or something?"

Buck shook his head, but he looked nonplussed when they got there. "*This* is your place?" Buck asked. They were standing outside a shuttered warehouse. Across the way, barbed wire guarded the subway yards. A dog barked, fierce.

"Yeah, this is my place," said Noonan. "Why?"

"You looked like better money to me, is all."

"Yeah well, up yours." Noonan walked over to the door and unlocked it. "You coming or not?" They walked in. Noonan didn't turn on the lights. He closed the door.

"Shit," said Buck in the black. "What are you playing at?"

"Wait for it," said Noonan, and he turned on the lights.

"Oh God," said Buck. The warehouse was empty except for small bundles nestled next to the supports and a half-dozen oil drums in the middle of the floor. Chained to the wall opposite the entrance were Ronald Hooks, Faith and Julie. Noonan locked the door. Buck looked at him, eyes wide, no longer interested now that they were playing for keeps. He backed away. Noonan stayed where he was, smiling. "Jesus, man," said Buck. "The hell is going on here? Who are those people?"

"Your new roommates," Noonan said. He started to walk

forward. Slow and easy. All the time in the world to enjoy payback for a shitty evening in a fudgepacker bar.

Buck shook his head, no. He ran over to the family. He knelt down in front of Hooks, who had his head down. The girls were crying, but very, very softly. Their throats were too cut and raw from the screams of days past. Hooks's eyes were swollen almost shut from bruises. His nose was broken. Buck made a noise in his throat, appalled, and stood up. Legs planted firm, he faced Noonan. Noonan laughed. He paused by the oil drums. He lifted the lid of one, and scooped out a handful of cocaine. Then he kept walking toward Buck. "You are a sick son of a bitch," said Buck.

Noonan shrugged. "Checkitout," he said. "You're dead. So who's worse off?"

Buck shifted from foot to foot, waiting for Noonan to get within range. His hands balled into fists. Noonan sneered. What a loser of a fighting stance, giving up all your grounding like that. This jerkoff wasn't going to be much fun at all. He took another few steps.

Buck lunged. Noonan threw the cocaine into his face. Buck snorted, coughed, spluttered. He staggered away, rubbing at his eyes. Noonan followed, waiting for him to get it together. Buck got his eyes clear, turned, and charged. Noonan stood still and waited for it. Buck cocked his right fist, and hit Noonan on the left cheekbone. The concussion shook Noonan's brain. His mouth filled with blood. The pain in his cheek, needlepoint and white hot, flashed out and dulled until his entire head hurt like an echoing bell. He loved it. "Nice," he said, and his blood poured down his chin. He hit Buck in the same place he'd taken the punch. He hit with purpose. He hit with training. He shattered Buck's cheek and orbital bones. Buck screamed and fell to his knees. Noonan strolled around behind him, grabbed his head with both hands, and snapped his neck.

Earlier.

Eddie was asleep. Flanagan sat at Holly's kitchen table and sipped coffee without tasting it. "So," he said. "Looks like I'm at war."

"I see." Holly looked at him. "Is that a good thing?"

"I hope it is."

"How much can you tell me about it?"

Flanagan thought about that. "I'm not sure how much you want to know."

"Would I be proud of you?"

"Yes, Big Sis, I think you would be."

"Then that's probably all you should tell me. There's a 'but,' though, right?"

"Yeah." Flanagan stared into his coffee. "That's what I came over to tell you." He took a breath. "I'm worried about creating a risk for you and Eddie."

Holly looked down. Flanagan saw the fear spread onto her face, the fear that the bullet in her spine had taught her, the fear that went with the lesson that some foes were better left unfought. "I really don't want to ask you this," she said, "especially given all the ragging you've had to put up with about having a cause. But here goes anyway: do you have to be part of this war?"

"I am whether I want to be or not. I have two options. I can do what I'm told, and be knowingly complicit with murderers. Or I can try to fight them."

The phone rang.

"Excuse me," said Holly, and she wheeled out of the kitchen. Flanagan sat and played with his mug while he waited. He turned it around and around on the table, smearing a ring where coffee had slopped. Now that he was here, he was feeling some of his fire dampen. Goddamned consequences and responsibilities. No wonder he never did anything. He was too frightened about whom he might hurt. And rightfully so, he thought.

When Holly came back, she looked a lot less frightened.

Her eyes had a shine. Flanagan knew she'd been talking to her man. The man who brought her flowers. The man who made her happy. Flanagan asked, "Am I ever going to meet this guy?"

Holly cocked her head. "Why don't you come tomorrow? He's taking Eddie and me out for dinner. Join us. His name is Ken Elton, and you can find out the rest then."

They were quiet for a bit. The weight of the other conversation came back. Decisions with sharp teeth threatened. Finally, Holly said, "So you're going to fight."

"Yes," Flanagan said, and the decision hurt all right. His resolution went supercritical. One word from Holly and he felt that he'd change his mind. But he still did his best to back the decision up. "I'm not sure you'd be safe even if I didn't. Rebecca's dead. And I don't know where her family is."

"Have you looked?"

"I wanted to talk to you first."

"So the bad guys don't know you're going to fight them?"

Flanagan shook his head. "We've got a bit of a breathing space. Couple of days anyway."

Holly took a breath. "What should I do?"

"Take a leave of absence. Effective immediately. I'll pay for your expenses. Leave town. Go stay with Sally." Holly's college roommate and still best friend. She lived in Oregon now, and the bulk of Holly's long-distance bill was calls to Sally. "Do you think you can do this?"

(Snip.)

16

Wednesday.

Doug Rhodes stood in front of Kroker's desk and kept his face still. He had been made an ass of and obviously knew it. That wasn't enough for Kroker, though. He wanted the point driven into Rhodes like a barbed suppository. He paced back and forth behind his desk, letting Rhodes see the storm clouds. Lutz sat at the back of the room and sent smoke Rhodes's way.

"Stop me if I get this wrong," said Kroker. "Noonan goes home. His lights go off at 2:14 am. He's gone to bed, you figure. And then this morning, the InSec Building team spots him arriving for work, with a monster bruise under his eye, no less, but you never saw him leave home."

"I don't know what happened," said Rhodes.

"No, you don't. And if you don't, I don't. Do you see the problem here? We have a shitload of hours unaccounted for, during which Noonan picked himself up some damage. Given that our boy is ex-Special Forces, I'd say that's pretty significant, wouldn't you?" Rhodes nodded. Kroker said, "Get out of here."

Lutz grinned. "Feel better now?"

"No, because you're with me for the evening shift on Noonan."

Lutz blew a cloud into his face. "Bite me."

Kroker sat down, stretched and yawned.

"Seen much of home lately?" Lutz asked.

"Yeah, right." And when he was home, it was Zombie Land. Neither he nor Louise had had the energy lately for anything more than a collapse into bed. Cop and marketing cubicle drudge, killer combination. Number One Son Jeremy was lucky if he ever saw his parents at all. And now he was hitting his teens and feeling the hormones bounce against the walls. Kroker had a recurring daymare that if he wasn't careful, he was going to see a lot more of his son, especially in front-and-profile, black-and-white shots.

"Bachelor life," Lutz said. "Has its advantages."

"No doubt. But spare me the details of you and your pad."

"Yeah, some pad."

Kroker closed his eyes. Office nap, he thought. Going to need it. Long shift this evening. And he still couldn't shake the sense that the worst of the shitstorm was waiting to hit.

Cabinet meeting over, Walter Campbell met Jim Korda in the Rose Garden. Sprinklers chuffed, spraying the roses. Campbell wondered what the point was. Lack of humidity in Washington wasn't the problem. It was the heat. June was going to be a nightmare, he could see that. He didn't want to think about July and August. "What's the latest?" he asked Korda. They stood next to a spinkler. The water was going the other way, but the noise was a useful precaution. Never hurt to screw up hypothetical mikes, even if only a little bit. Never ever hurt.

"Pembroke's off his nut," said the CIA Director. "You're not the only one he's called. It looks like he's got a new hobby phone-stalking the leaders of the OECD."

Campbell nodded. The phone call had been strange. Pass the MAI, Pembroke had said. Pass it or else. "How are the others responding?"

"Everyone's calling his bluff, but nobody's doing anything against him."

Campbell nodded. "Stalemate. He's wounded, so we don't have to jump when he says. But he's still a big man."

"Sounds to me like his usefulness is coming to an end."

"Yeah." Campbell clasped his hands behind his back and began to walk. Korda fell in beside him. "Tell me something helpful," Campbell said. "And tell it to me carefully." Translation: so the inferences can be plausibly denied. Now they weren't guarding against bugs. They were protecting themselves from each other's subpoenable memories.

They walked around the garden. Campbell watched Korda's face. The fat man never lost at poker, and his face was his ace card. Campbell had never seen it deviate from the pensive and calm. Never. But he knew what Korda was doing. He was framing his own deniable response. "Pembroke has been making a nuisance of himself with other heads of state," Korda began. He sounded like he was delivering testimony before a Senate committee. "He's currently weak, from a public relations point of view at least, and that has some real world ramifications. A united front on the part of the leaders of the G8 would, I submit, strike a very effective blow."

Absolutely nothing indictable there. So far this was a conversation that both men would be able to remember without a lawyer present if called upon to do so. Campbell tried to respond in kind. "A purely diplomatic maneuver, then," he said.

Korda nodded. "How ... completely do you want Arthur Pembroke's ability to harm the national interest reduced?"

Do we whack him? A tempting idea, and, because it was tempting, dangerous. That would be asking for it. Too many unknowns, nasty surprises and long knives down that path. Save that for an absolute last resort, for when the alternative would be even worse. They were a long way from that yet. Plus, a neutered Pembroke could still be useful. No sense in completely destroying what had once been a nicely working relationship between government and free enterprise. "Government does not belong in the boardrooms of Americans," Campbell replied. "I've always maintained that we should allow the market as free a hand as possible. It's when the market interferes with government that some ... curbing ... is necessary. But the hand shouldn't be too heavy."

"Christ, that's even quotable. Remember it come campaign time."

"Too kind."

"Anytime. Anyway," said Korda, getting them back on track, "if everybody takes a stand at the G8 summit, and my recommendation is that you actually mention the blackmail angle, then you cut him off at the knees. Credibility zero. Stalemate over, checkmate in your favor instead. Sound good?"

Afterwards, Pembroke thought that even the way the phone had rung was different, that the nature of the Call tainted everything, even the sound of its arrival. He had received the Call once before, and he had moved fast, but he'd been too late. Sylvia had been dead for ten minutes by the time he got there. That was one reason why he visited Nancy in the evening, the time when the Call was statistically most likely to come. He would never be too late again. And then Nancy refused the visits, and the threat of the Call, Pembroke felt, went up.

He was right. 3:13 pm. He was on the phone to Stepan Sherbina. The conversation was important. They were finalizing details for Noonan's arrival. Pembroke had ordered that there be no calls. Except for one. It came. Mount Sinai was patched through immediately. Pembroke stumbled an apology to Sherbina and got rid of him. He took the Call.

"Mr. Pembroke, this is Dr. Sheraton." Dr. Heather Sheraton. Never the voice of comfort. Always the trumpet of doom. "Your daughter has taken a turn for the worse—"

"I'm on my way."

Barbara Weber, Pembroke's secretary, had buzzed Lentricchia as soon as she had passed the Call on to Pembroke, and Lentricchia had the limo ready and running when Pembroke reached the parkade. Pembroke jumped into the back. He didn't have to tell Lentricchia where to go. I will not be late, Pembroke told the gods. This time, I will not be late. He warned the traffic not to get in his way. The traffic didn't care. It wasn't any better or worse than it ever was at this time of day. It was supremely uninterested in Pembroke's little crisis, and simply went about its normal stop-and-start routine. Lentricchia knew the tricks and the patterns, and made pretty good time, but a bicycle messenger still passed them three times. Pembroke almost opened the door against the cyclist, just to teach him not to overtake a desperate man.

Once they got to the hospital, Pembroke's importance reasserted itself. People cleared out of the way as he jogged to the elevators. Lentricchia shoved aside the slow. Sheraton met them outside Nancy's room. Sheraton's voice was cool, calm, firm. So was her face. So was her stance. So were her eyes. Sheraton was Authority. She knew it, she knew her business, and she used her monolithic unchallengeability to calm the first hint of a relative about to go frantic. "Catch your breath first," Sheraton said. "You're not going in there wild-eyed and foaming."

Lentricchia took a step forward. Pembroke waved him

off. He took a breath, gathered himself. "Tell me," he asked Sheraton.

"It's been very sudden," she said. "She's been using a lot of energy over the last few days, energy she hasn't had to spend." Her eyes, pale blue professionals, gave nothing away. But she was letting Pembroke know the InSec scandal had put his daughter's death on fast-forward. He didn't need it spelled out for him. He already knew. He nodded and went into the room.

Nancy's eyes were closed. She was propped up with pillows, arms stretched out on the covers. Her skin wasn't so much pale anymore as gray. It shone like dirty wax. Her hair hung lank and wet, already dead. Tubes ran into her nose, keeping the oxygen flowing, uselessly fueling a machine whose only goal now was to break down once and for all. The air hitched and stuttered as it went into the lungs, and gurgled over gravel as it went out. There was a five-second pause between each breath. A nurse stood by the bedside, waiting. Pembroke looked for her scythe. "Would you leave us, please?" he asked.

The nurse nodded. "I'll be just outside," she said as she left.

Pembroke sat down beside Nancy. He caught the rhythm of the breaths and timed the pauses. They weren't getting longer yet. He noticed that Nancy was frowning. She looked like she was concentrating. She looked like she was trying to expel something. Herself, perhaps. The effort was immense. Pembroke held her hand. It was warm, but not in any way that suggested life. Nancy took a huge breath. It sounded like a bridge collapsing. A pause at the apex, and then the air exited, shaped into a word: "Go."

Pembroke squeezed her hand tight. There was so little flesh there he could barely feel her in his fist. With his other hand he touched her face. Her body convulsed. Her neck jerked whiplash away from his touch. Her eyes snapped open. She looked at him, she glared at him, and her eyes were wide wide wide. They were cold with knowledge and betrayal and hatred. She did not blink. She held his gaze and let him feel a resentment, resentment that he had disturbed her biggest moment, resentment that reached all the way to the core of the Earth. Resentment that he made her use the last of her fire on him, instead of on seeing her way out of the game in peace.

Pembroke left Mt. Sinai. He said nothing. He tried to feel nothing. He wanted numbness. What he got instead was a huge, expanding membrane in his chest. The outside pretended anesthesia, but it trembled and thinned as it grew. The more it filled him, the more it promised pain ugly and corrosive as lye when it burst. Pembroke sat in the back seat of the car. He didn't watch the traffic. He saw only the membrane's progress. Lentricchia drove so slowly and smoothly it was as if he were tiptoeing. Halfway back to the office, Lentricchia's cell phone trilled. He answered it fast, shutting off any further beeps. The first had already made Pembroke jump. Lentricchia listened. Then he pulled over. He turned around in his seat, pale. The membrane burst.

Flanagan couldn't believe he was doing this. The foolishness of the risk sent the big-city paranoid in him into the shrieking horrors. But he also felt the first drips of combat adrenalin. It felt amazing. It shed new light on the crackle he had seen coming out of Blaylock's eyes, an eros of power and movement. He felt all this, and all he was doing was standing still, waiting for his guts to settle so he could do what he needed to do. The bile crept back down his throat, and he knocked on Karl Noonan's office door.

"Yeah?"

Flanagan opened the door and peeked around it. Noonan was putting some folders into a briefcase. Flanagan was struck by the sight. Noonan with the accessories of business looked wrong. He was about as convincing as a kid pretending to be a cowboy or a doctor, especially with this huge bruise under his left eye. But Noonan was handling the papers carefully, and there was an open safe behind his desk. Legit pencil pushing by Noonan?

"Howzit going?" Noonan asked. He closed the briefcase. "What's on your mind, Mikey?"

Flanagan started in. Play naïve, play stupid, play like you've always believed him. "I was just wondering, what with the industrial espionage you told me about and all—"

"What did I say, eh? Scary times or what?"

"Yeah. Um. And then with what happened to Rebecca—"

Noonan shook his head sadly. "Jesus. Can you believe that? But when I'm right, I'm right, whatcanIsay."

"Yeah." Wow, we're good, Flanagan thought. I know he's having me on, and he probably knows that I'm giving it right back. But he went on with the act anyway. If there was a chance that Noonan still thought he had Flanagan hood-winked, Flanagan wanted to reinforce it. "So like I said," he continued, "I was wondering about Ronald and the kids. Are they still under threat? Do they still have to remain in hiding?"

Noonan picked up his briefcase, and walked over to Flanagan. He put a hand on Flanagan's shoulder and squeezed, avuncular as Stalin. "Checkitout: quite the friend old Ronald's got. Well listen, Mike. What I told you before Rebecca got herself whacked still holds. Remember: you're the one these nasty boys want to put the squeeze on. So they got Rebecca. That would make you even more pro-tective of her family, wouldn't it?"

Flanagan nodded. He stared at Noonan's carpet. "I'd just like to see them," he said.

Noonan squeezed again. "'Course you do. Tell you what. I'll see what I can do." Noonan clapped him on the shoulder and opened the door for him.

Back in his office, Flanagan got the sweats. A stupid part of him had hoped that he'd learn whether Hooks and the

kids were still alive. "I'll see what I can do" could be code
for everything from "next Friday" to "not without an exhu-
mation order." Of course, by keeping them alive, Noonan
could use them as leverage on Flanagan, exactly the way
those mythical Colombians were supposed to be doing it.
So that was a good thing, sort of, wasn't it? Wasn't it? Yeah.
But even better leverage would be Holly and Eddie. He
wanted them out of town *now*. He picked up the phone and
dialed Holly's number. He hoped she would remember to
keep her side of the conversation coded against bugs.

"Hello?" Holly answered after the third ring.

"Hey," said Flanagan. "Change of plan. Can you leave
tomorrow?"

Silence while Holly thought. "Yes," she finally said.

"Good." Relief sank in. If they left tomorrow, and he was
seeing them tonight, that would cut the risk factor way
down. He glanced at his terminal, then at his watch. He still
had to put in an hour or so of work if he didn't want eyebrows raised by his departure. "I might be a few minutes late
for dinner," he told Holly. "Don't go without me."

"Of course not."

"You'll apologize to Ken for me?"

"Checkitout, Mike: he's not that anal about time."

Flanagan's blood flash-froze. "What did you just say?
Where did you get that expression?"

"I must have picked it up from Ken. He—"

"Holly, he's Noonan! Ken is Noonan!"

He ran from his office, almost crying with fear because
Noonan was also on his way, and Noonan had a good head
start.

"There he goes," said Lutz.

Kroker jerked awake. He rubbed his eyes clear of sleep in
time to see Noonan drive past in a minivan. He was hard to
miss with his face smashed an angry purple. Lutz gave him

a block and then pulled out to follow. Kroker grabbed the radio and filled the other teams in. Noonan drove across town and got on the Williamsburg Bridge, and then hung tight on the Brooklyn–Queens Expressway. He kept going. His pace was steady. He was the simplest tail Kroker had ever seen. "This is easy so far," said Kroker.

"He's really being a very good boy," Lutz commented a few minutes later. Noonan was observing the speed limit religiously, even when the traffic opened wide. He didn't even honk when a muscle car cut him off.

"Anybody that polite is up to no good," said Kroker.

Noonan finally got off the Expressway. In Astoria, he pulled up in front of a one-step-up-from-shabby apartment building on 46th Street. He left the van in the loading zone and went inside. "If he's got some ex-wife we haven't heard about, and this is visitation day, and he's just taking his kid to play soccer somewhere, I'm not going to be hugely impressed with you," Lutz told Kroker.

They waited.

It looked like the gods were smiling. Flanagan didn't have to wait for the elevator: he got to it just as a load of freed cubicle drones were piling on for the trip down. He was double-lucky: the elevator only stopped twice before it got to the ground floor. Chris Grant got in with him, excited and bouncy as NAVCON's completion drew closer. The engineer wanted to talk about all the latest bells and whistles that were going into the system. Flanagan couldn't listen, couldn't contribute, could only nod and grin a rictus. But that was all Grant needed. He was happy with the sound of his voice. He jargon-frothed a mile a minute and chortled over the triumphant arcana of techie humor. But he was going home, and he took off as soon as they reached the ground floor. He didn't slow Flanagan down.

Triple-lucky: Flanagan caught a cab the instant he hit the

street. Quadruple-lucky: the traffic flowed in a way that rush-hour Manhattan rarely did. They made good time. They might even be gaining. Flanagan watched the hands of his watch crawl. He sweated. The gods seemed to be smiling. He knew that they were laughing.

Noonan climbed the stairs to Holly's apartment. He didn't take the elevator. He had too much energy combusting, for one thing. And for another, he wasn't fond of the old, squeaking, rickety cage. Its mechanism ran much too loudly to be healthy. He could hear it now. *Clankety-clankety-hitch-hitch-vrrrrr.* He grinned. The sound was a long, long way from the smooth meshing of all the machinery he had thrown into gear. The engine of his moves was purring to make an engineer weep poetry. He could do no wrong.

He really must be living well, because Heaven had given him a blessing and a gift. When he'd driven away from the InSec Building, he'd seen that today Kroker himself was in his tail car. Unbelievable. It was all just too beautiful. He'd made sure he paused and looked around when he got to work, so whoever was watching would catch the bruise. He wanted to stand out bright and big today. But to have Kroker swallow hook and bait was so perfect he wanted to sing. The whole scenario he was building was going to play out even better than he'd hoped.

He reached Holly's door and knocked. He knocked again. He pressed his ear against the door. He couldn't hear anything. But he suspected the silence. It was the stillness of suspense, of intaken breath. "Holly?" he said. He smiled when he said it. He kept his voice gentle, but he knew the humor was leaking through in his tone. He thought he could hear the silence behind the door change quality. He sniffed for panic. There, that was a sweet whiff of it, yes? Yes.

"Holly?" Then he couldn't help himself. He laughed. What the hell, the game was over now, wasn't it? He kicked the door off its hinges. "Checkitout: I'm here!" he called. The silence didn't break. She's good, Noonan thought. The kid too. He would have expected one of them to have squealed or whimpered by now. He walked into the apartment. He could see the traces of panic. Books and clothes were piled up on the sofa and the floor. A number of the shelves were empty. Noonan frowned. "Holly!" he called, not kidding now. He tossed the place. There was no one there. The silence had been playing games with him, all its promises false. He found a half-packed suitcase in the bedroom. A green woolen sweater hung out of the case and drooped over the edge of the bed. Hangers had fallen to the floor in the closet. Panic all right. Packing interrupted in a hurry.

He remembered the sound of the elevator. He ran to the living room window. It looked out onto 46th. He threw it open and leaned out. There, just reaching the corner, he saw Holly and Eddie. They'd walked right past Kroker. The joys of unmarked cruisers. Small miracles.

Noonan ran from the apartment. He grabbed the bannister and jumped down the stairs four at a time. But he made himself walk to the van when he got outside. He didn't want Kroker's adrenalin pumping yet. He got back into the van, pulled out and did a U-turn. Holly and Eddie were now gone around the corner. He pulled his revolver out of his pocket as he drove. It was still loaded with Glaser rounds. He wanted any shooting to match the pattern of the Smith killing. Dot every i.

He checked his rear-view mirror. Kroker and the woman cop were following. Okay. The play is to go smooth. He rounded the corner and there they were, mom and kid, half a block up. He slowed the van to a crawl as he drew next to them. He lowered the passenger window, and felt the heat walk into the van like a slow wall. He leaned forward. "Hey Holly!" he called, all smiles. Holly didn't acknowledge his presence. She kept going. "Listen," said Noonan. He kept his tone gentle, playful, quiet. Anyone more than a few feet from the van wouldn't be able to make out words, and wouldn't hear anything that didn't sound like happy banter. "I've got a gun. If you don't get into the van right now, I'm going to shoot both of you."

"You wouldn't dare," said Holly.

"Fine," said Noonan. He cocked the gun. He kept it below the head of the passenger seat, so Kroker wouldn't be able to see what he was doing, but he knew Holly heard the sound. She stopped.

Lutz held the car at the end of the block. They watched the van slow and stop next to the woman in the wheelchair and the kid. "This is really clumsy," Lutz said. "He must have made us. If he hasn't, he's an idiot."

Kroker shrugged. Curtailing Noonan's movements hadn't been part of the plan, but he could live with it. "So at least we know he'll behave today," he said.

Noonan climbed out of the van and opened both the rear and the passenger door. He lifted the woman out of the chair and put her in the passenger seat, then hefted the chair into the back of the van. The boy climbed in after the chair. From this distance, Noonan looked like the picnic-outing uncle, smiling and laughing at whatever the other two said. Then he got back into the van and drove off.

"We stay with him?" Lutz asked.

"We stay with him," Kroker said.

"Wait here," Flanagan told the cabbie. He jumped out of the car and was halfway to the entrance of Holly's building when he noticed a car hesitating in the middle of the road at the corner. The passenger looked familiar. He stopped, looked again, then walked towards the car until he could make out the face clearly: Kroker. The car pulled away.

Flanagan hesitated. He looked up at the apartment, saw the breeze move the curtains in the open living room window, and knew that if he made a mistake now, he'd pay for the rest of his life. The realization: Kroker had been looking at something. He ran back to the cab. "Can you go around that corner?" he asked. Flanagan spotted the car two blocks ahead of them. "You see that car?" he said. "The blue Crown Victoria?"

"Yeah."

"Follow it."

The cabbie grinned. "You're kidding, right?"

The van led them to Corona. "Nice outing," said Kroker.

"I always take my nieces here," said Lutz. "Good for them to get the full spectrum of experience, you know? Trees aren't the only valid form of outdoors, you know?"

The van stopped outside a warehouse. "There," said Lutz. "See? Warehouses. Not enough kids get to visit warehouses. And you know what? I think you should call for backup."

"Doing it."

Noonan unloaded the woman and kid, and took them inside.

Lutz got out of the car. She took her piece out of her shoulder holster. "Warrant," said Kroker as he waited for confirmation of backup.

"Do what you can," said Lutz. "You've got two minutes. After that, screw it." She started across the street.

When Noonan locked the door behind them, Eddie started to cry.

Holly rolled her chair to the wall where Hooks and the girls were chained. "Ronald?" she whispered. Hooks didn't react. Julie was unconscious, breathing shallow and limbs twitching in bad sleep. Faith looked at Holly with eyes that had known the death of hope, and with it coherent thought. Buck's body, mustache shaved off with a knife, lay next to them. Eddie clutched at his mother.

Noonan looked at his watch. He walked to the center of the floor, where there was a large drainage pipe. Made to order, nice little back door. "So here's the deal," he told Holly. "I want you to scream."

Holly looked around. Noonan could see her trying to figure what the play was. She couldn't, but she decided to work against it anyway. "No," she said. "If you're going to kill us, get it over with. But I'm not going to give you the satisfaction." She put her arm around Eddie.

Noonan left the pipe and walked over to them. "Scream," he said.

"No," said Holly.

Noonan trained his gun on Eddie.

Kroker heard a shot and screams. He and Lutz looked at each other. He saw murder in Lutz's eyes. They ran for the door.

The cab turned onto the street and Flanagan saw Kroker and Lutz pounding at a warehouse door. He jumped out of the car. He saw Lutz shoot at the door. He ran towards them. The air in front of him rippled, stretched taut, and tore.

The warehouse exploded.

17

What Flanagan saw: he saw an attack kaleidoscope of images random and topsy-turvy, a flashcard assault of blur and tumble, fire and blood. He saw light, flamed into a boiling fist. He saw cars parked in front of the warehouse lift up and flip, screaming, across the street. He saw the cab sliced in half by a beam. He saw metal blow through the driver's chest. He saw the warehouse's facade fly towards him. He saw the building collapse.

What Flanagan felt: he felt pressure squeeze his eardrums to pulp. He felt the shock wave bat him, knocking him end over end back across the street. He felt a shrapnelweb of pain as he slammed into a wall and crumpled to the sidewalk. He felt horror and loss and the shock of the end of the world.

What Flanagan did: he screamed. He screamed loud enough that he could almost hear himself. He picked himself up, weaving, bleeding. He ran. Wavering, stumbling, howling, crying, he ran.

What Flanagan knew: at last, he knew war. He knew hatred, real and pure. And he knew he would fight until he saw Pembroke and Noonan burn.

Noonan climbed out of the sewer. He could see the smoke cloud, black and huge, spreading wings over the sky to the east. He grinned. Sweet. Very sweet. He hadn't pulled a gag like this in years. He headed back home to pack. He had changed his flight so he would now be catching the plane out of Chicago. Getting out of New York and into a safe house in Chicago where he could hole up until Saturday was the next smart move to play.

His message light was flashing when he got in. It was Pembroke. Two words: "See me."

Pembroke had the news on the TV in his office when Noonan got there. The wreckage of the warehouse was still burning hard. The media were on it like piranha. Pembroke stood with his back to the door, facing the screen. "This is just a hunch," Pembroke said without turning to Noonan, "but my hunch tells me that this is your definition of tidying up loose ends."

"You'd be right," said Noonan.

Pembroke turned around. His expression was unreadable. "I need your assurances. And I need them to be convincing. I need you to prove to me that what I am watching burn is not a very important house of cards."

Noonan held his hands out. "What you're seeing is the end of a lot of problems."

Pembroke folded his arms. I'm waiting, his expression said.

"Okay, first, that cop, Kroker, was starting to sniff around where we really didn't want him. And Flanagan was. . . . Let's say I was getting a little uncertain about his commitment to being a team player."

Cold monosyllables: "Yes." Giving nothing, emphasizing authority.

"Yes," Noonan said, letting his tone get a touch defensive, as if he shouldn't have to be explaining the obvious. "So checkitout: boom, Flanagan's sister and her brat are toast, so he'll have some food for thought, and boom, Kroker is toast."

"Yes." Pembroke's voice was all ice and needles. His eyes had widened slightly.

Noonan realized he'd better finish the explanation or fear the reaper. "And right about . . ." he checked his watch ". . . now, One Police Plaza is getting a call from Colombia claiming responsibility for the bomb."

Pembroke blinked. "Colombia?"

Noonan shrugged. "I spoke to some friends in Cali. I don't know if they're going to use the explosion for their own ends or shift the blame to some rivals. Whatever. Either way the heat gets applied far away from us."

Pembroke nodded, once. The gesture was barely perceptible, but Noonan caught it. He'd done good. Pembroke kept his eyes lowered for a moment as he thought. When he raised them, there was still some frost. Noonan kept his own face straight and open, but he wondered if maybe he wasn't out of the woods yet, and why not. "The Colombia gesture is good," Pembroke said, "but you threw away our leverage on Flanagan." Noonan opened his mouth, but Pembroke held up a hand, cutting him off. "Subtlety. You really don't understand what the word means, do you, Karl? The *threat* of harm against his sister would have done just as well."

"How would he know we weren't just bluffing?"

Pembroke sighed. "Karl, remember the type of person we're dealing with. He is not one of your hard targets. All you would have had to do is growl at him and he would have imagined the worst. And all this time and effort spent getting close to his sister. This is how you use insurance policies? By cashing them in at the first sign of trouble?"

Noonan kept quiet. He held his body still. No way of getting Bossman on your side when he decided not to be. Just don't get him madder, that's all.

Pembroke waved a hand, dismissing. "Oh, go to Russia. I'll handle Flanagan. And Karl?" Pembroke pointed at the TV. The smoke still billowed on the screen. "Try not to blow anything up overseas." Pembroke's grin was cold and thin. "A premature explosion would be very painful."

The hours before night and action were long. Blaylock had killed most of the afternoon with the tube. She'd spent the rest of yesterday and this morning doing a recce of the *Bhopal's* docking area and buying what she might need. She'd taken her time, buying rope in one place, a grappling hook twenty blocks away, but she still had to wait the day out. She found that if her thoughts had too much space to dick around, they circled back to Flanagan. A little too much, a little too distracting, a little too frustrating in all the wrong and fun ways. So she zoned out with the box of idiots. It numbed, but it worked. Evening eventually showed signs of arriving. Only a few hours more.

Then the entertainment became genuine. She was kicking the collective ass of the other contestants on *Jeopardy!* when the network hollered joy with a Special Bulletin, and then it was all explosion and death. Blaylock watched, hooked. Voyeur and vulture, she dived on the proferred meal. She felt her mouth twitch into a hard grin, but she wasn't enjoying the show, at least not with the *schadenfreude* greed that the network wanted. Instead she saw smoke memories of Bosnia and of Winnipeg. She felt her anger build, and enjoyed that. She didn't even know who was involved in the blast, but she felt her breath and pulse quicken with the free-floating need for violent justice. And she enjoyed that. She felt her fingers begin to tingle with the ticktictick lust-hate adrenalin of war.

Flanagan walked the streets, marching hard on random pilot, until he noticed people trying not to notice him. He stopped, suddenly aware of the wide berth he was being granted. He looked down at his clothes, and the tears and the burns and the blood registered. He rubbed his face, and his hand came away with still more grime and red. He leaned against a building and began to weep. His eyes stung with dirt, and that got him moving again. It took him several minutes just to figure out where he was. He stood for another three as he worked out how to get back to Battery Park City. Then he was walking again, but at least he was conscious, and he knew where he was going. He took his time, though. He didn't want to get to his building until after sundown. He was drawing enough averted stares as it was. He didn't want to deal with cops if he could avoid it, and he didn't want to attract the wrong attention as a dirt-and-blood ghoul stumbling toward high-end housing.

No problems. It was dark when he got back. No one raised a fuss. No questions at all until he walked in the door of the building. "Mr. Flanagan?" Bernie Walmsley, doorman extraordinaire, johnny-on-the-spot. "Are you all right?"

"Bit of a car accident. Looks worse than it is." He headed for the elevator. While he waited for it to arrive, he thought, no more questions, no more questions, I don't have the energy to keep the lies sounding good. For that matter, he doubted the first one had rung at all in tune.

No other passengers on the ride up. No one in the corridors to dispense pity, worry and suspicion. Flanagan got in the apartment and stumbled out of his clothes and into the shower. He turned it on hard, needle spray almost drawing blood with the force of its blast. The damage of the day sluiced down the floor of the tub in a foam of pink and gray. And now that the tears could come with impunity, now that there was nothing to do but stand and crash into the shock and misery and rage, the only water that ran down his face was fluoridated.

When the steam became oppressive and breath difficult, he stepped out of the shower. He toweled off, shrugged into a bathrobe and walked into the bedroom. He threw himself down on the bed. He stared at the ceiling. He waited. The tears still didn't come. There was a rock blocking them. A big rock, granite hard but lead poisonous, heavy and round and jammed in his chest. It wasn't letting anything through. Nothing good, anyway, nothing cleansing, nothing that might start the process of grief and healing and working through the iron-shod march of time. The only movement was vapors, toxic and full of torture. Hatred was there. Hatred of InSec, of Pembroke, of Noonan. But hatred too of himself, of Mike Flanagan the coward, who acted too late, too small, too wrong. Who was sure to find out a little bit more every day and in every way how he contributed to the death of his sister and her son. The ceiling disappeared into fuzz as he stared at it, unblinking. His vision hazed in the night of his anger and agony.

When he was ten, his father had owned a seventeenth-century Bible. It was a mystical object, accorded the veneration one would have expected if it had arrived in the States with the Flanagans. It hadn't: it had beaten them there by two hundred years, and it had been acquired by Flanagan's grandfather in 1923. But that didn't matter. It was still a family Holy Relic. And it was worth a mint. It had its own antique lectern, and was permanently open, as if in constant study. Flanagan had rarely actually seen it used except at Thanksgiving, Christmas and Easter. The book was almost always open in the middle, to a random psalm.

It was a Saturday. Flanagan's father was at work, about the bank's business, putting in those extra hours. His mother was in his parents' bedroom, having a post-housecleaning nap. The lectern stood next to an oak wall unit. The wall unit was new. It had come in along with a real oak dining room table: substantial furniture replacing the cheap and transitory as Flanagan Senior's career solidified. At the top of the unit were four vases. One of them, already ridiculously tall and top-heavy, was loaded with past-prime peonies. It had been moved dangerously close to the edge when Mother had been dusting there. Flanagan was playing with his cars. He set up an almighty traffic jam, then brought in a tanker truck to careen through an intersection, flip over and engulf downtown in flames. He backed up on his hands and knees, aimed the truck over the linoleum of the kitchen, and let fly. The truck rolled through the kitchen, hit the line of commuters, and boy did it flip, boy did it fly.

"Cool," Flanagan started to say. But then the truck's arc took it through the living room where it hit the wall unit. The contact sent barely a whisper of vibration through the oak. The front door slamming would have caused ten times the commotion. But so what. It happened now. The peonies rustled, restless, and knocked the vase over. It fell off the unit and smashed its ugly self on the floor. But not before pouring dirty peony water all over the Bible.

Flanagan's mother was there ten seconds after the crash. He was in his room ten seconds later, on his bed, instructed to remain there until his father's wrath walked in the door. He lay there quaking with impotent fury at the unfairness of the world, torn between wishing he could make everything explode and teach people to be sorry, and wanting to immolate himself for destroying the crown jewel of the House of Flanagan. It was a stupid, pitiful, useless, wasted anger, runt son of guilt and injustice. And he felt it again now. It was even worse because it now carried the additional charge of infantilizing him.

He cursed Noonan, Pembroke, himself, the anger. He pushed himself up and swung his legs off the bed. He sat hunched and clasped his hands, pressing his nails deep into flesh. He had to act. Sleep and grief were murdered, and he couldn't wait for whatever chess move Blaylock wanted to make next. He needed to make InSec bleed, and bleed now. He needed a pyre to flame for Holly and Eddie.

All right, then. The *Bhopal*. Earlier that day, he'd asked about touring the ship to get an idea of how to fine-tune some of NAVCON's specs. Noonan had given him the brush-off, letting him know that engineering had it covered, and would let him know if anything relevant came up. Need to know had been the message, and he didn't have the right need. Well, now he did. He got up and turned on the lights. He opened his closet. He rooted through with no clear idea, hoping his hands would close on something that could cause some serious damage. But no rocket launcher materialized, no long-forgotten flame-thrower lay in the corner. The only things harder than a shoe were his golf clubs. He'd bought them two years ago when there had been a series of tournaments immediately prior to a swath of downsizing. Once the smoke had cleared, the tournaments evaporated, and he was $1200 poorer and the owner of a set of Calloways. He had taken part in the tournaments because he'd thought it was the done thing, the smart move, and for no other reason. He couldn't play worth shit. In fact, the games had meant nothing. They were just a short blossom of fun before the pain came down on pink paper.

He picked up a five-iron. He stepped away from the closet, gave the club a good swing. This could hurt something delicate, big smash, if he found a decent target. It would have to do.

He dressed in jeans and a T-shirt, both black, and runners. He caught a glimpse of himself in the mirror as he walked out of the room with his club. Weekend gangbanger, executive style. Not even a good joke. Not even a gun. The thought made him pause and look at his club. As weapons went, it would work only if his opponent was prone to incapacitating laughter. He went into the kitchen and pulled a chef's knife out of the cutting block. He looked at the blade, imagined plunging its eight inches into a stomach, and felt sick. Then he pretended it was Noonan's stomach, and he felt hungry. Good enough.

He held the club and knife, and wondered how he was going to transport them without drawing attention. He also didn't want to stab himself with the knife. He thought for a moment, then went back to his closet and pulled out a backpack. In went the knife. Then back to the kitchen where he opened the odds-and-ends drawer. He pawed through it until he found some red ribbon left over from last Christmas. He cut a length and tied it in a bow around the shaft of the club, just below the head. There. A birthday present. For the first time that day, he felt a twinge of pleasure, grim and small as it was. He felt clever.

The dockyards.

Flanagan couldn't believe he was doing this. Any minute now, if there was any God at all, he would wake up, and it would be time for work, and the day would start all over with Holly still alive and a world of mistakes unmade, and he would not be clambering around in an area he normally would have shied away from during the day. But the night stayed warm and hard and real. He could feel the clam of sweat on his forehead and under his arms. He could feel the sick fear-beat of his heart. His stomach was tight and closed as a walnut. And the rock was still there in his chest, damming up the terror and anger. He stubbed his toe against a train track, and the hurt had clarity.

The yards were still busy, which was good. He didn't have to sneak into the port and run a gauntlet of security guards and dogs. The cargo loading was done for the day, but crews still worked under arc lights, last-minute repairs stretching into late hours. Now the golf club looked completely ridiculous, Flanagan knew, but he decided really stupid was still more dismissable than just odd, so he kept the bow on. He tried to walk like he knew where he was going, but he didn't try to pretend that he belonged. That pretence would be smashed in a stevedore minute. And so would he, if he wasn't careful. He stayed out of the light as much as he could, and out of the way all the time.

Finding the *Bhopal* was easy. He just looked for the biggest ship around, and the *Bhopal* was currently the only superfreighter in port. It was docked in the new hub port, the multibillion-dollar concrete phoenix that had risen over Brooklyn's Red Hook piers specifically to harbor the new monsters and steal some of the shipping pie from New Jersey. Flanagan made his way over to the monster, its bulk a deeper steel shadow in the night. There was nothing to be loaded here. The ship was just in town for its test run. The shipyard activity dropped down to nothing as Flanagan got closer. He slowed and hugged the shadows. There would be security here. Good money on that. InSec protected its toys. But here was his gamble: the *Bhopal* was such a big toy that nobody was likely to walk off with it. It was hardly a likely target for much of anything, right? Right. So when it comes to security, we're not going to talk motion detectors, laser beams, rabid dogs and automatic police calls, right? Right.

He reached the ship. He walked its length, hoping to catch sight of its name. It would be a treat to be sure he was in the right place. Nothing more hilarious than misdirected sabotage. But the lights here were minimal: bare-bones illumination for security. No spots shining on the prow to announce the ship's pride. He did get the impression, even in the dimness, of one filthy ship. That surprised him a bit, but hell, what did he know from ships? He had to assume this was the *Bhopal*. Right place, right time, right size. And what was one more uncertainty?

He found a ramp leading up to the main deck. There didn't seem to be any other way on tonight. Shop closed, call again. The ramp was lit. He'd be a black bug on a white wall during the climb. Anyone watching from shore or looking down that side of the ship would see him. He hid behind the wheels of a gantry crane and watched the ramp and the decks of the ship. His heart hammered up its beat. The adrenalin pumped, building a critical head of steam. Vent it or use it, crunch time.

He broke cover and made for the ramp. He walked up it. Didn't run, didn't creep, just walked. Slowly, though, putting his feet down softly, trying to keep the ramp from creaking and jingling and shouting *here he is!* It still made noise, metal still whinged to metal, but he kept on, didn't run, risked that heart attack, that shout of discovery, that bullet between the eyes, and thought over and over, inane as hope, I'm supposed to be here, just walking up to give my good buddy his birthday golf club, nothing to see, nothing to see.

He reached the deck and ran to the first shadow he saw. He cowered under an overhang of the bridge superstructure. His eyes flicked in random everywhere patterns, no time to blink. He felt an urgent need to piss. Eyes flicked, flicked, flicked. No one around. He hugged steel until he found a door. It was unlocked. The first thing he noticed in the utility-light glow was that if the ship's hull looked like a pigshit wallow, the interior was showroom clean. It even smelled new. He felt like he should remove his shoes.

He reached the bridge. He blinked. Greenlit high-tech city. He ran his eyes over the banks of instruments. Looked for a wheel, saw what looked like a tiny model of one. This steered the ship? He brushed his fingers over the console. Not what he'd imagined as the bridge of a freighter. An aircraft carrier, maybe. Made sense, given NAVCON, he supposed. Was this par for all freighters? If he pushed the right button, would he nuke Baghdad? He felt the rock heat, begin to turn molten. He wanted to smash? No better place to start. He hefted the club.

He heard footsteps on the stairs. There were two doors

leading from the bridge. He'd come in the starboard side. He waited, breath held, trying to hear past the pounding of his heart to see if he could tell where the sound came from. Metal echoed, fooling him. He rolled the dice and ran for port. He threw the door open. The metal swung and collided with the man on the other side. The man staggered back, clutching his forehead. He lost his footing and fell down the first flight of stairs. There were still footsteps coming. The other door opened. "Hey!" The voice sounded familiar.

Shitshitshit. Flanagan trotted down the stairs and swung his club, catching the first man on the forehead as he tried to get up. The sound was *thunk*, heavy and dense. The shock of impact zipped up the shaft into Flanagan's arms. The shock of the sound contracted his stomach. The man slumped again, blood pouring down his face. Flanagan jumped over him. The other guy was right behind.

Down the stairs, clatter-scramble and he would have been screaming if he'd had the wind to spare. The fury of God pursued him. Down, down, one landing, two, three-fourfive. The superstructure was huge. And then behind him, two voices.

"You got him?"

"Just about!"

So much for taking one out. Useless. Flanagan almost gave himself up on incompetence alone. Then the stairs ended and he was out on the main deck. He ran for the ramp to the dock. It was gone. They must have pulled it when they realized there was someone aboard and decided to come at him from both sides in the bridge. Flanagan's breath came out as a whimper.

Footsteps closing. He ran down the deck. All hatches closed, it stretched ahead of him like an airport runway. He dropped the golf club and ran full tilt, arms pumping for flight. A giant fly buzzed his ear, and there was a loud *crack*. They were shooting at him. He started to zigzag, waited for the end, and ran for the bow, finishing line on the four-hundred-yard dash. He heard more gunshots. But nothing else whizzed as close. Then he heard footsteps again. Running. What were they doing now? Could he lose the time to look? He glanced back, still running. One guard coming up hard behind. The other he couldn't see.

His left foot came down on the unevenness between hatch and deck. He fell. His shoulder hit the metal hard. He grunted, rolled and scrambled, trying to get to his feet and get at the knife in his pack at the same time. The guard was no more than five seconds away. Flanagan was on his knees and his hand went into the bag and grasped the knife. The guard slowed as he closed. His legs were spaced, each step friend to gravity and ally to menace. His arms swung, death wrapped around bone. Flanagan finally saw his face. Derek Hirsch. Who hadn't been seen at the downstairs desk for a couple of days. New and important duties, it seemed. Hirsch grinned when he recognized Flanagan. Deer in the head-lights, Flanagan froze, his hand sweat-tight around the han-dle of the knife. Hirsch leaned down. He grabbed Flanagan by the collar and hauled him up.

Flanagan went up fast. He wasn't thinking. His hand and the rise did it all. The knife came out of the bag, point up, and slid *tchhhhhik* into Hirsch's belly. It went deep and trav-eled high. Flanagan felt the edge grate against bone in Hirsch's chest. Hirsch stared at Flanagan, eyes dimming with disbelief. He shook his head. The gesture was an animal spasm. He took a breath, and it hitched three times, each worse than the last. He let the air out, and he sounded like a man gargling chicken bones. Blood leaked, sudden-flow, from the corner of his mouth. He let go of Flanagan. His arms fell to his side. He shrugged once, as if startled. He went down. Flanagan still had his hands around the knife, and as Hirsch slid, the knife went up the rest of the way, finally coming out at the throat, the tip knocking Hirsch's chin up.

Flanagan released the knife. His hands began to tremble. He felt something warm and wet and not his sweat slicking his palms. He took a step back. Then another. Blood, dark-shadow, pooled out under Hirsch's body. Something near his stomach caught some light and showed a pink Flanagan had never seen before. Flanagan screamed.

Footsteps. He whirled. The other guard, anonymous vengeance, closing in for the locomotive finish. Flanagan waited, all done.

A shadow shot up from the deck and raced up behind the guard. It threw something. The something became a grappling hook that *chunked* into the guard's shoulder. He yelled and rolled into the pain, avoiding a bigger and better tear. He turned to face his danger. Flanagan heard another chunk. This one wetter. The guard went over backwards. His foot jiggled a bit, then stopped. There was a knife sunk deep into his left eye. Flanagan screamed again.

Blaylock stepped into the light and yanked her knife out of the eye. She looked at Flanagan. He stopped screaming. He started shivering.

They were silent during the drive. Flanagan was only now getting the shivering under control. He'd collapsed on the deck of the *Bhopal* and lain there, fifty kinds of useless, as Blaylock dragged the bodies to the rails and heaved them into the river. She had re-deployed the ramp, then hauled Flanagan to his feet and supported him all the way off the ship and through the yards. She took him through shadow-paths so dark he hadn't realized they were there. Her route did a connect-the-dots of linked cover, and they never passed anywhere near the remaining workers on site.

Outside the port area Blaylock had a car waiting. She bundled Flanagan into it and drove off. And finally, the trai-tor twitches in Flanagan's body began to wear off, and he tried to sort his thoughts, tried to make himself functional again. It didn't go well. There were too few thoughts to sort, and too many huge emotions out to batter him into the ground. The rock was still there in his chest, still the anger and the guilt. It was heated to molten red, ready to erupt and he didn't know if it would free him or kill him. And now there was terror of a new kind. Terror so huge, so new, so *unique* that he could barely recognize it out of fear for his sanity. But it was there, unavoidable as its feel on his skin. Its feel was blood. Cold blood now, thick and sticky, going brown underneath his fingernails. Blood that did not come from his body, but that was his anyway, because he had summoned it out, pulled it from another body. He felt ill. But the rock glowed hotter, moving to incandescence, and because of the rock there was a part of him that, now that it knew he could kill, wanted him to do it again. So the terror gathered strength and stormclouds, and loomed huge and lord over all his horizon.

He kept his eyes staring straight ahead, registering nothing of the streets. He allowed his eyes to move only once. He let them jig to the left to sneak a peek at Blaylock. There was thunder in the set of her jaw. Her eyes were moon-cold glitters. He didn't look again.

Blaylock drove to the Lower East Side safe house. She parked across the street, turned off the ignition, and sat for five minutes, scanning, before she got out. Flanagan followed. As he walked around the front of the car, the AVIS plate caught his eye. He stared at it, stupid detail in a chaos night nagging at his fractal thoughts and trapping him in iterative loops, nailing him to the spot, until the sign of a rental finally put two words together for an articulated concern: "paper trail."

Blaylock must have seen him staring. "Taylor," she said.

They went upstairs to 323. Flanagan stumbled inside while Blaylock locked the door and turned on the light. Then she turned around to face him, and her anger boiled the air ahead of her. "*What*," she threw her kit bag to the ground, "*the HELL were you doing there?*"

At first he didn't say anything. But he felt the rock grow bigger, and instead of embarrassment and shame, he felt anger that she should challenge his right to act, that she would infantilize his own war. "I had every right to be there!" he shouted. "*They killed my sister.*" He was all anger as he spoke, and it felt like a strike more real than sinking the blade into Hirsch's gut. "They killed her. They blew her up, and they blew her son up, and everybody else up." His voice went away. It wasn't tears blocking his throat. It was the rock, shutting off the words with a rage beyond articulation.

"The explosion at that warehouse?" she asked.

Flanagan nodded, choking.

Blaylock nodded back, kept nodding. She started to walk around the room, nodding, nodding. The heels of her boots kicked against the floor, as if stabbing deep into the under-bellyflesh of Noonan and Pembroke with every step. She walked faster, circled the room three times, building to her own explosion, every movement the promise of violence. Then she turned and walked straight at Flanagan. He took a step back when he saw her eyes, saw something shining so hard he thought it was broken glass. She hit him with a backhand slap that spun him around. He lost his footing and crashed to the floor. She crouched over him and grabbed his T-shirt, yanking his head off the floor. She shook him. "*So even more what the hell?*" she yelled, in his face and roaring fire. "*You want to die?*"

It wasn't broken glass. It was tears.

"*FUCK YOU!*" she screamed. And then she kissed him.

18

Dawn. Flanagan was curled in a ball on his side, the flow of tears finally taking the rock out, grief having its say, taking him down the road to being human again. Blaylock lay next to him, curving her warmth around, protecting. "I killed my sister," Flanagan whispered.

"No, you didn't."

Flanagan closed his eyes against her voice. The floor pressed, penitent's stone, against his bones.

"Listen to me." Blaylock squeezed his shoulder. "Do you know when InSec first got interested in Holly?"

He thought. Yes, yes, he did know. Holly's mystery date around the time of NAVCON's inception. Before Blaylock, before any boat-rocking. Weapons being lined up against him and his before he even knew there were hostilities in the air. "Yes," he said, and there was a little more strength in his voice. A little return of the anger.

"So who killed her?"

"Noonan," he said finally. "Noonan did it."

"Right. Not you. You did not, in any of a hundred what-if parallel universes, kill your sister. Karl Noonan did, because that's what he does. He kills people. And he enjoys it."

Flanagan frowned. "How do you know that?"

"His eyes."

Flanagan sensed something being held back, the answer incomplete, but he let it go. Something else popped up, the bigger question, the scarier one. "We kill too." He curled tighter, trying to block access to the image of Hirsch's deathface.

"Not the same. You killed in self-defense. Trust me, you would be dead if you hadn't had that knife." She paused, then probed, "Did you enjoy it? Do you want to do it again?"

"Oh Christ, no." Nausea went through him in a wave at the idea.

"Then you won't have to. But you have to hit back." There was an old knowledge of revenge in her tone. "So what can you kill?"

The question opened up the answer to him, rosebloom. "InSec," he said without hesitation.

"What do you want?" she asked.

"To stop Pembroke and Noonan. But I want to kill InSec."

"So that's what you'll do."

"And you?"

"Killing people is what I do."

The way she'd said Noonan's eyes told his joy. Flanagan thought of turning around to look into Blaylock's and see what they had to say. But he couldn't.

"We'll work our strengths," Blaylock went on. "All right? You leave the strategy to me now, and you stay out of the field."

There was something in the way she spoke. That and the memory of her tears earlier made him turn around after all. He did look into her eyes. They shone in pinpoint sparks lit by the gray light. He didn't see a mark of Cain. He didn't see the thrillkill he knew lived in Noonan's gaze. Not now, anyway. Instead, he saw exhaustion. He saw the strain of perpetual strength, of always having to be the steel, of never letting the guard down. Of having to be strong for two now. Of loneliness. Of fear. Fear for him. "I'll stay out," he said.

She ran her fingers down his cheek. Gentle now, a feather touch trembling with curiosity and disbelief. It was the touch you give an object new and fragile and precious, an object you never expected to touch, and that you fear will be taken away. She smiled, sad. "As much as you can," she said.

He smiled back. "As much as I can." He could hide in logistical support and run from the front lines all he wanted. The lines would catch up sooner or later.

Blaylock shook him awake at six. "We have to move," she said as he rubbed his eyes. She dragged him to his feet and tossed him his clothes. When he was dressed, she said, "We have to get you to work." All business and strategy again.

"Does it matter? Nobody's pretending anymore."

"It might not matter, but we don't know. How vital are you to NAVCON?"

Flanagan thought for a moment. "Depends. I think I can make myself vital all the way to the end. Put in some specs that complicate the user interface. Passwords, stupid little bugs and routines. Wouldn't be permanent, and there are plenty of computer engineers who could take care of the problem sooner or later."

"Can you make it later?"

"Yeah, I think so. No, scratch that, *I know so.*" He grinned, mind tracking flow charts that led to a first-class screwing of Pembroke. "Pembroke wants the system usable only by him. So the specs are already in for a single user. I just make it usable only by me until the last minute. Simple."

Blaylock nodded once. "Do it. Make it so getting rid of you is not an option. And if there is anything left to pretend, we might as well keep up our end. No point showing our hand before it's called. Agreed?"

"Agreed."

"Fine, so let's go. You can't show up for work looking like that." She gestured at his clothes. They were torn and stained. The stains showed rust-brown on his white runners, giving the game away. "And we have to make a stop by my place too. Just because we're playing the game doesn't mean we aren't going to cheat."

The nearest parking space to the other SRO was four blocks away. By then it was close to seven. "Come on," she said to Flanagan, and set off at a good clip. He had trouble keeping up with her.

"So no safe house this time?" he asked. "I'm really going to see the sanctum?"

"We're just going to a place where I keep more stuff and I sleep more often, that's all."

He saw what she meant when they reached the hotel. It was another dwelling as holding pattern, everything in or near cases for instant packing. Flanagan thought he would have gone insane within days if he'd had to live like this, finger just a jab away from unfreezing the pause button and sending the action into fast forward.

Blaylock opened a case and pulled something out. "Here," she said and tossed it to Flanagan.

He caught it, looked at it. A cufflink. "No, wait," he said. "Don't tell me."

She nodded. "You got it."

"They really do make bugs like this." He shook his head. "An InSec special. Picked it up at last year's IMTEX."

Flanagan grimaced. "Of course you did. And why do I need this?"

"Chances are, what with the way things went down yesterday, that it's going to get harder and harder for us to keep in touch. I need to know what's going on in there, and you might not be able to contact me. I might also need to know what you know *right away*. So you're going to be wired, and I'm going to monitor."

"You think they don't do routine bug sweeps?"

She shrugged. "So they find it. So it won't change much. It's not like you haven't already been targeted." She saw him wince. "Sorry," she said, and her tone made it clear that she meant it. "What I mean is, if they find it, it won't significantly change our position for the worse, and until they do find it, we have an edge. Yes?"

He nodded. "Yeah." Then a worry: "Hey, this works for you to keep track of me, but what if you need to get in touch with me?"

"I'll think of something. Okay?"

Work. On time, in his office, at his desk, no comments about the cufflink that looked just a bit more polished than the other. To Flanagan it stood out like a searchlight. He'd expected the security gates to shriek ballistic as he walked through, but no, big fat anticlimax of nothing. Which suited him fine. And so another start to another day at the office. Just another cycle of the routine, yes? Yes, until midmorning. Flanagan wondered idly what Blaylock was doing, if she was sitting somewhere with a bank of instruments, bored silly as she listened to him clatter at his keyboard and field calls. The reassuring tedium, false silence in the war.

At nine-thirty there was a knock on his door. Mary Bottomore poked her head in. "There are policemen here to see you," she said, face deeply serious. Flanagan felt for her. It was bad enough when the cops had come by after Blaylock had killed Smith III, but for them to come *again*. This sort of thing didn't sit with the kind of office she tried to run.

He thought he knew what they were here for, and he braced himself. He nodded. Mary gave him a long look, equal parts concern and disapproval, and withdrew. A moment later she ushered in two plainclothes detectives. Flanagan didn't recognize either one. Their faces were serious, which he expected. But they also looked angry. For the first time since the explosion, Flanagan thought of Kroker. There hadn't been any room in his grief for anyone other than Holly and Eddie, but he saw larger repercussions now. "Michael Flanagan?" one asked. He was the older of the two. Cropped white hair standing on end. Eyes wide as if always surprised. "I'm Detective Oatley. This is my partner, Detective Miles." Miles nodded. He was in his forties. He had the face of a man who wasn't on speaking terms with his digestive system.

Flangan gestured for them to sit down. They did.

Oatley said, "I'm sorry to say that we have reason to believe that your sister is dead."

Flanagan didn't have to fake his reaction. Hearing the news of Holly's death this way was like seeing a death certificate. There was a finality to it, an official seal, that sent him into shock all over again. He stared at the detectives, then wondered why his vision went blurry. He rubbed his eyes and his fingers came away wet. "How?" he finally asked, forcing himself to stagger through his role, to hear the plot of the tragedy spelled out once more.

"You heard about the bombing in Queens yesterday?"

Flanagan nodded. Yeah, he was vaguely aware of that, all right.

"Two of our officers, Detectives Kroker and Lutz, as well as a cab driver, were killed in the street by the blast." Oatley flipped open a notebook and kept his eyes on it. Flanagan noticed that his eyes didn't move. He wasn't reading, just avoiding contact with bereavement. "Rescue crews have found six bodies in the wreckage. Two of them we have tentatively identified as those of Holly Flanagan and her son Edward."

"Eddie," Flanagan whispered, and it was still no act.

"We're very sorry, sir," said Miles.

Oatley said, "They were killed in the explosion, not the collapse, Mr. Flanagan. It would have been quick."

Flanagan nodded, nailing himself with the cold comfort image of Eddie ripped to pieces in light and heat.

Miles asked, "Do you have any idea what your sister was doing there?"

Flanagan opened his mouth and got ready to lie his head off. Last time he'd spoken to the police, he'd been hiding his knowledge from Noonan. Now he'd be hiding his own role. Covering his bloodstained tracks. "No," he said. "I can't imagine what she was doing there." And he followed that up with a question of his own. "You said there were six bodies."

"That's right," said Oatley. "We were hoping you might be able to give us some help on that matter too." As if he'd been any help on the other so far. Oatley looked at his notebook again. This time, when he spoke, Flanagan noticed that Miles was watching him closely. The notebook trick was magician's misdirection. Oatley kept the subject's attention while Miles recorded the reactions when the guard was down. "We believe that three of the other bodies are those of Ronald Hooks and his daughters Faith and Julie."

"Oh Jesus." He couldn't believe he'd forgotten about them. They'd vanished off his internal radar as the threats had homed in on him.

"They appear to have been chained to the wall," Oatley continued.

Flanagan closed his eyes. He began to rethink his inability to kill again. "And the sixth?" he whispered.

"The height and weight match those of Karl Noonan, whom I believe you also know."

Flanagan opened his eyes, snap. Noonan dead? Sure, that was up there with flying pigs, homecoming cows and barking lobsters. The bastard had faked his death. He wasn't sure what the implications were, except that they weren't good. "Yes," he said slowly, "I know him. Knew him."

"You see why we wanted to talk to you," said Miles. He cocked his head slightly. "InSec seems to be having a pretty high casualty rate among its employees and their relations."

Flanagan nodded.

"And don't forget Rebecca Harland and Johnathan Smith," Miles pushed on. He crossed his arms and leaned far back in his chair. "Frankly, I think you're damned lucky you're still alive."

Flanagan blinked a few times as what Miles had said sunk in. Big trouble loomed close, breathing down his neck. I'm about to total the war, he thought. He felt the blood withdraw from his skin. He knew his face must now be paler than his shirt. "Do you mean...?"

The two detectives said nothing at first. They sat quite still, and then Oatley smiled slightly. They were pissed enough about the deaths of Lutz and Kroker that they were willing to play cat-and-mouse games with someone they didn't even consider a suspect. "No, Mr. Flanagan. We don't think you set the blast off. Your record doesn't really point that way. But we do need all the help we can get, and whatever is going on, you appear to be close to it. Tell me: how aware are you of employee travel patterns?"

"Not very. Just whatever someone happens to mention to me. I knew about Rebecca in Paris, of course."

"What about Colombia?" Miles asked. "People or shipments going there?"

Flanagan was willing to bet there was a healthy amount of trade going on there. "My secretary will show you the records we have here, if you like," he said.

"Thank you," Oatley said. "Tell me, how do you feel about the recent news stories about your firm?"

Flanagan looked him straight in the eye. "I'll shortly be looking for another position."

They left after that. When they were gone, Flanagan sat with his elbows on his desk, hands clasped in front of his mouth. "Did I do good?" he whispered at the cufflink.

He jumped when the door of his office opened.

"Oh, Mary—" he began.

It wasn't Mary. "She's on coffee break," Pembroke said.

Blaylock sat on a bench in the Trinity cemetery. She was wearing what looked like a Walkman. She choked on her Sprite when she heard Flanagan say, "Mr. Pembroke, please sit down." She was getting the Dark Lord himself on tape. Big morning. Keep cool, she thought at Flanagan. Don't lose it now. You're going over the trench, soldier. Do me proud.

Pembroke didn't sit. He shut the door and walked over to Flanagan's desk. He stood two inches from it, arms crossed. "Let's get the cards on the table, shall we?" he said. "Let me start by saying that I do not approve of Karl Noonan's latest endeavors. They were unnecessarily flamboyant, and I'm not convinced that the risks didn't outweigh the benefits." He shrugged. "But what's done is done."

Flanagan kept his mouth shut. Fury bubbled as he listened to Pembroke's nonchalant reference to the murder of nine people. But he wasn't going to react. Wasn't going to say anything until he absolutely had to. No mistakes here.

Pembroke reached into his inside vest pocket. "Show me your left wrist." Flanagan flinched as he stretched out the bugged wrist. "Nice watch," said Pembroke. "But here's a nicer one." He pulled a watch out of his pocket. Flanagan's watch had been a present from Holly, but he took it off and slipped on the one Pembroke gave him. Pembroke reached out and pushed a button on the watch. It beeped once. "I want you to think of this watch as representing me in spirit. When you wear it, I'll always be looking over your shoulder. It's a bug. It's got some other nice features too. It's waterproof. So you won't have to take it off ever, not even in the shower." Flanagan knew what he meant. Don't take it off. Don't even fantasize about it. "And now that it's been activated, it's doing two things. It's sending out a homing signal, so I'll always know where you are. And it's keeping track of your pulse, so I'll know if you take it off. You follow so far? Good. Let's see if you can follow the rest."

Pembroke leaned forward, placing his palms on the desk. "This project is important to me. You are important to the project. Not absolutely irreplaceable, but important enough that I would much prefer to keep you on it. But if you do anything other than what I am paying you to do, if you try anything to interfere with or sabotage NAVCON, I will have you killed. Not someone close to you. You. Still with me? Excellent." Pembroke's voice was getting lower and lower, turning into a hiss that filled Flanagan's world. "So this is how it's going to be. You will do your work. And you will go home. And then you will come back to the office and work some more. That is the shape of your days. You will do nothing else. You will make sure NAVCON works. If it doesn't, you die. If it isn't completed on time, you die. If I don't like the shape of the control unit or the color of plastic, you die. And when it is all finished, when you've satisfied me that NAVCON will do everything I want, then you are going to stay close and make sure it *keeps* working.

"Now, another thing: you like nature, Flanagan? You know, trees, birds, fish. Do you like that? Good. Then you'll enjoy your holiday. With me. Beginning of August. We have this wonderful lodge in northern Ontario. No one to bother us, just you, me and . . ." he paused, and a grin flashed, crazy-cheerful, ". . . a few guests. And you're going to make sure I can work my new toy. Sound good?"

"Wonderful."

"No, it doesn't. Don't lie to me again. This sounds like Hell on Earth to you, and do not pretend otherwise. You're scared to death, and well you should be. It didn't have to be like this, Flanagan, but you rocked the boat. Just be thankful I'm not throwing you to Karl."

Flanagan swallowed.

"That's better. A good, silent, vague response. At least it's not a lie. Now I'm going to tell you one more thing. You're wondering what happens to you if all goes perfectly and I'm pleased as Christmas with NAVCON. Well, good. Keep wondering. We'll just have to see, won't we?" He straightened up and stepped away from Flanagan's desk. He waggled a finger. "Be good." He turned to go, actually had his hand on the doorknob, but then turned around as if he'd just remembered something. "One more thing. That woman you went out with in April. Whatever happened to her?"

"Date didn't go well." Flanagan had never put so much effort into a single lie before.

Pembroke bought it. Seemed to, anyway, and that was enough to be getting on with. "If she ever approaches you again, run away. If that bug catches one word of conversation between the two of you. . . . Well, you know."

Her Sprite had turned to warm syrup. She hadn't touched it while she listened to Pembroke's speech. She didn't touch it afterward as she played the tape over and over, trying to read deeper, divining goat's entrails made of sound. There was something off about Pembroke's tone of voice. Not the menace and threat. They were present, but that was all right. They were expected. No, there was something else, something behind the sarcastic jocularity. She rewound the tape, played it, listened, tried to get behind the voice. There. A slight quaver, as if the jokes might really be funny after all. As if he almost laughed. She listened again. Yes, almost laughing, but not cheerfully. Bad laughter, not quite hysteria but related. Something had come loose inside the man. There was a bolt bouncing around the machinery, and if it got caught in the right cogs it could rip everything apart. And from the sounds of it, the shrapnel would take a lot of people out when it flew.

She put another tape in the machine and took the headphones off. She thought strategy. She would monitor for another couple of hours, but the god of war had given so much this morning that expecting any more would be greedy and might be seen as asking for it. Pembroke slapping a monitor on Flanagan was sweet and sour. Sweet because no one at InSec would be looking for another bug now. Too funny. Too lucky. She had her ear inside the building now, and there it would stay. But sour too. Contact was out now, the risk just too high. It would take a drastic new phase before she could see him again. Time to go back underground. She'd be leaving for Montana soon now, from the looks of things. Preparations to be made.

She thought about last night. She thought about holding, about being held. She thought about being able to stand at ease for once, to be off the forced march, to let go, let in and not be alone. That was the worst of it. Taking the risk. Deliberately making a chink for the enemy to shoot through. Judgment could be affected. Action was no longer free. Critical areas could be compromised. She closed her eyes and smiled. He could compromise those areas all he wanted. It had been so long. So screw false regrets. She opened her eyes and focused on the hard facts the tape had picked up. A deadline for NAVCON, and something big in northern Ontario at the beginning of August.

By the end of the day, Flanagan figured he'd lost at least five pounds to sweat and adrenalin. No more scary visits after lunch, but the fear and the worry were strong and pumping. Armpits soaked, fingers slippery on the keyboard, hair lank with the humidity of terror. He didn't eat lunch. Was scared Pembroke would see it as goofing off and the watch would explode. Was scared a SWAT team would descend on him if he stepped outside. Was scared his anger would not see him through. Was scared he was failing already, failing Holly, failing Blaylock, failing himself. Was scared for his life.

He worked late. He skipped dinner. Didn't matter, his stomach would have rejected any overtures. Tried to find room for his anger. Tried to see himself as still at war and not caving in. Tried to tell himself he was biding his time, being the good boy until the opportunity was right. Tried to tell himself he was being smart. He knew this was true. He knew this was exactly what Blaylock would have him do. He knew that the payoff from this morning was huge, that a jackpot prize of strategic information had fallen from the skies into their laps. He knew all this. But he was still shit scared. And felt the guilt of cowardice.

He left the office at eight, and went straight home, good boy, just like he was told. He stopped at the entrance to his building and checked his mailbox. Two bills and a letter. He looked at the envelope as he took the elevator up. There was no stamp on it. Someone must have handed it to Bernie Walmsley to slip into the box. The handwriting was feminine.

He waited until he was in the apartment before opening the letter. There was one sheet of paper, and when he unfolded it, a pressed tiger lily petal fell to the ground. He picked the petal up and read the letter.

Brave Soldier,

I heard it all, and ya done good. Yes, it's scary, but hasn't it always been? You've got what it takes, don't worry.

I'm going to pull another powder on you now. It was probably going to have to happen again soon anyway. The Bad Guy just speeded it up a bit, that's all. Don't worry, though. I'm going to fix things, and you won't have to bow and scrape too much longer. Do it for now though. Make it a good act. And then we'll hit them hard.

Burn this. Burn the envelope. Do it now.

But you can keep the flower.

He went to the kitchen for matches. He carried the tiger lily in his right hand, seeing in it all the fragility of his strength, of his hope. And in the black and flame of its color, the smiling gift of rage.

19

It was June when Blaylock got back to Montana. She flew to Spokane, where she'd left her truck, a black, mountain-battered Ford, in a long-term parkade. From there she drove out of Washington and across the Idaho panhandle. Night was falling when she entered Montana. Twenty minutes past the border, she reached Hexton, population 270. There was only one road in, crossing a single-lane bridge over the Clark Fork River. Behind the town, the Cabinet Mountains rose, the granite guard, the wall of night and stone. Hexton was the perfect little *festung*. Any force trying to take it would find it a royal pain. This was the pride of Hexton.

The pavement stopped at the far end of the town. After that, it was gravel, at best. The route Blaylock took went uphill fast and was a dirt track defined by tire grooves. It wasn't maintained at all. Rain had cut deeply in the trail, gouging gullies across it, here and there shoving large chunks over the mountainside. The truck bucked and sank over the ruts and holes like a ship in high seas. Blaylock bounced hard. Without her seatbelt, her head would have hit the roof. She drove up the trail the only way possible: slowly, carefully. No charging up the slope, pedal to the metal. Which was precisely the idea. The track turned a sharp left and, still at a steep incline, came to an abrupt halt at a wooden barrier. Blaylock stopped the truck, put on the emergency brake, and flashed her lights. Two short, one long, one short. Then she shut them off.

After a few seconds, a figure approached, flashlight bobbing. Blaylock stuck her head out the window so she'd be easier to see. The flashlight beam shone in her eyes, blinding her. Then it moved aside. "Hey, Joan," said Sam Rivers. "How's it hanging?"

"To the ground, Sam, to the ground."

"Heard you was coming back. What's up?"

"Judgment Day. Charlie in?"

"Everybody is."

"Good." Blaylock started up the truck and drove into the compound.

Assembling an army had not been difficult. Once Blaylock had settled on a profile for her soldiers, search and recruitment had been a dream. What did she need? Men with guns willing to believe the worst of large corporations. Where did she find them? First on the Internet, where Joan Taylor came into being. Joan Taylor had been to Bosnia, and she frothed at the mouth on all matters patriotic and Second Amendment. It wasn't long before she was invited to conventions. She met the Rivers brothers at the Patriot's Clarion Call in Billings, Montana. Charlie, Danny and Sam. They were angry. They were armed. They and Charlie's wife Susan were the Liberty Raiders, a militia of four that needed a leader.

The Rivers brothers had been farmers. The farm hadn't been a good one. The land had been too thin, the roots of the mountains too close to the surface. But it had been theirs. It was family. It was history. It also had oil. At least, that's what the survey had said. Corporate will, backed by government fiat, had made them an offer they couldn't refuse, and then politely shown them off their land. Turned out there wasn't any oil after all, but by then the funds were committed, and the exploration went on, just because it had to. The land was gone.

The Riverses bought some new land outside Hexton. It was even worse for farming. It was great for defense. They knew they would never be forced away again. But big deal when they were on a scrap of almost vertical dirt that no one would want anyway. So that wasn't enough. They had to strike back.

The first thing Blaylock did was establish what experience the brothers had. Charlie had served weekends in the National Guard for a while twenty years before. He had done his best to pass on what he remembered of his training to the others. They saved their dollars and sent Susan to Texas for a weekend of training at some ranch outfit called Packing Thunder. The brothers went on a paintball cruise offered by *Soldier of Fortune* and stormed the Florida beaches. If Overlord happened again, they'd be ready. When they told her about their training program, they sounded proud.

Blaylock gave them a real program. She turned them into blades. And word got out about the new leader, the leader who had done damage in Bosnia. The membership of the Liberty Raiders grew. Some of the locals weren't happy, least of all Sonny Butler. He was big man, six-five mean by three hundred ugly, and he let it be known that real men should join with him, and not some woman. Blaylock faced him down in Hexton's bar, and very publicly broke his arm. Then, just as publicly, she kissed his forehead, called him strong and invited him to become part of the cause. Butler wasn't even out of his cast when he signed up.

There were twenty of them before a year was out. And they knew how to fight. Gradually, Blaylock let them in on the target. She beefed up their arsenal with regular orders. Every few months, Charlie and Danny would do the cross-continent drive to Miami to pick up a new load, adding to the illusion of the Colombian LR INC. It was a long and expensive bit of misdirection, but their paranoia fit beautifully with Blaylock's need to be careful. Plus they loved the new toys, and the idea that they were going to use the enemy's own weapons to take it out.

Sometimes Blaylock would lie awake at night. Her eyes would be open in total surrender to the insomnia of guilt. She would think about the people she was living with. She would think about how they trusted her. She would think about how she had chosen them because she wanted cannon-fodder, people whose lives she could sacrifice if necessary. She would think about how she was starting to like some of them. And she wouldn't sleep. So she would wrestle with herself. She would pour energy into keeping up the hate and contempt that she needed to feel. Militias were a societal brain tumor. These people were walking arguments against universal suffrage. The kind of world they wanted was the inbred offspring of the worst of the frontier West and '30s Europe. She looked at their intolerance, their jacked-up, wacked-out patriotism and God-riven babble, and she saw Jesse James in jackboots. So screw 'em. Twice.

These were the things that she would tell herself, all the while trying not to think about how deeply she was gazing into the abyss. These were the things that helped her do what she had to, but they did nothing to help her sleep. She accepted her good conscience as another casualty of the conflict. She did her work. By the time she left to start the New York phase of the campaign, her Montana war machine was primed.

Lock and load.

20

NAVCON had its test run at the end of the first week of June.

Flanagan stood next to Pembroke's chair. Pembroke had the modified laptop open on his desk. He had his eyes on the start-up screen. Next to the laptop was a speakerphone connecting them to the bridge of the *Bhopal*, Captain Vincent Willson, commanding. Pembroke spoke to the phone: "Are you ready?"

"Yes, sir," said Willson. The *Bhopal* had left the harbor and was moving east into the Atlantic at a crawl.

"All right." Pembroke addressed Flanagan. "Explain this to me."

"There are basically three systems working together here," Flanagan began. He felt like he was giving a sales pitch. And if the mark bought the car, then he got to hang onto his life for another few weeks. "Firstly, the *Bhopal* has got some pretty refined Aegis technology on board, or so

Engineering tells me, so you'd have to try pretty hard to run her into anything. NAVCON will let you know in plenty of time if you're going to run aground or collide. And if you don't react to the problem right away, it will start screaming. There's a fail-safe that will take over navigation if you still do nothing."

"Unless I use the override." When Flanagan didn't answer, Pembroke glanced up at him. Pembroke's grin was barely visible, but its condescension ran deep. "Every contingency, Flanagan. Every contingency. You've never heard of sacrifice moves? Destruction of evidence?" He turned back to the laptop. "That said, I'm not planning on wrecking my new ships. How do I know what's going on out there?"

"That's where the other two systems come in. Like we talked about at the start of the project, the ships are locked into the Global Positioning System, and both they and your end of NAVCON are speaking to each other on the cell phone bandwidth. When you turn the laptop on, it dials up automatically, and the commands go back and forth instantly."

"Cell phones are not secure."

"The encryption is solid," Flanagan said, "and will be updated constantly. Once you're satisfied with the system, you punch in your key and that will be the one and only way in." Except for my back door, he thought. "Now here's your way to monitor." Flanagan leaned over Pembroke and called down a menu. "Each of these options takes you to the instrument of your choice on the ship of your choice. All of the information is in real time, and so are your commands. So when you tell the ship to do something, you'll see the result on your screen at the same time as the captain sees it on his instruments. And here are the camera views." He toggled through screens looking fore, aft, port and starboard, and one showing the bridge. Willson, a twenty-year freighter vet, moved past the camera in jerky freeze-frame as the image updated.

Pembroke didn't look ecstatic. "Those are a lot of screens to keep track of."

"That's right. So most of the time you'll be using one of two summaries. There's this." He brought up a screen showing an illustration of the *Bhopal* in relation to the New York coastline. At the top right of the screen were the *Bhopal's* speed, bearing, latitude and longitude. There were also two other categories: *Destination* and *Comments*. They were blank. "And there's this." The screen shrank to one-eighth, reducing the diagram to a sketch, but keeping the information. The other seven boxes were blank. Flanagan pointed to them. "Those are for the rest of the ships when they come on-line."

"*Destination* means where I want the ship to go, presumably," Pembroke said.

"Yes. Right now you haven't told the *Bhopal* to do anything. NAVCON is in passive mode, just monitoring. The ship is under Willson's control. Once you plug in a destination, he might as well go down to his cabin and play solitaire for the rest of the trip."

"So the captain doesn't need to know where his ship is going." Now Pembroke sounded cheerful. He was almost laughing.

"Someone with a lot of experience would be able to figure out generally where he's heading, but you could alter the course without warning. So he'd never know for sure what the final destination was."

"Good. And *Comments*?"

"That's multipurpose. But most frequently it would be for storm or shoal or collision warnings."

Pembroke nodded. "Show me how to take control."

Flanagan went to another menu. A map of the world appeared. "Use the trackball," he said. "Center the cross-hairs on the region you want to go to."

Pembroke moved the cursor around the screen. Latitude and longitude numbers moved with it, blurring as they adjusted to the changing location. Pembroke stopped the cursor over the US east coast. "Now what?"

"Click on the left button."

Pembroke did. The screen zoomed in to show eastern North America and the Atlantic. Pembroke kept clicking and the view became more and more focused.

"This is all GPS, to the military, not civilian, specs," Flanagan carried on. "You could send the ships to this office if you wanted to."

Pembroke moved the cursor and started clicking. Flanagan saw that he had put it on land. The land became Manhattan. Lower Manhattan. Battery Park City. The InSec building. Pembroke asked, "Right button to input destination?" He clicked. Then he called up the summary screen for the *Bhopal*. The numbers were already changing.

"Sir?" Willson's voice crackled on the speakerphone. "Have you gone active?"

"I have. What's your status?"

"We've changed heading." There was a moment of silence. "And the helm is no longer responding to my commands."

"Thank you, Captain. Stand by." Pembroke steepled his fingers and watched the screen. The *Bhopal* steered itself back into New York harbor. *Comments* blipped a collision warning once or twice, but the ship altered course on its own and avoided three tugs and a small tanker. No fuss, no muss. "Nice," Pembroke allowed. A few minutes later NAVCON beeped. "Collison Course" appeared as a comment. The ship began to slow and change direction. Pembroke hit OVERRIDE. The *Bhopal* headed back towards the Financial District.

"The Port Authority—" Flanagan began.

"Quite. Now shut up." Pembroke continued to watch. NAVCON continued to beep at him. The ship continued on a suicide run. Pembroke waited until the *Bhopal* was just shy of triggering Port Authority alarms, then disengaged the override. The ship's engines stopped, then went into full reverse. Flanagan's mouth dried as he watched the *Bhopal* takes its forever-time to stop moving forward. It finally slowed to a halt, uncomfortably close to shore, then began to back up.

Pembroke touched the intercom. "Barbara," he told his secretary, "call the Port Authority and give whatever apologies and explanations are necessary, will you? And no calls from them." To the speakerphone he said, "Back to dock, Captain." He turned to Flanagan. "So that's it, then. I might as well be on the bridge of the ships."

"We call it telepresence. A lot of the same technology as they've been using on the Mars explorers." Still in pitch mode, still pointing out the cool features to the mark.

Pembroke's eyes shone clear with cold amusement. "Frightened, Flanagan? You should be. You're nowhere near being out of the woods yet. But this," he patted the laptop, "does you a world of good. I take it that you are confident NAVCON is ready for action?"

"Yes."

"Good boy. You've done well today. Now go back to work, behave yourself, and don't forget your holiday in August."

June 15.

Jim Korda let himself into the Oval Office. Walter Campbell gestured for him to take a seat facing the desk. He went back to reading the letter he held. He'd already read it a dozen times. He knew the words by heart. But he didn't know what they were saying. Not really. He handed the letter over for Korda to read. Its tone was polite, conciliatory, which worried Campbell a lot more than the ranting threats on the phone. Pembroke apologized for any misunderstanding. It was all his fault, he didn't mind admitting. He promised full cooperation with the new investigation, complete openness and total disclosure. Campbell asked, "Mind telling me what investigation he's talking about?"

"There's nothing new. Nothing he hasn't been fighting for weeks now. And nothing too. ..." Korda trailed off out of deference to the recording tapes.

Campbell knew what he meant. Nothing too top-flight. The various agencies had agreed to keep the investigation at street level, and, if it ever tried to get up, to spin it off into dead ends and let it die. The whole thing was just too poisonous. InSec bleeding could stain everybody. And with that thought, the meaning of the letter clicked. "Openness, disclosure, transparency," he recited. "Christ, Pembroke's going to sing. He's going to take us down with him."

Korda placed the letter on the desk. "Not necessarily," he said, pointing to the last paragraph. *I look forward to future frank discussions,* Pembroke had written. "He's saying he'll talk to you before he talks to the press."

Campbell looked at the next line. *I trust you'll have a pleasant and productive August.* "At the G8?" he asked.

"Maybe not at the summit itself. But in and around then."

Campbell frowned. "I don't like being blackmailed."

"I think we should see this as an opportunity. We might as well get this over with, and if he wants to meet privately, so much the better. We'll be in a stronger position, then." He looked at Campbell significantly.

Campbell took the meaning. The more private the meeting, and the further away they were from cameras and tape recorders, the better his chances of fighting back unencumbered. And with a full security contingent on-site, even better opportunities presented themselves. Who knew what desperate measures discredited arms dealers might attempt to resort to? Who knew how extreme the prejudice might have to be in stopping them? "Okay," said the president. "Let's get in touch with him. Say we want to talk. Find out where and when he wants to do it. Encourage him to make it as private as possible."

On June 20, the InSec fleet set sail for Russia. The *Bhopal*. The *Taegu*. The *Dhanbad*. The *Flixborough*. The *Ludwigshafen*. The *Oppau*. The *Wankie*. The *Texas City*.

On July 1, Blaylock spread the map out on the Riverses' picnic table. The make-work sentries had been given the afternoon off so the full contingent of the Liberty Raiders could be present for the briefing. All twenty of them crowded around the table, shuffling, taking turns pushing forward to see the large-scale topographical map of northern Ontario. It was the last treasure she had brought back from New York. She'd saved it as a psychological peak now that there was less than a month to go before deployment. At the beginning of June she'd told them what she'd learned from the bug on Flanagan. She'd told them that the target was going to be a lodge, and that Pembroke, Archfiend in the Raiders mythology, was going to be there. She'd stepped up training, dropping all pretence of defending the turf of the Rivers ranch, putting everything into offence. But she'd held back a couple of items. The striptease wasn't quite finished yet.

She'd spent her last days in New York chasing the identity of the lodge Pembroke had mentioned. Knowing its general location narrowed the search, but there was still a lot of combing through records to do. She ruled out resorts open to the general public. Then she worked her way through InSec's maze-layers of owned corporations, looking for one that would deal in real estate, and had interests in Canada. It was a safe bet InSec wouldn't be directly connected to the lodge. She hit gold with Jewel Properties. In the mid-eighties, it had acquired a sizable chunk of forest near Red Lake, and then built a luxury lodge. That was the last public record Blaylock could find. There was no mention of the lodge opening, or anything else. The legalities observed, whatever had gone on at Red Lake had been allowed to disappear into the fog of bureaucratic Alzheimer's. But she knew this was it. The location was right, and she could trace Jewel back to InSec. She was willing to bet that if she could see InSec's private records, she'd find mention of the lodge all right. Probably for top-level executive retreats. A great deal-making locale, especially with hostile parties. Give them all the luxuries of friendship, but keep them isolated until they give in. Simple. Effective. So she was pretty sure she knew where her target was. But that was it.

She began her briefing. "The objective is twenty miles south-southwest of the town of Red Lake, Ontario, Canada." She pointed to a small lake. "The enemy's base is here, at Ember Lake. He owns property, and has constructed a lodge. That is what we'll be after. But what you see on this map is the sum total of all we'll know before we get to the site. We know where the property is, and we know there is a lodge there. That's it. And not only is the property quite extensive, it might as well be several times larger than it is because it's in the middle of nowhere. Red Lake is the only development around. As I see it, there are two likely locations for the lodge itself: either somewhere on the shores of the lake, or here." She pointed to a level area. It was about three quarters of the way up a valley that sloped up northeast from the lake.

Butler frowned at the map. His face had a huge welt where he'd been hit by simulated ammunition. He hadn't scrubbed all the blue paint off yet, either. "I don't see any roads," he said.

"That's because there aren't any."

"So how are people supposed to get to this lodge?" Sam demanded.

"Helicopter or float plane," Blaylock answered. "Pretty common practice in that part of the country, but I suspect this lodge will be bigger than most of the places serviced that way."

"So we're going in on foot," said Charlie.

"We're talking true guerilla warfare here, people. So we're going to have to think long and hard about what we can carry. There is an upside to this, though: plenty of cover for our approach. The big downside is going to be a lack of proper recon."

She rolled the map and climbed up on the table so everyone could see her. "I'm not going to lie to you. There are a few basic principles to LIC." Low Intensity Conflict. By sweet holy Jesus these guys loved the acronyms, so they were going to get them. Least she could do if they were going to get themselves killed for the sake of her vendetta. "And I'm sorry to say that we're going to be violating just about all of them. I want you to be aware of our weaknesses, so you don't get cocky. Our IPB is shit-poor." Intelligence Preparation of the Battlefield. Talk that talk until they walk your walk. "Look at this thing." She gestured at the map. "That's all we've got. This is our terrain analysis? There are no roads, fine, but it would be nice to have some kind of trail overlay, wouldn't it? We can assume a fair degree of cover and concealment, but we don't know precisely where and how much. And let's not even mention avenues of approach, since we don't know where what we're approaching is supposed to be. Weather analysis, threat evaluation, all of this is going to have to be done on-site, and that is going to be limited to what we can see at a distance. How big a distance, I wish I could tell you."

The troops were looking grim but steadfast. Sure, there were problems, but the problems were expressed in cool terms, so that was okay. Blaylock could see in them an adolescent conviction of their own invincible immortality. "What we do know is this," she continued. "Sometime in early August, something big, something very important to InSec, is going down there. Pembroke himself will be present. This is our best chance to hit InSec in a way that will cause some real damage. The mission is to wreck their plans.

We also have a man inside, whom we'll have to get out. Questions so far?"

Danny Rivers put up a hand. "Any hard targets?"

"Pembroke. But he's mine. That clear? Good. As for targets of opportunity, feel free. Watch out for possible hostages, though."

"So the Rules of Engagement...." Danny prompted.

"ROE is shoot to kill. Identify the enemy and wipe him out. No prisoners. They have the advantage of home turf, of budget, of technology, and quite possibly of numbers. So don't be doing them any favors."

Susan had her hand up. She still looked a bit uncomfortable in her fatigues, as if they were not functional at all, but a dubious costume. She clearly had mixed feelings about the guns too. Blaylock wondered how much she really believed in what was happening around her, and to what degree she had been pulled over the event horizon by her husband and now couldn't get out. She asked, "What will be the nature of the opposition?" Nervous or not, she had the lingo down.

"We can assume top-of-the-line security from InSec," Blaylock answered. "How much depends on how big the event turns out to be. I'm hoping we'll have a clearer idea before we go in, but...." She shrugged.

She noticed Sam staring at the ground. He looked worried. Root whatever this is out quick, she thought. "Sam?" she asked. "Some concerns?"

"Well." He kicked at a stone. "You make it sound like we're up shit creek before we even begin, is all."

She nodded. "Glad you were listening." She raised her voice again. "You hear what Sam said? I hope so, because any SOB here who thinks this is going to be a cakewalk had better tell me now, because I don't want any morons on my watch. We go in there overconfident, we get our asses FedExed back here. I want you to think about what we'll be up against, and I want you to realize that the reality is always worse. But we do have some points in our favor. Anyone want to tell me one? Sonny?"

Butler was smug to the core. "They don't know we're coming," he said.

Blaylock said, "Give that man a gun."

21

I, Noonan thought, am in the armpit of the world.

It was July 4th. He'd been cooling his heels in Moscow since he'd arrived. Everything was supposed to have been greased up slick by the time he got here. He'd had ideas of taking care of business inside of a week, then heading off to gamble and screw on the Riviera until he had to go back across the Atlantic in August. But no. And nothing he did got him any joy. He yelled at Leon West a lot, and that made him feel better, but it didn't make anything happen. West was the head of InSec's Russian division, a red-haired twenty-something with a rash of initials after his name, given this office because of his fluent Russian and geek knowledge of local armaments. It had been his responsibility to handle the deal at this end. As far as Noonan was concerned, he'd done a piss-poor job.

Noonan spent most of his time in his hotel, going

ticktock mad with boredom. The hotel itself, the Lux Ultra, was fine. West had done that much right. It was a new luxury hotel built with dirty money. West had chosen it for that reason. Security and privacy were easier when management was a business partner. The Lux Ultra had the tacky glory of Las Vegas mixed with a soupçon of old-style Soviet stolidity. The fountain in the lobby was just a tad too powerful. There was a marble half-shell burbling water at the entrance to Noonan's room, and it looked like it could survive ground zero. The colors were no-nonsense and emphatic. Noonan liked it. It was a man's hotel, with not a pastel in sight. The bed was comfortable, the toilet paper soft, the call girls attractive, the downstairs bar well-supplied, and there hadn't been a single power cut. But even so, after a week, the endless cycle of getting drunk and laid while waiting to roll out got to him.

There was no action. Nothing to do. The one casino he'd checked out was so baldly rigged that he had stormed out without dropping a dime. It had crossed his mind to fix some faces as he left, but now was not the time to ruffle the Russian mob's feathers. They were deep into the deal, and no matter how much he abused West, he knew that they were the real problem. InSec had to keep the mob happy, or the deal was off. The mob knew they had to be kept happy, and that the street didn't run both ways. If InSec didn't like the deal, there were other options for the merchandise. It was easy to move, and there were plenty of customers in the Middle East. That was the last thing in the world Pembroke wanted. It wasn't just a matter of one big project falling through. If the wrong people got some bright ideas, InSec might face a serious rival for the first time. This was, among other things, a pre-emptive strike. If it fell through, Noonan's head would be the first to roll.

It was late afternoon. Noonan lounged on his bed and stared at the TV. He had it tuned to a porn channel piped exclusively to the hotel and other mob concerns. It was the only channel where Noonan could understand what the hell was going on. Someone knocked. Noonan grabbed the remote, thumbed the TV off, and jumped off the bed. He picked up his Glock 30 and padded over to the door. He looked through the peephole, saw West. He shoved the pistol down the back of his pants and let West in.

"I've got good news," West said. He plunked himself down on an armchair near the window. The view was of the red-brick Petrovsky Palace. The palace had once been a stopover for the tsars commuting between Moscow and St. Petersburg. But Moscow had stretched wide since then, and now the palace was spitting distance from the business district. "Sherbina says he'll see you. I think we're finally good to go."

"Yeah?" said Noonan. He leaned against a dresser. The gun dug into the small of his back. He liked it. "So where do I meet him?"

"His club, tonight at eleven."

Noonan nodded. He did some quick calculations. If Sherbina really was going to come through, then they could still make the schedule. Just. But there was no more room for fooling around. He thought about how close they were to deadline, and he began to wonder if Sherbina's timing was totally coincidental. "Did he happen to say why all the delays?" he asked West.

West shook his head. "No. Goddamn game player is all, if you ask me. Like I keep telling you, everything was set before you got here." He said it as if Noonan was to blame.

Noonan didn't like that. He didn't like that West was cocky and mouthy now that it looked like things were going to work out. He took a step away from the dresser, towards West. Something occurred to him. "You didn't mention our timetable to anyone, of course."

"No! No, I never said anything!"

"Never mentioned August 8? To anyone Stateside?"

"I reassured Mr. Pembroke, of course, but—"

Noonan saw what had happened now. But he dug a bit more to make sure. "You spoke to Pembroke. On the phone?"

"I told him that—"

"You mentioned the date too, I bet." Noonan stepped forward and slapped West, hard enough to knock the chair backwards. West's head jerked to the left. Blood spurted from his lip onto his suit. "Your job is to do what you're told and not screw things up. You screwed up. Didn't you do your research? Who do you think you're playing with?" He leaned into West's face. "Checkitout: Sherbina is ex-KGB. How long do you think your phone has been bugged?" He broke West's nose.

Noonan hit the Club Nomenklatura at eleven sharp. It took up the top floor of a low building overlooking Red Square. A trio of bouncers the size of T-72 tanks manned the entrance, making sure the club lived up to its name. You had to be somebody-plus to get in. Tonight, Noonan qualified. They frisked him. Noonan wasn't packing. They looked surprised. He smiled at them, locking gaze with the head muscle. He sent his message: I don't need hardware. The bouncer, twice his size, looked away. They stepped aside. A maitre d' led him in.

The club was gangland class. The interior of the building had been preserved and restored, the hardwood floor gleaming mahogany luster. A trio played whisperjazz in one corner. The music had just enough of a beat for a half-dozen couples to slow-dance. A lot of the men looked like middle-aged bureaucrats. There wasn't a woman in the place who wasn't a pro.

The maitre d' brought Noonan to a table next to a huge, arcing bay window. The table was flanked by leather armchairs. Noonan sat down and eyed the man facing him: Stepan "SS" Sherbina. A man born with his mouth glued to the main chance's tit. Former fair-haired boy of the KGB's dirty tricks department, now he was the Syndicate Apollo. He was dressed in a dark suit whose cost would have fed the population of Novgorod for a year. His hair, cropped close, was so blond it was almost gray. His eyes were clear pools of trust-me blue. His jaw was heroic. His features were airbrush perfect. He didn't look Russian. He looked like whack-off material for Himmler. "Mr. Noonan," he said. "Very pleased to meet you at last." Not a trace of accent. He sounded like Yale. He made Noonan feel like the rube cousin.

Fine. He'd be the hick. "Where's our merchandise?"

Sherbina smiled. "Yes, there have been a number of delays. Please accept my apologies. Can I get you a drink?" He leaned around the armchair and signaled a waiter.

"I'll accept you living up to your end of the deal," Noonan snapped. "And I'll take a scotch."

"Of course, of course, of course," Sherbina said. He murmured to the waiter, who nodded and withdrew. Sherbina turned back to Noonan. He crossed his legs and adjusted a crease. "Let me reassure you, Mr. Noonan. The merchandise is available, ready for your inspection, and can be loaded as soon as it meets with your approval. There's nothing to worry about."

"So why did it take so goddamn long?"

"Ah. Well, some facts have come to my attention, facts that suggest your Arthur Pembroke might not have been bargaining entirely in good faith." Sherbina looked pained. "And people say Russian businesses aren't to be trusted."

"What facts?"

"Let me back up a bit." He paused as the waiter brought Noonan's scotch. "At first, I didn't think that your order was more than what it appeared, and I have to say that the initial bid was quite generous."

"So? What's the problem?" Noonan sipped his scotch. It was good.

Sherbina uncrossed his legs and leaned forward, clasping his hands. The close friend, about to make a confession. "I was lying awake one night— This happens to me quite a bit, you know." He simpered. "Insomnia. The stress of the job, but of course you'd know that. I do so envy the lady wife. At any rate, I was lying awake, and I began to wonder why InSec would be so interested in so much material and be offering more than market value."

Noonan remembered the day the deal had been made. Pembroke hadn't been as cheerful as he should have been. The mistake, Noonan decided, had probably been West's. The geek was looking for a long fall down the corporate ladder. "Go on," he said.

"I tried to come up with an answer. Was InSec stockpiling, hoping to create a shortage? No, that didn't seem likely. Certainly not sensible. And if the head of InSec ceased to be sensible, then where would we be, eh?" Sherbina's smile was pleasant, and Noonan had no doubt that Sherbina knew where he would be: ready to step in and fill the gap.

"So?" Noonan prompted.

"So, then some information concerning a deadline came my way." Now Sherbina's grin was shit-eating, telling Noonan: I'm up your ass all the way, buddyboy. He pretended to wrack his brain. "Something about international waters and August 8. That's right, isn't it? Yes. Yes, I think so. Now, why August 8? I did some research. And do you know what else is going on around the same time? No? August 8 falls the day after the conclusion of the G8 summit." Sherbina leaned back, summation concluded.

Mouth dry, Noonan said, "So? I should care about that?"

"Mr. Noonan, I admire your disingenuousness. It's very good. But stop playing games. What I am seeing in my crystal ball has the potential for being, at the very least, the biggest extortion gambit in history. And if Pembroke thinks we're not going to get our cut, then he doesn't know us very well. He hasn't done his research. I can't tell you how important research is to the smooth functioning of a large commercial concern."

Noonan realized that he was gripping the arms of his chair. He wanted to drive the asshole's teeth down his throat. But he knew if he tried, he'd have some massive exit wounds inside of a second. To say nothing of screwing what remained of Pembroke's deal. He made himself relax. He asked, "What kind of cut are we talking about?" He looked away from Sherbina as he spoke, looked out the window at the Square. He could see the lights of the Kremlin opposite. The Square was huge, shrinking the walls of the fortress with distance, but the building still gathered a sense of mass and power around it. But the sense was an illusion, Noonan knew. The real power was inside the Nomenklatura.

Sherbina stroked his chin. He pondered theatrically for a minute. "I'd say that, oh, twenty-five percent of the gross wouldn't be out of line."

"You're kidding, right?"

"Hardly. We supply the material, we get it to port, we take care of the paperwork and the bribes. Really, now. Without us, where would you be? And a little bird tells me that you are in no position to negotiate. Twenty-five, take it or leave it. And we're going to need a portion of our cut in the form of an advance. Up front."

"How much?"

"Shall we say quadruple the original figure?"

Noonan winced. Pembroke was going to shit a brick. Noonan looked at Sherbina. The Russian gazed back, calm, placid, beyond the ability of any force to ruffle. Noonan wondered what it would take to make Sherbina lose his temper. He would have given his left nut to be the guy to make Sherbina lose it, and then slap him down. But that wasn't going to happen tonight, or tomorrow, or any time until Pembroke had what he wanted. Noonan was going to have to give in to this asshole because of forces beyond his control. But Sherbina was on his shit list now. Business here would not be truly concluded until Noonan could put a checkmark beside Sherbina's name. And Noonan could keep his accounts active for years. "I'll have to run this by Mr. Pembroke," Noonan said.

"Of course you will," Sherbina echoed right back. He reached inside his vest and pulled out a cell phone. "No time like the present, is there?" He handed the phone to Noonan. "It's mid-afternoon in New York."

Noonan glared at him as he dialed Pembroke's private office line. He got through on the first ring. "Me," he said, and thought for a moment. Cell phones were the worst security in the world. He had to say something completely unindictable. "Our partner is demanding renegotiation of the contract terms."

Silence. Then: "How much?"

Noonan told him.

"And the goods are there?"

"He says so."

"Make sure."

"I will."

"All right. I'll cable the money. Pay him. But make sure." Pembroke hung up. Noonan held the phone to his ear a minute longer, pretending to listen. Pembroke had taken the news very calmly. He hadn't sounded cheerful, but he hadn't sounded like he cared about the money, either. There was intensity in his tone only when he told Noonan to verify the merchandise. Maybe Noonan had underestimated how much cash this gambit was going to generate. Maybe they were still getting off cheap. If so, he didn't want Sherbina to clue in and double or triple the price again. He did his best to look like he was being chewed out. Then he said, "Yes, sir," turned off the phone and passed it back to Sherbina.

Sherbina cocked his head. "So?"

Noonan waited a bit, then nodded once, curt. "But I see the stuff, and I see it tomorrow."

Tula was a city of 600,000, a hundred miles south of Moscow on the Moscow-Yalta highway. Its layout was Moscow's smaller twin: concentric circles of roads with a kremlin at the center. It had history: it was one of Russia's oldest cities, and boasted Leo Tolstoy as homeboy. It had poison: heavy engineering and textile industries coated the land gray and the water brown. The ghost of Chernobyl still haunted the crops. It had samovars. And it had weaponry.

Sherbina's limo pulled into the base near the eastern suburbs a little before seven. There were more concentric circles to go through, all of them razor-wire and guarded by concrete barriers and armed security. Noonan looked at the sentries as they drove past. Their uniforms looked almost, but not quite, military. There was the same weird blur about the base itself. It felt like army. It had been originally. But there was a sign at the entrance with the logo that Noonan recognized as that of Kornukopia, Sherbina's front company. There were no government symbols in sight. Sherbina caught Noonan's frown. "You're wondering about the troops. Former Red Army, now Kornukopia. Private armies are much better. More loyal."

They drove toward a group of huge bunker warehouses. They had to weave their way through the biggest fleet of trucks Noonan had ever seen. He could see a hundred, absolute minimum, parked near the warehouses. There were more arriving all the time. And on the road down from Moscow there had been a monster convoy. Noonan had had the impression that the limo was the only car on the road. Everything else was trucks. He was impressed. The actual logistics of what they were pulling off had been an abstraction until now. When he saw just how much hardware was being mobilized for Pembroke's plan, when he thought of the superfreighters that were waiting in St. Petersburg, he began to understand what it felt like to be God.

The limo pulled up to the nearest warehouse. The driver got out and opened the door for Sherbina. Noonan got out on his own. They walked to the open bay. The merchandise waited inside. Guns. The elephant graveyard of guns. The home of all good AK-47s. The late harvest of the Cold War, stacked and forgotten, waiting to be called into use again. Waiting for InSec to bring light to their barrels.

More AK-47s were produced than any other rifle. Simple, reliable, damn near indestructible. Kalashnikov's genius made metal. Find a military force operating anywhere on this sweet screaming Earth, and you will find the AK-47. Even US forces in Vietnam were known to dump their M-16s if they got hold of the waterproof AKs. The AKs had flowed off the production lines like a river in flood. They flowed out of the Soviet Union to legion liberation armies. And then the Cold War ended. And the Soviet Union ended. The world still screamed, but there was only one Big Player left, and the power games were smaller. The guns stacked up. By the mid-'90s, there were twenty-six million surplus assault rifles stashed in the arsenal cities of Russia. Twenty-six million guns. All lubed up and nowhere to go. Now InSec had come calling.

Noonan wandered through stacks four storeys high of crated rifles and ammunition. He felt overwhelmed by riches. This was it. Here we go. Pembroke's master plan ticking over and *look at all these guns.* Pembroke was going to cream his pants when these beauties were loaded up and in his possession. Sherbina walked over to a crate. He gestured to the driver. The driver picked up a crowbar and pried the top of the crate open. Sherbina reached in and picked up a rifle. He tossed it to Noonan, who caught it mid-barrel. "I'm sure you'll want to do some spot checks for quality."

"Damn straight," said Noonan. No way he was going to take any chances of anything else screwing up. But he already knew what he would find. It was going to be a slick slide in from this point on. He test-fired two dozen AKs. He chose them randomly, from different heights in the stacks, from different stacks, from different warehouses. They all worked. They were all the distilled music of death. They were perfect.

He was in a good mood when they left the base. He was almost willing to forgive Sherbina the gouge. He looked out the back window as they drove away, watching the trucks load up. God, it was beautiful. Deployment worthy of war.

"Satisfied?" Sherbina asked.

"So far," Noonan qualified, but he grinned.

"Excellent. On to our next stop, then."

Noonan frowned. "Where are we going?"

"Obviously this isn't *all* the guns."

Obviously. But he was more concerned now with being in St. Petersburg for the loading up. He could do some more spot-checking at that end. "Yeah, but—"

Sherbina held up a hand. "Tut tut. I insist. Kornukopia treats its clients properly. We respect their need for proactive quality control." He chuckled. "Plus, I've got a surprise."

Izhevsk in heavy rain.

Capital of the Udmurtskaya Republic. Slightly larger than Tula, but five hundred miles east of Moscow, well out into the vast nowhere of the western Urals. Noonan saw lots of timber as Sherbina's private plane flew in, but he also saw the smokestacks. More heavy industry, more metallurgy, more defence. Another limo met them at the airport, and took them out to more Kornukopia arsenals. Noonan was starting to get bored and tired by this time. The rifles all worked, and he didn't have to make this trip to have it proved to him. And Sherbina's constant smile was getting on his nerves. If there was going to be a surprise, then bring it on already.

Sherbina saved it for late in the day. One more base. One more horn of plenty. And this base was different. It was much further out from the city than the others. The security was tighter. More and higher fences. More AKs on active duty, instead of in boxes. The limo stopped outside a thicket of Scotch pine that stood in the middle of the base. As they got out of the car, a truck rumbled by on its way to join the waiting fleet. It wheels splashed through a puddle. Mud flew, spattering Sherbina. He didn't flinch. Didn't lose his cool over a thousand-dollar overcoat ruined. He hardly seemed to notice. He wiped absently at a splotch of mud on his cheek as he led the way into the woods. Noonan had a sudden vision. He saw blood flying into Sherbina's face instead of mud, and the same lack of concern. He filed this away, and reminded himself not to underestimate the man when it came time for payback. They walked down a wide mud track that the trucks could handle but would bog down the limo. The bunker they approached was sunk halfway into the ground and heavily camouflaged. Its metal door rolled up as they drew near. The track became pavement that sloped down into the depths of the bunker. The interior was dark.

"The hell is this?" Noonan asked, antennae reacting to potential threats. He tried to calm them. If Sherbina wanted him dead, he didn't have to go to these lengths. A quick slug in his hotel room would have done the job just as well.

Sherbina said, "My surprise." He bowed, elegance in mud, and gestured for Noonan to proceed. "I realize this is a slight breach in protocol, that surprises are not generally kindly regarded by men in our line of work. But I think you'll be in a forgiving mood when you see what it is."

Noonan started down the ramp. As he did, the lights flickered on inside the bunker. At first he thought it was just another AK depot. More stacks and stacks and rows and rows of crates. Then he noticed the boxes were a different size. They were longer, but otherwise smaller, as if each held only one item.

"Our deal called only for guns," Sherbina said behind him. His voice echoed against the concrete. "But I thought to myself that Pembroke is a good businessman, who wouldn't balk at an unexpected deal. So I would be remiss if I didn't make this bonus available. At a competitive price, of course."

There was one crate sitting by itself in the middle of the central aisle. The demo model. Noonan accepted the invitation and walked over to the box. He pulled off the lid. He stared for a good long while at what he saw inside. It was a Grail SA-7 shoulder-fired infantry missile. It wasn't exactly the Excalibur of surface-to-air missiles. It was only good against very small aircraft and rotary wings. Its heat-seeking mechanism could only home in on the exhaust nozzle of the target. But it was very light, very portable. Big mayhem in a little package. In multiple packages. Noonan looked up from the missile and gazed around the bunker. The place felt like it was the size of a football stadium. He had no idea how far it stretched, how many thousands of the missiles were here. He turned to Sherbina. "I think I'm going to need to use your phone again." His voice felt thick, stunned.

22

Click, click, click of gears meshing. One at a time, starting off slow, but each one starting up another, clickclick build-up, the mechanism winding itself tight, tight. Each tick of a day through July brought August closer. Momentum ruled the day now, and not a single cog could be turned back.

July 31.

Summer had gone full bore and become a heathen roar, a withering breath over the continent. The newspapers were full of heat and fire. In the midwest, and on the prairies, the farmers had given up on the hope of rain, and were praying for an early winter. In Chicago, the elderly were being culled. In Ottawa, they were beating the red carpet for the G8 summit. The air-conditioning systems in the residences and conference rooms hummed at full strain. Outside, the air was death-still and pressed down with suffocating lake moisture. Mere movement was an invitation to heat hysteria. In New York, Flanagan pulled his suitcase out of his closet. The air conditioning was working fine in his bedroom, but he was still sweating. He did that a lot, these days. At Ember Lake, it was business as usual in the false calm of the hurricane eye.

Ian Dix sat down on one of the twin sets of porch steps leading up to the south-facing, enclosed front deck of the lodge. He wiped the sweat from his forehead. The interior of the lodge was like the black hole of Calcutta. The air was so still it was a wall. Breathing curled the inside of his lungs. Out here it was a little better. There was shade from the overhang, and something that was almost a breeze touched his cheek. It was his lunch break, but he didn't think he could eat. The heat had sent his appetite away until further notice. Maybe tonight. Maybe. But these days the temperature didn't drop more than a few degrees overnight. Sleeping wasn't much fun, as the building released the heat it had stored up during the day. The indoor temperature hadn't dropped below ninety degrees in more than two weeks. And meanwhile there was the air conditioning, first class, top of the line, lying dormant. No wasting of fuel on the hired help. It would not be turned on until the day before the guests arrived. Dix looked forward to that day. It was going to be better than Christmas. He saw the tops of the Jack pines and the spruce that surrounded the lodge wave slightly. His nerves reached out in anticipation of the breeze. It didn't come.

This was his sixth summer at the lodge. The other five had been great, and he had been convinced that he'd found *the* utopian seasonal job. He'd spent the summer after his first year of university tree planting, and that had damn near killed him. He'd loved being in the woods. At least at the outset. But the first straight week without a shower got to him. As did the bugs. But what finished him off was the work, the back-shrieking, two-steps-bend-down-dig-and-plant rhythm of it. He'd survived, barely. Come the end of second year, he'd had no other job lined up, and he couldn't afford to pass up the money. Then a miracle: one of his fellow planters, one of the converted for whom the whole experience was a holy Zen meditation, turned down the opportunity to work at the lodge, and passed the tip on to Dix. That summer, Dix wondered what god he had accidentally contrived to please so hugely. The job was an afterlife reward. It was deep in the woods, the whole nature thing writ large, but with running water and real beds. And the work itself was a breeze. Dix helped out with general maintenance, fixing whatever he was told to fix, hauling this, repainting that. The idea was to keep the lodge in top shape, should it be required. The beauty was that the wear and tear beyond what the weather brought down were minimal, because the place wasn't occupied more than a week or two each season. During his second summer at the lodge, there were guests for only four days. The third year had been so rainy and miserable that no one had showed at all. He and the rest of the staff didn't have to do anything more than keep the place up and look after themselves. It was a paid summer vacation. In luxury.

You reached the lodge by float plane or helicopter. The aircraft dropped you off on the shore of Ember Lake, a glacier-carved pothole in the Canadian Shield just under a mile in diameter. You walked four hundred yards through forest up a path that sloped just enough to make it feel like you had earned the first view of the lodge. The building filled a clearing. Two storeys of rustic decadence. Its log frame wedded it to its surroundings. Its base, a series of squat stone pillars joined by arcs, lifted it off the cool of the ground. Its conveniences were more appropriate to a CEO-only club in Manhattan. Twenty-two guest rooms on the upper floor of the two wings. Downstairs: billiard room, dance hall, bar, on-site doctor. Don't worry about leaving the city—it'll meet you in the bush. The staff quarters were on the ground floor of the east wing. They might not have king beds and jacuzzis, but they beat the hell out of cots and tents. For that matter, they beat the futon Dix slept on in his bachelor suite in Winnipeg. And he'd had a chance to try out the jacuzzis upstairs.

The job was even better than government work. Dix had every intention of staying on this gravy train until he finished grad school. He'd just finished his Master's in English at the University of Manitoba, and was heading off to Edmonton in the fall to start his doctorate at the U of Alberta. He figured on at least another five summers at the lodge. If he survived this year, that is. He got the feeling that the karmic watchdogs had twigged to his scam and were doing an audit on him. He hated heat. This summer the lodge grounds felt like some of Dante's real estate breaking surface. Death was a long and sweaty proposition. And the work this summer was heavy. The word had come down from on high: the lodge was going to be full, and the guests were going to be VIPs of the first water. Perfection was the watchword. Anyone who said "Good enough" or "That'll do" got shipped home. Dix had already seen it happen. And after so many years of goofing off, he resented each job he was assigned as if it were a slur on his mother.

And still the heat. Always the heat. Nothing but the heat. It defined and tortured the world. The only good thing about it was that most of the bugs had shriveled up and died.

Sucks, Dix thought. He puffed his cheeks, blew air, leaned back on his elbows. He heard a door behind him open and close. Footsteps on the stairs. A voice close. "Hey. Join you?"

Dix tilted his head back. Marianne Louden in upside-down perspective, fanning herself. There was another door from the deck, with a whole other set of stairs five yards to the left. She could have gone there, no? It was too hot to have someone sitting so close. Especially Louden.

He hadn't thought so last season. Then he'd sized up the entertainment coordinator and her short, perky, brown ponytail, her perky, round face with its surprised mouth, her perky ass, and decided that he'd known who this year's jacuzzi partner was going to be. It had taken until late August, but the home run had finally come, and then she had surprised him. At first pleasantly. But then she'd wanted to explore the whole spiritual side of what they'd just done. He'd been hopeful that she was going to trot out some toe-curling tantric sex technique. But oh no, it was all planetary alignment and goddess belly babbleshit. He'd dismissed her as a flake case and made sure he was busy and exhausted for the last week of August, which for the first time hadn't come fast enough. He'd left for Winnipeg on a relief high.

But then this summer she'd wanted to pick up again. He couldn't believe it. Hadn't she ever heard of the summer fling? She seemed oblivious to his attempts to stay clear, and kept wanting to talk goddess, as if this held the *slightest* interest for him. He vaguely remembered acting fascinated last summer during his bed campaign, but he'd only been half-listening, and hadn't thought that she tried to live her precepts. Now it seemed that it was all she wanted to talk about, and she would not leave him alone.

"It is so hot," said Louden.

"Yup. Like you said." He was only being minimally civil, and that only because they had to coexist together for another month. But if she started up on Earth Power and Moon Strength or whatever, then screw it. There was only so much he could put up with.

Louden said, "I can't remember when there's been a heat wave this long over such a wide area. And look at all the records that are being broken. This is the lead story on *The National* just about every night, Ian."

Dix shrugged. There weren't any new and interesting

things happening in the Middle East, the economy wasn't a sexy story, and Peter Mansbridge had to have *something* to anchor, now, didn't he? "So it's El Niño again or something. I don't know. Freak stuff happens."

"I think it's global warming."

"Whatever."

"It doesn't worry you?"

"Sure." Not really a lie, but then it wasn't something he thought about much. Only when he channel-surfed by CBC and David Suzuki was scaring people on *The Nature of Things* again. "Not like I can do anything about it." He stood and walked down the stairs.

"I know you're skeptical, Ian, but if you heard me out, I think you'd change your mind."

He stopped, but made it clear that he was hovering, waiting for the slightest pause on her part to take off. "I doubt it."

"But how can you know—"

He lost his temper. The heat had him snappish. He knew he should just walk away, that you never win arguments like this, but all he felt was the need to do the mad dog snap. "Because I know I have better things to do with my time than sit in a circle, beat drums, tootle flutes, clap my hands, and indulge in weepy hugs and oh-we're-so-empowered laughter. What, you think sitting on your ass has any effect on the goddamn weather? What are you going to do, write 'greenhouse effect' on a slip of paper and burn it, and all will be well? And if you think lighting any kind of a fire is a good idea, then you are *really* out to lunch. Give me a break." And he left.

Not his brightest moment, he knew. The unwritten rule was not to come right out and insult people you had to live with, no matter how much they drove you nuts. Once the shouting started, the teams were drawn up, everybody was sucked into the mess, and the air would become poisonous. Like it wasn't hard enough to breathe already.

The view from the lodge was of swaying boreal forest. But walk into the woods and here was a revelation: the band of pines on the west side was very narrow. Beyond them was the ugly death scar of a 1991 windstorm. The wind had come through like a battering ram and had smashed the forest flat in a long band that ran from Kenora to Red Lake. The blowdown was a gray band on the land, hundreds of thousands of trees jumbled on top of each other, branches bleached by the sun into brittle javelins. Needles still clung to many of the branches, petrified in place by the suddenness of death. The corpses tangled together into a mass, huge, dense and sharp. Nature building the better barricade.

The stand of trees that had gone down at Ember Lake had been a graveyard to start with. Many of the trees had been balsam fir killed by budworm infestation. They had stood snap-dry, their own tombstones, until the wind had come. The storm had been a purging, taking out the infection, leaving the healthy trees on either side. The stand around the lodge was just wide enough to block the view of the blowdown. Chris Wurman, who managed the lodge, viewed this as sure proof that there was a God. The lodge had barely been completed when the storm had hit, and she had had visions of a career decapitated the first time an InSec VP showed up and saw a lodge sitting in the middle of a moonscape.

Wurman had initially made arrangements to have clearing equipment helicoptered in to try to clear the InSec land of the blowdown. But when Pembroke saw the aerial shots, the increased isolation of the lodge struck him. The blowdown blocked the path of even the most obstinate land-based vehicle plowing through the forest. He saw potential use. He ordered the work halted and filed the information away. It was a decade later, when he started working on the Kalashnikov and MAI deal, that he saw in the lodge the key to finalizing the sale.

His goal for the operation had now changed. The lodge's

usefulness had not. If anything, the inaccessibility was even more important.

Dix walked through the fringe of trees and reached the blowdown. This was his spot. It wasn't the usual choice. There was a small creek that ran past the northeast edge of the lodge's lawns, and a lot of the staff liked following the creek upstream until they were alone with it in the woods. Dix liked the blowdown better. He liked looking at it. He liked its size. He liked its attitude. He liked trying to come up with an image adequate to the task of describing what he saw. A timber river was the latest one he was working with. A frozen timber river. In raging flood. Not bad, but he wasn't sure about the water theme. It didn't deal with the way the sun radiated off the wood. And it didn't quite capture the hostility that he saw. The needles and spikes of branches warned him off. He knew if he tried to climb the damn thing he'd be asking for the gift of a broken leg at the very least, and an impalement or two as a bonus.

He leaned against the trunk of one of the standing pines while he thought. It was ninety-five degrees in the shade, but the creak of the trees somehow made him think he wasn't quite as miserably hot as he really was. His brain cooled down a bit, anyway. He felt a couple of guilt flashes. He fought them down. You weren't doing anyone favors by coddling stupidity. Still, would it hurt to apologize? If only to make the rest of the season run smoothly. And if that didn't work, at least he would have staked out the moral high ground for the coming campaign. Sure, what the hell. If he played this scene right, it might even help him get a leg over Evelyn Robinson, who seemed much less interested in things long term. Pleased with himself, he pulled away from the tree and headed back. He heard someone fire up a chainsaw. Probably Howie Gordon, stockpiling the firewood. Like they were going to need it.

Louden had been busy while he was gone, he saw as he approached. She'd collected some stones and had arranged them in a circle. She was sitting cross-legged in the middle of the circle, hands resting palms-up on her knees. She was breathing very consciously. Out in the sun. Without a cap. In the heat of the day. Dix felt his resolution evaporate. He almost kicked her circle apart. Instead he said, "You're going to get heat stroke." Louden opened her eyes and gave him a look that was equal parts accusation and pity.

"Well, isn't this just a kick in the pants," Blaylock said.

They'd gone as far as they could towards Ember Lake without dealing with the blowdown. But now they were entering the area purchased by Jewel Properties, and Blaylock knew that the blowdown lay between them and the lake. She'd hoped they'd be rid of the dead trees by now.

They'd rolled out of Montana on the 24th, a convoy of twelve trucks, staggered thirty minutes apart to avoid attention. They hooked up again every night. In North Dakota they went north, stopping just shy of the Canadian border. They gathered in Walhalla, hung around until nightfall, then found a gravel road running parallel to the border, and drove along it until they got to a treed area. They unloaded the weapons and carried them across the border, hiding them in the woods. Half the team stayed with the guns. The others went back to the trucks, drove on and, big gaps between each truck, crossed the border at the main Interstate 29 checkpoint, bold and smiling. They backtracked, picked up crew and weapons, then headed north through Manitoba. At Winnipeg they took the TransCanada. East then, into Ontario, through the Canadian Shield, until they hit 105, which took them up towards Red Lake. The turnoff to Ember Lake was a logging trail, and even that petered out miles before the target area. They were on foot for the last day. It wasn't fun, bushwacking while backpacking heavy firepower, but they made good progress, and here they were, with no sign of hostile forces. Except for the blowdown.

Blaylock shrugged out of her backpack. She kept her binoculars around her neck, and her C-7 slung over her back, and started to climb the trees. The blowdown was taller than she was, and there was no regularity to the pile. She had to go up three yards, then down two, then back up again, at the mercy of the world's biggest game of pick-up sticks. She took it slow, feeling good about her handholds before she moved her feet, testing each branch before she gave it her weight. A lot of wood snapped, smokepuffing dust. She could see places where she could have crawled under the trees if she'd wanted to. Shoots of green were pushing up from the ground.

She reached the top, and saw more wrecked timber stretching out ahead of her, a rough topography of angles and gaps. The blowdown was about two hundred yards wide, hugging the western wall of the valley, and then the forest started up again. To her left, going north, the ground rose. No sign of a lake, but she knew they were close.

So what now, cross the blowdown? It was doable. But she was reluctant to have the fallen timber at her back before she knew exactly where the target was. As an avenue of retreat, the blowdown sucked elephants.

Then she heard it: a chainsaw. The growl was coming from the stand of trees at the top of the rise. Objective located. She scrambled back to the militia. She gave them the thumbs up as she made her way down the slope of the dead trees. "Found it," she opened her mouth to say, but the new sound stopped her. They all heard it at the same time. They all looked up. They all saw.

Dix had just reached the deck when he heard the sound, the chopchopchop of helicopter blades. Forestry service out spotting for fires, he assumed, and started forward again.

Stopped. The noise was getting closer, and it sounded awfully loud, not so much chopchopchop after all, more the WOP WOP WOP of Vietnam movies. He turned around and went back outside to take a look.

Louden had forgotten her breathing and her circle and was staring straight up. Dix's eyes widened. This was no Forestry flyover in a Bell 206 Long Ranger. There were two helicopters, and they were big, twin-engined, and they were coming in low. They slowed as they came over the clearing. Their thunder filled the world. One of the birds hovered while the lead lowered into the lodge's front grounds. The wind from the blades made his eyes water. Something went hysterical at the back of his mind and said that it was nice to feel a breeze.

Dix's jaw flapped. The idiot going snake in his head launched into stupid, missing-the-point panic. We aren't ready, he thought. We weren't expecting anybody until the 7th. Then he decided there were probably other problems looming. The Bell 212 hesitated just above the ground. Its doors opened. Its interior had been stripped out, and it was packed solid with men in camouflage fatigues. They jumped out. Huge bundles were tossed out after them. Then the chopper lifted off, and the second one came down.

By the time the 212s had unloaded and flown off, all twelve of the seasonal staff had gathered in front of the lodge. They stuck close to each other and to the building. Evelyn Robinson was three feet away from where Dix stood at the bottom of the steps, but he didn't put his arm around her. He was too much in need of a hug himself.

There were thirty men on the grounds, busying themselves with the bundles. The men all looked big. One of them stepped forward. His hair was so blond it was almost white. His skin was sun-darkened leather. A spiderweb of white scars radiated out from the corner of his mouth, only partially hidden by his mustache. He said, "Who's in charge here, then?" He sounded South African.

"I am." Chris Wurman had emerged from the manager's office and stood at the top of the stairs. She was still holding a pen and a handful of papers.

"Ma'am," the man said, nodding a greeting. He pulled a pistol out of his waist holster and shot her in the forehead. She toppled sideways off the staircase and hit the ground with a loud thump. The back of her head was smeared on the door. Someone screamed.

"Medic!" the man called.

No one answered. Dix looked over to where Dr. Fuller was standing next to Robinson. Everyone else did too. "Ah," said the South African. Walked over to Fuller. He said, "Sorry, but we've got our own," and shot him too. The South African looked around. "Any questions so far?"

The screaming stopped. The echoes of the two gunshots ricocheted through Dix's head, working their way down to his gut.

"Great stuff. Now that we've laid down the ground rules, maybe we can get to work." The South African brushed past Dix. "Excuse me," he said.

Dix felt urine pour down his pants leg.

The South African marched up the stairs, opened the lodge door and stepped inside. He paused. "First thing we're going to do," he called out, "is get some bloody air conditioning going here."

23

August 1.

The *Bhopal* was the last of the freighters to pull out of St. Petersburg. Noonan stood by the gangway, ready to go back ashore as soon as he finished with Willson. "Vince, you still don't look happy," Noonan said. The captain didn't. He didn't look happy at the best of times, with basset hound eyes sunk deep in sea-wrinkled flesh. But today he was definitely a Prozac candidate.

Willson rubbed the gray stubble on his cheeks. "Just not wild about not knowing what I'm carrying and where I'm going, is all."

"You're going to the mid-Atlantic. That's pretty clear, you ask me."

"That's no goddamn destination."

"It is as far as you're concerned. Your need to know stops there. Seems to me you're being paid pretty generously to know nothing and do nothing. Or am I wrong?"

Willson shook his head quickly, but still looked pissed.

Noonan shifted his weight back and forth from heel to heel. The seaman was a full head taller than he was. Inflicting some corporal discipline would be a pleasure. And Noonan thought, amused, about Willson's reaction if he knew how many surface-to-air missiles he was carrying. The *Bhopal* was taking the bulk of the SA-7s. "Let's make this clear," he said. "Checkitout: you're being paid *not* to know. You're being paid *not* to care. You're being paid to do *squat*. Now that sounds like a pretty sweet deal to me. Wish I could land a gig like that. I mean, jeez, get paid twice the going rate to sit on my ass with my dick in my hands? Let me in on the scam."

"All right," said Willson.

Noonan clapped him on the back. "Atta boy. Now get this tub the hell out of here. You're already five minutes late."

He walked down the gangway to the dock. Sherbina was waiting for him, leaning against the limo. "Problems?" Sherbina asked.

Noonan shook his head. "Nah. Usual stuff. Just gotta crack the whip sometimes, is all."

Sherbina nodded knowingly. "Believe me, I've been there. But it's amazing what a little discipline will do for productivity."

Noonan couldn't fault Kornukopia's productivity. Once the price had finally been settled on, the weapons had been transferred here from Tula and Izhevsk with Stakhanovite efficiency. An armada of trucks had brought the whole works to St. Petersburg, and the loading had gone faster than Noonan had hoped. Hoops he had expected to have to jump through evaporated. No one had opened a single crate to inspect. He hadn't caught a whiff of a customs official, or any other uniform. The level of legal blindness impressed Noonan, and he made a careful note of it. If Kornukopia had this much clout, they were going to have to be watched. He behaved himself around Sherbina now, glad–handing and joking. He still hadn't forgiven him for the games, but he didn't want Sherbina thinking he needed taking care of. Not yet. Not ever. When the time came to whack Sherbina, he didn't want the Russian to see it coming.

"So," said Sherbina. "Our business comes to a conclusion."

"Yeah." Thank Christ, Noonan thought.

"Time for a drink at the club?" Sherbina asked.

Noonan looked at his watch. "Love to, but I should get to the airport." A lie to be gone: there was plenty of time before the plane.

He had three hours to kill at the airport after they left him. He paced, bored and edgy, wanting out of here and back to North America where the game was his, as it should be, and where the action was going to be. Then the wait finally ended, and he was off. Off to Ottawa. Off to the endgame.

August 5.

Ottawa. The G8. The gathering of the gray men. They'd arrived on the 1st. Roll call for the duly elected supreme wills of the people. Playing host, Frank Palliser, Prime Minister of Canada. Palliser stood and beamed as each head of state landed. They stood and beamed together for the press. They beamed as they shook hands all round. They beamed for the benefit of the television viewers. They beamed for the benefit of their people. They beamed for the benefit of history. They beamed for their image as the movers and shakers of the globe. They beamed for power. Outside the glare of the flashbulbs and arclights, they beamed not at all.

The Chateau Laurier was taken over for the duration of the summit. A grand old luxury dame of the Canadian Pacific, the Laurier was a green-roofed aristocrat of a hotel, chateau in appearance, chateau in service. It should have been able to make its dignitaries beam. Phone calls and messages from Pembroke made sure that they did not.

They had their meetings at the Congress Centre, safely isolated from the tear gas and the protests. They did the whole summit routine. It felt like even more of a farce than it usually was. They used words like "substantive" for the press conferences, but privately knew it had been a long time since any of them had come close to the reality of the term.

This evening there was the reception in the entrance hall of the National Gallery. Four storeys high, outside wall a huge pattern of windows sculpted into an expanse that was somehow both glass cathedral and schooner at full sail, the hall held a temporary exhibit of twentieth-century sculpture, moved out of the main galleries and supplemented just for the event: a really big show to entertain the shimmering glitterati of insubstantiality. First Wives and First Mistresses, ambassadors of the also-ran states, top-dog diplomats, the whole crew sipping champagne and nibbling caviar, rustling and sycophanting among the ignored trophies of High Art. Frank Palliser moved through the crowd, doing the beaming, and feeling the gray leach from his suit into his bones. He thought about how far he had fallen to get this high, and he didn't want to have anything to do with himself. Where did the university idealist go? Swallowed by the political pragmatist. Sent running by the realist, who knew there were compromises necessary in order to get things done.

It had been easy when he was on the back benches of the Opposition. The glory days of the early '90s, the days of unexpurgated opinion, of standing up and being counted, the take-no-prisoners terrier of the left wing of the Liberal Party. Even then he thought he was being realistic, the caring lawyer, the hard-edged fighter for social justice untainted by the dewy-eyed romanticism of the New Democrats, the cold-hearted, deficit-cutting, tunnel-vision of the Conservatives, or the bigoted psychosis of their up-and-coming bane, Reform.

But then came the fall of 1993, and the Liberals had been in power ever since, hacking and slashing at programs with a ferocity that stunned the obliterated Tories and stole thunder from the loose-cannon Reformers. And he had toed the line. Loyalty above all else. Play the game, that had been his new strategy. Do what you have to, then reform the system from within. And meanwhile there were things like the anti-landmine treaty he could throw in with, getting behind the Foreign Minster and earning his stripes. The treaty looked good in the PR, even if the major mine players had stayed home, and it reaffirmed his credentials for human rights even as he played footsie with the right wing headed up by the Finance Minister. And when the time came for a new leader, he was the compromise leadership candidate for the compromise party.

By then it was hard to remember what he had gone into politics to fight for in the first place. Now there didn't seem to be anything left but the game: the fight to keep the Party in power, the speaking of comforting lies, the asking of "how high?" whenever Moody's or Standard & Poor or the other high priests of the supreme deity Market said "jump." There were times, when he yammered convoluted nonsense he didn't for a moment believe, that he shuddered at the accusing memory of Pierre Trudeau. There was the Prime Minister whose actions had called him into the Liberal Party, if only to save it. He hadn't always agreed with the man, had often been horrified by his arrogance, but now thought with bitter envy of the politician who could approach the press with a grin like a shark closing in on a bleeding seal.

And look at me, Palliser thought. Who the hell really cares? He could remember, at the far end of the dim tunnel of his past, a young man, a fighter whose stomach wasn't a paunch, whose blond curls were not gray, and whose vision wasn't a bifocaled strain. A fighter who used the phrase "making a difference" and actually meant it. Now, he was supposedly in the position where he could make that difference, and he was even worse off than when he had started. Before, he had lacked the power to make that difference. Now, he knew that that power did not exist. And he didn't even have the will to fight for change anymore. Only the regret.

At least he wasn't alone. That was the real reason for these summits. The deals that meant something, even if they were expressed in droopingly unsexy legalese, were the Finance Minister summits, where Wall Street and Bay Street and all the myriad Exchanges had their say. The meeting of the G8 leaders was the support group for figureheads, where they got together to deny impotence. They talked tough about Iraq and terrorism. They took stands. They signed treaties with no details but lots of good words. They made each other feel better.

Palliser watched his cohorts move through the gallery, fellow passengers on the glamor train of obsolescence. Walter Campbell, the molded patrician, born and bred and wed to the game and no longer conscious of anything beyond it. Vladimir Belinski, eyes shadowed from the strain of presiding over the guttering flames of his country's stab at democracy. Matsushiro Kitamura, handed the job of standing witness to his economy's further decline and fall, the World Bank officiating. Edward Willis, Bernard Lévi and Werner Feher, revamped social democracy's great white hopes, gone gray as their illusory colors washed away. Of them all, Damiano Fulci seemed the most relaxed. There hadn't been an Italian leader who'd lasted long enough to matter since the war, so he was relieved of the pressure to perform.

Palliser snagged another champagne flute from a passing

waiter. It was his third glass, and he'd have to start watching it soon, but for now it was just making the evening more bearable. Someone touched his shoulder. Palliser turned. "Frank," said Willis. He moved his head towards the windows. "Join me a moment?" They walked over and stood beside a floor vent. Cool air wafted up. It felt nice. Beyond the huge window was a bush garden, kept green in spite of the drought by constant sprinkling.

Willis stared past the garden, looking toward the Parliament buildings. "I've been canvasing the others," he said. He looked like a man who hadn't been sleeping out his jet lag well. "Have you been approached by Arthur Pembroke?"

"Oh," said Palliser, "the whole InSec fiasco." They were speaking freely. The gallery had been swept and re-swept by overlapping and competing security forces. Anybody who got a bug in deserved to be rewarded. Palliser nodded. "He's been after everybody with that creepy letter promising full cooperation."

"Campbell thinks we should meet with him."

"If Campbell thinks that, it sounds to me like Pembroke has got his claws in deeper than Campbell would like."

Willis grimaced.

"You?" Palliser asked.

"We're pretty badly tangled. It's that bloody end-user certificate business. We brought down a law that pretended to ban sales to countries that are under UN arms embargoes, but it was toothless and a fiddle with Pembroke. If everything comes out, we'll be hammered."

"It would look bad for us too," said Palliser. Canada wasn't as big a player in the arms trade, and the direct government dealings with InSec weren't as big and as damning as the ones Willis was facing. They didn't have to be. Anything at all would look bad. Canada was still spearheading the drive toward the sequel to the landmine treaty: a clampdown on the international small-arms flow. Palliser's credibility would toilet dive if there was even a whiff of connection to InSec. And the treaty would be knocked into intensive care.

"I don't understand," Willis complained. "Is the man mad?"

"He seemed really angry about the MAI being scuttled again."

"The rest of us aren't throwing dangerous tantrums."

Palliser hadn't been that disappointed with the MAI going down. The agreement's revival had become a real hot-button topic in Canada, receiving the same kind of media attention as the Free Trade battles in the late '80s, and was generating the same kind of screaming matches as abortion. The Liberals had gone along with the MAI because they'd had no choice, but nobody was happy with what backing the agreement was doing to them in the polls. "He must have had a lot invested in it," he said.

"That's what worries me." Willis turned his head to look hard at Palliser. "Pembroke must have had more to gain with the MAI than we thought. Based on what we know, what he's doing is completely irrational and inexplicable. So there must be something else. It's as if InSec were about to go bankrupt without the deal."

Palliser snorted. "I'd find that hard to believe."

"So would I. But if it isn't that, then there must have been some huge gain involved, something that we didn't see."

"A power grab?"

Willis shrugged helplessly. "I don't know! I keep hoping someone knows, but so far nothing."

"I have something new since the last time we spoke, Edward," Vladimir Belinski broke in. They turned to face him. Belinski's voice was the deep Russian bass. It always sounded odd coming out of his slight frame. He was holding a champagne flute too, but his was filled with Canada Dry. Palliser knew that there were at least four Russian tabloids that had a standing reward offer for anyone who presented documented proof of alcohol passing Belinski's lips. So far, no one had collected. "I did not mean to eavesdrop," he said. He smiled apologetically.

Willis asked, "What's happened?"

Belinski looked even more apologetic. Frustrated too. "I wish I knew. I know that InSec has been involved in something very big in my country. But what?" He raised his hands. "Mystery. When I tried to discover, I was told to mind my business." He sipped his ginger ale.

The others looked away, as if avoiding the contamination of impotence. Belinski made no secret about the degree to which the mob had his hands tied. He had fought hard during his first year in office. Three of his strongest allies had been shot dead in their homes. Now the best he could do was complain, the best he could be was bitter.

"We," said Willis, "are being made to dance."

Palliser scanned the reception. "Is Pembroke here?" The Prime Minister's Office had extended an invitation to Pembroke in a placatory gesture. It was devoutly hoped that he would decline.

"No," said Willis, "but that Chatman toad is." He pointed.

Chatman was paying court to Walter Campbell. The president's wife, Helen, looked charmed. Campbell's face was very still. Belinski started in their direction.

"What are you going to do?" Palliser asked him.

Belinski shrugged and kept going.

"Might as well corner the rat," Palliser muttered, and followed.

"Careful," said Willis, keeping step. "Rats bite."

Bernard Lévi stood in front of a Henry Moore. The piece was huge, dominating the center of the floor. Across the room, through a hole in the sculpture, he saw Edward Willis and Frank Palliser walking toward Walter Campbell and

Terry Chatman. Right now Lévi wanted to put his big hands around Chatman's neck and squeeze. But right now he couldn't. Right now he had to listen to the High Commissioner from Australia. Right now he could feel his blood pressure rising to painful heights. He knew his face was flushed deep crimson.

"My government doesn't have any love lost for InSec either," the commissioner was saying, "but they're inclined to believe that the promised documentation will be pretty solidly supportable." She leaned forward, so he couldn't avoid her gaze unless he turned his head. She wasn't giving him any room to maneuver. "I don't think you want a repeat of the Rainbow Warrior mess, do you?"

Lévi worked to keep his voice down. "One. You are not New Zealand. Two. Bougainville is not your sovereign territory. Three. Australia's policies in that area are hardly blameless." Australia had been supporting the government of Papua New Guinea in putting down the Bougainville Revolutionary Army. Papua New Guinea depended on the Panguna copper mine on Bougainville for twenty percent of its GDP. The mine's majority shareholders were Australian. The natives of Bougainville didn't see a red cent. They got mad. The army got brutal. There had been nastiness on both sides. But it was the government that had burned villages. "I'm sure InSec could tell us some interesting things about Australian involvement with civilian atrocities."

The commissioner didn't blink. She'd been in the game longer than Lévi, and knew how to play hard and dirty. "But they're not threatening to do that, are they? What they are offering to be most helpful with is details of French gun-running in the area, an activity that has exacerbated the conflict. And don't tell me you've been letting this happen out of the goodness of your heart and concern for the oppressed indigenous peoples. That's a nice mine they have there."

"I really don't know why you're telling me this." That

was code for "What do you want?" But he wasn't going to give her the satisfaction of asking right out.

"I'm just suggesting that you back off," she said airily. "That would be a good way of making sure this particular scandal doesn't come to light. Of course," she gestured with her glass, "from what I hear, there are plenty more that are going to be keeping you busy. How's tricks in Rwanda?" She patted him on the arm and left. Her perfume lingered a moment, a laughing insinuation. Lévi clenched his fists and glared across the gallery at Chatman.

Chatman charmed the wives. Chatman showed his teeth. Chatman invited the gray men to meet with Arthur Pembroke at his lodge. And the gray men huddled.

Werner Feher asked, "Do we go?"

Palliser grunted. "Do we have a choice?"

"We always have a choice," Campbell said.

"But not always a good one," Belinski put in.

"He's enjoying this," said Willis, spitting bile and helplessness. "He's blackmailing us and rubbing our faces in it."

Palliser sympathized. It was bad enough to have to dance to the multinationals' tune. But at least they usually had the grace to give you some kind of illusion of autonomy. Pembroke's out-and-out blackmail was crossing the line, trashing the illusions. Why bully so outrageously? It wasn't necessary. Unless. "Why is he blackmailing us?" Palliser asked. "Here's what I think: he wouldn't be this unsubtle if he had a choice."

Campbell shook his head. "I don't know, Frank. We've checked into InSec's finances. They're taking a hit with all the negative publicity, but that's temporary. They're still deep in the black. I don't think Pembroke even knows what red ink looks like."

"Well, then, it's something else."

Matsushiro Kitamura was nodding, grinning. "You're

right. And if he's desperate, that means he's weak somewhere."

"So we go?" Belinski asked.

Campbell nodded. "What about security?" he asked, looking pointedly at Palliser.

They all knew what he was asking: were they going to stand in the way of his agents? It wasn't really a question. Belinski wasn't likely to object. Given the shifting sand he stood on, he probably trusted Campbell's troops more than his own. No one else had the resources Campbell could summon. And Palliser doubted they were inclined to let the RCMP handle this. Covert had never been their strong suit. "Okay, Walter, your boys," Palliser said. "But listen: Pembroke walks away. You want wet work done, you do it in your sandbox."

Campbell looked amused, gave him the smile you give a chihuahua trying to be fierce, but nodded. A favor granted. Belinski laughed and clapped. His drink slopped over the glass.

24

The briefing was finished. Paul Kuhn stood to leave. They were in the president's suite in the Chateau Laurier. It was late, but they were both used to working these hours. Campbell watched as the Secret Service man gathered up his briefcase. The case always looked like a theatrical prop when Kuhn carried it. He wasn't a suit-and-attaché man, and it showed. It wasn't that he was huge, or that his face was a killmap of scars. It was the way he moved: his center of gravity never shifted to a position where he could be pushed off-balance. He was a machine on perpetual stand-by. His face was poker-bluff calm, though his eyes moved a lot. Right now, though, they were staring straight down at his case. That meant Kuhn was thinking. "The option that Mr. Korda discussed with me in Washington . . ." Kuhn began.

Campbell knew what Kuhn meant: the hit on Pembroke. "Keep all options open," he told Kuhn. "But I'm not anticipating needing that particular one. What I want, above all else," said Campbell, "is total control over the space. Got it? Not even unauthorized insect movement."

Kuhn walked down the hall to his suite. He was impressed with himself. He'd kept a straight face during the entire briefing.

Noonan met Jack Lentricchia in the bar of the Hyatt-Regency. Pembroke was staying here: in Ottawa, so he could keep on top of the chess movements, but away from the Laurier and the political action. If any of the G8 leaders wanted to speak to him, the only way that was going to happen was if they came to the lodge. The two men sat in a corner booth, knocking back the Guinness.

"You're right," Noonan said. "He is different." He'd needed the two-month absence in Russia to see the change when he got back. Lentricchia had mentioned his concern when Noonan arrived late on the 1st. He'd watched Pembroke carefully over the last few days.

Lentricchia said, "He's squirrely. I mean, look at the money he blew on the Russia thing." They shared sorrowful looks. The more Noonan had thought about it, the less happy he'd been with Pembroke's cave-in to Sherbina. Lentricchia went on, "It started after his daughter died. You don't think...." Lentricchia stopped and glanced around the bar, as if Pembroke might suddenly loom up behind.

"I don't think what?"

Lentricchia didn't answer. He'd come as close to the heresy as he dared.

Noonan shook his head. He downed the rest of his Guinness and opened another. They had each bought three cans to start with. This conference was serious business. They didn't want to interrupt it more than was absolutely necessary. "He knows what he's doing. I mean, sure, we're spending a lot. But this is high-stakes stuff. The payoff is going to be goddamn huge." He wanted to believe this. Lentricchia didn't look convinced. He was picking at a bar coaster, stripping the cardboard into little curls. "You ain't buyin'," Noonan said.

Lentricchia backed off. "Well, maybe. I dunno." He looked down at his hands. He tore the coaster in half. "Damn it, you haven't been with him all the time, Karl. He's reckless." He whispered the last sentence. By Lentricchia's standards, he had just spoken outright mutiny.

Noonan opened his mouth to argue, changed his mind. He didn't know for sure. He had his own doubts. Lentricchia had been much closer to the scene of the action. So let's say Lentricchia was right. Let's say Pembroke was playing on the edge a lot more than was normal. Was this bad? Figure it out. "Checkitout," he told Lentricchia. "What's the worst that could happen?" Lentricchia said nothing, waiting for Noonan to work out his thought. "Maybe InSec takes a bath on this deal. Is that gonna kill you and me?" Lentricchia shrugged. Noonan spread his hands. "The Christmas bonus ain't so hot. We don't get those swimming pools we wanted. We still pay hookers by the hour instead of the night. So?" He was minimizing a bit. Pembroke's hard men earned generous percentages. And Noonan hadn't had anything less than a top-flight call girl since 1993. That wasn't about to change. He and Lentricchia weren't about to go bankrupt. It would take more than one bad deal to queer InSec seriously.

"Yeah," said Lentricchia, "no biggie." He sounded subdued.

"But checkitout, Jack. If Bossman's taking some chances and swinging wide and hard, I'd say we might be looking at some righteous action." His gambit in New York had wetted his appetite. Having to hold back and be polite in Russia had made him antsy. The prospect of playing with triggers made him very happy. He reached over and punched Lentricchia on the shoulder.

Lentricchia didn't look up. He sighed. It was a big sigh, raising his shoulders high and slumping them down again, catching three times when he inhaled, hissing out long when he exhaled. "Dunno. Getting old."

"You thinking of getting out?"

Lentricchia shrugged, shook his head. It wasn't the answer Noonan wanted. The shake did not mean *no*. It meant *don't give me a hard time*. "I'm just getting tired," Lentricchia explained. "It's getting to be too much like work."

August 6.

More choppers. Not civilian this time. US government crests on them.

"You see them?" Blaylock asked Charlie.

He had. He looked grim. "Those other birds weren't American," he said.

"No. Probably rented privately and overhauled. But not carrying tourists."

Charlie watched the helicopters through the binoculars. "When do we attack?"

"Not yet. Pembroke's not here."

"How do you know he isn't?"

"Our man inside. He'll be coming with Pembroke, and he has a bug on him. When he gets to the lodge, he'll be within range again and I'll start picking the bug up. Hasn't happened yet." She watched the helicopters as they circled the area. "I think we should fall back a ways," she said. "Get everyone under good cover. These guys are taking a hard look at the ground."

"So far, so good," Paul Kuhn told the pilot. "Looks clean. Let's go down."

The Bell 205 dropped. There was barely enough room for it to land in the lodge's front grounds. The back and sides were even worse.

The staff of the lodge was gathered outside to watch. They looked scared. Kuhn smiled at them as he disembarked. The rest of his team, all suits and earphones, followed behind. The 205 flew off to the helipad on the lake. "Hi," Kuhn said to the staff once the sound of the rotors had faded. "My name's Paul Kuhn, and I'm with the US Secret Service. We're here to secure the site for the G8. We'll be needing your cooperation, naturally, and I thank you in advance for it." The staff stood still. They didn't look either surprised or thrilled at the prospect of playing host for the world leaders. They did still looked scared.

"I was wondering if I could have a volunteer?" Kuhn asked. No one stepped forward. "How about you?" He pointed to a woman who was actually *trembling*. She almost fainted when she saw he was talking to her. He walked over. "Hey there, don't freak out. We're just here to make everything safe." He held up his hands. "Look: harmless." He paused, then asked, "Do you think you could be my guide around your fine establishment? Show me and my team the various facilities?" She nodded, and he walked back to the other thirteen agents. "Okay. Anderson, Fields, Rothermel, you're with me. Keeley, you stay with the staff. The rest of you, spread and do the grounds. I want a fine-tooth comb, people. There's a lot of cover here."

The Service went to work. Kuhn turned to face the lodge staff again. "I'm going to ask the rest of you to wait outside with Agent Keeley. And even before that, we're going to have to check you for weapons." He shrugged an apology. "You know how it is." When the frisks were done, Kuhn turned to the trembling woman. "Okay, Miss . . .?"

"Louden."

"I'm all yours. Give me the ten-dollar tour. After you."

The enclosed deck was first, five sides of an octagon.

Then the entry to the lodge proper, with the grand foyer: a full octagon, staircases hugging the walls east and west in a circular climb to the second floor. The foyer opened up into a huge diamond divided lengthwise by a wall made up of a massive stone fireplace. The left side of the diamond was a lounge. The right was the dining room. The color in both rooms was deep brown. The brown was oak tables and chairs in the dining room, deep leather armchairs in the lounge. Each half of the diamond had a massive wag-onwheel candelabra hanging from the ceiling. "Nice," Kuhn commented. And then, "Where is the generator kept?"

"There's an outbuilding in the back. It's where we keep the generator and the propane."

Kuhn nodded. "We'll look at that later."

Louden took them through the lounge. Doors opened into the manager's office, a billiard room, a trophy room and the kitchen office. A hallway led off the left-hand corner of the lounge. Louden led Kuhn down it. Storage, electrical, washroom, doctor's office. Dance floor and, at the end of the wing, a bar with an enclosed patio. Everything clean, every-thing top of the line.

They went back to the lounge. A door in the rear led to the kitchen. Kuhn took in the hanging utensils, the gleam-ing steel. The floor here was tile. The other three agents checked the two storage and two freezer rooms. Kuhn looked out the rear exit. He saw the outbuilding Louden had mentioned, blending in with the trees. Beyond the trees, he could see the rise of the valley. It couldn't get more picturesque. He looked at the kitchen again, nodded to himself, then followed Louden into the dining room.

Off on the sides were another bar and a private dining room. The bar in the other wing had been rustic-casual in theme. The bar in this wing was darker. The theme was still in the country, but now the tone was lord-of-the-manor. A painting of a fox hunt. Embossed horses' heads. Wood so dark it was almost black. You would speak quietly in here.

The private dining room was the same class. The table and chairs were Old World. The hallway in this wing had the conference room on the left. Long table, papers and pens all laid out, chairs less elegant than in the dining room, but a lot more comfortable. Big windows for staring off into space. Beyond the conference room the corridor doglegged, and Louden stopped.

"What's up next?" Kuhn asked.

"The . . . the staff and manager's rooms." Louden's eyes were jumping.

"Is something wrong?"

She shook her head, trembling.

Kuhn left her behind, took the dogleg, and checked each room. Louden was staring at him, eyes very big, when he got back. Anderson, Fields and Rothermel looked a question at him. "Come with me," Kuhn said.

Ron Whitmore reached the blowdown. He exchanged looks with Larry Biswell. Biswell said, "Looks even worse from the ground."

Whitmore nodded. They'd seen the blowdown from the air, but the magnitude of the problem hadn't registered. He wished that they'd spent a bit more time on the aerial recon, so he'd know if there were any more surprises like this. There probably were. The place was a security nightmare. The blowdown did have one solid advantage. If they could secure it, it would make a fabulous perimeter guard on this side. No one was going to get over it in a blink and a flash. But the problem was how to secure it. Whitmore gazed at the jumble of trunks, and saw thirty great hiding places just in the stretch nearest him. It would take weeks to sanitize this mess.

They walked along the edge, seeing more problems all the time. Partway to the lake, Whitmore crouched down and saw a crawl space beneath the trunks. He couldn't tell how far it went. He shook his head. "This can't be for real," he said, straightening up.

"I don't think we're going to be able to use this," Biswell said.

"Yeah. But what do we do with it, then? We can't exactly rake it up and leave it at the bottom of the driveway." He still liked the idea of turning the blowdown into a defensive wall, but Biswell was right. There was no way of plugging all the holes on this thing. It would never be an ally. It was always going to be a risk. If someone was in there now, they probably wouldn't find him without smoking him out. Whitmore broke a branch, felt it snap loud and dry. No. Smoke would be a bad idea. "Secure the area, my ass."

"All agents," Kuhn's voice spoke in Whitmore's earphone. He and Biswell stopped to listen. "Immediate rendezvous kitchen of lodge," said Kuhn.

Whitmore and Biswell acknowledged, and started to run.

"Gentlemen," Kuhn said, "we have a problem." He kept his voice low. They were gathered in the kitchen, crowding around the central counter. The staff of the lodge had been ordered to remain outside.

"I'll say," said Biswell. "You have to see this pile of dead wood, Paul. I don't think it's resolvable."

"It's worse than that," said Kuhn. "And keep your voice down."

Uh oh, Whitmore thought. "Hostiles?" he asked. Kuhn nodded. "Where?"

Kuhn put his finger to his lips. "Let me show you something," he said. He moved to the rear exit door. Opened it. Stepped out. Whitmore began to think *no*. Then the back door, the doors to the dining room and the lounge, and the door to the storage rooms and the freezers all opened at once. The kitchen was filled with men with assault rifles. There was really only a second's pause. Whitmore still had time to think *surrounded* and *turkey shoot*. He dropped, reaching into his vest for his gun.

Death was a standing O, the harsh CRACK CRACK applause of the rifles going off. Muzzle flares and the wet slap of meat hitting the wall. Somebody screamed. Whitmore felt a body land on him, pinning him down with dead weight. His head hit the floor and pain blossomed. He ignored it, fought his way out from under the body. He got up, crouching, to return fire. Mistake. A round hit him in the chest. His Kevlar vest took the damage but the impact knocked the breath from him and threw him backwards. He willed himself through the pain, twisted as he fell and had his gun up as he hit the floor. He fired and took the merc at the door in the throat. The man fell. The doorway was clear. Opportunity. He took it. He scrambled up, feet sliding, nothing moving fast enough. He heard a shout behind him. He launched himself forward, looking back as he did. A gun muzzle had him dead on. Biswell jumped in the way. Biswell jerked, the side of his head disintegrating as the bullet exited.

Whitmore hit the door and rolled out into the dining room. He fired back into the kitchen. A merc had followed him out, and Whitmore's round took him in the knee. He collapsed, yelling, and blocked the door. Another gift of two seconds. Whitmore ran. Something sank fangs deep into his left shoulder, and he lost feeling in his arm. He kept going. Two other bullets whistled by him and dug wood out of the wall. Then he was through the dining room, into the foyer, and the exit was ahead.

Kuhn ran for the helipad. He had his pistol drawn. In the distance, he could hear the chatter of guns coming from the lodge. The pilot, Newell, had the door of the helicopter open and was leaning out. Kuhn ran up and shot him between the eyes.

A bullet snicked Kuhn's vest and ricocheted off the helicopter. He whirled. Whitmore, blood pouring down a limp arm, coming down the slope, yelling. His right arm up, gun pointing. Kuhn ducked and threw himself to the left. The second bullet hit the ground in front of his nose. Whitmore was a crack shot. If he hadn't been wounded, Kuhn would be dead. Kuhn fired, no time to aim. He got Whitmore in the chest, smack in the goddamn Kevlar. Whitmore fell down anyway, his third shot going wild. Kuhn had the time to aim. He took it, nailed Whitmore good and dead.

Kuhn stood, leaned against the helicopter and caught his breath. He listened to the gunfire. It tapered off quickly. Soon there was just the occasional burst. Mop-up, he thought. Jacob Van der Wat and the boys preparing the lodge for its guests. Time for Kuhn to sink the 205 in the lake.

25

August 8.

Flanagan struggled up the last of the climb from Ember Lake. He wasn't carrying much—clothes for four days and his computer—but the heat was sucking the strength from him. Sweat poured into his eyes, stinging. He paused and shifted his suitcase to his other hand. He'd dumped a lot of what he'd packed in Ottawa, convinced he wouldn't be needing it again. The case had felt light this morning. Now it weighed a ton. The climb from the moored helipad had been a coalwalk through Hell. Pembroke was up ahead, not carrying anything (he had Lentricchia to do that, who had shifted from helicopter pilot back to bodyguard and porter), but dressed in a dark business suit. Flanagan knew Pembroke was sweating, could see it, but the man moved as if it were New York October outside. Bastard.

They reached the clearing. Flanagan took in the lodge. It

looked nice. So this, he thought, is where I'm going to die. He supposed there were worse places. He hoped Pembroke thought so too. I'm not the only one going down, Arthur, believe it.

"Whaddaya think, Mike?" Noonan, dressed like a TV ad for African safaris, had come up next to him. When Flanagan didn't respond, Noonan continued, "Hey, cheer up. You're on holiday." Noonan flashed a grin that had eaten much shit, and marched on to catch up with Pembroke.

Flanagan noticed a tall antenna that had been installed on the roof of the lodge. A relay tower to boost the cell transmission from NAVCON. Pembroke was making sure that there was no way his new toy wasn't going to work.

Two men in camouflage, cradling M-16s, stood by the two sets of stairs to the lodge. They snapped salutes for Pembroke as he drew near. He acknowledged them with a nod. The lodge door opened and two other men walked out. One of them was huge, with evilbad scars on his face. The other was dressed in a suit darker than Pembroke's. Noonan whooped and embraced the man in the suit. Lentriccchia and the giant punched shoulders. Flanagan gave them a wide berth and followed Pembroke into the lodge.

Someone who looked for all the world like a student on a summer job came running to meet him. He tried to take Flanagan's bag from his hand. Flanagan glanced ahead. Pembroke was already being led up the left-hand staircase by someone else. Flanagan took another look at the man standing beside him. He looked terrified. He had a name badge reading "Ian Dix." Maybe he really was a student, after all. "Do you like working here?" Flanagan probed, letting go of the suitcase.

"Oh yes, sir, wonderful job, sir." But he'd paled when Flanagan asked.

"Lucky you," said Flanagan, low and sarcastic.

Dix stared at him. Flanagan nodded slowly, trying to

convey knowingness and fellowship. Dix smiled slightly. It was a frightened smile, with no real hope. Just as well: Flanagan wasn't sure he had any to give. But there was gratitude: at least you aren't all monsters. At least there's another one of us.

The central part of the upper floor was open, looking down on the diamond of the lounge and dining room. Dix took Flanagan down the west wing, and stopped at the next-to-last doorway on the right. "Mr. Pembroke is in the next room down," Dix said.

"Your best suite, I take it."

Dix nodded. He unlocked Flanagan's room. "It connects to a room on the other side. Very spacious."

"Is Mr. Noonan staying in that adjoining room?"

"Yes." Dix opened the door. Flanagan stepped into his room. It was big. A window dominated the outside wall, looking out onto the lodge's front grounds. The bed was king-sized, four-poster. Ridiculous in the surroundings, but so what. There was a walnut desk next to the window. Dix put Flanagan's case down next to the bed. He turned to go.

"Thanks," Flanagan said, and automatically reached into his pocket for a tip.

Dix laughed, weak and bitter, and shook his head. Flanagan nodded and dropped his wallet on the desk. "Enjoy your stay, sir," Dix said, in a tone that indicated a black joke between them.

"Thank you. I will," said Flanagan, just as dark.

Dix left, pulling the door closed behind him. Flanagan turned slowly. The room should have been a cell, either monastic or condemned. He sat on the bed, and the mattress tried to pull him into its embrace. Another joke with him as the butt. All this comfort, and what the hell was the point? He was going to die. He believed it. He accepted it. And it was accepting the fact that allowed him to get past the worst of his fear and gain strength from his anger. He got up, walked to the window and looked down. More

InSec mercenaries strolled past. He shook his head. A lot of firepower out there. Blaylock was good, but she couldn't be *that* good. It would take pretty miracles to get out of here alive. He wasn't going to count on them. So yes, he was going to die. But he was taking InSec down with him. Somehow or other, between him and Blaylock, there was a big corporate fall coming up. Give him the opportunity, give him the right moment, hive him the right fulcrum so he could use the lever of his back door in NAVCON, and it would be crash and burn time for Pembroke.

"Thank you. I will," Flanagan's voice crackled out of the receiver. The reception was iffy, but good enough. He was in the lodge. So was Pembroke. So was Noonan. The ducks were lined up. Blaylock was on a forward recon. She was crouched behind a log halfway across the blowdown. At the militia base camp they had heard the Astar approach, and Blaylock had moved forward to see if she could tell who it was this time. They had heard the firefight yesterday, and Blaylock guessed who had won. She'd seen some nervous faces in the militia while they'd listened to the echoing *pock-pock-pock* of the guns. No games this time. Live fire, playing for keeps. It had sounded small, like firecrackers, but the meaning was huge. Blaylock had taken advantage of the lesson. "Let's not make any mistakes," she'd said.

Now she put her binoculars down. She wished she could get closer. She couldn't see anything through the screen of trees. Never saw anyone except when a patrol would walk past the eastern edge of the blowdown. She'd noticed that they seemed relaxed, which was good. They didn't believe anyone else was out here, and were only going through the motions of mounting a guard. Advantage to the visiting team. She also had an idea of their numbers. With two Bell 212s, there couldn't be any more than thirty. Maybe they'd taken some losses yesterday. If they had, there weren't many more of them than there were Liberty Raiders. Though she had no doubt the training would be on the InSec side. As for disposition of forces, who knew? Getting close enough to find out would probably mean engaging. No good. She wanted to engage on her own terms. If what she was setting up worked, then she would get what she wanted.

She rested a hand against a branch. It had been bleached smooth by wind and sun, and was so hot it almost burned her skin. She tightened her grip on the branch until the heat faded, beaten. She thought about Flanagan, deep in the lion's den. She wanted to get him out now. She wanted to storm the battlements and haul him out on the back of her charger. And that was all well and good, that was a nice thing to want. But her armor had stopped shining a long time ago. It was stained pretty damn dark. She sighed. She would have to live with that. There was worse to come. She hoped the worse wasn't Flanagan dying. *I'm going to get you out, Mike, I promise.*

But she still had to wait. It wasn't enough that both Pembroke and NAVCON were there. She could have killed him in New York if that was all she was working for. When she'd first arrived there, that had seemed like enough. But she still didn't know what Pembroke was planning. She had to know what it was, had to know that the assault would be enough to stop it, had to know that the timing was right. If she hit too soon, she would never get another chance. If she was going to have the weight of many deaths on her conscience, then she had damn well better win the war.

She started back over the blowdown. She wanted to see that the ambush was being properly set up. The attack wasn't for now, but it would be for soon, and she wanted Pembroke to know that he was facing real opposition, a war machine come to tear up his stratified organization.

The sunlight caught it, dagger glint in the sky. She saw it before she heard it. She stopped and raised her binoculars. She heard the buzz of the float plane at the same time as it

David Annandale

came into focus in the glasses. She thought, *Now* who is this? The plane was going down. It was going to land on the lake. Blaylock moved back to her lookout spot. She waited to hear what Flanagan's bug might tell her.

"Those are not your men," said Belinski.

"*He* is," Campbell said, pointing to Kuhn.

They had all just walked up from the lake, sweaty and grumpy that they hadn't been brought in by helicopter and deposited on the front lawn. Pembroke already showing them their place? Likely. Campbell had seen an InSec helo on the helipad. Pembroke had no doubt arrived in style. Either that or he'd deliberately walked up from the lake just to grant himself some kind of specious moral superiority in the bargain. Campbell wouldn't put it past him.

"Perhaps he is your man," Belinski answered. It was clear that he thought Campbell's trust misplaced. "But the others are not."

The Russian was right. Campbell knew it. Had known things had all gone wrong as soon as he had seen the unfamiliar faces and fatigues. But he hadn't wanted to know it. Kuhn had radioed in that the operation was successful. And there he was, kicking back under the overhang of the deck's roof. He was giving Campbell the thumbs up. Campbell didn't like the agent's grin, but he still wanted to believe that Belinski was making a mistake. Then Terry Chatman jogged past him, made a beeline for Kuhn. Campbell's heart sank. The two men talked briefly. Kuhn laughed. Campbell knew he was screwed.

Chatman turned to face the gray men. "Gentlemen, on behalf of Arthur Pembroke and Integrated Security, welcome."

The G8 rooms were in the east wing. Campbell changed suits, then sat down on the edge of the bed to think through his options. He couldn't think of a single one. He had been frisked when he stepped into the lodge, and his cell phone had been taken from him. So no outside communication. He and the others would be missed if they didn't return home per the schedule, but Pembroke *had* to have taken that into account. He was taking too lunatic a risk to play it stupid. So he still had two days, three at the outside, to do whatever it was he wanted. Campbell's options: play along, do what Pembroke wanted, or ...? Here's what you do, he told himself. Know the layout. Find the angle. Slip through the loophole. There was always a loophole. Clinton had shown that, and Campbell could top him. He didn't have his apparatus of friends here, but the principles still held. Ferocity was weakness. Pembroke had calmed down since those first crazy phone calls: no screaming and threatening, just presiding in the shadows like a goddamn Dark Lord. But the craziness had been there. That impulse had been first. It might be buried, but it was still there. That was the weakness. So dig it up. Grab it. Twist it. That would open up the loophole.

He stood up. Layout first. Time for an infobinge. Grab everything and anything he could. He strode to the door, tried it. Wasn't locked, at least. He was going to be allowed to wander. That was already a mistake. He opened the door and stepped into the corridor. Kuhn was lounging against the wall opposite. Now *there* was someone who was going to learn a thing or two about payback. Campbell felt rage boil up, but he held it down, kept it cold.

"Mr. President," Kuhn said. He didn't straighten up. He lowered his head, peered over his sunglasses at Campbell. He didn't smile, but the grin was all over his body. "Getting settled, I hope."

"Tell me, Paul," Campbell said, eyes lidded, "how long have you been a traitor?"

Kuhn looked at him seriously now. "Never. I've always been loyal. Just not to you."

Campbell snorted and turned away. He was just reaching the end of the hallway when Kuhn called out: "Mr. President!" Campbell looked back. Kuhn was still leaning against the wall. He wasn't even looking in Campbell's direction. "And what are you loyal to, Mr. President?" Kuhn asked.

Campbell didn't answer. He stormed away from Kuhn and down the staircase to the grand foyer. He felt sick to his stomach. This isn't good, he told himself. You're the one supposed to be doing the cage-rattling. Let them get to you and you might as well just give up. He walked out of the foyer into the lounge. Damiano Fulci was sitting back in an armchair, brandy at his side, reading *The Globe and Mail*. He looked completely relaxed. Campbell was floored. He walked up to the Italian prime minister. Fulci looked up from his paper. "Walter," he said. "Sit down and join me?" He folded the paper and put it aside.

"You seem to be very calm about everything that's going on here."

Fulci shrugged.

"You *do* know what's going on." Campbell was beginning to have his doubts.

"I do not know all the details," he lilted. His accent always distracted Campbell. He found it hard to take the man seriously. Then again, he didn't take the prime minister's country seriously, either. "I do not know what precisely Mr. Pembroke has planned," Fulci went on. "But I do know that we are at his mercy. These guards," Fulci looked around. There were none there at the moment. "These guards," he repeated, "are not our friends."

"And that doesn't bother you."

"It does not please me. But I know when I am helpless." He sipped his brandy. "This is excellent. You should have some." When Campbell stepped away, Fulci picked up his newspaper again. "You will exhaust yourself with all this struggling, Walter," he said as he leafed through to find his page.

"And have you ever exhausted yourself?"

Fulci nodded. "Very much so. Every day of my life until the end of my fourth month as prime minister." He looked up at Campbell and smiled, beatific. "Then I finally learned what good all my struggles were doing. None."

"So what are your plans? Are you just going to go along with Pembroke?" Campbell didn't try to disguise his contempt.

Fulci wasn't bothered. "I think that is very likely, unless a reasonable way of resisting is proposed. Which I doubt. And then I will go home, and when my term ends," he laughed at the preposterousness of the idea, "or my coalition collapses, I will retire, and cultivate my garden. For now, however, I will read my newspaper."

Campbell left him to it. Fulci was useless, had already surrendered. So don't count on him. Campbell wandered the halls, memorizing the floor plan. He didn't know what good that would do, but the exercise helped. It felt like action. He didn't see any of the other leaders in the west wing, and he understood why. This was merc country. There were a dozen of them in the billiard room. When he poked his head in, they turned and gazed at him as if he were a fourteen-point buck in hunting season. He ducked back out quickly, his throat drying. There were more of them in the bar and on the patio. The dance hall had been turned into a barracks. There were two guards posted outside, and Campbell didn't catch more than a glimpse into the room as he walked past. He saw bedrolls, and he saw weapons.

He saw the strangulation closing of any loophole.

26

There is a nightmare weather formation called an Omega Block. It is shaped like a horseshoe, and the prevailing winds move around it, taking changes in the weather with them. Within the horseshoe, there are no changes.

The drought and the heat were continent-wide. It felt like an Omega Block sat over all North America, killing the land with stasis. That wasn't the case. A Block wasn't the only way to dessicate. Where there was an Omega Block was over Ontario, and here was the true stillness of the summer furnace. On August 9, the Block wavered slightly. Not much, not enough to disturb seriously the hellfire stability of the atmospheric conditions over Ember Lake, but enough to make a wind. It blew from the west. And with that, free will ceased to be a factor.

Pembroke kept the gray men waiting. They got through the night in a limbo of sleepless staring, cold-sweat sheets and a fear of guns. And they did not know what he wanted. They got up in the morning expecting the ultimatum, but instead they got breakfast served by the frightened staff. In the lodge and on the grounds, they saw the guns, and got the message. But they did not know what he wanted. They got through the morning one breath at a time, and the tension was honed fine by boredom and confusion. Chatman moved through them, glad-handing and speaking volumes of nothing. They wanted to hurt him. They wanted to kill him. But Noonan was never far away, and even if they didn't know him, they feared him.

But they did not know what Pembroke wanted.

Breakfast was held in the main dining room. The G8 sat clustered around two central tables that they had pushed together. Flanagan ate a few tables away, watching the leaders. He felt a number of things, but none of them was awe. An epiphany, colored the dirty despair of coal fog, spread ill and draining through him. He was looking at what his old belief system told him were the elected rulers of the world. He was looking at what should have been a nexus of power. What he saw was eight anxious and gray men. They were the crowns of society, but they were constitutional monarchs, the magna carta of capital and market stripping them of all but stewardship, the ability to choose between minor variations on a theme. Select one war from column A and one initiative from column B. Deviate and be slapped down. These men were not power. They were its front men. And they were turning into the weeping softness and disappointment of impotence.

Flanagan wondered: Is Pembroke power? At first he thought yes. The whole game proved that. But then he wondered. The game was too elaborate, too desperate in its deaths, to be the simple deployment of power. If Pembroke was absolute, why was this necessary? A new image came to mind: Pembroke riding the power flow, able to tap it enough to lightning-strike his opponents, but still not owning it. Riding it, riding it, adapting to the wild bucks, going where it wanted, giving it the lead. Riding it. Why? To tame it. To finally control it and *be* it.

A short circuit was needed. The power had to slip from Pembroke's grasp and electrocute him. Flanagan received no hope from the epiphany. He saw only enormity and impossibility. He saw the impotence as a brave acceptance of truth. He felt brotherhood with men of greatness. He felt kinship in shared helplessness. He wondered how many of them knew what he knew about power. He wondered how many of those accepted the knowledge. He didn't accept it, did he? He felt the helplessness, but the anger was still there, the refusal to bow and scrape, the need for vengeance that was the truly human steel. He was still going to fight.

1400 hours. The summons finally went out. The gray men filed into the conference room, gray in their faces and gray in their souls. Pembroke sat at the head of the table, flanked by Chatman at his right, Flanagan willy-nilly at his left. Noonan and Lentricchia stood behind and watched the room. Flanagan glanced at the notebook computer that sat on the table in front of Pembroke. It crossed his mind to grab and smash, end NAVCON now. He dismissed the idea. He'd have both his arms broken before he'd even fixed his grip on the machine. He raised his gaze and saw that Pembroke was looking at him. Pembroke's mouth was neutral, but there was sick amusement in his eyes. Flanagan let him see the hatred in his own. The war was not over. He wanted Pembroke to know that. It would not be over until one of them was dead.

Pembroke spoke. "Gentlemen. I think we can now finally get down to business. Mr. Chatman?"

Chatman opened his attaché case and pulled out a stack

of reports. He distributed them around the table. Flanagan looked at the cover of his copy. THE MULTILATERAL AGREEMENT ON INVESTMENT, it read. PROPOSED TEXT OF THE AGREEMENT, AND A STUDY OF ITS BENEFITS. Chatman moved to the other end of the room, where an overhead projector and screen were set up. He turned on the projector, and put a transparency up on the screen. He brandished a laser pointer. "This graph," Chatman began, "shows the current level of international trade, in US dollars, compared to the projected level two years after the implementation of the MAI. Now, if you will turn to page three of your reports, you will see—"

Rumbles from the gray men interrupted. This was all a rerun.

"I thought a refresher was in order," Pembroke said. "I was under the distinct impression that the benefits of the MAI had not been fully appreciated by you gentlemen."

"*This* is what this is about?" Campbell asked. "All this. Everything. . . . Just so you can rush this through?"

Pembroke gave him a patient smile. "If you turn to the last page of your documents, you will see a line for your signatures. Fill in the line, and our business here is concluded."

"That's it," said Campbell.

Pembroke nodded. "That's it. Not so painful, is it? And Mr. Chatman will be more than happy to demonstrate the very clear advantages to your economies to do so."

Chatman bowed.

"No," said Palliser.

Pembroke turned to him. "Of course, all those paranoid fantasies your anti-MAI loonies cooked up. You didn't believe those, did you? NAFTA didn't destroy your country, why should this?"

Flanagan was only half-listening. He was leafing through the document, trying to see it through the eyes of Blaylock, of Harland, of his sister. Something had spooked Harland in Paris. She had seen something in here that was bad enough to risk her life over. He flashed back on the argument with Holly and Blaylock over dinner. He flipped through Holly's arguments. He'd heard them often enough, he should have them by rote. He thought about the gift of litigation the MAI was going to bestow on the transnationals. He flipped to that section of the agreement. Read the wording, thought it through. And he saw it. He saw the implication that Pembroke was going to use: local laws restraining dangerous goods would go down if the goods were legal elsewhere. Flanagan caught his breath. He looked up. "You son of a bitch," he said to Pembroke. "If you get this thing through, you could legally challenge all gun control laws, and the WTO would have to back you. You could bring them all down."

Pembroke's eyes flared, and he smiled. "Clever boy," he purred.

I've just danced to his tune again, Flanagan thought. But how? Why would Pembroke want this known?

"I'm not signing this, Arthur," said Campbell. His voice was still flat and dead, but there was the echo of will in its tone.

"Even if we did sign," said Lévi, "we would be doing so under duress. We would make that clear when we left, and the agreement would never pass in any form. And if we do not return, that will do you no good, either."

"Exactly," said Pembroke. His voice was a velvet snake that coiled around the room. "You'll need a permanent inducement to honor your signatures." He opened the laptop, turned it on. On cue, Noonan and Lentricchia opened cases beside the table. Lentricchia hauled out communications equipment. He plugged a mike and receiver into the computer. Noonan set up a digital projection unit that put the computer's display up onto the screen.

"President Belinski," Pembroke began. He typed as he spoke, entering passwords and setting up screens. "When you return to Russia, you'll find that your country is some millions of Kalashnikov assault rifles lighter. Also, one super-freighter worth of Grail surface-to-air missiles. I am, at this very instant, at the helm of a fleet of superfreighters loaded with these weapons. I can send any ship anywhere I choose. The commands I send cannot be overridden." He hit a key, then turned on the mike. "Captain Willson," he said.

The receiver crackled static. A few seconds later, Willson's voice came out, breaking up but just clear enough. "Yes sir."

"Are you ready?"

There was no Omega Block in the Atlantic. The storms and rains absent on the North American plains had moved out here. The waves were peaking at sixty feet. Even on a ship the size of the *Bhopal*, they were enough for Willson to notice. Wonderful, he thought as he communicated with Pembroke. Just the kind of weather for Pembroke to play video games in. "All right, boys," he shouted, "get ready for a ride. The bastard's got his toy out."

"Captain Willson," Pembroke typed in a command, "can you tell me what is happening now?"

A pause. Then the sound of a background hum getting louder. "Our engines have just gone to full ahead."

"Please stop them."

"I can't."

Pembroke let that sink in. On the display, the *Bhopal*'s speed was climbing. "Thank you, Captain." He turned off the communications and the projection. He moved the trackball, clicked in some settings. Then he shut down the computer. "Gentlemen," he said, "I have given my fleet their directions. Each ship has a particular port of call now, subject to change at my discretion."

"We'll stop them," said Campbell.

Pembroke shrugged. "Possibly. But first you have to find

them, which you won't. Not in time. They have a way of blending in with other shipping vessels. So what will you do? Shut down global trade? Something else I should tell you. You're all aware of the amalgamation of arms dealers that InSec represents." He waited for the nods, then went on. "Good. Now follow me carefully. Do you remember at the end of 1998, when Executive Outcomes closed up shop?"

It had been a third-string wire-service story that year. Executive Outcomes, the top-line South African mercenary group, had up and dissolved itself. After some fairly spectacular successes. A couple of people scratched their heads, then everyone moved on.

"You absorbed them," said Willis, very quietly.

"Among others." Pembroke leaned back and folded his hands over his chest. "Wherever the ships go, I have the manpower to put the weapons to good use. Now let me mention some names. Red Brigade. Action Directe. Front de Libération du Québec. The militia of your choice. Aum Shinrikyo." He waved a hand. "I could go on."

"More rubbish," said Willis, desperate to be right. "Most of those groups haven't been active for decades."

"They were merely examples. Ones you would recognize. Every one of your countries has the right kind of seeds in it. If you do not pass the MAI, and *keep* it passed, and enforced, I will water those seeds. Trust me, you won't like what blossoms."

Flanagan wondered if Pembroke was bluffing. He was proposing chaos on a massive scale. Huge supplies of arms funneled to the psychotic fringes, pumping them up, priming them, giving them the toys and the confidence to go completely berserk. Mercenaries, now under the same monopoly control as the arms industry, moving from country to country and turning the nuts into war machines. The potential for a million massacres, the sandblast and pneumatic drill erosion of the rule of law. He had to be bluffing.

Flanagan looked into Pembroke's eyes. They had gone dark, with a cold, pinpoint shine at the center of their depths. Flanagan's skin chilled.

Lentricchia looked at Noonan, puzzled. "Is he nuts?" he whispered. "This doesn't sound like a goddamn goldmine to me."

"Shut up," Noonan shushed. "Sure it is." He felt the adrenalin pump. Pembroke was painting a future of unlimited action. Valhalla was opening its doors wide. Lentricchia was wrong. There was huge money to be made here. The destabilization Pembroke was promising would push the demand for weapons through the roof. But Lentricchia was also right. Pembroke was paddling in the deep end of his sanity. Dying was the best thing that daughter of his had ever done. Pembroke was changing the agenda. The threat of domestic terrorism had only been meant to be that: a threat. But Noonan could hear it in Pembroke's voice. He could see it in the way Pembroke was sitting: apparently relaxed, but with a slight quiver of tension. There was a growing part of Pembroke that wanted to release the hounds. Noonan was going to nurture that part until it dominated. Whatever agreement got hammered out today, Noonan was going to see the InSec nightmare scenario explode.

"That is no choice at all," said Kitamura.

"Of course it is." Pembroke sounded cheerfully reasonable, as if this were just another day of takeovers on Wall Street. "You don't have to like it, but you do have a choice. It's between total chaos and regulated chaos. If the MAI goes through, InSec will make sure that its privileged customers—that's you, gentlemen—will get advance warning of upcoming events. You'll be busy, but I think that's preferable to the alternative, don't you?"

When no one answered, Pembroke stood up. "I see you need to think about it. Fine. Talk. Discuss. You have until dinner. At which point I will consider these negotiations concluded. See you then." He picked up the notebook and walked out of the room, trailed by his retinue.

Flanagan sat still for a moment, and then, very slowly, very deliberately, very calmly, he took the watch off his wrist. He put the watch on the floor, stood up and ground it under his heel. "I hope you heard all that," he whispered to Blaylock's bug. "If you're here, Jen, stop him. Stop him now." He looked around the room, gauging the spirit. He saw the full palette of shock and horror. He sensed that Pembroke was about to get his grip, iron and immovable, around the powerflow. It had left these men completely. They were approaching absolute helplessness. "Fight him!" Flanagan yelled, frustrated. The air conditioner hummed, the oxygen filtered into sterility. "I need some real air," Flanagan muttered, and went to the window. He threw the sash open. Heat poured in, but with it true movement of air, and the sounds of the wind in the trees. The noise of a world real outside the conference room. Flanagan turned back to the heads of state. "For God's sake," he said. "Even if you don't know how, you have to fight. You have to. This is for keeps."

Palliser and Campbell exchanged looks. "I don't know," Campbell began, and the negative sounded like a death knell to Flanagan. "I—"

The *crack!* and its echoes cut Campbell off. Willis looked up. "Was that a gunshot?"

27

"Go," Blaylock radioed.

Noonan and Lentricchia were in Pembroke's room. They barely heard the gunshot through his closed window, but they heard enough to know what it was. Noonan rushed to the window, looked out. He saw birds flapping up beyond the blowdown. He watched a few moments before saying, "Hunter?"

"Find out," Pembroke said. "Neutralize whoever it is."

Noonan nodded. Lentricchia stayed, his stance already shifting back to bodyguard mode, while Noonan went downstairs. The heat was a molasses wall he hit the instant he stepped outside. He found Van der Wat in the front grounds. "You hear that?" he asked.

Van der Wat nodded. "Rifle. Definitely."

"You send someone in?"

"*Ja.*"

"How many?"

"Six. I think that will be frightening enough."

Noonan smiled, leaned back against the wall of the lodge. He could feel the heat of the wood through his shirt. It was like having a fireplace at his back. God, the heat made him feel lazy. It was the contrast of in and out that was screwing him up. If it was always hot or always cold he could handle it. As it was, he didn't even mind that he was missing out on a hunt. He was too sluggish. The air inside the lodge was so artificial it made him feel fuzzy, as if a headache were just about to get going. And outside it was too hot to move. The wind was picking up some, at least. It was furnace breath, dry and parching, but at least the air was moving.

Noonan jerked away from the wall. He looked at Van der Wat. The South African had made the connection too. Hunters? There had been no planes in the area. They were far from any settlement. Where had the hunters come from?

"Ah, shit," said Van der Wat.

Blaylock scanned the ambush area, final mental checklist. She finished applying the cam sticks to her face, and got into position. Here we go. Three days to find the right spot and prepare the trap. If it went wrong now, she'd know whose fault it was. A hundred yards in from the blowdown, a trail cut through the woods. The ambush site was three quarters of the way down the gorge from the lodge. The trail leveled off here for a bit, actually sloping up slightly, before taking a sharp bend deeper into the trees and continuing its descent. The bush on either side was thick. Good cover.

Blaylock had gone for an L-shaped ambush. She used ten of the Raiders to form the attack element. They spread out along the path, six on the straight, four on the bend. Six to fire on the flank, four to interlock the bullets. For support, they had two M-60 light machine guns, bipod mounted at either end of the L. Blaylock spent two hours with Danny Rivers, making sure that he would observe his limit stakes planted just ahead of his position and respect his field of fire. He was at the tip of the short arm of the L, and would be firing diagonally through the kill zone, upping the kill factor of the overlapping fire still further. But if he rotated too far to the left, he'd start taking out his own assault element.

Tammy Harper and Billy Duke were up in trees, sentries guarding both approaches to the kill zone. Sonny Butler was back of the main assault force, one-man security element and tank. He was loaded down with his Mk 19 machine gun. An automatic grenade launcher, the Mk 19 weighed seventy pounds, fired a hundred rounds of 40 mm high-explosive shells per minute, and was intended to be mounted on a vehicle. Butler had glommed onto it as his baby and let no one else carry it the entire trip. He could swing it one-handed. He refused to use a tripod, no matter how much Blaylock got on his case for accuracy. He had the weapon suspended at chest level, rotary drums of ammunition belts hanging from his web belt. Butler was solid, but wouldn't be moving either quickly or with stealth.

There are point ambushes, and there are area ambushes. A point ambush is a set-up at one point and one point only. An area ambush is interconnected point ambushes. Blaylock didn't have enough personnel for a proper area ambush, but she did her best. Six of the other seven Raiders were set up further back along the trail as a second point hit. They were going to come into play only if more than one party showed up and took the bait of the other squad coming under fire. Blaylock was counting on that happening. This was a destruction, not a harassment, ambush. She had to get the numbers of the InSec troops down fast. She didn't want to be outnumbered by the defenders when she launched the assault on the lodge.

That left Charlie Rivers on the suicide ledge. He was dressed in hunter's orange vest, plaid shirt and cap. He was carrying his old rifle. His M-16 was in the bushes at his feet. He was wearing Kevlar under the vest, hoping that he was going to get shot in the bright target area.

Long pieces of string connected the arms of the entire militia. The string would break, given a sharp tug, but light tugs would work as silent signals. Two short tugs, starting from the lookout, would mean the enemy was approaching.

Blaylock squatted down next to Sam, at the corner of the L. From this position she could see down the path. She aimed her C-7, which now had an M-203 pump action grenade launcher clipped underneath. She had two magazines taped together in the rifle, ready for a quick reverse to reload, and another four on her belt, giving her 180 rounds. She gave her own signal. One long tug to pass down the line. The last step in setting the trap. Click click click through the forest as the safeties went off. Charlie used the cue and fired into the air again. Ravens squawked, in on the game.

Two tugs.

Trevor Scott, hunt leader, on point, spotted him first. He stopped and held up his hand, halting the group. Guy Chappell came up behind him. Scott pointed. Chappell nodded. The hunter had his back to them. He was looking up in the trees as if he'd shot something five minutes ago and was still waiting for it to drop. Moron, Scott thought. This hunt was nothing. The job was going bust fast after a good start with the Secret Service rumble. He had a nostalgic flash for Sierra Leone. Now there was a place with some fine merc action. That had been home after he'd left England, and things never got boring there for more than a few months at a time. But Van der Wat had called, InSec had issued orders, and here he was. Tracking down poncing Canuck hunters. What a joke.

His radio crackled, noisemaker. He shut the radio off. This close and the hunter would hear them. If they were going to do such a candy-ass exercise, they might as well do it properly. Van der Wat didn't trust him to blow his own nose. Scott stood motionless, waiting to see if the hunter had heard. He hadn't. There was enough noise from the creaking of the trees. The wind was getting strong. Scott wondered if they had a storm coming. The hunter started walking away. Scott scanned the woods, didn't see anyone else. If the hunter had some friends, they weren't nearby. Scott gestured. The team moved in.

"He doesn't answer," Van der Wat said.

Noonan thought for a moment, thumb hesitating over the transmit button on his own radio. Scott not answering didn't necessarily mean trouble. He might not be receiving. They hadn't heard any gunfire. They could still be dealing with a party of losers who were about to wish they'd gone golfing. But if he thought that, and was wrong, who was the loser then? He pushed the button. "Assume hostiles," he told Van der Wat.

It had taken them a full minute to arm up and get on the chase. They'd taken the bulk of the InSec troops, and left the lodge double-quick. Lentricchia and Kuhn were at the lodge with a reserve of six men, more than enough to keep the lid on civilians unarmed and soiling their pants. The other sixteen were split into three groups as they worked through the woods. There was a group of six on the path, moving fast to catch up with Scott's team. Van der Wat and Noonan each headed up a squad of five. They were off the path, deep in the woods, Van der Wat's men on the side close to the blowdown. The three groups formed a v-shaped moving ambush. The lead team was the bait, a moving target locked and loaded.

Unbreakable ambush rule: coordinate the fire. To coordinate the fire, use a precise signal to trigger the ambush. Do not whistle as a signal. Do not yell. That would give the enemy reaction time. The signal should take casualties.

Blaylock watched the mercenaries approach. Six of them, single file, three yards apart. They had their eyes fixed on Charlie. They walked into the kill zone. Blaylock triggered the signal.

Noonan heard it. Shit, he thought. He started to run. There was enough noise now to cover their movement.

The path exploded as Blaylock squeezed the handle on her static line remote. A bank of Claymore mines went off, each one spewing 1000 BBs out to make ground meat. The Liberty Raiders opened fire with the boom still echoing. For a few seconds there was nothing but dust and gunfire and yells. Something landed next to Blaylock. She didn't stop firing, but she looked. It wasn't a weapon. It was a leg.

The wind cleared the air enough to see. Flames licked the underbrush at the edge of the mine craters. Two of the mercenaries had been blown apart by the mines. Blaylock saw the second man in the line, screaming wet and gargling, trying to crawl while his legs tangled in his intestines. Blood pumped out of his mouth. The other men were going down fast and shredded. The fire from the two legs of the L interlocked, bullets crossing perpendicular, Swiss cheese city. Two more men were dead before their first reaction. The chest on one blew out, courtesy M-60. The other spun once on his feet, dead already but kept up by the impacts. A fifth leaped into the bush, away from the fire. Blaylock tracked him, stitched the forest with bullets. A giant's hand slammed the man down, blood jetting splash from his back.

The squad leader had been thrown flat by the Claymore

blast. He rolled, keeping underneath the horizontal hail. He returned fire, spraying the forest wild, no aim. Blaylock felt a bullet-wind kiss her cheek, heard the rattling *tack-a-tack-a-tack* of hard rain against the tree trunks. Beside her, Sam grunted and fell backwards. Blaylock lowered her aim and the squad leader's body vibrated hard against the ground, nail-gunned.

Blaylock looked at Sam. He was clutching his left shoulder, blood between his fingers, face going shock-pale. Luck was a bitch.

There was a tug on the string on her left arm. "Can you move?" she asked Sam. He nodded. "Can you fight?" He nodded. "Then get back into position, soldier. More coming."

The initial sounds of battle lasted less than thirty seconds. The silence that followed went on just long enough for Noonan to begin wondering if they were going to be heard approaching after all. Then the rifles opened up again, but a lot closer this time. Two different ambushes.

Corner of his eye: movement to the left. He stopped, looked at a fir thirty yards away, near the path. One of the branches a third of the way up was moving up and down. Not a wind gesture, that. He sent his squad on and crouched low, closing on the tree. He looked hard, focusing through the needles, searching for the pattern he knew would be there. He saw the lookout. Camouflage fatigues, right there, thank you very much. The woman had her back to him, was watching the way back up the trail. Good discipline, not looking at the firefight. Bad inexperience, forgetting about her back. He raised his M-16, opened up, punched through flesh. The body fell from the tree.

He ran to catch up with his squad.

The trail's straight stretch was long, over a hundred yards of descent before it took its little climb. The second ambush point was at the start of the straight run, at the spot where you could first see what was happening at the other point. Jimmy Chase, middle boy of the waiting trap, had been fighting the shiverchills since the first group of mercenaries had gone past. The shakes got worse when he heard the Claymore blast and the opening of war. He almost fainted when he felt the tug signaling another group of the enemy on its way. Fear was squeezing bile back up his throat. He had to work at keeping a grip on his rifle. He managed, but he couldn't stop the barrel from shaking back and forth.

The enemy came. His enemy, his targets. Last second before he'd be in the war. His bladder gave way. The Claymores went off. Chase screamed and fired.

The mines only took out one of the squad, blasting straight up his groin. The men had been moving fast, and the lead two actually got out of the kill zone before the explosion. They jumped into the bush on the far side of the path and shot back. The other three were winded and down but still active elements, rattlesnakes cornered but not defanged. On their butts, pushing themselves backwards with their legs, they fired into the ambush line.

Chase wasn't aiming. His rifle was shaking too much from recoil and fear. It jerked to the right and he saw his bullets thud into the chest of one of the men on the ground. The mercenary arced into the bullets, his rifle jerking up and shooting the sky. Chase's bullets stopped and so did his screams. His rifle was empty. He hung fire, slack-jawed, brain scrambling to catch up with the information that he had just killed a man. Bullets zipped past. He didn't notice. Bullets took off the top of Howard Bugbee's head. Chase noticed. He fumbled another magazine into his rifle. Another mercenary was cut in half, but the third managed to reach the bush and cover. The Raiders had better cover, but the InSec troops had the skill. They all but disappeared. Chase couldn't see anything to aim at. He fired anyway.

The return fire suddenly got a lot heavier. Another Raider was hit, went down screaming. Susan Rivers, on Chase's right, pulled a grenade out of her pouch. She yanked the pin, counted slow, and threw. The trees blocked most of the fragments, but the blast got someone. The rate of fire dropped slightly, but it was still far too much for just two people. Susan grabbed another grenade, pulled the pin. She stood up to throw. She pitched forward, chest exploding out. The grenade rolled in front of Chase. He yelled and threw himself back. The grenade went off, thunderclap. Something sharp slammed cold and tearing into his left thigh. He screamed. He tried to get to his feet, but his left leg gave out and he fell. He sobbed into the dirt, and the image of Susan's death finally registered. Falling forward: hit from behind.

Now he noticed the *brrrrrt* of automatic weapons fire was louder yet. Now he saw the bullets flying by from the rear. Now he heard more Raiders going down. He pulled himself forward, hugging the ground, until he got to a large tree. He grabbed hold of the trunk, managed to stand up. He leaned against the tree and gingerly put some weight on his left leg. Blood had soaked his trousers. The leg felt weak and howled pain, but he thought he could run, a bit. He crouched and stumbled away from the tree, moving uphill, away from the crossfire.

A little man with a rifle popped up in front of him. Chase stopped dead, threw up his hands. "Checkitout," the man said, and fired.

Blaylock heard the gunfire. She heard it heavy, and she heard it coming closer. She sensed big trouble. She tried to hail Tammy Harper on the radio. Got no one. She tried Susan Rivers. No one. Their forward positions were gone.

Somehow they were being flanked. Time to move. If they stayed where they were, they were fish in a barrel. "Frag," she radioed. It was the code to abandon the ambush position. A widespread scatter, fragmentation, get lost in the bush. Regroup if possible, and ultimately head for the mansion. That was, in the end, the mission after all. Get there by any means possible and kill anyone armed. Blaylock figured their odds were dropping like an iron bomb.

"Butler," she radioed. "Back. Way back." Move the tank further to the rear, flank the flankers. Butler double-clicked acknowledgment. Blaylock stood up. She looked at Sam. He'd lost a lot of blood. He was looking sluggish. "Move out," she told him.

He shook his head. "Don't think I can run."

"Run or die, Sam."

He staggered to his feet, stood wobbling. "No good," he said. He looked at her, knowledge of his end a grim illumination on his face. "Machine gun," he said, and staggered. Blaylock understood. She put an arm around his waist, had him lean on her shoulder, and supported him to Danny's M-60 position. Danny had already followed the order and run. Blaylock settled Sam in behind the gun. He looked unstable even sitting.

"You want to do this?" she asked, wondering if she would really be able to help if he changed his mind, and wondering where her ability to discard these people had gone. Sam nodded, grabbed hold of the gun, aimed it down the trail. Blaylock squeezed his good shoulder and took off into the bush. Enemy fire was close. She could hear the running tramp of boots. A bullet cut through a branch just above her head.

No more ambushes. Every good plan turns to shit, and hers had just done so. She hadn't expected anything else, knew they were lucky that even the first hit had gone so well. Now it was full-out guerilla war, the hunt-and-shoot between dozens of armies of one. Smoke from the smoldering vegetation got into her nostrils. Shit, she thought, we've got ourselves a forest fire.

Van der Wat and his squad hit the path roaring blitzkrieg. They'd struck the up-slope ambush hard, giving covering fire to the surviving members of the forward element and adding them to their strength, then pulling out when Noonan's team had arrived to clear out the enemy from behind. Van der Wat stayed in contact with Noonan, letting him know where they were, keeping down the risk of friendly-fire exchanges. They were working their way down the slope in alternating steps now, Van der Wat attacking first to drive the enemy back, Noonan arriving to mow down the retreat. That was the plan. One nest down. Next one coming right up.

Flames were crackling up and down the bushes as they closed in on the trail. Smoke blew straight into Van der Wat's eyes, stinging tears. He blinked them away, jumped over some waist-high flames, landed next to the body of Trevor Scott and dropped, firing the whole time. Someone in the forest ahead screamed, but there was no return fire. They were already in retreat. Reed Anderson landed next to him. The rest of the squad was just behind. A fire was gathering strength on the opposite side of the trail too.

"What do you figure?" Anderson asked.

"I figure in half an hour I'll be buying the beers," said Van der Wat. "Come on, mop-up." He moved forward, gesturing for the squad to follow.

He had reached the flames when the M-60 started up. He heard its full-throated rattle and dived. Anderson erupted in multiple geysers. Van der Wat went through the flames. He hit the ground on the other side and rolled, his fatigues already starting to smolder. Then he was up and running deeper into the bush. He got himself some cover, then dou-bled back towards the sound of the machine gun. The gunner was firing a continuous burst. No pauses. His belt was going to be gone soon. Van der Wat caught a glimpse of the trail through bush and smoke as he closed in. Three more men down, looked like. Van der Wat reached the gun emplacement just as the firing stopped. The gunner sagged against the gun, then seemed to look for another belt. His movements were sluggish, confused. His left side was all blood. Son of a bitch had nailed three pros while barely conscious. "Hold your fire!" Van der Wat yelled. He wanted the bastard for himself.

The gunner heard him. He turned around, fumbling at his belt for a handgun. Van der Wat waited until he had it in his hand, then walked up to him and kicked the pistol away, breaking the man's fingers. The gunner screamed and fell back against his M-60. Van der Wat pulled out his own 9 mm Browning. He rammed the barrel hard into the gunner's mouth, smashing teeth. He made sure the gunner was looking into his eyes, was seeing what was there, before he pulled the trigger. Brains flew up in a high arc.

"Form on me," Van der Wat called. The men gathered, down to five again. Van der Wat looked around. He doubted now that he was chasing a rout if the enemy had had the time to leave a sacrifice to cover the retreat. He wanted to consolidate forces before taking the next step. The situation had changed again. Tactics had to too. He called Noonan. "What's your situation?"

Noonan didn't answer right away. "We caught one coming from your direction. You get the others?"

"No. You saw no one else?"

"They've scattered."

They were going to have to track them and kill them one at a time. The beers receded into the distance. "We're moving your way," said Van der Wat, already running. "Make sure you don't kill us."

They hooked up with Noonan and his team two minutes later. They were much deeper into the woods now than initially. Noonan had had a hard chase to catch the runner. Noonan kicked the corpse as Van der Wat joined him. His eyes flickered as he did a head count. "Five two-man teams," he said. "Track them and kill them. Go. Jacob, you're with me."

"Have you warned the lodge?" Van der Wat asked as the other men headed off into the woods. His gut was uneasy. The enemy had lured them out here. He'd hate to think all this mess had just been against a diversionary force, and that he was missing the main assault.

"I got them to put four men on watch at the blow-down," Noonan said.

Van der Wat heard a noise. He turned. He had time to think: This can't be happening, not to me.

Noonan jumped back, splattered as Van der Wat exploded. There was a deep and heavy *dugdugdugdug,* and he was running hard, the ground and small trees going up around him, blasted by high explosive shells. Noonan danced, Noonan deked, Noonan moved fast as he ever had in his life. He zigged around the trunks of the larger trees, but their cover was bad, the HE shells punching and splintering through. Noonan saw an unevenness in the ground where Shield rock poked up. An MK 19 round hit the rock a second after he leaped up. Granite shards cut his face. The blast sent him flying. He landed hard and tucked himself in tight against the slope of the rock. There was a pause, then more firing. Explosions above, making the forest jig. He could hear the crackle of new flames. Son of a bitch wasn't using HE any-more—he was firing Willie P, white phosphorous incendi-aries. With the forest tinderbox dry, he might as well be using a flame-thrower.

Noonan wiped the blood from his eyes, waited for the enemy to stop and reload. When the silence came, he was up and running, putting in the distance before he could stop and counterattack. He hadn't gone far before the explosions started again. But the misses were wider this time. The gunner was further away, blocked by the wreckage and flames he had created.

The shooting stopped, another reload. Noonan spotted a hollow and jumped into it. He lay flat, poked his rifle over the lip. He couldn't see far for the smoke and fire. He waited for the flames to die down. They didn't.

28

This is the way the world burns.

Your basic fire, moment of genesis. Ignition: heat the fuel until its water evaporates and the runaway chemical breakdown takes place, liquid tars oozing out and flammable gases roiling at the surface. Keep the heat up, and sooner or later the process takes over and goes it alone: combustion. Look at a flame. In the invisible center: the vaporized gases waiting to burn. In the orange: carbon particles heated until they glow the special color of Hell. And flickering blue at the edge: the combustion zone, the moment of death for the carbon. Rising above, the smoke: gases, water vapor, soot, hydrocarbons. Don't breathe in.

Boom. Birth. Infancy and growth. Spread: the edge of the flames heat the adjacent fuel to ignition and combustion, and so it goes, the cycle getting faster, stronger, more violent. The spread moves out like a ripple from the point of ignition, pushed by the wind into an ellipse. One fire, the basic model, with no complications. Dry your fuel enough, and ignition won't take very much. Multi-thousand-acre conflagrations don't need a lightning strike to get going. A bad campfire will do it. A tossed cigarette. Sparks from a train. The firefights had already led to multiple starts. The fire had been conceived, and its implacable life was assured before Sonny Butler opened up with his MK 19. He just accelerated the process, gave the fire speed, fast-forwarded it through the stages of childhood and straight into adolescence.

Butler knew he had made a mistake. Blaylock had told him high explosive, but he hadn't thought that was good enough. He took his responsibility as a tank seriously. Tanks were heavy hitters. He was the big firepower, and it had occurred to him that phosphorous would up his strike capability enormously in a forest. The rounds would be that much more devastating. They were. And when he felt the heat against his skin, he remembered that he wasn't a tank. He backed up, coughing. He squinted, trying to peer through the smoke and spot the man he'd been shooting at. No good. All he could see was the fire's growth. He lifted the MK 19's barrel high and began to jog through the trees. He headed west, against the wind, still operating on Blaylock's last orders. Flank, flank, flank again. Work around the fire, find that asshole and finish him off.

Pumped by Butler, the burn at this end, most of the way down the valley and well west of the lodge, was already a strong surface fire, the main river that the other fires would feed, tributaries of spread. It needed a ladder to move into adulthood. It found one. The undergrowth was dense and burning close to trees. Young trees burned strong and passed the gift on to their bigger brothers. Dead branches, the driest limbs of a forest already so dry it was close to spontaneous combustion, picked up the fire and lifted it higher. Minutes into life, the fire was already beginning to crown.

Pembroke saw the smoke. He had his suite window open and the air conditioning turned off so he could hear the sounds of the firefight. They had diminished from a constant rattle to the occasional burst. But now there was smoke rising from the trees. The air around the lodge was starting to change. Pembroke could smell burning wood. "Jack," he said to Lentricchia, "I think we might need to leave fairly soon." In the distance, the smoke, dirty gray, puffed higher. Pembroke saw a tongue of orange peek their way.

Dix saw the smoke. He was cleaning the billiards room, scooping up ashtrays and re-slotting cues, when he looked out the window and saw the billow. He watched the smoke, and felt a fear new and visceral. He thought he'd been afraid of dying before, thought in fact that he was almost resigned to being shot. But now he realized how much he'd been hoping for rescue, for escape, for mercy. As long as a gun wasn't pointed his way, he could pretend he was going to be okay. Now he was looking down a gunbarrel. Fire moved uphill, he knew that much. If there was a fire down below, it was law that it was going to reach the lodge unless somebody stopped it.

Through the fear, an hysterical stab of hope. The fire would change things. It wasn't going to listen to the InSec goons. They were going to listen to it. It was going to incinerate their house of cards. Maybe they will abort. Maybe we can all go home. He left the billiard room, looking for Kuhn or Pembroke. Some god he could propitiate. He tried the manager's office first. He had last seen Kuhn in there.

The room was empty. Dix started to go, then spotted the radio on the desk. He stared at it, hesitating. He knew how to use it. The staff had all received instruction on how to call for help in case a fire broke out. Dix poked his head out the doorway and looked left, right. No one. The G8 leaders were still in the conference room, arguing, their voices the ebb-and-flow roar of distant surf. He couldn't see Kuhn. He looked back at the radio. If you do this, and you get caught, he thought, you die.

If you don't, you die anyway. Close to throwing up, he walked over to the radio, picked up the transmitter. His fingers were so slick with sweat he fumbled the switches several times before he finally got through to the nearest forestry station. "This is Ember Lake Lodge," he said. His hands trembled. Through the window, he saw the smoke build like a fist. "We have a forest fire in progress, and we—"

The radio was snatched from his hands and he was shoved to one side. Kuhn knocked the radio off the desk and stomped it. Then he looked at Dix. He sighed. "I don't know." He shook his head, disappointed. He pulled his gun from his shoulder holster. "I thought we'd made things clear, but...." He shrugged and shot Dix in the gut.

The Red Lake Fire Centre.

Jim Pyne was Fire Response Officer when Dix's call came through on the radio. He'd been on twenty-four-hour call for a week, and was running on coffee and fumes. When Dix's voice cut out, Pyne tried hailing the lodge. Nothing. Christ, this was all he needed.

There were currently 117 active fires in Ontario, twenty of them big project fires. The season was blowing at high do. Most of the fires were in the full response zone—areas where active suppression was the rule. The resources weren't stretched thin: they were *gone*. Ditto across the continent. Ontario had been trying to get more water-bombers and firefighters in from the other provinces, or the States, but they were all up to their asses in alligators. Nobody was in a giving mood. It looked like the burn records of 1989 were going to be beaten.

There were still a couple of initial attack crews being held in reserve. It didn't matter how hot things got, there was always a reserve, otherwise they'd be asking for more fires to get out of control. Pyne hit the intercom. "Ehorn crew, dispatch," he called. Then he got on the horn to Pete Arno in Dryden. "Need another tanker group from you," Pyne said. "We've got a lodge threatened at Ember Lake."

"Tell me you're kidding."

"I'm not kidding. And Pete—we've got people at the lodge."

Butler was confused. The fire disoriented him. It was bigger than he had thought. He was having to go much farther west than he would have expected to get around the flames. He was starting to move uphill on the valley wall, and the fire was beating him to it, racing upslope wherever there was enough shelter to slow the wind. Butler ducked around the first barrier of flames and found a new one. He avoided that and lost his bearings. He looked around, and the compass had fire on all quadrants. Smoke raked his lungs and stung his eyes to tears. The forest was getting dark. He had only the slope of the land to go by now. He ran forward, weaving between flames, MK 19 pointing ahead, turret cannon. Screw strategy, screw stalking, screw everything.

Noonan thought at first that a bear was heading his way.

He'd been driven from his shelter by the fire, but the flames had also given him cover. He couldn't see whoever had been firing the grenades, but he wasn't being bombed anymore, either. He wanted to find a blind and set himself up an ambush, but the fire kept him moving. He crouched low, keeping below the bushes as much as he could. The air was better down here too. He moved west, and kept his travel as slow and careful as he could. If he circled around and caught the SOB from behind, great. If not, he still wanted first reaction, which he would get if he saw the enemy first. He froze when he hear the crashing in the bush. Big animal, coming fast. He dropped to one knee and braced his rifle. He hadn't thought a human would be stupid enough to make so much noise. Then the biggest piece of white trash he'd ever seen careened out of the smoke, Mk 19 swinging like the world's premier erection. The angle of approach was fluke right. The trash saw him at the same time. The trash roared and pulled the trigger on the Mk 19, still running. Noonan, choice gone, put his faith in inaccuracy and took the trouble to aim. The Mk 19 shells went wide and blew up behind him. Something hit the back of Noonan's jacket and started to burn. He ignored it. He emptied his clip.

His bullets hit the trash chest center. The trash was bull stupid and didn't realize he was dead at first. He ran forward three more steps into the bullet stream, feet piledrivers of momentum, voice the yell of war. Then he was rearing back and screaming, wounded animal in the rage of death. The Mk 19 went up and around in a wide swing. The trash's finger convulsed on the trigger and kept it down. Incendiary shells swept the arc. Back heating to pain, Noonan went flat and kept down until the belt feed ran out. Orange and heat exploded.

Noonan rolled, putting out the fire on his back, then stood and tore off his jacket. Stupid. He should have taken the time to get into camos before leaving the lodge. But oh no, smart boy thinks it's enough to grab his weapons.

Okay, he thought, let's have a sitrep. That was easy enough: fire. He looked downslope and saw it marching his way. He heard a sound like a giant's cough and a tree disappeared in flames ten yards high. Noonan knew bad, and he was seeing it. There was a new player in the war, and Noonan didn't have the means to oppose it. Honor the threat, he thought. Get outta Dodge. In less than a minute he was running. He didn't worry about being shot.

Packing sprinklers, equipment and full initial attack crew, the Bell 205 lifted off from Red Lake. To the south, the smoke was a huge invitation. "Red Lake Fire Centre," Allison Ehorn radioed, "this is Helitack 66 with Ehorn crew on board, off Red Lake, bound for fire designated Red 113. Uh, we're not going to need any coordinates for this one. We can see it fine." Ehorn rolled her eyes at Ralph Whitney. The pilot rolled his back, but he was grinning too. Big honking fire, big adrenalin job. "Red Lake," Ehorn continued. "Advise District this one is not walk in the park. We're going to be here a while. Any other crews or tankers dispatched to this fire?"

"Dryden has dispatched Birddog 7 and tankers 998 and 999," Pyne answered. "You'll be fire boss at this time."

"Copy that, Red Lake."

Ehorn hailed the birddog pilot, and got an ETA of thirty minutes for the tankers, twenty for the birddog. "Going to be our show," she told Whitney.

"That's what I like. First come, first served." He aimed the helo at the siren call of the burn.

Danny saw the discarded rifle and hunter's vest. It was in a line southwest of where he'd last seen Charlie. He ran the line, hoping. Blaylock's instructions were for a wide scatter, followed by a regroup in a clearing at the southern end of the gorge where they had stashed the rest of their supplies. But without his M-60, all he had was his Colt .45. Charlie should still have his M-16. Danny reached the clearing. No Charlie. Nobody at all. He waited five minutes, getting antsy, smelling smoke. He heard rapid fire explosions. Sonny, he thought, and couldn't stand the wait anymore. He felt exposed sitting still. He went looking for Charlie. He knew Blaylock would slap him stupid for this move. He was being bone dumb. Odds of finding Charlie, alive or corpse, in the woods were a sucker's bet. He wasn't even tracking in the most rudimentary sense. He was doing a run from cover to cover and hoping for the best. The only thing he wasn't doing was shouting Charlie's name.

He got partway up the hill again. Visibility was getting worse, the natural darkness of the thick forest gaining smoke strength. He saw the fire and steered clear of it. It didn't return the favor. He heard a crackle and felt heat. He looked over his shoulder and saw an arm of fire cut off the way back. It licked up the hill toward him. He moved faster, searched less, got farther away from the heat. The sucker won. He saw Charlie. He was uphill and to the left, crouched behind a fallen tree. He was holding his leg. Danny ran towards him. "Charlie!" he shouted, too dumb to live.

Charlie saw him. "Down!" he yelled, and the bullets were digging up the ground around him at the same time.

Danny didn't go down. He was between cover. If he ate dirt, he'd be a prone target begging to be nailed. He took another sucker's bet and ran hellfire for Charlie. He won again. He curled up behind the trunk. About two yards of ground were between the dead tree and the firs standing behind them. Rounds pinged off the log and the trees. Danny looked at Charlie. He'd been hit just below the knee. He was holding his leg tight, squeezing with fading strength against the flow. "How bad?" Danny asked.

Charlie's lips moved. His teeth were gritted. "Bone's broken."

"Can you walk at all?" Charlie shook his head. Danny took Charlie's M-16. "Do you know where they are?" He dug through Charlie's pockets and found three magazines.

Charlie nodded. "Two big trees, really close together, one o'clock."

There was a pause in the gunfire. Danny poked his head up, sprayed bullets in the general area Charlie had said. He saw the twin firs, caught a glimpse of movement behind them, and ducked down in time for the shooting to start again.

"Goddamn pinned," Charlie grimaced.

"They gotta run out of ammo eventually." Charlie grunted, face gray. Eventually wasn't looking too good to him.

And then thunder. A random rain of 40 mm shells coming down and french-kissing the area with fire. "*The hell is Sonny doing?*" Charlie roared, losing his grip on his leg. Blood jetted. Charlie screamed and clamped hold again.

Danny moved fast. He was moving before the last of the shells had hit. He was moving so fast his body had committed to the action before his brain had a chance to veto. He had seconds while the enemy took cover from the bombardment. He had initiative. He was on a sucker's streak. He tore over the open area between him and the two trees. He ate it up, legs pumping fire-speed. He got to the trees as the two mercs were sitting up again. He dropped, sliding into second, firing all the way. He bagged them both. Call it three for the sucker.

Burning, all around. Fire in the forest, fire in the hole, fire roaring hallelujah. Time to leave. He started to scramble back to Charlie, and saw the new fires were being joined by the one he thought he'd left behind. He looked up and saw that Satan was loose and laughing at sweet Jesus and dancing in the treetops. He saw an independent crown fire. Pushed by the wind and its joy, the fire was doing Tarzan jumps from the top of one tree to another, racing ahead of the surface blaze. He couldn't hear the wind anymore. The fire's crackle was deepening, size and intensity multiplying the noise into a roar. The fire drew in its breath and spat. Danny saw embers fly out and land deep in the forest, birthing anew. The fire was spotting now, doing Sonny one better, showing how it was done.

The trees behind Charlie were torching. Danny ran back. He slung the rifle around his neck, put his arms around Charlie's waist. "Gotta go, brother," he said. He glanced up. The tree was raging orange and showering them with sparks. He heaved Charlie up. From above, loud splintering cracks. Danny looked. The top third of the tree collapsed, falling down at him, the burning fist of luck bringing his streak to a halt.

Billy Duke had been unrighteous. That had to be the explanation. He had been sinful, and was being punished with a losing war. It was either that or the end of the world, and since he hadn't been called up in the Rapture, he was screwed regardless. He had dropped out of his tree when the "Frag" signal had come. He'd forgotten his training and run wild at first, but then he saw a hollow formed by some tumble boulders, and he threw himself in. Mouse in a hole, he tried to wait out the war. But then the fire came, and with it the heat and the smoke and the noise of the anger of God. This was divine intervention, death come burning on both sides of the war. Duke stayed in his hole for as long as he dared, but the heat turned into a physical blow, and the air began to flee from him. He stumbled out. He decided to make for the rendezvous point. He knew Blaylock was wrong now, and that leaving his country to fight on foreign soil had been a mistake, but being alone was worse. He had to find the others. Halfway to the RV point, coughing and tearing, he saw Brenda Miller up ahead. He almost didn't spot her. She was crawling, staying flat with every unevenness in the ground. Superslow and overcautious. She was never going to make it. The fire would catch her first. He caught up to her. "Brenda," he said, bending down and grabbing her arm.

"No," she said.

"Come on." He raised her. "We've got to move."

A bullet passed through her head. Her left eye jumped foward and fell to the ground.

"Got one," Steve Fosberg said. He trained his rifle on the man.

"Hold it." Wade Ohler put a hand on his arm. "Let's follow for a while. He might flush the rest of them out, now that we've got him panicked." Ohler lifted his radio.

Blaylock heard the crackle-rasp of a radio. It was nearby, if she could hear it over the fire. Once clear of the InSec pincer movement, she'd tried to retreat strategically. She moved slowly, and thought offensively. She evaluated each point she paused at not as cover, but for ambush value. She was not being hunted in the woods. She was loose in them, a roving mine keyed to blow up any InSec merc who set a foot wrong. She planned to take out as many as she could on her way to the RV point, clear the forest for a counterattack in force. She kept hearing bursts of gunfire, but never close enough. The radio noise was the first opportunity she'd had.

She was standing against the downslope side of a thick trunk. She'd been here five minutes, motionless, listening to the forest. The fire was a problem, throwing up white noise, covering the sounds of approach. She hadn't heard the men coming down the hill until the radio spoke up. They were almost on top of her. "Fosberg and Ohler nailed one," a merc said, putting away his radio. "They're tracking another. They want us in on it." The two men moved past her tree. They didn't look behind. They were being cocky. She lowered her rifle. She made kissing noises. The men turned. She cut them into meat.

"Sir," said Lentricchia.

Pembroke got up from the bed and looked out the window where Lentricchia was pointing. A helicopter had just overflown from the north. It paused, hovering, then headed in toward the smoke. Pembroke said, "Take it down."

"Well, it's definitely occupied," Ehorn said. She'd seen people moving on the manicured lawns of the lodge. They'd looked up at the helicopter and watched, but no one had waved. They all seemed really busy. Odd. She picked up the radio. "Red Lake, H-66."

"H-66, Red Lake," Pyne came back.

"Are you in contact with the lodge?"

"Negative, 66. No contact since they called the fire in."

"We have visual." She looked ahead. "Be advised that the lodge is right in the fire path." The gorge was acting like a chimney, and was going to suck the flames right up to the building. Ehorn took another look at the blowdown and shook her head. The whole deal had bad written all over it. "Initial attack will be futile."

"Any opportunity to get the people out?"

"Working on it. 66, clear." She turned to Whitney. "Let's finish this recce fast and evacuate them."

Bad turned to worse as they flew downhill. The fire was already pumping big smoke. There was muscle below them. They might as well go ahead and declare it a campaign fire now. Nothing much they were going to be able to do. There was a good chance people were going to burn. Once a fire got big enough, you could throw all the CL-415 water-bombers in the world at it, and it would still do whatever the hell it wanted. The Ember Lake fire had spread so quickly it was bucking for conflagration status.

Whitney was flying over the south end of the fire. "Hey," Ehorn said. Something caught her eye. "There's somebody down there." There was a clearing below them, and she saw someone run into it and start waving at the helo.

"I see them," said Whitney.

A second figure joined the first. Then three more. Ehorn hailed Pyne again. "We have a second visual contact. Three persons at the rear of the fire." They had to get these clowns out of here too. A change in the wind and they wouldn't be behind the fire anymore. They'd be in its jaws. "Red Lake, we're going to land here, dump the equipment and take these people and the crew to a safe area. I'll remain with the pilot when we go back for a second load at the lodge."

"Copy that, H-66. Do it fast and safe."

Whitney took over the radio. "Birddog, this is Whitney in H-66. Am currently putting down in a clearing. We have visual contact with persons in need of aid." He brought the helicopter in for a landing.

"Hey, Allison," said Paulson, "are they wearing camouflage?"

She looked more closely. "You're right. They look freaked too." The figures were running toward the helicopter as Whitney touched down. Ehorn pushed the door open and dropped to the ground. The rest of the IA crew followed her. She stared at the men scrambling across the clearing. They looked like participants in a paintball tournament gone wrong. They were yelling something Ehorn couldn't make out at first over the noise of the rotors.

The group reached the 205, shouting. "*Go go go go go go!*" Ehorn heard now. The rearmost man fell down and there was blood everywhere. Ehorn's jaw dropped, nothing computing, and then she heard the bullets clang against the helicopter's fuselage. She turned and crashed into Paulson. "*Back!*" she yelled.

Panic time, scream and stumble, twice as long to get back inside the 205 as it took to get out. Ehorn's feet tangled, dropped her. She grabbed onto Paulson's back and almost pulled him out of the helicopter. He scrabbled foward, kicking back. His boot caught her in the chest and she fell over. She jumped back up, got her hands on the machine but now her feet slipped off the boarding step, wouldn't find the purchase to lift her in, and still she was already screaming "*Take off!*" at Whitney. He did. Bullet hits starred the windshield. The floor of the cabin lifted against Ehorn and the ground dropped away. She heaved herself in. One of the men below grabbed hold of the skid and held on. Another had been hit in the jaw and was down, screaming. The last two were lying flat, covering their heads with their hands as if it made a damn bit of difference. The clearing sang with bullets. The 205 lifted higher.

Kuhn aimed the Stinger's sights at a point above the trees where they had seen the helicopter descend. He turned off the Identification Friend or Foe interrogator. The missile was going to fly at whatever was airborne.

The sound of rotors built in speed and intensity. "Here it comes," Lentricchia said.

Kuhn grunted. "To me, babe, to me," he whispered. The helicopter appeared in his sights. He cooled the passive Infrared seeker, waited for it to sense the 205's exhaust. It growled, locked on. "Fire and forget," Kuhn commented, and let fly.

The gas generator shot the Stinger from the tube, giving it safe flight from Kuhn and Lentricchia. The dual-thrust motor kicked in and the missile streaked to prey at 700 yards a second. No challenge. The prey didn't evade. The Stinger had almost no maneuvering to do. Simple as death, it flew into the 205's exhaust port beneath the main rotor and the impact fuse did its job.

Blaylock ran the last stretch of descent to the clearing, called reckless by the rattle of gunfire and the chop of rotor blades. There were four InSec troops at forest edge, spraying with confidence. She skidded to a halt, didn't even look for cover before opening fire. Bagged two. The other two ate dirt. She jumped sideways as they shot back. A bullet chewed through her left sleeve. She felt the burn of its crease. She rolled twice, fired again, saw a body twitch with her hits. One more to go.

Slow motion then, a couple of very big seconds. Her

finger twitched off the trigger and she stopped firing and turned to look into the clearing. Her opponent stopped firing too, distracted by the *boom* into the same mistake. She saw two Raiders running back towards the forest, bullets safer than beneath the helicopter. A fireball flowered huge where the rotors met the fuselage. The main rotor detached and flew wild, a spinning scythe. The helicopter, burning, crashed and disintegrated in a second, bigger fireball. The rotor tilted to vertical and slashed down. It cut one of the Raiders in half and then thunked and twisted itself to death in the bigger trees. Flames washed out of the clearing, the tide rushing in. A cloud of black smoke came in ahead, drawing the curtain.

Blaylock coughed, tried to locate the last merc. She couldn't see more than ten feet ahead. No sign of him, and no more shooting. She coughed again, her lungs in full revolt. The merc had run. So should she. She got to her knees and was kicked flat, her rifle skittering away. A body fell over her. She was up and on him, knife out and ready to slash before she recognized Billy Duke. "Stupid ass," she muttered, and hauled him to his feet. She picked up her rifle. "Let's go," she ordered and started to jog uphill.

"Back?" Duke sounded horrified. He bent over, gagging from the air.

"We're still at war," she told him and ran on. She didn't check to see if he was following, but she heard his footsteps a few seconds later. She moved fast, not worrying about opposition. There was still one merc left, but he had the same problems. If they wanted to reach the lodge, they had to cross the blowdown, and the fire was racing them to it.

The forest was a roar of red and heat and wind. Blaylock noticed that the wind was no longer just blowing from the west. It was shifting, gusts sucking back into the forest, a dragon inhaling. Running was hard as her lungs struggled with the smoke. Twice she felt the tap of the fire on her shoulders as burning branches fell and lovebrushed her.

Duke was crying, useless deadwood. They reached the blowdown a third of the way down the slope from the lodge. Random miracle had kept the fire from it until now, but the countdown was minutes or less. Duke stopped still in front of the blowdown, trembling as he stared at the world's biggest pile of kindling. Blaylock started to climb. She didn't bother to tell Duke that the glow of the fire would silhouette them for any defenders on the other side. Past a certain quantity, bad news becomes meaningless. She tried to move fast. The blowdown resisted. Logs shifted, trying to break her legs. Branches, weathered into spear points, slashed her hands. She slipped and a limb jabbed into her throat. She pulled up, bleeding, and kept moving, still fast, dancing with impalement.

Halfway across. She looked back. She saw three things. She saw Duke grabbing a handhold and hoisting himself up stupidly high. She saw a figure climb up onto the blowdown and take aim at them. And she saw the fire, the whole forest now, flames climbing twice the height of the trees, reach out for the blowdown. "Get *down*," she yelled at Duke, knowing it was pointless, seeing it was pointless as the bullets slammed his body back and forth. She stared for a full second before she realized she wasn't just seeing exit wounds. There were bullets flying both ways across the blowdown. She looked towards the lodge. The smoke had spread over the entire area, killing the day, and she could barely make out the edge of the blowdown. But she could see the muzzle flashes, and she knew they could see her.

Pinned. Wood chips exploded around her, slashing her face. If she tried to move, she'd be hit. She looked back at the fire. No more minutes, just the last few seconds before it ignited the blowdown. It was going to connect just downhill from where the merc was standing and shooting. She pumped her M-203, aimed at the muzzle flashes and fired. She reloaded and fired again, reloaded and fired again. The edge of the blowdown exploded, wood and smoke and dirt flying, a cloud of cover where the flashes had been. The gunfire behind her paused and she stood and ran, leaping from log to log, daring the blowdown to kill her. She put her weight down hard on a branch and it collapsed into a hollow. She fell with it.

Fosberg slammed a new magazine into his rifle and saw the woman disappear, and then realized his jacket was smoldering. Asshole, too busy shooting. Hadn't realized the fire was coming so fast. His skin was pulling taut, and the heat stabbed in, a burn all the way through his skull. He staggered back from the flames, slapping at his jacket. He saw the fire hit the blowdown and started to run.

And then something new. Fosberg screamed. The radiant heat torched him. The fire ate the blowdown with triumph, and this was no burn. This was explosion.

29

"Wow," said Kuhn.

He and Lentricchia shielded their eyes from the incandescent blowup of the fire. They felt the ambient temperature shoot up from furnace to blistering. We're gonna cook, Lentricchia thought. I'm gonna die in a goddam forest fire. The old boys in Queens were going to love this. His radio crackled for attention. "Yeah," he answered.

It was Pembroke. "Jack, I think it's time to go. Fetch the chopper."

"We're outta here," Lentricchia told Kuhn. He started to jog down the path toward the lake. The heat got worse every step. He felt like he was running down into the devil's throat.

Blaylock landed in a tangle of clawed wood. Daggers slashed her camouflage and skin. A spike stabbed through her left cheek. She tasted blood and wood in her mouth. She grunted and jerked her head, pulling the spike out. She felt warmth pour down the side of her face and down her neck. She shunted the pain aside, turned it into an adrenalin boost, cranked the killing machine up another notch. Her brain revved with the anger, situational awareness a high blast of sheet lightning information. Less than five seconds after she fell, she saw the gap between the ground and the trunks. She pressed herself flat and began to squeeze under.

She heard a huge *whoompf*, and her ears popped. Air started blowing against her face. The fire had hit the blowdown and was sucking wind. The heat radiated through to her, the sun come down to earth. Move or burn, she thought. She moved, shoving her rifle ahead of her, crawling as fast as she could from gap to gap. It began to get lighter, but it was bad light, flicker light, red light, hot light. Her path twisted and angled. She tried to see a way back up to the top of the blowdown, but the timber roof was solid. She was committed now.

She found the tunnel. She laughed, harsh and snarling, at the dumb-luck miracle. The crawl space was close to a straight-line exit from the blowdown. She moved faster. When she breathed, she felt the fire reach inside her chest. She saw the exit. And she saw boots. She couldn't hear voices. All she could hear now was the basso profundo breath and heavyfist cracking of the fire.

She paused, getting her rifle into position. She had seconds to decide. Were the feet going to go away? They were shifting, dancing, anxious to get gone. So go, she thought. I'll give you to ten. She crawled forward until she was just shy of the exit. Ten. The feet were still there. She fired. Ankles blew out, screams and yells, and a body went down. Blaylock propelled herself out of the blowdown, gambled to the right and won. Three more mercs were coming her way, but they were staggering, ducking down from the blast of the fire, jerking black silhouettes against orange. Blaylock fired another burst, squinting blind, eyebrows burning away, spraying until her clip ran empty. She forced her eyes open, and saw three bodies on the ground, all broken. She dropped the empty clip, grabbed another.

Something grabbed her legs from behind and pulled her down. She dropped the clip and it bounced away. Her rifle, useless, was under her back. The man she had shot in the ankles, the man she had forgotten to finish off, climbed on top of her, pinning her. He rammed his forearm into her throat. Her vision purpled, her brain stammering as the oxygen ran out. She threw a punch but the angle was wrong and her fist glanced off his shoulder. She couldn't reach her knife. He had his out. He raised it. She reached up and grabbed his wrist with both hands, pushing back. He leaned harder. Purple shifted to black. He was heavier, stronger, had the leverage. The knife started to come down. She pulled suddenly, taking the knife in toward her, but then shoved to the left. He stabbed the knife *thunk* into the ground. She kicked against his ankles and he screamed, losing his balance. She heaved him off and rolled away, drawing in a breath that was barbed wire and broken glass. He got to his knees, and was reaching for his knife again, but she was up first and kicked him in the jaw, breaking it. He sagged, howling. She reached down to her leg and pulled her knife, swung it hard as he tried to twist away. The blade sunk missile-sure into his left ear, stabbing brain and crunching skull. His eyes fluttered, and the light went out.

Blaylock wove away from the corpse, swearing, instinct and habit colliding in her brain and knocking sense out of the running. She stood still, swaying, dumb from heat and pain. Each breath that forced its way down her bruised throat was poisoned with the fire's touch and cooked her lungs. The heat slammed into her like a wall and dropped her to her knees. The fire was the universe now.

Then the burn climbed over another threshold, and made her move again. She forced herself to her feet, picked up her rifle and ammunition, then moved back to the body and tried to pull her knife out of the skull. It was stuck. She grabbed the merc's knife instead and stumbled uphill. Her lungs grated, wailing for clean air that would clear her mind and give her the energy she needed. She fought the fatigue that clamped on her like shock, trying to get her to lie down and give it up. She fought the animal fear that wanted her to run, get past the fire somehow, get downhill and out of the way. Flee the burn. She fought it all, and moved uphill, into harm's way, up the fire's path, always and forever at war. She dredged up the roar inside her, called up the anger and the rage and denied her body its pain except as a goad to move faster. Behind her, the ground glowed red with preheating. Then she heard helicopter blades.

The west wind dropped just enough to slow the fire's run. The crown fire was already a plague, long since graduated to full conflagration. When the wind eased, the last obstacle to the fire's will evaporated. The burst of intensity from the blowdown ignition pumped the fire up one more notch, and the metamorphosis was complete. Firestorm.

A huge convection column formed over the blowdown and marched towards the lodge. The flames hit five hundred feet in height. In minutes the smoke column climbed into a mushroom three miles high. The weather outside the fire area was now irrelevant. The fire made its own weather. As the fire burned oxygen, it sucked the air into the convection column on all sides. The winds going into the flame shot up to fifty miles per hour, and kept climbing.

Lentricchia was down the rabbit hole, deep down, way past Wonderland now, falling into regions more dreadful and strange. He was eyes wide and heart-hammering scared. He saw a wall of flame high as a Manhattan canyon. He heard the continuous roar of a jet plane close at hand that never took off. The wind threw him down twice, and once it tried to pick him up and float him into the fire. When that happened, he screamed for the first time in his life.

He had the helipad in sight when he saw how the fire took its steps. It was spotting, hurling flaming matter high. Some of the debris was landing miles away, fathering a new generation of flame. Some landed much closer. Something huge and humming, bumblebee gargantua, flew by, and it was a chunk of tree the size of a telephone pole. Lentricchia ducked, yelling disbelief, and the trunk hit meteor in the forest to his left. More flames.

Lentricchia was howling by the time he got to the helicopter. He clambered in, and started thinking about prayers as he started it up. He had no idea if it could fly in air this thick. The engine caught. The rotor turned. So far no grief. He pulled back on the collective, powering up. He had the floods on, but could barely see ahead. The wind slipped in under the skids and tried to steal control from him. He increased power, grip tightening on the collective and the cyclic. Mine, he told the wind. Mine. He began to rise.

There was a huge crack of timber going down. A tree in full torch fell and rolled, bouncing down the hill, flaming steamroller, coming maximum rock and roll at the helipad. Lentricchia yanked hard, get-me-outta-here reflex. The engine roared abuse, and the Astar shot for the sky. The log smashed into the helipad, bounced up, and crashed onto the float plane. The plane burned slowly at first, half sunk under the weight of the tree. Then its fuel tank caught and it went up. Flames moved over the forest floor like liquid, red flowing horizontal, quicksilver Hell.

Lentricchia giggled, shaking hands with hysteria. He climbed until he was above the forest's flames. Now he was in smoke. Finding the lodge was going to be a question of hopping up and down in low altitude and trusting that he didn't touch fire or treetop. He thought about climbing above the whole deal and heading south. Out of this. Early retirement. He thought about it for a whole minute, struggling to maintain a hover. Then he headed north. He would do this thing for Pembroke. He would do this one last thing.

"It's over the hill and *gone*," Hank Martin radioed to Jim Pyne. He was piloting an Aerostar, flying birddog for the two CL–415 water-bombers. His plane was their airborne air-traffic controller. The valley was invisible, smoked in by a cloud that looked like a Hiroshima flashback. There was no work here for the airtankers. There was no way to tell where the fire was. Even if he could locate actual flame, the attack would still be pointless. This big, the fire would swallow whatever water they dropped and keep on smiling.

"You sure?" Pyne sounded upset. Another fire lost. Just what he wanted to hear.

"Positive." Positive about an absolute negative of a day. Martin's gut was an ulcerated knot, had been since he'd spotted the wreckage of the 205. He knew Whitney, didn't know how he'd blown the landing. The clearing should have been a cakewalk. A stupid fluke, must have been, and they had casualties. The first in years. And the badness wasn't done yet.

"There're people in there, you know," Pyne reminded him.

Martin sighed, fatigued to the marrow. He knew there were people there. He knew it very well. And he also knew the meaning of what he saw. "What do you want me to tell you, Jim? There's nothing to bomb, and there isn't going to be an airlift."

"Okay, better— Hang on."

Martin waited. When Pyne came back on, his voice was the worst Martin had ever heard it. "Hank, I just found out who's in there. The heads of the G8."

Martin eyed the smoke. "Doesn't change a thing. Doesn't suddenly make an airlift possible."

"Army's on the way."

"They're going to have to go in on foot." And that would be too late and a half.

Pyne didn't answer.

"Jim?" Martin asked.

"Sorry," he came back. "I've got the Prime Minister's Office yelling at me at the same time. We need that drop, Hank."

The drop would be like spitting at the sun, and Ember Lake itself was covered too, so the water-bombers wouldn't be able to pick up any more water. But longshot odds said they might buy the people down there a few minutes. Martin looked down at the smoke cover. It was an iron lid. The world below was gone, swallowed by terminal limbo. He had no idea where the lodge was. "I'll see what I can do," he told Pyne. "Birddog 88, clear." He kept the 415s circling. He knew they were in the vicinity of the lodge, but vicinity wasn't good enough. They had to nail it. Come on, *come on*, he told the smoke. A little break. Just a little one.

Confident it already had its victims, the smoke decided to play. An eye billowed, and Martin caught a snapshot of a building below, blink and gone. He guided the bombers in.

Noonan made it back over the blowdown with healthy minutes to spare, and checked back with Pembroke. He was with him when Pembroke ordered Lentricchia to get the helicopter. He watched the fire and he fidgeted. He couldn't help it. Pembroke said, "You're nervous. I don't think I've seen that before."

Noonan shrugged.

"Bothered by the odds?" Pembroke asked.

"Some, yeah." He wasn't enjoying this action. "I'd make sure there was a second option in case things don't pan out with Jack and the helo."

"All right, then." Pembroke walked to the door of the

suite and gestured for Chatman to come with him. "I'll have a final word with our guests. You find us a back door."

Noonan looked for shelter. If the helicopter didn't fly, they were going to be stuck here until the fire moved on, and that meant hiding out of its way. He checked the lodge's ground floor and ruled it out. The building was wood top to bottom, and would be a collapsing death trap. No basement, either, and that really sucked. He tried the rear grounds. Not much promise here, either. The generator shed was wood too, *and* it held the propane tank. Seriously bad news. He was about to give up and try the front when he spotted the pump. It was a hand pump for getting water into buckets in case the freeze and thaw of the ground wrecked the pipes for the indoor plumbing. The pump was on a raised platform with a wooden cover.

Noonan looked at the platform, then ran over to the firewood stacks and grabbed the axe. He went back to the platform and hacked away. Five minutes later he was through. He crouched and looked down into a well. It was about five feet in diameter and went down about fifteen. He couldn't tell how deep the water was, and there weren't a lot of handholds on the side. Getting in and out would be a scene, but as alternatives went, this was the best he could see.

He straightened up and sniffed, puzzled. He suddenly had the feeling it was about to rain.

Not rain. Christmas. Six tons of water, chemically foamed, came down. White, soft, sticky, it clung to the trees, a retardant winter, Monsanto wonderland. One of the trees was dead. Deep-rotted, the snag fell over. Dead, but heavy. The generator shed got slammed flat. The generator howled sparks and cut off. The propane tank shrieked metal and rolled into the yard, glancing off more sparks. Noonan threw up his arms, but the explosion didn't come. He lowered his arms, stared at the wreckage, and started to laugh. He laughed even harder when another load of white nonsense fell, deeper in the forest. He had proof now. God was an Irish drunk.

Flanagan stayed with the G8 by default. He still had nowhere else to go. Some warrior—useless civilian camped out with the impotent generals. Campbell and Palliser kept quiet, but the others argued in panicky futility as the wind carried the sounds of battle to them. Soon it was carrying smoke. Flanagan shut the window, but the smoke still found its way in. The sky darkened, and they moved to the deck to see. They didn't stay there long. The smoke drove them back inside, and they went to the private dining room. It had a good view of Hell, and the air conditioning kept the worst of the smoke at bay.

The gunfire seemed to have stopped. Flanagan wondered if the war was over, and if so, who had won. Maybe no one. He tried not to think of Blaylock shot or burned. Instead, he focused on doing a headcount. Outside, he had seen Lentricchia and Kuhn, and then Lentricchia had gone running off a couple of minutes ago. He hadn't seen any other InSec thugs outside. Inside, he saw two in the lounge, holding guns significantly as they watched staff and world leaders. He knew Noonan was around. But no one else. Think about that, he told himself. They still have the guns, they still have the experience, but they do not have the numbers any more. He totaled up the figures. Ten staff that he'd seen, eight leaders, himself. Nineteen. Pembroke, Chatman, Noonan, Kuhn, Lentricchia and friends. Seven, you think? Opportunity had a door that much bigger to knock on. Flanagan felt hope spike, and then he looked outside and it dropped again. The fire was going nova, and was minutes from making goodguy badguy trivialities moot. No one was arguing now. They stood and watched the reification of destruction.

"And what a view it is." A voice from the doorway. They

all turned. Pembroke stepped into the room. Chatman followed, the stack of MAI copies under his arm. Hal Schroeder and Burt Gunn marched close behind, M-16s begging for someone to give some lip. Pembroke waved a hand at Chatman's load of paper. "You forgot your copies in the conference room," he said. "I didn't want you to worry you had lost them." Chatman started to distribute the copies on the dining room table. Pembroke wasn't carrying anything. Flanagan checked the doorway. Nothing there, either. The NAVCON notebook wasn't in the room.

No one was paying attention to him, so Flanagan sauntered toward the room's doorway. Nobody cared. Chatman was passing pens around, Pembroke was being the smiling overlord, and the mercs wouldn't swallow without a direct order. Flanagan reached the door, stepped into the corridor. Pembroke glanced his way, but didn't appear to register him. He was irrelevant: no longer useful, inconceivable as a threat.

Flanagan was starting up the stairs when he heard a groan. He paused, listened. Another groan. Someone else shushed. Flanagan moved back down the stairs, trying to locate the source of the voices. To the left, he thought, maybe from the billiard room. He took three steps, then jumped heart-attack high when he heard an almighty crash from outside and the power went out. He froze, waiting for the thumping in his ears and the kettledrum pain in his chest to stop. He thought about investigating, but then heard Noonan laughing, loud and crazy, and decided no, bad idea. Another crash, not as loud. Don't ask, he thought. Just don't ask. He made his way through the dim twilight of the lodge to the billiard room.

He found the whole staff. He'd noticed a big herd instinct in them. They clumped together, threatened cattle, whenever they weren't on specific duties. Now they'd homed in on the billiard room. Flanagan was surprised at first, wondering why they'd chosen one of the merc hangouts. Then someone got out of his way and he saw Ian Dix on the floor, bleeding from the gut. Marianne Louden was trying to staunch the flow. The puddle took up most of the floor and was still spreading, thick and rich. Dix's face was waxy gray. He was unconscious but twisting and groaning in the pain that reached his dreams. Louden looked up at Flanagan.

No, he thought. I can go play with a computer and try to stop something about as relevant to you right now as storms on Jupiter. But I can't stop the blood, the guns, or the fire. I can't save you, me, anyone. Can only help stop someone, and a fat lot of good that does you. Louden looked away. Flanagan studied the floor, the pooling blood. Over the silence of the room, the jet-roar of the fire, getting louder, shook the walls. Then new sounds. Helicopter blades. Shouting. Gunfire.

Pembroke said, "I imagine you've realized that this conference is going to have to conclude a little earlier than planned." He looked sure he wasn't going to be touched even with skyscraper flames laying siege minutes away. He glanced at his watch. "I'm afraid I have to leave. Other appointments." He grinned, a shark. "If you sign, you can come with me. Otherwise...."

"There isn't room for all of us in that Astar," Campbell said.

Pembroke shrugged.

"My God," said Lévi. He turned to the window, seeing more than the forest burn. "What will happen to our people?"

"Nothing that wasn't going to happen anyway," said Campbell. "It doesn't matter. Makes no difference."

Palliser, hearing truth, met his gaze. Campbell's eyes were a mirror, reflecting back a self-loathing and disgust with the game. But there was more too, and Palliser knew that he and

Campbell were going to fight. They'd lose, like they would have lost every other struggle to make a difference, but this time the fight would be real, uncompromised. Go down blazing.

Palliser heard a helicopter approaching. And then there was Fulci. "I'll sign," he said. Campbell glared. Fulci ignored him, picked up his pen and flipped to the end of the MAI document. He read quickly, then frowned. "One question," he said, walking over to Chatman. Fulci appeared to stumble. He brushed past Chatman and collided with Schroeder. He grabbed Schroeder's M-16, pointed the barrel at Gunn and forced Schroeder's finger on the trigger. The blast blew Gunn backward, dead in the air. Chatman hit the deck, rolled under the table. Schroeder yanked the rifle from Fulci's grip and slammed the butt against the Italian's head. Fulci staggered back. Schroeder drilled him. Campbell leaped over the table and landed on Schroeder. Both men went down, grappling. Palliser ran for the corner where Gunn lay slumped. Pembroke was already there, leaning down, and Palliser rammed him with his shoulder, slamming Pembroke into the wall. Palliser snatched up the M-16.

Schroeder had thrown Campbell off. He leaned over Campbell, picking him up by the shirt collar. His fist, huge, hit the president's jaw, a rock against meat. Campbell slumped. Palliser fired. The rifle bucked in his hands. The noise terrified him. Bullets pocked through the wall, smashed the window. Everyone was yelling and ducking.

Schroeder was dead. So was Fulci. Palliser whirled and trained the gun on Pembroke, who froze, hands reaching for the holster on Gunn's waist. "No," Palliser told him. Campbell brushed by, mouth bleeding, and took Gunn's pistol. He held it to Pembroke's head. Palliser crouched and pointed the M-16 at Chatman. "Get out of there," he said. Chatman, shivering, crawled out from under the table and stood, arms up. Campbell got Pembroke in front of him. He put an arm around Pembroke's throat and kept the gun at his temple. "Let's go," he said. He led the way out of the dining room door. Palliser came next with Chatman.

With the G8 conference concluded, the delegates went to greet the helicopter.

Flanagan stepped into the hall. He saw Pembroke being frogmarched out of the dining room. He heard the helicopter's rattle slow. It was landing. "Come on," Flanagan told the billiard room refugees. "Bring him," he pointed at Dix, "and let's get outside."

The air in the lodge was hazy with smoke. The temperature was shooting up with the death of the air conditioning. But it was still better than outside. Outside, Hell was screaming. Flanagan tried to turn his face away from the fire, but there was nowhere to turn now. The flames were everywhere.

Lentricchia had the Astar hovering just above the ground. Kuhn had opened the passenger door, and was standing frozen as he watched the reversal of fortune walk down the steps. Noonan, done with the laughing jag, was beside him. His hands were twitching and he was doing his little Noonan dance.

"Anybody reaches for a gun and your boss dies," Campbell warned. He had to shout. The fire's roar was thunder without pause. Lentricchia started to lift off again, but Campbell gestured him back down. He marched forward.

Flanagan's joy took a hit. Between staff and politicians, he counted seventeen people, exclusive of himself, hoping for a ride. The Astar could carry pilot plus eight. Wind slammed through the lodge's grounds. It was blowing beyond eighty now. A gust slammed into the helicopter, knocking it sideways. The skid hit Noonan in the back and he fell, stunned. Flanagan saw Palliser doing the same kind of death math he had just done. He was looking around desperately, as if the numbers might resolve themselves into the magic solution, instead of a final one.

I'm not booked for this flight, Flanagan thought. NAVCON was still waiting for him in Pembroke's suite.

Palliser caught Campbell's eye. They were still sharing the communication of desperation. We're trying to do the best thing we've ever done, Palliser thought, and it's going to feel like the worst. If they lived, the guilt was going to make them wish they hadn't. The moment stretched out. God did not come down and make the decision for them. And the fire surrounded the lodge grounds. Its march was stately but juggernaut, and the lack of trees on the lodge grounds was only good for a short pause.

"*God damn it!*" Campbell yelled. "*You.*" He pointed at Louden. "*You.*" Evelyn Robinson. "*You.*" Howie Gordon. "*Take him.*" Dix. "*Get in!*" Campbell was weeping. He pointed randomly at the staff. "*You. You. You. You.*" And that was it.

Louden and Gordon picked Dix up and carried him to the helicopter. The others raced ahead and got in first. Campbell stepped aside, pulling Pembroke with him. He was sticking close to the Astar so he could fire on Lentricchia if he needed to. Palliser had Chatman and Kuhn covered. Dix was loaded into the Astar and was being strapped in by Louden. Robinson had her foot on the step. Gordon was waiting behind her. They got that far before everyone else did the math and the panic set in. There was a mob rush at the helicopter, a wave of trampling instinct and screams half-drowned by the fire. Campbell turned to ward them off. As he did, he took a step back, the fear shoving him, a wall. Noonan, jack-in-the-box, popped up behind him. With one hand, he grabbed Campbell's gun arm and pulled it out straight, aiming at nothing. He wrapped his other arm around Campbell's neck and squeezed. Campbell choked.

Palliser felt it all dying. He couldn't shoot without taking out Campbell, the helicopter and everyone by it. Noonan twisted Campbell's wrist. The gun dropped. Noonan let go of Campbell's wrist, pressed on his head and snapped the president's neck. He dropped down with Campbell's corpse, picked up the gun, and fired. A stone, fire and ice, hit Palliser in the chest. The numbness was instant, total. His body went slack. He tried to stay standing but he crumpled instead. He fell, but didn't feel it when he hit the ground. He lay on his side, seeing through a slow fade to black.

Kuhn snatched the M-16 from him. He and Noonan fired into the mob. Gordon and Robinson piled into the helicopter. The Astar hovered in place. Chatman was curled up in a ball, yelling for everything to *stop*. Pembroke was reaching for the Astar's door. Kuhn and Noonan were grinning, blasting through screams and scattering flight. Flesh piled up in the yard. Then Pembroke was yelling, storming, left behind as the helicopter lifted off.

30

The firestorm was at peak. Sun-hot and bright, its intensity was that of a two-megaton nuke. A huge mother indraft was sucked into the convection column. It hit a vertical wind, and an eddy was created. The eddy spun. It turned into a vortex. The vortex, muscled, put on flesh and walked into the lodge grounds as a fire whirl.

Brimstone at her heels, Blaylock reached the lodge. She ran into its clearing, and quicksnapped a mountain of data. She threw herself to the ground before her brain could process the whole range of sights she captured in one look. She saw Flanagan, on the lodge porch, run back inside. She saw Noonan and another man slaughtering civilians. The survivors were scattering, some into the lodge, others running around the sides of the building. She saw Pembroke screaming at an ascending helicopter. She saw a tornado made of fire, and that was what made her hit the deck, what almost made her brain stop computing. It was huge, a twisting tower of apocalypse. It snatched up debris and flung them wide, scouring the ground of combustibles. A tree branch shot out, javelin, and sunk itself into the roof of the lodge. The fire got its foothold on the building. Pembroke gave up on the helicopter and ran for the shelter of the lodge. Cobra-moving, the whirl slewed toward the Astar. The helicopter jerked out of the way, but its ascent slowed. It hesitated in the air.

The whirl swallowed the helicopter into its core, spun it and burned it. The roar was so loud it smothered the engine and the screams in the passenger compartment. Desperate for engine power, Lentricchia yanked hard on the collective. The engine couldn't keep up with the demand. The main rotor bled off rpm and stalled. Warning lights flashed. He lost tail rotor control, and the helo went whole hog into the whirl's dance, spin uncorrectable. A flaming branch punched through the windshield. It pinned him to the seat, and the fire poured in as the Astar dropped. Lentricchia screamed, joining the chorus. His chest was an explosive burn. The world was maelstrom, nothing but fire in kaleidoscope angles and fury.

Blaylock heard the engine whine high, then cut out. The helicopter went into a crazy dive, nose first, spinning like a drill and burning hard. It hit the ground and exploded. The whirl torqued the wreckage, shrapnel flying on high curve and slicing meat. Metal thunked into the lodge's deck. Wood ignited. The whirl hit the lodge. The size and look of a tornado, its winds weren't in the same league, and it couldn't move the building. It dissipated, but left its kiss burning over the façade.

Blaylock stood. Low flames licked across the lawn, smothering bodies with their love. There was only one other person standing—the man with the M-16, Noonan's massacre partner. He was close enough that Blaylock could see that he still had the trigger depressed. Ammo gone, though. He dropped the gun and looked around, stunned. "Noonan?" he called, trying to make himself heard over the fire's voice. Blaylock couldn't see Noonan, either. He'd disappeared behind the helo's wreckage. Blaylock recognized the voice from some of Flanagan's bug transmissions: Kuhn. She looked at the bullet-ridden bodies and went full feral. She ran at Kuhn, knife in hand. She dropped her rifle as she closed in. No bullets here. Nothing quick. Justice was messy. She hit him from behind, swung her blade hard and severing into his spine. Kuhn's legs folded up under him and he fell over, yelling. He flopped, landed fish, and flames licked forward to check him out. Blaylock watched and hesitated, but in the hesitation what came through was not regret or guilt or doubt but the realization of stupidity. She was cat playing with mouse, but didn't have that luxury. The point was driven home. The blow to her side knocked her down. She clicked her jaw shut and bit her tongue to blood. Her knife skittered out of her grasp. She rolled out of the way and tried to shake the stun, tried to draw breath.

Noonan said, "Explain this to me. Why does it make perfect sense that you're here?" He was bleeding too, cut on forehead, lacerated on chest. Burns charcoaled over his face and arms. He stepped over Kuhn, who was screaming, writhing, and starting to smoke.

Noonan came at Blaylock fast with a kick. She tried to absorb it, but it sent her flying again. Noonan closed in, pressing advantage, not giving her a chance to get up. In the second before the connect, she caught the way he moved. Bouncing, floating, feet ready for gravity shift, hands exploring air for best strike position. The danger she'd seen coiled in New York was out in the open and flexing. Then another kick, sudden lightning. She half blocked it, but was still knocked back, stars in her head and blood from her nose. The block was good enough to let her stand up this time. She backed up, bracing.

Flame, smoke and heat drove Edward Willis from the deck. He moved into the lodge on a disconnected wander. The panic was leaking out of him. Nothing replaced it. He'd run with the mob when he'd realized what Campbell and Palliser were proposing, and had felt only a nanosecond of shame. He'd run again, direction and hope scattering wild, when Kuhn and Noonan had started killing. And then there had been nothing but explosions and fire and death. Kitamura had been cut in half, his blood showering Willis. When he reached the lodge, Willis's batteries had run flat-line. He'd seen Belinski go in ahead of him, but the Russian hadn't stopped.

Willis stumbled into the lounge. He didn't know where to go. Someone should tell him. Maybe Belinski would. He wondered where Belinski was. He went looking. He tried the private dining room first, the last site of the conference pulling him in like a lodestone. Belinski wasn't here. There were only corpses. Willis looked down at Fulci, and an echo of shame rang inside, then faded.

The fire called him to the window. The heat through the broken panes was huge, but the gorgon pull was stronger. Willis looked outside, and saw madness. A woman and Noonan were fighting while the fire closed in, towering to the sky. Kuhn was lying down. What did the man think he was doing? He was on fire, and he was screaming. He should roll. He should put the fire out.

The woman made a strange move. She took a step forward, her left arm moving horizontally away at chest level while her right hand shot forward, palm open, wrist first, at Noonan's chest. Noonan jumped back very quickly. He looked alarmed, Willis thought. He threw a punch at the woman, who knocked his hand away. But the punch turned into a blurred kick to her stomach, and she stumbled backward.

There was a pause in the wind, a breath being held. Then a rumble, locomotive incoming. The wall of the lodge vibrated. A loose pane fell out and shattered. There was a vacuum in the clearing, and then the locomotive came. It was a horizontal run of fire, sucked with the wind toward the main convection column. A billowing explosion, it hit the lodge at ramming speed. Willis stepped back, hands up, jerked into fear at the very end. He saw red boiling and unfolding. He started to burn. He was hit by a freight train of wind and sound.

The radiant heat of the fireblast sideswiped Blaylock. She was still staggered from Noonan's last kick, and the explosion gave her an even better reason to go down. She didn't. Noonan had covered his face. His killer rhythm of footwork faltered. Blaylock stepped forward, grounding herself, and gave him a right punch. Her fist hit his kidney with all of her weight behind it. Noonan buckled. Blaylock flowed into another move, slamming her heel down against his ankle. Noonan started his counterattack at the same time, and his foot rotated. She bruised his ankle instead of breaking it, but threw the momentum of his kick off. It broke a rib instead of killing her.

Blaylock backed off, feeling the bone move. She spat blood. Noonan, limping, pressed the attack. He kicked. She ducked. He missed, but then got her on the forehead with the edge of his hand. She lost her balance, reeled into heat. He'd pushed her all the way into the burning wing of the lodge. The fire dropped onto her back. It bit into her hair. She yelled rage at the pain and the fire and Noonan, and did the thing he could not have imagined. She rammed her head into his grinning face, smothering her flames against his flesh. Noonan screamed, eyes scorched by burning hair. His hands clawed at the hurt and the blindness. He staggered forward. Blaylock grabbed him and swung him along his own momentum headfirst into the fire. He fell into the flames and they embraced him bodylength. He tried to get up and she kicked him back in.

The pain on her back was a new revelation, and overwhelmed Blaylock's rage. She dropped and rolled, beating herself on all sides until the pain was of impact and the fire was out. She was still yelling. She looked up, and saw a flame with two legs stagger out from the fire. She scrambled over to Kuhn's cremation, got her knife, then ran, bayonet charge, at Noonan. She sank the blade into his chest and stuck him to the wall of the lodge.

Big cracks from above. She yanked the knife out and got out of the way. Noonan sank to the ground, screams turning to a hiss, and the overhang of the deck collapsed on him. Blaylock bent over, hands on her knees, gasping air and pain, watching to make sure he was dead. She gave herself thirty seconds, and then it was back to war. The deck was almost completely engulfed, but the right-hand door to the deck was open, and the flames were still small enough that they left a gap. She ran up the steps and through the ring of fire.

Flanagan heard the helicopter explode. He knew what it was. He refused to deal with it. There was plenty of death to go around, and he'd face it when it was his turn. He took the steps three at a time, racing the smoke. He needed to beat the lodge's burn. He was dead, Pembroke was dead, NAVCON was dead. But the initial settings Pembroke had transmitted would hold. The ships would get to their destinations, and he had no doubt that Pembroke had all of the machinery up and rolling, and InSec's mercenary divisions would pick up the weapons and distribute them. Pembroke's doomsday anarchy would be carried out whether he was around to laugh or not.

Flanagan hit Pembroke's suite, found the notebook on the desk, turned it on. He rolled the trackball, double-clicked on the NAVCON icon, and waited again while the satellite link was made. The pause almost killed him. He was terrified the fire would interfere with the signal. Terrified that, with the generator down, and the booster disabled, the desktop's transmitter wouldn't be strong enough to make the link. A map of the Atlantic with the ships' positions and routes appeared for a second, and then was replaced by a screen asking him for his password. He typed RETALIATE.

ACCESS DENIED. He stared at the screen. He must have typed the password wrong. He tried again. ACCESS DENIED. He shut the computer down. Start over.

Downstairs, a huge roar. The lodge shook, earthquake. Flanagan shut it all out and stared at the screen, tunnel-vision consciousness. The computer went through the start-up routine again, connected with the ships, asked him for the sign. RETALIATE. ACCESS DENIED.

"Not working, is it?"

Flanagan jumped, looked over his shoulder. Pembroke was standing in the doorway. His suit was torn and filthy with soot, but he still wore it as the mantle of the corporate king. He was smiling, and the smile was bad. The different elements of his face weren't connecting properly. He was misfiring and loving it, reveling in the burn and the end. He had the shine. He was bestowing a legacy, and that would be the crown fire spread worldwide.

Pembroke walked into the room. "What did you think?" he asked as he approached. "That we don't have multiple redundant safety protocols? Bill Jancovich found your back door. Good man, Jancovich. Does what he's told and only what he's told." Pembroke pulled a pistol from his vest pocket. It was a tiny .32 ACP Guardian. It all but disappeared in Pembroke's hand. "Your area was design, Flanagan. The big picture. Leave the software to the experts." He chambered a cartridge.

Flanagan looked at the pistol. "Isn't that pointless?"

Pembroke laughed and shook his head. "I'm not going to kill you. You're not getting out of being burned, you treacherous little shit." He shot Flanagan in the right leg. Flanagan screamed and fell off the chair. He clutched his leg. The bullet had shattered bone.

Something stormed into the room, a war demon of smoke and blood. It rammed Pembroke off his feet before he could turn and fire. The gun skittered across the floor, out of reach. The demon planted a boot on Pembroke's chest and kept him still. "Have you got it working?" the demon asked Flanagan in a hissing rasp. Flanagan gaped, hearing the voice. It was distorted by fire and rage. He barely recognized Blaylock. Her fatigues were hanging in tatters, vanishing in the dark of burns and blood. Where the skin of her face wasn't scorched and charcoal-smeared, it was a green and black war mask. Her cheek had a hole in it, and dripped blood onto the floor. Her hair had been burned to stubble. Smoke rose from her, the aura of flame.

Flanagan said, "My password won't work." He pointed at Pembroke. "It has to be his."

Blaylock looked down. "Tell him," she ordered. Pembroke spat at her. She reached down, grabbed his right hand and took hold of his little finger. "Tell," she repeated. Pembroke shook his head. She snapped the finger. Pembroke shrieked. It was the best sound Flanagan had ever heard. He wanted to hear it again and louder. He wanted to get in there and summon that melody too. Blaylock moved her boot to Pembroke's throat so he couldn't scream, and broke his index and middle fingers. Pembroke's body arched. His mouth strained wide. His eyes bulged. He jerked his head. Blaylock stepped off his throat.

"Metastasis," he gasped.

Flanagan let go of his leg, crawled back onto the chair. He was grinning rictus, teeth clamped against the pain. He typed. The screen changed to the North Atlantic. Flanagan twisted around in the chair. "We're in," he said.

Blaylock pulled her knife out of its sheath and drew it across Pembroke's throat. Pembroke made choking and gargling noises. His blood spurted, spraying Blaylock's face. She walked away from him and came to look at the computer.

Flanagan stared at Pembroke. His feet and hands were drumming against the floor. The music wasn't sweet anymore. The rhythm made Flanagan want to puke. Blaylock nudged him and he turned back to the computer. He shut off the safety measures. "All yours." He turned the laptop over to Blaylock.

She selected each ship and changed its headings. "Full steam ahead," she said, and cranked the engines on all eight superfreighters. When she was done, she asked, "This the only controller? Is there anything that can change what's going to happen now?"

Flanagan shook his head. "The ships are locked in now."

Blaylock looked down at NAVCON. Flanagan saw her eyes quiver as she took in the power. He saw an oilsquirm of greed. She shook her head, no. She smashed the notebook's keyboard with the hilt of her knife. The screen froze. Flanagan looked and saw what she had given as new coordinates for the ships. "Do you know what you've done?" he demanded. Blaylock stopped in mid-smash. She stared at the screen. It went out, dead. She looked at Flanagan. He saw the war fury in her eyes flicker and her momentum slowed. Human thought crept in again. Something that looked like fear followed it. "*What about the crews?*" Flanagan shouted.

Blaylock winced. Her face blanched. Guilt and horror thundered in with the fear. "Maybe they'll see what's happening in time," she whispered, hope in her words but none in her voice.

Willson was sitting in the captain's chair on the bridge when he felt the *Bhopal* turn hard to port. The hum of the engines grew loud. Christ, he thought, not more silly games. This wasn't the weather for Pembroke's bullshit.

"Sir." Art McPhee, at the radar. "Look at this."

Willson sighed, heaved himself out of the chair and went over to McPhee's station. He looked at the radar and his bowels loosened. They were on a head-on collision course with the *Flixborough*. Willson grabbed the radio and hailed Marv Starkey on the other ship. "Marv," he asked, "you seeing what's happening?" Then he noticed the *Oppau's* new course. He checked the headings on the rest of the fleet. They were all heading at max for the same point of ocean. "Oh shit," he whispered. He and the other captains had disobeyed company orders and opened up crates to see exactly what their cargo was. Now he wished he didn't know. Minutes only to the bang. "Get everybody off, Marv," Willson said. He signed off and hit the klaxon to abandon ship. He ran with his crew from the bridge, pulling on his lifejacket.

By the time all thirty-four crewmen were loaded into the two lifeboats, the other ships were in sight. By the time the motor winches were lowering the lifeboats, Willson could hear, over the wind and the waves, all the klaxons, wailing a chorus of useless warning. No ship was going to blink first. The sea heaved. The *Bhopal* was broadside to the waves, and Willson wondered if she might capsize before the collision. His lifeboat banged against the hull, then swung away as the ship rocked back. McPhee almost fell out.

The water came up huge below. Willson yelled for the lifeboat to be detached. They cut loose and splashed into the hump of the wave, and then they were dropping, roller coaster. The crew of the other lifeboat didn't time it right. They detached too late. The sea had already peaked and was sinking again. When the boat released, it fell thirty feet before it sliced into the side of a wave and capsized. Willson looked away from the men in the water. They disappeared almost instantly. Another mountain of water picked his boat up and carried it away from the *Bhopal*. The superfreighter plunged ahead, wailing for the company of its mates.

Spray slashed over the lifeboat. There was so much water in the air it was hard to breathe. If the storm worsened, they would drown without leaving the boat. Willson leaned forward to McPhee and yelled into his ear: "Is the beacon on?" McPhee nodded, face twitchy with terror and despair. Rescue was a prayer in the devil's fist.

Willson watched the ships. They were huge enough, and still close enough, that he could see them clearly through the foam and the rain. They came together, a metal city coalescing on the ocean. The *Taegu* and the *Wankie* collided first. The boom of impact and scream of metal blasted through the storm, nature briefly dwarfed. The *Dhanbad* came in next. Riding high on the top of a wave, it hit with enough speed and height to ride over the *Wankie*, capsizing it. Willson saw fires begin. They spread fast, explosions building as each ship came in and buried itself in the hulls of the others. The fuel went up first, big and bright. The blast fed a firecracker string of secondary explosions as ammunition cooked off. The *Bhopal* slammed into the wreckage. It started burning immediately. It was rear-ended by the *Ludwigshafen*, then lifted up by the *Texas City*, getting it in the side. Willson watched the mass of twisting and burning immensity, and he thought about the *Bhopal*'s cargo, and what would happen when the explosions got to the thousands of missiles. He didn't bother to order any attempt at rowing. They would be out of range or they would not, and that was the storm's business. Nothing to do but watch the show.

It took ten minutes. The metal city was glowing with flame and fireworks. There were enough booms and rattles for a decent-sized war. There was escalation. And then the big one went down. The missiles detonated. Willson actually saw the shock wave as it raced for him.

Belinski was in the kitchen, soaking towels. The water was still running, and he'd repeatedly filled a pot and dumped the contents over himself. When the towels were water-logged, he wrapped them around his head and draped them over his shoulders. He was going to run. There was fire on all sides, and the lodge was burning fiercely. He kept coughing on the smoke pouring into the ground floor. He couldn't stay here. There was no shelter that he could think of, so he had to run. He wanted to make it downhill, into the area already burned. But he had to get through the flames first. He covered his mouth with a wet towel and approached the kitchen doors. He felt them. They were warm. Fire in the lounge and dining room. He couldn't go out the back, though. It was worse out there. He backed up to the rear of the kitchen. He breathed through the towel, inhaled deeply, held it, and ran. He was going full-tilt when he banged through the doors and hit the lounge. The room was blazing. He ran straight into a floor-to-ceiling wall of flame. The first thing his wet clothing did was scald him. Then the synthetics in his suit melted into his flesh. He stumbled, and he let his breath out. He breathed in to scream, and the moisture of the towel turned to steam and boiled his lungs. He made it to the foyer before he collapsed.

Lévi was at the head of the pack that ran around the west wing of the lodge to escape the bullets. He saw the open well as soon as he reached the rear lawn. He didn't hesitate. He ran for it and jumped in. The fall was just long enough to terrify him, but then he hit water. He sank over his head, touched bottom immediately, and came back up, gasping. He treaded water, and felt around the sides of the hole for something to hold on to. He heard footsteps, looked up, and the hole was blocked by another body. He hugged the side of the pit, and was knocked back under water. He gagged, surfaced, and was hit again. He started to thrash, getting tangled up in someone else's limbs. Air, and then a fourth body. Down again, thrash with the others, panic. Someone went underneath his feet and he stood on the body, propelling himself back up. He scrabbled at the wall, and his fingers found a hold. He clung, pressing his face into muck, and tried to find a grip for his feet, tried to climb the rest of the way out of the water. Hands grabbed his legs. Lévi looked down, made out Werner Feher's mud-smeared face. "*Lâche-moi!*" Lévi yelled, feeling his grip slip. He tried to kick, but couldn't get leverage against Feher. He lost his grip and fell back into the water. He fought Feher, who splashed over to the other side of the well. One of the staff was flailing between them. Lévi's feet touched the body below again. There was no struggle. Whoever it was had drowned. Lévi sank and then stopped. The body was giving him the height he needed to be able to stand and keep his mouth out of the water. It was close. He had his head tilted all the way back, water covering his ears. When someone splashed the water, he choked again, but he was getting air.

Red light, harsh and painful. The fire was burning directly over the well. There was a hollow vacuum roar, and the fire sucked the air out of the well. Lévi felt breath stolen. He panicked again, climbing up, chasing oxygen. His lungs pulled hard. The fire pulled harder. Nothing came in. Heat came down. Lévi tried to scream. He couldn't.

Blaylock tore Pembroke's trousers into strips. The floor was growing warm, the countdown locked in and approaching the end, but she had to do this or Flanagan would die in this room. She broke the notebook's cover into two pieces and used them as splints for Flanagan's leg. She tied them on with two of the strips of cloth, used another to bind the wound, and handed him another. "Put this around your face," she told him. She pulled her scarf out of her pocket and tied it around her own face. She picked Flanagan up, draping one of his arms over her shoulder. He hopped on one foot and they made their way to the door. When he moved, he bumped against her broken rib. The pain was keeping her alert, anyway.

The corridor was smoke heavy, worse than the room, and they started coughing immediately. Illumination was a red and jerking glow. They reached the end of the corridor, and it was this far no further. The foyer was acting like a chimney, pushing the fire up to the second floor. The stairs were on fire all the way.

Craig Szebin had been delirious for the last couple of days. His knee, pulverized by Ron Whitmore's bullet during the lodge takeover, had become infected. Bad enough that he had no feeling in his leg below the knee, his whole leg had swollen and his brain had started frying neurons. He'd been sweat-sleeping for most of the war. The fire woke him up. He lay still for a minute, confused, wondering why he couldn't stop coughing, why he was so hot, why he couldn't hear anything except an airplane roar. When he finally put it together, he crawled off his cot. When his leg bumped the floor, he felt no pain, but a buzz like poison flushed up to his face. He shivered, and started to drag himself over the dance floor. The space stretched out infinite, the crawl an afterlife punishment. He had almost made it across when he saw smoke creeping in under the doorjamb. He stopped, splayed frog nailed to the floor, and listened to the flames on the other side eat the lodge. His mind raced stupid circles, hyperfiring a search for an option that wasn't there.

Wood cracked and popped, gnawed by the fire's jaws. The sound intensified, and Szebin began to crawl back. The noise was so big it sounded like the fire was in here with him. Then he looked up. The fire was here. It was eating the ceiling. The cracking was the timbers above him giving way. He stared, rodent to serpent. His mind gave up the search. The ceiling fell in.

Blaylock backed away from the staircase. She and Flanagan had reached the nearest guest room on the south-facing side of the lodge when something very big crashed. She looked to her left, and saw a third of the west wing collapse. The fire exulted. Heat rolled at her, a wind of pain. She shoved Flanagan into the room and closed the door, blocking some of the smoke. She hauled him over to the window and looked out. The window opened onto the sloping roof of the deck. The fire had finished with this bit and moved on, leaving a smoldering skeleton waiting for its moment to collapse. The lawn below hadn't been touched yet. It was a twelve-foot drop to the ground. She only had five feet of rope in her web belt. "Wait here," Blaylock said, and made Flanagan lean against the wall next to the window. She stripped the bed, tied the sheets together, added her rope, attached the whole thing to the bedstead. She pushed the bed. It resisted, but finally scraped over the floor to the window. She lifted the sash and tossed the line out. It reached the ground.

Flanagan gasped, "Does this gag really work?"

She yanked hard. The sheets didn't come apart. Time to gamble. She looked at Flanagan's face. Under the soot it was very gray. She didn't know if he would be strong enough. "Can you hold on to it?" she asked. When he nodded, she said, "I'll go first and guide you down. Copy that?" He nodded again. She squeezed his shoulder, then clambered onto the bed, grabbed hold of the rope, and climbed out.

Chatman was weeping. He had uncurled from his ball when the fire whirl had grabbed the helicopter. He'd known that

God was not going to make this stop. He'd known that immobility would mean death. So he had run from the crash, flames chasing him around the lodge. The rear wall, untouched by the fire, lured him with the illusion of shelter. He flattened himself against it, all running done when he saw that there was nowhere to run to. He curled in smaller and smaller as the fire took over the rear grounds. He saw Lévi and three others jump into the well. He was going to follow, but then he heard what sounded like shouts and screams coming from the well, and then flame had pounced over the opening, raptor on prey.

Chatman began to gibber. Red walls that flickerdanced and roared circled in. Sparks fell at his feet. He looked up and saw the roof above him flaming. He stood up, legs trembling in useless nowhere-to-run flight reflex. He saw the fire wash into the forest on the uphill side of the lodge. The trees that weren't coated with foam erupted. A giant's hand, shining red supernova, yanked the weak up and threw them into the grounds. Chatman watched as a fluke played out. He saw one of the hundred-pound propane tanks that lolled on the grounds, waiting for an invitation. It was pointed at him, dormant torpedo. A tree came down and smashed the release valve. Chatman's eyes widened.

It was a clumsy rappel, but Blaylock got down, and she didn't want to strain the sheets any longer than she had to. "Okay!" she called. It was several seconds before Flanagan even appeared at the window. He was moving very slowly. Blaylock forced herself not to look at the fire, not to gauge how much time they had. Flanagan would take the time he needed, and then they both escaped or neither did. Flanagan held onto the rope and tried to swing himself out gently. It didn't work, and he jerked down. His broken leg bashed against the windowsill on the way out, and he howled. Blaylock winced, expecting him to drop, but he held on. He lowered himself hand over hand. She lifted her arms, reaching for his legs to give him support on the way down. She just had hold of him when a sheet gave. Flanagan fell the rest of the way, knocking them both down in a heap. He screamed again, and Blaylock felt strange movement in her lower chest. Stay put, she told the rib. If it detached completely, it would flail and kill her from the inside.

She stood. Flanagan shook his head when she reached down for him. "Can't," he whispered. Blaylock had to read his lips. He was inaudible in the furnace thunder. Then a boom that punctuated the fire's sound, an exclamation point. Blaylock ducked at the sound, and a steel fist punched through the lodge, splintering wood, collapsing walls. The disintegrating missile flew low, superheating the air where her head had been a second before. The propane tank buried itself in the cauldron of the forest.

The lodge creaked. It was a creak that vibrated through the entire structure. The lodge leaned forward. Support beams splintered. Momentum built. "Have to go, have to go," Blaylock said. She heaved Flanagan up so she had him in a firefighter's carry. The lodge trembled. She scanned the grounds, wincing as the flames marched in, bright and high and wide, radiant death. She could count the seconds to being trapped. She looked right. Smoke was thick near the side of the building, as if the burn was done on that bit of lawn. The grass would have gone up quickly in the wake of the fire whirl. Now it smoked, obscuring, choking. But not burning. She moved, stumble-jog. The smoke swallowed them and she coughed, fingernails scraping her throat and lungs, heat and grit stabbing needle-pain in her eyes. She could see only two steps ahead. Tears smeared her vision.

She was gagging by the time she made it to the rear of the lodge. She stumped forward on momentum, desperate to get out of the smoke. It lifted when she came near heat. Flames ahead of her. The lodge moaning behind. But there, in the woods, a band of dark. Something wasn't burning.

Not yet. The last path open. There were flames between her and the foam-soaked trees, but they were low, grassfire, no more than three feet in height. It was a thin enough barrier. "Hold your breath," she said. She felt Flanagan inhale and hold. She took four rapid breaths, filled up, closed her mouth, and ran. She closed her eyes as she hit the flames. Behind her, she heard wood begin to fall. She was racing an avalanche.

There was a feather touch as she went through the flames, and her pants caught fire. She dropped, throwing Flanagan off. He thumped but this time did not scream. She rolled the flames out, then lifted him up again. Her knees buckled under the strain. Her rib stabbed deep. She was walking pain. She trembled, and the next step wouldn't come. From behind, incentive. Deeper thunder yet, suspense over and here we go, the lodge going down, front walls collapsing first and sending the whole building eevy ivy over, spreading its death wide. Blaylock ran, she actually ran, as a tidal wave of wreckage and flame swept forward.

The dark band narrowed. The suppressant was surrendering. The fire closed in around her, final hunger. The smoke reflected the flames and turned the air red. Heat slammed its walls down. Branches fell flaming. She saw the creek. Final adrenalin burst, zigzag through the last little bit of untouched forest, the chemical gift on the trees giving her a dotted-line way through the flames. She howled against her body as it tried to collapse. She couldn't hear herself over the fire's Armageddon shout. She didn't know if Flanagan was screaming or dead. She dropped him into the creek, then splashed in beside him. The red scream was seconds away. "Go under!" she yelled, but there was no way he could hear. She held her breath, grabbed his head and pushed down. The water was just deep enough for them to submerge, and then the storm was there in final judgment.

EPILOGUE

The eye of the firestorm passed over them. Blaylock held her breath, held Flanagan under, until the orange began to fade from the water. She didn't dare let either of them surface to take in a lungful of burn. Then the fire moved on, bored. The rest of the valley and the forest beyond called. Orange turned to gray and darkness. The heat left the water. Blaylock surfaced, gasping, pulling Flanagan up with her. He spluttered and choked, but was alive. They'd been under just over thirty seconds.

Smoke came and dampened down the red light. It replaced agony with discomfort. Blaylock climbed out of the creek and hauled Flanagan onto the bank. "Are you okay?" she asked. He nodded, coughing. With evening coming on, an inversion was holding the smoke in over them, and the smoke would come down further yet. The air hurt, but they could breathe. There was still enough fire glow for visibility.

She looked Flanagan over. The break in his leg had been aggravated, and the smoke inhalation wasn't doing either of them any good. Her own wounds began to make their demands felt. She sagged. They needed hospitalization. She was losing a lot of moisture from her burns. She could think of at least a half-dozen reasons why she should die.

From somewhere above the smoke ceiling, she could hear helicopter blades. Search and rescue. She wondered if the pilot was brave enough to try to descend blind. If yes, then she and Flanagan had better be in the clearing or they'd miss the ride. She smiled at Flanagan. "Cavalry's coming." She struggled to her feet and began to undress.

"What are you doing?"

"Better look like a civilian." She stripped down to her underwear, rubbed the paint from her face, tossed her fatigues to cremate slowly in the bones of the forest. She helped Flanagan to his feet, and they stumbled back downhill toward the rubble of the lodge. They sat, now at energy's absolute terminus, when they reached the dead planet of the lawn.

Flanagan gazed around the flickering destruction. "They're all dead," he said, voice awed by horror. His eyes locked onto hers, pleading. "What happens now?"

"What happens where?"

He gestured vaguely. "Everywhere. The world. I mean. . . . Oh my God, what have we done?"

You mean what have I done, she thought. Part of her was back on the road from Kuwait City again, gazing over smoldering responsibility and guilt. Only this time it was all hers. All of it. Here. And in the Atlantic. "Nothing happens," she said. "You think this is going to make a huge difference? Not much it won't. A bit maybe, but not much."

He stared at her, face a shadow-mime of horror and despair in the flashlight's glow. "You make it sound like the war isn't over." She didn't want that stare. She wanted him to stop. She saw in his gaze, in its recoil and its accusation, a summation of everything she had lost, and would lose yet. She saw him staring at a monster.

She thought about what she would have to do to wipe out that look. She thought about laying down arms, finally, and working for a peace. The temptation was huge. She almost surrendered. And then she looked at the lodge, and the wreckage spoke to her. It was an iceberg tip. However much blood she had drawn, however much she had defiled herself with her own Highway of Death, there were plenty of Pembroke's brothers-in-night to step in and fill the gap in the system. And they would, if she laid down arms. "It isn't over," she told Flanagan. That gaze was part of the price. Fine. She could pay it. Somebody had to. Somebody had to descend to the pit and fight the monsters as one of them. Fire with fire. The war wasn't about revenge anymore. And she knew it wasn't about power, either. She'd felt the tug when she'd stared at NAVCON, and had pulled back.

So no, it wasn't over. The war was immense, its fronts infinite, its laws non-existent. She would be the scapegoat, and allow herself to be blackened in combat so that Flanagan and the rest of the civilians wouldn't have to. She would be the necessary monster. But no more Highways of Death. No more Atlantics. Otherwise how would she know she wasn't a Pembroke?

The guilt. That was how.